WOLFEN TIME

Roxy Boroughs

Publisher: Baucis & Philemon

Cover: Croco Designs at http://www.crocodesigns.com/

Editor: Linda Style at http://www.EditingwithStyle.net and Mr. Ted Williams, Freelance Editor

Formatting: Anessa Books at http://www.anessabooks.com

ISBN: 978-0-9921271-1-4

Dedication and Acknowledgements

For Barry, as always.

Thanks to my critique partners Lecia Cornwall, Pamela Yaye and Sherile Reilly,

and to my beta readers, especially Sarah Castille.

A special thank you to my wonderful parents and my awesome big brother, for indulging my *Star Trek* habit.

CHAPTER ONE

RAFE GARRETT'S VISION swam as his stomach took a dive south—the usual byproducts of time travel. *Tripping* in human form had its disadvantages. But four leather-clad hunters materializing in downtown Seattle were far easier to explain than three stray wolves and a vampire.

Blaez, their team leader, looked around, the whites of his eyes bright against the dark background of his skin. Despite his years, Blaez's vision remained excellent, his muscles hard and his tracking abilities unsurpassed. He sniffed the air. "No humans. Good. We're clear."

Rafe allowed himself to relax a fraction, as he checked the *zeitmeter* on his wrist. "One-twenty hours before Zero Time. Right on schedule."

He scanned the deserted warehouse, one of their regular base camps when visiting the twenty-first century. It was past dawn, but little sun filtered through the cracked, grease-smeared windows. Shards of broken glass crunched under his heavy boots.

So fragile. So easily broken. Just like the humans whose lives they were about to invade.

"Our target rents an apartment within walking distance," Tala reported, her pimped-up GPS in her right hand, while she indicated the direction with her left.

Then her sultry gaze fell on him.

Rafe busied himself, checking his weapons, avoiding her eyes. Sure, she was attractive. Gorgeous, in fact. With long red hair and a body made for sin. The view from behind was enough to make most guys take a second and third look.

Not Rafe. He still missed Daciana, and wasn't in the market for another mate. First Pack approved, or otherwise.

And Tala would be a definite otherwise.

A quickie with no strings attached, now that would have suited him fine. But he liked his women with a pulse. Behind Tala's brown contacts, her eyes were red. And under her special sun block, she had the kind of skin that would burn to soot if exposed to daylight for too long. No wonder the cloudy West Coast was a vampire haven.

"An apartment, huh?" the fourth member of their group remarked. "Whadda we do? Go up and knock?"

Caleb was the youngest of the group, barely out of puberty and the joker of the team. There was nothing funny about being on the other end of one of his punches, however. The kid could fight his way out of any battle—with human, lycan, or vamp. Rafe was grateful to have his adopted brother at his back.

"We're too conspicuous trolling the neighborhood together. We'll meet there. Caleb and I will stake out the front of the apartment building. Rafe—you and Tala cover the back." Blaez topped off the command with a smirk.

Rafe cringed. Being under the scrutiny of the über boss's daughter made them all as ornery as a pack of sharks with free-riding remora fish stuck to their sides. With his order, Blaez had earned himself and Caleb a few minutes reprieve from Tala's watchful eye, and slapped Rafe with the job of keeping her entertained. Blaez winked and headed off, Caleb trotting behind like the good pup he was.

Tala smiled. "Paired again. I could get used to that." With her fangs retracted she could almost pass as a living being.

Almost.

"Don't." Rafe added a growl for punctuation and stalked off. He didn't want to be harsh but so far nothing else had deterred her. He followed the other males through the warehouse to the nearest exit, picking up speed until Tala's footsteps became a distant memory. She was well able to find the apartment on her own.

Besides, he needed some time away from everyone. To think and plan.

Alone, he walked the street, the old monorail gliding along above his head. Beyond it, the sky was overcast, the air around him slightly cool. Typical August weather for Seattle, the city of his birth—though that wouldn't happen for another two centuries.

He knew where he was headed. As prep for the mission, he'd walked these same streets weeks before—in his time and without a jacket, thanks to global warming. Now he passed a coffee shop, still popular in his era. And a hotel, the future site of *Were* War Memorial Park. Rafe marveled at the differences, smiled at the similarities.

He checked out vehicles cruising down the road beside him—brand new models to their owners, museum pieces to him. He glanced up an alley and sighed. A blood-red Ferrari Enzo shimmered with a light of its own. Rafe allowed himself two seconds of envy, before flattening his body against the wall.

The car didn't fit the neighborhood. Not the style, not the color. He picked up a scent, stale flesh splashed with expensive cologne.

The stench of a hungry vampire.

Rafe touched the communications device on his belt, sending the coordinates to his team members. Then he tossed his leather jacket to the ground and peeled off his shirt.

Fighting a vamp in human form would put him on the losing end. Vein Drains were too fast, too strong. And the older they were, the more powerful. Rafe would have to wolf-it if he had any hope of staying alive, and he didn't want to wrestle with the extra clothing when he morphed.

He stuck his *zeitmeter* in his pocket, then slung his jacket casually over one shoulder and made his way down the narrow alley. Just your average, everyday, bare-chested assassin.

The place was a death trap, tight passageways between towering buildings that surrounded him like a maze. He came to a corner where a cement-filled wheelbarrow rested near a pile of multi-colored bricks, evidence that someone was attempting to jazz up the frontage of an office space. He scanned the area, side to side, eyes alert, nostrils tingling.

A woman's scream pierced the drone of city traffic.

Rafe broke into a run, slowing only to pick up a brick before skulking around the red car. He peered across it to see two vampires. One betrayed the wild, glassy-eyed hunger of a recent convert. Rafe pegged the other vamp as a supercentenarian, and he was closing in on a petite blonde, his fangs poised over her neck, ready for a snack.

Rafe set the brick on the hood of the car for easy access. From his jacket, he withdrew a stake—silver inlaid with strips of ebony. He snuck up behind the fledgling and tapped him on the shoulder. As the vamp turned, Rafe drove the spike into his chest, crunching bone and piercing his heart. The bloodsucker had enough time to look at the damage before decomposing into a pile of ash.

Rafe stepped aside. No point getting dust on his boots.

One down.

His next target wouldn't be so easy. He reached for the brick, took aim, and whipped it at the older vampire's head. Counting on a few seconds of distraction, he dumped his jacket, shed his jeans, and transformed—claws flexed, teeth bared.

* * *

Moments earlier…

STACY CADELL'S HEART beat in double time as another scream crawled up her throat. On legs as sturdy as cooked spaghetti, she backed away from the murder scene concealed behind the dumpster and plowed into solid flesh.

Steel-like flesh, cold and unyielding.

She turned to see the…*prankster?* Surely the man wrenching her arm was someone's idea of a gag—his face as hard and pale as marble, and slathered with coconut-scented sunscreen, by the smell of it.

A ghoulish pina colada.

The guy had to be part of an elaborate practical joke, concocted by her friend, Perry, and his geeky comic book buddies.

Stacy looked for her pal, ready to laugh along with him and admit she'd fallen for his joke—walked right into a fake murder scene, perpetrated by a dude with a fondness for all things Transylvanian.

But she was alone, save for the Dracula groupie with the bloodshot eyes. Sickly sweet breath enveloped her as he bared his inch-long fangs.

Not plastic ones. These teeth were legit. And the fella's strength? Superhuman. However bizarre, this madman's attack was real. It was happening. If she spent another second trying to deny her situation, she'd be dead.

She swallowed her terror and yelled, "Fire!" Then thrust the heel of her free hand into her attacker's nose, as she'd been taught in self-defense class. She may as well have smacked the head of a hammer, for all the good it did her. The fancy move didn't even slow him down.

She was about to try a knee to the groin, when her adversary's head snapped forward, a large brick bouncing off his skull.

Unprepared for her attacker's sudden release, Stacy fell to the pavement butt first. Her teeth rattled, the impact shooting pain through her jaw. Sharp stones cut into her palms as she crawled toward her savior.

She expected a police officer. Maybe a pitcher for the Mariners. Not a naked man with the body of a mixed martial arts champion. Tanned and ripped, all six foot plus of him.

If she wasn't scared spitless, she would have stopped to salivate.

The guy could move, too. Before Stacy could draw a breath to call out to him, he'd dropped down on the other side of the car, out of sight. An instant later, another figure emerged. Not her rescuer but a huge dog—black and tan, like a German Shepherd, but twice the size. Its fur thick, its amber eyes glowing.

A new fear jangled up her spine as she realized the truth. It wasn't a dog, at all, but a giant wolf. Wild and dangerous.

Looked like she was still on the menu.

Growling, the beast reared back on its haunches, then sprang at her attacker, teeth snapping inches from the bad guy's throat.

How a wolf had maneuvered downtown traffic to appear in her hour of need, she didn't know. And she damn well didn't care. She had to take advantage of the diversion and get the hell out of here.

She looked for the naked man, hoping he was okay, but couldn't see him anywhere. Was he dead? Gone for help? Popped off to Macy's for some pants? Maybe he'd made a run for it. Just as she planned to do.

Vibrating like a caffeine addict on a Red Bull high, she backed away, keeping her distance from both adversaries as they snarled and grappled, slamming into buildings on either side of the alley. Whenever she saw an opening for escape, they changed direction, their struggles blocking her path.

They shifted again, giving her a chance to dart to the mouth of the alley and freedom. She heard a heavy thud and glanced back to see them rolling across the top of the flashy red sports car. A reeling mass of fur, arms, and legs, locked together in mortal combat.

Blood smeared the wolf's fur. Whether it came from the animal, or Pasty Face, Stacy couldn't tell. She feared it was the wolf's and told herself it wasn't her problem. But when it came time to make her feet move, her heart kept them locked in place.

The wolf had saved her. She couldn't leave it to die.

Stacy checked the street. There was no one in sight. Odd for this time of day when people were scrambling to get to work. Either her cries for help had sent someone off to gather reinforcements, or everyone had turned tail and run in the opposite direction.

And the naked man? He could be lying on the pavement bleeding. She had to help him, at least buy him some time—since she couldn't rely on the cavalry showing up.

Shaking, she picked up a brick and hurled it at Ol' Red Eyes. It clipped his head with an audible thwack, and she thanked the years she'd spent playing girls' softball.

Until he turned and glared at her, his mouth curved down with… *annoyance*. As if she were a bothersome fly.

Stacy ran for her life.

Even with a head start of several yards, the thing was on her in seconds. Vice-like hands grabbed her, lifted her five feet off the ground, and sent her hurling through the air. She crashed sidelong against the steel dumpster, her lungs on fire, unable to draw a breath.

She lay crumpled on the ground, sure her ribs were cracked, if not broken. Sounds faded, as though she were underwater.

She opened her eyes, but saw only blackness. That scared Stacy more than the thing that attacked her. A slideshow of childhood memories flipped through her mind, fear zapping her with the force of an electric current making her body shudder. No way was she going to die in the dark.

No way.

Stacy stretched out her hand, only to feel a sharp stab at her side. She bit down and forced herself to move, prepared to crawl all the way to Lake Union if she had to.

Slowly, her hearing returned to take in more growling, more crashing. Her vision, still foggy around the edges, was clear enough to see a black leather jacket, a mere fingertip away.

As she reached out, a metal object rolled from one of the pockets—a rod.

No. A stake.

Thankful for any weapon, she snatched it then looked up to get her bearings.

Mr. Long-in-the-tooth backed the wolf into a corner and stood towering over it. Undaunted, the animal rose up on its hind legs and tore at its attacker. The man wrapped his hands around the wolf's neck, his fingers disappearing beneath the creature's heavy fur.

For a while, the wolf kept lashing, reaching for the man's face. As its efforts weakened, those amber eyes turned to focus on Stacy.

They spoke to her. Asking for help.

She heard sirens in the distance and hoped to God the emergency crews were coming to her rescue. But they wouldn't arrive fast enough. She stood, supporting herself against the wall. Stumbling the distance, stake raised above her head, she reached her enemy and thrust the weapon into his back.

The wolf fell to the ground, hacking. The flesh and blood man who'd held the animal was gone. Only his clothes remained, smoke spiraling up from the pile.

What the hell?

Had the baddie crawled into a manhole? Nothing else could explain his Wicked Witch of the West exit but, when Stacy gave the area a visual search, she didn't see anything except solid asphalt.

And there was no time to worry about it. Just ahead, Stacy saw another powder-white man—leaner, meaner, and uglier than the first. His bleached hair was slicked back as though he'd come from a *Grease* audition, though his clothes wouldn't have matched the fifties-style musical. He wore a rust-colored suit with a European cut—expensive but tacky—the shade doing nothing to enhance his red eyes.

The wolf let out a sigh along with Stacy, as if experiencing the same *oh-shit* moment. In a heartbeat, the animal summoned its strength and dove between her and the rusty-draped man, protecting her once again. Its low growl, amplified in the enclosed space, vibrated in Stacy's chest.

The approaching wail of sirens failed to deter their new foe on his march toward them. However, the appearance of two more wolves and a tall redhead did.

Was the woman a rep from the Woodland Park Zoo rounding up escapees? Or a trainer taking her circus animals for a walk? Whatever the case, the newly arrived trio made an imposing sight. Rusty took one look at them and vanished in a blur of speed.

Stacy felt a tug on her sleeve. Her wolf hero held the fabric between his teeth. He gave it another yank, urging her from the scene.

"The police are on their way. I have to stay."

Why was she explaining this to an animal? One she should be backing away from in fear? Only she didn't feel frightened at all. This creature had saved her. She trusted it. Plus, it was about the most gorgeous thing she'd ever seen.

Boy, she needed a stiff drink. Maybe two. Or four. Especially when she saw the police cars race by, overshooting their mark.

She turned back to the wolf. "You see, the cops—"

Only the wolf was gone. The man, who'd first come to her rescue, now half-dressed, bruised and bloody, sagged against the wall, his leather jacket in his hand.

This guy had it all going on. Bulging biceps, sure. Six-pack abs, check. But it was the intensity of his copper-colored eyes that glued her to the spot.

While her mouth hung open, the bleeding man took a step toward her and clutched her arm. "We have to get out of here. Now."

She dug in her heels. "I can't leave. I'm a witness."

"To what? An attack from a bunch of clothes?"

Stacy looked at the still smoldering material and shook her head. "No. To a murder."

She pointed to the place behind the dumpster, her hand trembling. She didn't want to see it again—an older man, his throat ripped out, his unseeing eyes staring up at the cloudy sky.

* * *

RAFE RECOGNIZED THE corpse. It belonged to Paul Smiley. The man his team had been sent to find. The one they'd been told to protect.

They were too late. The renegade vampires had already changed history.

And the woman at his side? Not since Daciana had he felt such spirit in a female, such courage, and never before in a human.

She'd saved his life.

And compromised his mission.

An experienced time *tripper*, Rafe knew history didn't happen by chance. This woman's presence at Smiley's death scene was too coincidental. She was connected somehow, which meant trouble. The kind that gave Rafe a bellyache.

She'd seen too much. Knew too much. She was as great a threat to the future as the first two vampires had been.

As the third vampire would be.

Red lights flickered and sirens screamed as the police finally arrived on the scene. With no time to think of a better alternative, Rafe tossed the woman onto his shoulder and ran full speed down the alley—his teammates, Blaez and Caleb, still in *were*form, ripping up the pavement behind him.

CHAPTER TWO

TOMAS YANKED ON the padded stage door and slipped into his Maker's studio with little regard to the sound his entrance produced. On most movie sets, undue clatter could ruin a perfectly good take—drowning out dialogue and breaking the actors' concentration.

Andrion's films, however, contained few words.

And, with a quick perusal of the action before him, Tomas concluded a sonic boom would have done little to interrupt the two human women and the one male vampire as they writhed for the camera. All three wore police caps. Nothing else. They kept themselves occupied, sprawled over a detective's desk while exploring innovative ways to use a nightstick.

Tomas' Maker tossed an annoyed glance his way, then swung the beam of a Fresnel light in his face.

"Where's the girl? And what the fuck are you wearing?"

Tomas squinted, then bristled. Rust was the new black. At least in Europe. Andrion may have possessed the beauty of a renaissance painting and the grace of a chiseled Fred Astaire, but the vampire was a fashion neophyte. Luckily, Andrion looked stunning in everything. Tomas' Maker could have rocked a pink tutu.

"It's an Alexander McQueen. And the girl's gone."

In an instant, Andrion bolted across the soundstage, his directing project abandoned. "Gone? You mean dead? I told Teddy not to drink her."

"He tried. The girl staked him."

The roar that came from Andrion was actually enough to startle the ménage. The nightstick fell to the floor with a clatter. The male's erection took a similar topple, sans the noise.

"What about his apprentice?"

"Dusted, as well."

"That's impossible."

Tomas would have thought so too, since they'd gone back in time BBR. *Before the Big Reveal.* The average human lived in ignorant bliss of vampires and *weres.* They had no knowledge that otherworldly creatures roamed incognito among them, and wouldn't have the speed or expertise to kill one.

Yet this girl did.

"She had help." Tomas paused for dramatic effect. The naked trio weren't the only ones in the room with acting talents. "Rafe Garrett was there."

A nerve near Andrion's left eye pulsed. Other than that, he gave no indication of concern. But Tomas knew better. When Rafe tracked them down before, Andrion ran. To the past.

Tomas didn't want to uproot again. He liked it here. Liked the freedom, and the fashions, and the fast cash he was making on Wall Street. He liked it all too much to abandon his new digs without a fight. Unfortunately, Andrion wasn't the kind of Maker you bossed around. You had to plant seeds. Throw out an idea and let him take credit for it. Tomas spent most of his day feeling like a housewife from the fifties, developing the fine art of manipulation into an Olympic sport.

"We should get rid of that wolf, once and for all." Tomas waited for his words to germinate, watched Andrion's mind at work. His striking eyes, with those ridiculously long lashes, calculated the tactical risks the way Tomas analyzed the Dow.

"The girl's with Garrett? Did you see where they went?"

After the carnage in the alley, Tomas had watched Rafe and his colleagues from the safety of a rooftop and noted the direction of their retreat. "I'll find them."

"Good. Then deal with it, T.J."

Tomas sneered inwardly at the diminutive form of his name. A diminutive to diminish. Hardly a worthy tactic for a Maker. Tomas already knew his place, knew he got all the dirty work. Only this job would bring huge gains, as well—earning him the admiration and loyalty of the vampires in Andrion's nest. And put Tomas in a good position when it came to choosing sides.

Before his Maker could wander off, Tomas dropped the bomb. "Rafe brought a team. One that includes Tala Lamoureux."

Instead of balking, Andrion grinned. "That must fry his ass. Good. He'll be distracted." Then Andrion walked away, leaving Tomas to scamper after him, reduced in stature with each degrading step.

"I'll need a team of my own."

Andrion paused, his gaze sweeping over the cast and crew. "Use whomever you like," he said at last, flicking his hand as though bored with the triviality of it all. Though once out of the light where no one else could see, he seized Tomas by the lapels and pulled him close. "Just get the girl. Squash the others."

After Andrion sashayed back to the performers, Tomas used his palms to iron his suit coat and shrugged off the encounter. He may have lost face with some of the nest. But his garden had begun to grow.

* * *

RAFE DIDN'T STOP until he was safely inside the warehouse with his comrades.

And the woman.

He bolted the door and barked his intentions. "I'll be in sickbay. Tala, get ready to do your thing."

The infirmary was hidden behind a faux brick wall. As he neared it, he set the woman on her feet and turned her to face him, blocking her view as he opened the portal. He kept his hand on her arm, in case she fainted. Or tried to bolt.

"What's going on? Who are you?"

Strike fainting. This woman was demanding answers. Even with a broken rib, if his hunch proved correct.

He smiled. The female had spunk. Again, she reminded him of Daciana, in that way. But she was wholly different in every other—delicate and sugary on the outside with a fiery core, like a daub of meringue with a jalapeño center. *Aur-moot*, they called it, among his kind. And he longed to feel the sweet burn.

"Believe me, the less you know the better," he told her, as he guided her into the room.

Where the rest of the abandoned warehouse looked as an outsider would expect—with dust and debris on the uneven cement floors—sickbay was a germ's nightmare. High-tech and antiseptic, gleaming in white and chrome.

He secured the door behind him to prevent her escape, then lifted her onto the examination table.

She sat on the edge of it, her face pinched, as if every inch of her body screamed with pain. During the fight, the flow of adrenaline would have kept some of her discomfort at bay. Not anymore. He winced in sympathy and gave her a visual check.

She had a gash on her cheek and a swollen, bloody lip. Her short, dirt-smeared skirt exposed her knees. Both were scraped and bleeding. All injuries that could wait. He'd tend to any broken bones first.

"Take off your shirt," he ordered. When she hesitated he added, "Or I'll do it for you."

"Why should I let you touch me?"

Damn. That's all he wanted to do. Run his fingers through that mess of blond hair.

He gave himself a virtual rap on the knuckles. Were most humans so tempting? He hadn't dealt with the species enough to know. First Pack

14

mixed with their own kind. That's how they stayed First Pack. Now this human, this woman, had him wondering about the motives behind that segregation.

Maybe it was their shared experience in the alleyway. Or maybe he'd gone too long without a female in his bed. Whatever the reason, he was drawn to her. Like a compass needle to magnetic north.

He cleared the erotic fur ball from his throat and reminded himself she was a patient. "Suffer through the pain, if you want. Your choice."

Her eyes searched his, those baby blues filling with moisture. "What're you going to do to me?"

Rafe got the message. Her fear was far greater than her pain. Time for him to back off and give her some space.

He leaned against the cabinet opposite her, arms over his chest, ankles crossed. *Mr. Casual.*

"Sorry. I forgot my first aid etiquette." He used his most persuasive smile. "I have emergency medical training. I'd like to help you. If you'll let me."

Even from the other side of the room, he could smell her mistrust, see it quaking through her body. Still, she was defiant. "Why didn't you just... take me to a hospital?"

She had him there. They were only blocks away from a medical center. "I didn't want you to have to wait in line at emergency. Didn't know if you had insurance." He rested his hands on the counter behind him, opening his chest to her in what he hoped was a non-threatening pose. "Will you let me help you?"

She contemplated him a moment longer. Then reached for the buttons on her blouse, flinched, and let her arms flutter to her sides. "I can't."

He crossed the room in one step, behaving like a high school kid on his first date. Again, Rafe reminded himself he was an emergency medic.

He reached for the top button on her blouse and undid it. Then moved lower. Each release revealed more of her silky camisole, more of her skin. Her perfume—a crazy mix of lavender and apple—reached out and squeezed his lungs. But it was her personal aroma, the one concealed beneath the bottled stuff that imprinted on his senses—warm and earthy, like the forest after a sun shower.

On the fourth button, the heels of his hands brushed against her nipples, which pebbled beneath his touch.

This was such a bad idea. He should have let Blaez see to her injuries. He was older and more disciplined. He would be able to control himself.

"Why were you in that alley?" Rafe had to question her at some point. Doing it now might take his mind off her body. And his.

"Work."

A vague answer and spoken through gritted teeth. Until she was out of pain, getting information from her was going to be slow.

"What kind?" Rafe prayed her occupation had nothing to do with helping the renegade vamps. Killing her would be a damn shame.

"I design computer programs and web pages. I was meeting..." She gulped in air—a mistake given her condition. A grimace followed before she continued. "...a new client. At his office."

"The place getting a new brick facelift?"

"Yes."

"How'd it go?"

She shook her head. "He was a no-show."

Her lame explanation raised Rafe's suspicions. However, she didn't appear to be lying. Sure, her voice wavered, but she was hurt. Her eye contact held steady.

Rafe slipped the blouse from her shoulders, letting out a breath as she sucked in one. Gently, he felt her sides. The tips of her breasts, hard and pink beneath the sheer silk, made his mouth water.

He licked his lips. "What about the guy who attacked you?"

"I went to throw... some garbage in the dumpster. That's when I saw... the dead man. Then that psycho... grabbed me. If it wasn't for you... and that wolf—"

A hint of recognition glimmered in her eyes. Had she realized the truth? That he and the wolf were one and the same? Distraction was his best weapon.

He pulled away and pressed the control panel on the examination table. The artwork behind the woman shifted to one side and revealed the sickbay monitor. He hit a series of buttons and performed a quick scan. When the machine whirled, the woman tried to swivel around toward it.

"Hold still." Rafe looked at the screen and frowned.

"Is it bad?"

"A broken rib." He went to the far cupboard and returned with a portable *heilen*, a wallet-sized device they used in the treatment of breaks and abrasions.

Normally, he wouldn't have revealed it to a civilian. Nature could heal their cuts and scrapes. However, in this case, even after Tala erased the woman's short-term memories, she'd still have a broken rib. Difficult to explain, no matter how you sliced it.

He held the machine to her side and let it do its magic.

A half-minute later, her eyes widened. "It doesn't hurt anymore." She took a deep breath. "Well, hardly."

"The break's mended. But it'll be tender for a few days. Breathe normally, though. Otherwise fluid can build up in your lungs."

"That device—I didn't realize something like that even existed. Is it experimental? Something invented for the military? When's it going to be available to the public?"

Not for a hundred and fifty years. "Not till we figure out how to mass produce it," he said, pleased that she'd assumed he was with one of her government's agencies, and that she'd accepted his makeshift answer. At least, she didn't ask any more questions about it.

Now for the rest of her.

Bruises were to be expected. Humans managed to bang themselves up all the time, never remembering when or how. What concerned him most were those two visible gashes on her face. He retrieved a bottle from another cupboard and a couple of cotton balls from a drawer.

"What's that?"

"Antiseptic. I need to clean your cuts before I close 'em." He dampened the cotton and held it just above her cheek. "It's going to sting."

"I'm ready."

He dabbed her wounds. She responded with a hiss. Once both cuts were clear of dirt, he reprogrammed the *heilen* and placed it close to her head.

She reached up and touched her cheek where the cut had been. "Oh, my God. It's like nothing happened."

"Looks that way, too." He completed the same treatment on her mouth.

She traced it with her index finger, the exact move he'd like to perform with his tongue. "That's incredible."

As was she.

He figured she was in her mid-twenties—younger than him though his lifespan was quite different than a human's. Rafe could tell she was scared, but she'd overcome it and fought like hell in that alley to save herself... and him. Now, her eyes shone with wonder as she smoothed a finger over her lips. Did she have any idea what that did to him? Or how her creamy skin looked so darn touchable? And, framed with that blond hair, it gave her a luminescence—the first light to pierce the dark tunnel he'd fallen into a year ago.

"You're all set for kissing." Rafe swore under his breath. What a stupid thing to say. Seducing a twenty-first century human, was the most appealing idea he'd had in months, but not one he could pursue. He hoped she'd taken his comment as a joke.

She smiled and parted her lips. "Is that a promise?"

* * *

STACY WATCHED HIS brows rise. Okay, maybe she'd been bold. When was the last time she'd flirted so openly with a stranger?

Besides never.

But she'd never longed for a man's touch so much.

His eyes narrowed as he gave her a silent appraisal. "Feeling good?"

"Fantastic." Never better, in fact. A strange euphoria swept over her, as if she'd just thrown a ceremonial pitch at Safeco Field, right after accepting the Nobel Peace Prize.

"It's a side-effect of the treatment. Your brain wasn't prepared for the sudden release of pain so it's still producing endorphins. That I-wanna-go-hug-a-tree-feeling will wear off in a few minutes."

Except Stacy wasn't thinking about foliage. She was thinking more along the lines of I-wanna-hug-from-you, big boy. After her brush with death, she needed—craved—his arms around her. To feel alive and protected. And she was sure this one-man powerhouse could deliver.

Maybe they could consider it physio.

Stacy fidgeted, worried the gadgets behind her could read her thoughts as well as they diagnosed her injuries. "Who are you?"

He hesitated for a moment before answering, as if the information was top secret. "Rafe. I'm Rafe."

The way he said it, a half-smile on his lips, made her skin ripple. *Rrrr*afe. As in *rrrr*ough and *rrrr*eady. If a man's grin could be bottled and marketed as an aphrodisiac, this guy would be a zillionaire. Only she couldn't keep her eyes focused on his mouth.

Not while he was still shirtless.

Magnificent wasn't a word she used lightly. She reserved it for art museums, when strolling through their ancient Greek and Roman statues, from the collections displayed in her hometown to the Louvre in Paris. There she'd observed human perfection, the exquisite balance of form and function, beauty and strength.

This man had it in spades. She wanted to run her fingers over his oh-so-touchable skin... trace the flawless V of his torso to its base, hidden beneath the low-riding waistband of his faded jeans... and lick her way across his rippled obliques.

She couldn't wait till he turned around, convinced the rear view would be just as...

Magnificent.

And that's not all his body revealed. It showed every injury he'd endured protecting her. He must have stepped in after that thing threw her against the dumpster and left her semiconscious. No wonder she'd missed seeing him in action.

She sobered. Remembering the alley and all that had happened there cooled her desires faster than a dip in the waters around Antarctica.

"Why don't you show me how to use that little machine? Then I could heal you, too."

"I'll doctor myself up later, thanks..."

She filled in the missing word. "Stacy."

He leaned against the table, his hands on either side of her hips, his mouth within inches of hers. He looked away from her for a moment, before meeting her eyes again.

"Stacy...today you saw something you weren't meant to."

"The thing...the way it killed that man." Her voice caught in her throat. She lowered her gaze, ashamed that she hadn't insisted on talking to the police. Whoever the dead man was, he deserved justice.

Rafe slipped two fingers under her chin and lifted her head until their eyes met. "Don't beat yourself up. Not over him. He was an assassin. He would have been dead by the end of the week. You don't owe him a thing."

Stacy wrapped her hand partway around Rafe's thick wrist, needing to hang on to something. "How do you know that? Do you work for a government agency?"

She ate the last word as a loud bang obliterated the rest of her question. When Rafe pulled away, Stacy could see the red-haired woman standing at the flung-back door.

Up close, it was clear the tall beauty was no zookeeper. With her pale skin, she looked very much like the crazy guy that attacked Stacy in the alley. Only much prettier. And mighty pissed.

Stacy jumped off the table, positioning it between her and the newcomer. Without taking her eyes off the woman, Stacy reached out, searching for something to use as a weapon.

Rafe's strong hands cradled her forearms, holding her still. "Stacy, it's okay. She's on our side."

His voice was calm, soothing. Only Stacy didn't buy into it. "What side is that?"

He gave her a tired smile. "The one that helped you."

She couldn't argue that point. He had helped. More than once. But everything about him left her with more questions than answers.

"Blaez wants your report," the woman said, directing her words at Rafe, her jaw rigid as if it had been wired shut.

"This is Tala. She'll be giving you a further treatment." The pause before Rafe's last word was subtle, but there. Stacy knew, whatever was involved with this treatment, she wasn't going to like it. Especially coming from Tala, whose mouth flatlined as she glanced at Stacy's open blouse.

Stacy took the hint and covered herself. When she looked up again, there was murder in the redhead's crimson eyes.

CHAPTER THREE

TALA GAVE STACY the once-over. And disliked her immediately.

It wasn't entirely the human's fault. *Tripping* always set Tala on edge. It was okay for the *weres*. Though generally long-lived, their existence wasn't nearly as enduring as vampires. So Tala had the extra challenge of avoiding her past self. Scientists from their time bandied several theories about world consequences if a *tripper* entered the same space as their earlier incarnation. None of them good. Tala sure didn't want to end up as the individual who brought on the apocalypse.

At least that was her official answer for the cold, definitely unfuzzy feelings she had toward the human.

Unofficially, the reasons were more complicated. Rafe figuring prominently in all of them.

"What are you going to do to me?"

Tala had a vindictive urge to let the female stew. And might have. Except for her oath to safeguard humans. One she took seriously, in spite of her predatory nature.

Less nobly, a stewing subject made Tala's job more difficult. Erasing short-term memory was far easier with a calm, cooperative patient.

"I'm just going to check your vitals. You've been through a lot and we want to make sure you're okay before we send you on your way." Tala plastered on a bedside smile.

"I don't believe you."

Another reason to dislike the human. She could sniff out a lie as surely as a vampire sniffed out blood.

Tala's smile cracked. "Relax, this won't hurt a bit."

* * *

HEAD BENT, RAFE beat tracks away from sickbay. What the hell had he been thinking?

Never before had he revealed a future happening to ease the troubled conscience of a human. Never before had he fought so hard to keep from kissing one.

Thank God his redheaded colleague was set to perform her magic and erase all memory of the afternoon's events from the human's mind. Stacy would forget about the dead guy, the vampires, and him.

It would be good. For their mission, and for her. So why did he feel like a starving man holding a bowlful of plastic fruit?

Not a question he needed to be asking right now. He pushed it to the back of his mind as Blaez approached.

"How's the human?" Typical Blaez, always straight to the chase.

"Fine. Injuries healed. Tala's with her now."

"Good. Fill me in on what I missed."

Rafe recapped everything he knew. When he told Blaez that Stacy staked one of the vampires, his team leader let loose with an appreciative whistle.

"I didn't recognize the guy she dusted. But T.J. was in that alley, too."

Blaez scratched the stubble on his chin. "I saw. He was hard to miss in that suit."

"If T.J. made the trip back to this time... then Andrion isn't far away."

Blaez clamped a hand on Rafe's shoulder and drew him closer. "I know what you're thinking. You need to let it go. The mission comes first. Before any personal vendetta."

Rafe tensed. Was he that transparent?

He'd spent the last year looking for the scumball—signing up for any shit-mission he could, sure the bastard had escaped to the past. But Andrion was elusive, always on the move, and forever out of reach. Now that Rafe had seen one of the bloodsucker's henchmen, he could almost taste the cold, meaty tang of revenge. "Andrion's dangerous."

"Agreed. He's also smart. Still, he doesn't have the technical know-how to make the jump from our time back to this one." Blaez's features hardened. "Someone else got him here. That's the person we need to find. So we can stop this history tampering. Permanently."

Rafe shirked off his team leader's grasp, needing some distance. "What if Andrion gets in our way?"

"Then we cut him down. Unfortunately, the stakes here, excuse the pun, are bigger than any of us." He shifted to stand in front of Rafe, a deep line etched between his brows. "Millions of innocent people will die, if we don't put things back the way they were. And forget about going home to our time. We'll be stuck here to witness the destruction of the country we love. I need to know I can count on you, Rafe. If you can't keep your cool and follow orders, I'd rather you sit here at base camp and do crosswords."

"Killer Sudoku's more my style."

Blaez shot him a side glance. "Smartass. You know what I mean." He switched his tone to a fatherly one. "You're an important member of the team, Rafe. Vital to our mission. But I won't have you jeopardizing it because you're thinking with your heart and not your head."

"It won't happen," he promised Blaez, pretty sure he could keep his word, since he didn't have much of a heart left. "So what's next?"

"Plan B."

Rafe nodded, ready to hear it.

"The man we were sent to protect is lying dead in that alleyway. The renegades struck earlier than expected and have already altered the future. That leaves us with five days to restore history before our pickup, 'cause we sure as hell don't want to risk another trip back for this breach. So we move on to the focal point of our mission—the governor." Blaez walked over to the well-used map of twenty-first century Seattle they'd slapped on a wall and pointed to one of the harbors.

"There's a yacht party in his honor, here, Saturday afternoon. That's when the key event of our mission took place historically. So the vamps are sure to attend. We'll be there to intercept and crush them. With as few human casualties as possible."

Blaez directed the last line to Caleb, who'd joined them and was busy flexing his muscles. Some of the puffiness in the young lycan's chest deflated and wariness curved his upper lip. Was he reacting to the odor that curled around Rafe's nose?

He sniffed the air. Stale, rank... dead.

Vampires.

Rafe's heart kicked into overdrive. He took a wide stance, his hands fisting, as he checked every direction. Their scent was all around him. They were nearby. But where?

A shadow passed over the grime-covered skylights. Before Rafe could issue a warning, they were under attack, glass shards showering down around them like knives.

Shielding his eyes, Rafe shot a look upward. Four vampires, two on either side of the room, crashed through the skylights. Within seconds, they'd be at ground level.

Rafe ran toward the biggest vamp's projected landing site, casting off his clothes as he wolfed-it. That would leave Blaez to deal with the youngest and least powerful. Caleb could amuse the other two until Rafe finished with his.

Unless the big vamp finished Rafe first.

He was able to get in the opening blow, ripping a chunk out of the undead man's leg, before the bastard had time to recover from his leap.

Behind him, the grunts and growls of a life and death struggle echoed off the walls, imitating the sound of rolling thunder. The air thickened with the heat of hand-to-hand combat and the metallic odor of spilled blood.

Like a dancer leading his partner on a ballroom floor, Rafe began maneuvering his opponent around, so the vamp's back faced the rest of the room. Rafe wanted a clear vision of the battleground. He wasn't about to let one of those leeches sneak up on him.

Above the din, he heard Blaez shout his name. He turned in time to see one of Caleb's adversaries pointing a *zilva-kieg*, the barrel aimed straight at Rafe.

He dodged left. Silver bullets screamed past his ear and ricocheted off the brick wall with a high-pitched crack.

He let go a howl and charged across the room, shedding his wolf-form mid-stride. Another bullet whizzed by, parting his hair as he scooped up a section of the skylight's broken frame, and plunged the wooden piece into the gun-toting vamp's chest.

Naked and vulnerable in human form, Rafe rolled to his left and landed in a low crouch. Panting, he scanned the room and prepared for the next attack.

Caleb was dripping blood from a head wound, but stood triumphantly above the smoldering remains of the largest vampire. Tala, who'd joined in the fight, helped Blaez finish off his assailant with a dropkick and a spike.

That left one vamp on the loose, and long gone.

Rafe dragged in a breath and forced his battle-weary legs into a standing position. He wanted to collapse onto a bed and sleep for twelve hours. But their base camp was breached. There'd be no rest for them now. They needed to move. Fast. Before the vamps brought in reinforcements.

"Take whatever supplies you can carry," Blaez ordered. "Destroy everything else." Then he approached Tala, asking the question on Rafe's mind. "How did it go with the human?"

"I tried hypnosis, psychic touch, even brainwave treatment. She still remembers everything." Tala's eyes darkened. "Especially Rafe."

Caleb smacked him on the arm. "Way to go, buddy."

Rafe ignored him and focused on Tala. He'd hoped his colleague would uncover the truth behind Stacy's involvement in Smiley's death. That information was locked up tight in the human's mind, along with the rest of her memories. "Where's Stacy now?"

The redhead looked over at the sickbay portal, her mouth opening in a silent O. "She was right behind me."

"Which means she either escaped during the fight," Blaez concluded, "or the vamp that got away snatched her."

Alarm, hot and swift, surged through Rafe's body, obliterating his weariness. Had the vampire renegades infiltrated the warehouse hideout with the sole purpose of kidnapping Stacy? If so, why?

The wolves kept their missions covert. Their adversaries weren't so careful. Ensuring Stacy's silence wouldn't have been a motive.

23

Unless she was a threat to them in some other way.

Rafe clenched his fists. He'd brought her into his world. It was his duty to safeguard her. He'd track her, by scent alone, if he had to. Because the thought of those bloodsuckers harming her—even so much as touching her—made his skin crawl.

But...

If Stacy had escaped on her own, then he had something even greater to protect—the future. She'd seen a piece of it and that made her more dangerous than Rafe dared to imagine.

CHAPTER FOUR

STACY WRAPPED HER arms around her middle, holding in a bad case of the shakes, as she fled the warehouse. She stumbled over cracked pavement—muscles quivering, brain on overload.

Oh. My. God.

She faltered, the pavement slanting as images of the afternoon bombarded her.

Stacy flung out one hand to steady herself, used the other to claw at the neckline of her blouse, which felt like a noose tightening around her throat.

Since finding the dead man behind the dumpster, she'd been in a near-constant state of fear—threatened and held against her will. But, through it all, she'd believed there was a rational explanation for everything. Even fanged creatures that drank blood.

Then, in the warehouse, she'd seen a man transform into a wolf. A man she knew as Rafe.

Tears streamed down her face, while her heart drummed out a military beat. When she'd first met her rugged savior, she'd thought he and the wolf were separate entities, both struggling to rescue her.

Now she knew the truth. Hard as she tried, she couldn't deny what she'd witnessed firsthand.

Nothing in her daily life had prepared her for the sight of a person morphing into an animal. Conjuring computer magic for politicians didn't come with supernatural hazards. Public officials didn't like controversy. Which made her perfect for the job. In spite of her dad's profession, she'd managed to stay anonymous, invisible, and had always planned to keep it that way.

She needed to fight her way back to that life now. Or risk losing her sanity. So she focused on the practical, the tangible, the familiar.

Stacy started by taking control of her panic attack. She wiped her cheeks and employed her usual distractions—stamping her feet, clenching and unclenching her fists. Able to run again, she took off at a jog to the alley where all the craziness began, bent on retrieving her purse, laptop and offering the police whatever information she could to aid their investigation—without disclosing anything that would land her in a padded room.

She hoped the police hadn't contacted her father yet, and needed to get to a phone to let him know she was all right. Before he sent out the National Guard.

Thank goodness she'd slipped a few dollars and a credit card in the pocket of her skirt. At least she could find a cab and get home after collecting her belongings. Just as she settled on her plan of action, she heard footsteps coming up alongside her. A hand fell on her arm.

She was ready to swing and bust a nose. Then she saw the cop's uniform, and the tall officer inside the outfit. Stacy was so relieved to see him, she almost wept again.

"Excuse me, Miss." His gaze traveled down her body. "Are you okay?"

Stacy snuck a peek at her clothes, stained with dirt and blood. She'd seen dressier roadkill.

"I'm fine. I—" Her words dried up mid-thought as she spied the items in his hand—her laptop and purse. "You found my stuff."

His brows reached for each other, doing the skeptic's dance. "Your name?"

"Anastasia Cadell."

"Same as on the ID in the purse. Good." He nodded and passed the items to her. "We've been looking for you, following up an incident that occurred nearby. In an alley. That's where we recovered your belongings. Did you witness anything unusual there, Ms Cadell?"

Stacy played with the strap on her bag, stalling. What was she going to tell the policeman? A tale filled with vampires and werewolves? Till now, she hadn't let herself say the words. Avoided thinking them. How could she begin to explain the existence of these fantastical creatures when she couldn't work her own brain around it?

The officer pushed his mirrored sunglasses higher on his nose. "I need to record your statement, while everything's fresh in your mind. My partner's investigating a related disturbance in a warehouse one block over. We can interview you there, or drive you to the station."

Chewing her bottom lip, Stacy weighed her options. How best to keep a low profile? "I'd really like to go home and clean up—"

"Understood. We'll interview you at the scene then, and get you on your way. Follow me, please."

He pulled out a walkie-talkie and spoke into it as he led the way, reporting that he'd discovered a witness. Stacy tagged along at his side, mentally rehearsing her statement.

Within minutes, they found a squad car parked outside a large brick structure, the windows of which were covered with black plywood. The officer reached for the door on the building. "After you."

Stacy stood at the threshold, blinking as her eyes adjusted.

Large, bright movie lights illuminated a couple of set pieces. One was decorated as an office, the other as a jail cell, where two topless women were fondling each other, their tongues intertwining.

Several men operated equipment, none looking terribly interested in the action in front of them. In fact, the cameraman yawned. Another forty-odd people meandered about the set—some human, some most definitely not.

No one alive was that pale.

Stacy grabbed the door frame, determined to stay on the sane side of the entrance. Before she could make a break for it, the officer pushed her into the warehouse and closed the door behind them.

He came up beside her and bared his Chiclets-white teeth. "Okay, I'm not really a cop. Just an actor. Johnny Hardbit. Maybe you've seen some of my movies."

"I don't think so." She attempted a casual smile, as she went into reverse and made her way for the exit, praying for a quick end to the terror-filled day that had just got a whole lot worse.

She took two steps and collided with something solid. The door, she hoped. She reached behind her, feeling for the handle.

A voice with a faint German accent hissed in her ear. "A little lower and you might get my attention."

She jerked her arm to her chest as she spun around. There, in front of the door, was Rusty, her nemesis from the alley, fangs in full view.

"With hand action like that, this little girl could be your new costar, Johnny."

The would-be actor took off his sunglasses, revealing a pair of brake-light red eyes. Stacy now saw where his tanned pancake makeup ended and his alabaster skin began.

Both men inched closer, salivating. A choked scream burned up the back of Stacy's throat. She lashed out with the only weapons she had, her purse and laptop. She whirled them around, becoming a human propeller, as she aimed for flesh.

"Stop playing with your food, boys," a booming voice chastised over a loudspeaker. Both Rusty and Johnny took a step back and damn near genuflected. She almost did too, happy for the reprieve, however short-lived.

Stacy looked in the direction of the voice. A darkly beautiful man, with glowing scarlet eyes, emerged from the shadows and drifted toward her. She couldn't say *walked*, as he seemed to glide over the floor.

He'd forfeited the hair on his head in favor of a neat chin-strip goatee. Beefy arms ended in giant hands that flowed out of an incongruent pink T-shirt. Though Stacy suspected the wording on it suited him perfectly. It proclaimed, *I eat vegetarians.*

She registered it all in a few seconds. In a blind panic, heart and lungs pumping, she launched herself at the door, praying she'd strike it lucky.

She didn't.

Stacy let out a wail as strong arms caught her—Johnny's and Rusty's. With one on either side, they suspended her in mid-air. She kicked at their legs, connecting with bone, which brought only snickers.

No matter how hard she fought against her captors, their grip remained the same. Solid and sure. Physically she was no match for them. She had to use her brain, and fast, if she was going to make it out alive.

She bit back tears and forced herself to stop struggling, though she couldn't stop trembling. It started at her knees and worked its way up to her teeth, which chattered away like the windup dentures in a joke shop. Her only hope was to conserve her strength, wait for another opportunity to escape, and be ready when they let their guard down.

She looked up at the man with the goatee. "What do you want with me?"

"You impress me, Stacy—rational in the face of adversity. I must send my compliments to your father on his parenting skills."

Her father? Is that why they'd taken her hostage? Did they expect a ransom?

She kept her mouth shut. Maybe they hadn't made the connection yet. Perhaps that was in her favor. However at this point, she wasn't above using her last name as a bargaining tool.

The man with the goatee tilted his head, eyeing her with curiosity. "Since you're to be our guest for a while, I should introduce myself. My name's Andrion. As you can see, I'm a filmmaker."

He swept his arm to indicate the set, on which the two women were now naked and taking turns twirling on an enormous purple dildo. Hardly *Gone with the Wind.*

Panic hit Stacy again, as if a giant fist had reached into her gut and hefted it up into her throat. Did they want her to perform in front of the cameras? Maybe kill her in the process? She'd heard snuff films were urban myths. What if these wackos didn't know that?

Andrion grinned. "Oh, we're not going to be filming you, my dear, if that's what has you worried. Certainly you're pretty enough to be on camera, but we have quite a different role for you to play."

Stacy snuck a breath into her lungs. "What role?"

This time, the man laughed full out. "You're our bait, Stacy." He came closer and chucked her under the chin. "Such tasty bait."

So they wanted a ransom, after all. That meant she had a little time. They'd make her call her father. Maybe keep her around for a few days, in case he needed more urging. But she'd seen their faces, which meant they had no plans to let her go.

Ever.

She was sure they could hear her heart thumping out a mad beat. Stacy worked to keep her expression neutral, as if she trusted them to let her go. Maybe then they'd get lazy, make a mistake, give her an opening to run.

"I'm sure my dad will pay," she said, to reassure them.

All three toothy men laughed, but it was Andrion who spoke. "Oh, honey—you're not bait for your father. You're bait for Rafe."

Rafe? Why would they think he would come for her? How would he find her, anyway? Confusion must have read on her face because the man with the goatee continued.

"He and I are old pals. We've drunk from the same cup, so to speak." He gestured to the man in the rust-colored suit. "T.J. tells me the wolf put up quite a fight."

So Rusty's name was T.J.—for Total Jerk, she imagined. No doubt he'd reported all the details of the battle in the alley to Andrion in living color.

But why did these people think she and Rafe had any connection? "He hardly knows me." She cursed her honesty, as well as her voice, which came out squeaking. Let them believe Rafe was mad about her. That he'd crawl through a cobra's nest, if it would save her. "But I'm sure he'll come."

Andrion hummed in agreement. "Rafe never could pass up a damsel in distress. And he obviously made an impression, since you recall him after your close encounter with Tala Lamoureux. I can only assume she attempted a little memory washing with you."

Cold fear crawled up Stacy's spine. Was that the 'treatment' the redhead had tried to perform on her back in Rafe's medical room? Mind probing? Stacy felt invaded, violated.

"What happens once Rafe finds me?" Stacy swallowed two or three times, before Andrion answered.

"Then we'll let you go, of course. It's the werewolves we want. They're a dangerous bunch, as you've seen. All brawn and no brains. They mean you harm, Stacy. Believe me."

He drifted closer, his gaze slipping to her breasts before meeting her eyes again. "Tell me, my dear... do they know who you really are?"

She wasn't sure what answer would buy her more time. So she said nothing.

"I'll take that as a no. Clever girl." He caressed her cheek with his index finger, which could have been an icicle for all the warmth it exuded. Still, she tried not to pull away. No sense in antagonizing the man who called the shots.

"You're a threat to them, Stacy," he purred. "The enormity of which they haven't even begun to understand. So guard your secrets well."

Stacy intended to. She wasn't sure she trusted Rafe. But she knew damned well, she didn't trust these guys.

Apart from the attempted 'memory washing,' about which she only had her captor's word, Rafe and his friends had done nothing to harm her. They had only confronted people who were already committing violence.

But she'd seen the vampire in the alley murder someone, unprovoked. And she knew it was only a matter of time before they'd kill her too.

CHAPTER FIVE

STACY SAT IN one of the folding director's chairs that littered the studio, munching on an apple that one of the vampires had tossed to her, calling it lunch. They'd left her untied and free to roam, as if she posed no threat to them.

She supposed she didn't and—in spite of her fear, in spite of her relief at being unfettered—the fact they gave her so little credit pissed her off. She felt like a child again, at the mercy of a charmingly cruel, emotionally bankrupt adult.

Back then, she would have cried. Hell, even an hour ago, she'd indulged in some waterworks, as she fought through her confusion and came to grips with the existence of these non-human creatures. Now, she wanted to even the score. If she was going to die anyway, she might as well take a few of her captors with her.

She wandered from her perch, wondering how close she could get to the door. The answer was, *not very*. Always Johnny—or T.J. when Johnny was filming, showing off his notable physique, and pleasuring both male and female, vampire and human with gusto—would step in front of the exit, arms over chest, a bigger barrier than the door itself.

Stacy eyed the huge movie lights above her head, all balanced on tripods. Blinking afterward left red and blue blobs dancing in front of her closed lids. If she could topple one of those lights, she might be able to take out a couple of vampires. Then, in the confusion, make a run for it.

She looked away, not wanting anyone to guess her plan, and noticed a vampire script girl (as if anyone in the movie had bothered to memorize lines), looking her way, hunger in her eyes. Stacy pulled her neck into her blouse, hoping to keep her jugular vein out of sight and out of mind.

In another corner, two humans sat with Andrion, one on each knee. Though Stacy doubted they were telling him what they wanted for Christmas. The twin twentysomethings, both topless and displaying their silicone assets, wore identical Daisy Dukes, their spiky hairdos dyed to match their denim shorts. Their eyes rolled back, either in pain or ecstasy, as the vampire took turns feeding from them.

A scene that was both erotic and gruesome.

Stacy shivered and glanced over at the action on the set. The sexual encounters displayed there were almost yawn-worthy by comparison, with textbook positions and fake sighs. Andrion's off-camera antics were far more interesting.

She watched him, torn between disgust and curiosity. He and the twins had changed positions. One girl, now naked, was bent at the waist, her feet and hands on the floor, while Andrion, still somewhat clothed, took her from behind. The other twin, defying gravity, sat atop her sister's hips and faced the vampire, her legs wrapped around his waist, his fangs buried in her neck. If the porn industry didn't pay off for the trio, they could easily find work with the Cirque du Soleil.

In the midst of it all, a bare-assed Johnny barreled onto the office set with a gun in his hand. He popped off a few blanks at another man and exclaimed, "A pistol's not all I'm packin'."

More shots rang out. Except they didn't come from Johnny's gun, the one he was holding or the one that withered as he looked toward the exit.

Stacy sucked in a breath. There, silhouetted in the open door, was Rafe—carved of flesh and bone, clothed in jeans and leather. He had a high-tech machine gun in his hand and looked as lethal as a Roman gladiator, as hot as the June hunk from her firefighters' calendar.

She'd never been so happy to see anyone.

"Drop to the floor or die," he told the assembly.

Only the humans complied. As Stacy hit the ground, the beat of rapid fire played a staccato bassline, accompanying cries of pain, which resounded like a chorus above her. She flinched with every deafening blast, the harsh roar of gunfire juxtaposed with the bell-like ping of each bullet casing as it hit the cold concrete.

Acrid smoke filled her lungs. A cloud of sulfur circled around Rafe, framing him, his biceps taut as his arms fought against the gun's recoil.

He locked eyes with her and jerked his head. She understood and began crawling to him, keeping her head low. She reached Rafe just as his ammunition was spent. He tossed the gun to her along with a fresh clip.

"Reload it, if you can. But keep moving."

Her ears were ringing so loudly, she could barely make out his words. She examined the weapon, her hands shaking, her spirits sinking.

How in hell did the thing reload?

She'd once dated an egocentric gun enthusiast, who enjoyed showing off his collection to her, but this weapon was unlike anything she'd ever seen. As she struggled with it, Rafe reached into his jacket and withdrew a handful of stakes. He shrugged out of the leather and flung the blades at the approaching vampires with the skill of a professional knife thrower.

A flick of a switch later, Stacy discovered the magic combination to reload the gun, just as Johnny charged at them, teeth bared like the rest of him. Panicked, Stacy aimed and squeezed what appeared to be the trigger. The recoil knocked her a foot back, while pain rippled up her forearms. She recovered in time to see her bogus policeman glance down at the hole in his trunk, and collapse into a pile of dust.

Rafe's quick smile of approval filled her with pride. "Good shot. I'll take it from here." He eased the weapon from her aching hands. "Get behind me."

She didn't argue the point, just followed his instructions.

He continued the onslaught with a dozen more stakes and another round of bullets. All found flesh, but not all penetrated vampire hearts. The wounded fell but, to Stacy's shock and horror, the same ghouls reappeared a few minutes later healed and hungry for revenge.

Weapons once again spent, Rafe used the butt end of his gun as a bat, knocking three more attackers in the head before a fourth managed to get close enough to jab one of the discarded stakes into Rafe.

Blood, dark and thick, spread over his T-shirt, drenching the area near his shoulder. There was a collective gasp in the room and two dozen pairs of fangs clicked into place—the sound of hungry vampires, ready for dinner.

Stacy looked up at Rafe, his face drawn with pain. While his chest heaved from the exertion of the last few minutes, she found it impossible to draw breath. He nudged her with his foot, signaling for her to continue to the door and escape on her own.

Only she wasn't going anywhere. Not without him.

She reached for the handle and pulled herself up. With her other hand, she clasped his belt and tugged him back with her, ready to open the door and make a run for it.

But the vampires were already on them, crowding around, teeth snapping, all set for a bite.

In a flash, Stacy was holding onto a belt and pants, but no man. Before her emerged a snarling wolf. It lashed out at one vampire, tearing off an arm, blood spurting over them.

As the droplets hit the floor, someone grabbed Stacy around the waist and slid a cold blade against her throat. T.J.'s German-spiced voice reverberated in her ears.

"I've got the girl, Rafe. I'll slit her throat, if I have to. You know I will."

The wolf turned back to look at her. In that moment, the vampires lit on him, their swarming bodies obliterating him from view.

Above the din, and Stacy's scream, came a single word—"Stop"—and all action froze. The crowd parted as the Red Sea had for Moses, and Andrion emerged before them, his long, silk dressing gown torn and stained from the battle. He took in the bloody mouths surrounding him and the injured wolf on the floor.

"This is a set-up," he shrieked. "A diversion. He's been buying time so his teammates can storm the building."

He motioned to the beefiest vampires. "Secure him. The rest of you, search the perimeter."

As one bodybuilder made a move to lift Rafe, the werewolf returned to human form. In the end, it took two steroid-popping guys to hold him up.

Stacy could see the extent of Rafe's wound clearly now—a gaping hole near his shoulder, blood smeared across his chest and trickling down his arm.

She slapped a fist over her mouth to keep from sobbing. She had to be strong. To find a way out. For both of them.

"Your hero needs some clothes, honey. Pick 'em up."

The sarcastic sweetness of Andrion's words, followed by his harsh order, sickened her. He was like every schoolyard bully she'd ever met, with an army on his side. Yesterday she was a pacifist. Today, not so much. She'd never thought of herself as someone capable of murder, but she'd already killed two vampires. A third would make her day.

She gathered Rafe's jeans, jacket, and bloody T-shirt—wondering if she could hide a stray stake within the layers of material, but there were none to be found.

A glint of something in Andrion's hand caught Stacy's eye. A second later, she registered the item as a switchblade. He flicked it open and brandished a nine-inch knife under Rafe's chin.

Somehow, Rafe managed to look unimpressed.

A smile played on Andrion's lips. "You're a brave wolf. But a stupid one."

"Not stupid enough to be a puppet. How's *your* master, Pinocchio?"

The vampire's eyes burned with sudden rage. Then he laughed. "If I didn't know better, I'd think you were trying to provoke me—so I'll treat you to a fast death. Instead of the slow one I have planned."

"I'm game," Rafe replied. "If you make it worth my while." He delivered his one condition with a nonchalance that made it appear as an afterthought. "Let the girl go."

"You're hardly in a position to negotiate. You are, however, in the perfect position to suffer."

With his blade, Andrion skewered Rafe's T-shirt from the top of Stacy's pile. He twirled the knife until the shirt wrapped around it, like spaghetti on a fork. Then he dug the works into Rafe's wound.

Stacy closed her eyes, not wanting to see this final torture. When she opened them again, Rafe was slumped between the two muscle-bound vampires, his face the color of Wonder Bread. Above him, Andrion waved the blood-soaked shirt like a flag.

"Thanks, Rafe. I'll use this to capture the other members of your team. We'll show it to them and tell them to play nice…if they ever want to see you alive again."

The vampires tittered, a death rattle sound. Andrion acknowledged their appreciation, then gestured to the men holding Rafe to lift him higher.

"The thought of revenge has weakened you, Rafe. Made you reckless. Some women like that in a man. Did yours?"

Andrion grabbed a fistful of Rafe's hair—used it to yank his captive's head back, so they were eye to eye. "She was particularly good. Must have been that extra ingredient she was packing. Frankly, I didn't know dog could taste so delicious."

Bile climbed up Rafe's throat. He'd prepared himself for the pain. For the taunting. Not for a vivid recap of Daciana's death.

He fought back with the only thing left to him, head butting Andrion with as much power as he could muster.

The surprised vamp staggered. When he regained his footing, Andrion's face was twisted with rage, his screech as high-pitched as a boy soprano's. "Lock them in our jail cell."

Rafe allowed himself to sag as the goons holding him followed their orders. Why should he make their job easier? Let the bastards carry him.

Andrion's voice was the last thing he heard before darkness wrapped him in a painless void. The vampire's words shook the room, amplified through a speaker, like the voice of God.

"That's a wrap for today."

CHAPTER SIX

RAFE WAS THANKFUL their cage came equipped with a bed. He had to sit down, before he fell over.

He'd known the weapons he carried could also be used against him, but the pain of that stake jammed into his shoulder—cool going in, hot as blazes coming out—had almost brought him to his knees.

Now, it hardly hurt at all. Probably not a good sign.

He took in the room beyond their cell. Filming had stopped, most of the participants engaged in protecting the building, or gone into hiding. The two beefy guards who'd held him were at a nearby table, playing cards. A few scattered humans were busy cleaning up the debris from his attack. Even if he could break out of his confinement, they'd be on him in a moment. In his present state, he wouldn't be able to put up much of a fight.

More important, Stacy might get hurt in the crossfire.

She looked bad enough as it was. Not injured—at least, not on the outside. But something was eating her alive as she paced up and down the cell, holding his clothes to her chest like a security blanket.

"They let you have my jacket?"

She looked at the bundle in her arms, eyes wide, as if she'd forgotten all about it. "After checking it for weapons. I told them I needed it to keep you warm." She dropped his jeans on the bed beside him, then slung the jacket around his good shoulder and draped it over his back.

"Thanks." Rafe smiled. "I love this jacket."

It had been a present from Daciana, for their third anniversary. Everything about that night had been perfect—a great dinner, a run through the woods in wolf-form, and a tumble in their bed afterward. How could he have known there would never be another evening like it?

Seeing her murderer again fueled Rafe's body with hatred. All he wanted was to live long enough so he could kill the motherfucker.

"If I had some water, I could clean your wound," Stacy said, cutting in on his thoughts. "I asked for some, but they just laughed." She was back to her pacing. When she spoke, her voice came out as rapid and shrill as artillery fire. "It was suicide for you to come here by yourself. You against thirty vampires? I mean, I appreciate your efforts, but what the hell were you thinking?" Her frantic back and forth movements gave him vertigo.

"You nervous?" She froze and he sent up a silent hallelujah.

"Why do you ask?"

"Because you're blabbering." She was close enough that he could tug on her arm using his good one. He pulled her down to sit beside him. "What's the matter?"

Her sigh carried a tone of exasperation. And blind panic. "Beyond the obvious?"

"Yes. Beyond the obvious." Rafe leaned back against the bars. Not the most comfortable position, but at least the steel was cool against his head. "Are you claustrophobic?" He slurred the words like a drunken man.

She tensed. "I don't like locked doors. Unless I'm the one doing the locking."

Definitely a story there. But she wasn't offering it, so he didn't pry. "Look on the bright side. We may not be able to get out, but they can't get in, either."

"They have the key."

He shrugged. The resulting pain made him wish he hadn't. "A minor glitch."

Her laugh warmed him. At least he'd reassured her enough to earn it.

"Aren't you the eternal optimist?" She sobered and placed her hand on his. "Thank you for trying to rescue me. Again."

"Don't get used to it."

He turned his hand over and threaded his fingers through hers, stroking them. They were soft and dainty next to his. He wondered what she'd do if he brought her hand up to his lips. And slipped one of her fingers into his mouth, to roll his tongue around it.

Before he could act on the thought, she flipped their hands over, reversing their positions. With a fingertip, she traced the roadmap of lines that crisscrossed his palm—her touch as intimate as a French kiss.

"How did you find me?"

"I tracked you."

Her voice pitched up a notch. "You put a GPS on me?"

She jerked away. With her warmth gone, a chill crept through his body. "I don't need a GPS. Your scent is branded in my mind. And will be, for the rest of my life."

Which wouldn't be long the way he was going. His racing pulse wasn't entirely from Stacy's nearness. If he didn't get medical attention soon, he'd succumb to shock. He pulled his jacket closer.

"Speaking of minds, your redheaded friend was playing with mine. What did she do to me?"

"Nothing. Not that she didn't try." He glanced at Stacy, as much as his drooping eyelids would let him. She was doing her defiant act again, arms crossed over her chest. "You're what we call a *memansaan*—someone whose short term memory can't be erased by our methods."

"You mean I'm tenacious."

"More like stubborn. Too bad. Because you've seen things you shouldn't have."

"Like you turning into a wolf?"

That would certainly be at the top of his list. Along with the sickbay equipment. In the hands of the wrong person, those devices could be actualized before their time—even warped and used as weapons. The *heilen*, his shifting—he couldn't explain either away with smoke and mirrors to someone as intelligent as Stacy. Or blame it on little green men like he did when they traveled back to the 1960s.

"You've definitely seen too much. And for that, I should kill you."

* * *

STACY WIPED THE perspiration from her upper lip, shamed by the liquid fear seeping from her pores. She didn't underestimate Rafe's threat and had no doubt he could kill her. Even in his present condition.

He was a warrior. The kind of man who'd go down fighting. The only reason he'd stopped his assault on the vampires earlier, was to keep her from getting her throat slashed. And protecting her could very well prove the death of him.

"You risked your life to save me, so you could... *murder* me?"

The corners of his mouth twitched into an ironic smile. "No. We're here to help. But it does mean I'm going to have to trust you." He made it sound like an awesome burden. "The vamps don't concern themselves with witnesses. So why are they interested in you?"

Stacy didn't dare tell Rafe what she suspected. Not after Andrion's warning. Senses on alert, her brain whirled as she sought an answer that would satisfy him. "They said I was bait. That you couldn't resist a damsel in distress."

His expression revealed nothing, but he finally nodded. "Let's hope that's all it was. But until our mission's over, you'll have to hang with me."

"Hang?"

"Stick to. Like glue."

"How long will that be?"

He closed his eyes. "Five days."

Was he nuts? She had clients, and a major deadline due before the week was out. She had friends and family, all who'd be worried sick about her. She couldn't abandon them for Rafe's mission, whatever the hell it was.

She leapt off the bed. "Look, I had a nice, quiet life until you and your orthodontically enhanced friends came along."

"And hopefully, you'll be able to go back to it. But until I say otherwise, you're with me."

What guarantee did she have that he'd keep his word and let her go when it was all over? She wanted to ask him the question, but kept her mouth shut. She'd escaped from him once. She'd do it again, as soon as she saw an opportunity. Until then, she'd use him to help her break free of their current prison. Though, right now, it didn't look like either of them was going anywhere.

The cell may have been part of a movie set, but the bars were real, the steel door solid. She eyed the lock, forcing each breath into her lungs as old fears bubbled to the surface. For a short time, he'd distracted her. Even put a name to her nemesis—*Claustrophobia*.

She was glad Rafe hadn't pressed her for details. Not like the doctors. She'd whiled away a good part of her childhood on therapists' couches—enough to call herself a cushion. And even more time locked in her bedroom closet, quietly crying herself to sleep. She'd spent hours in her dark, tiny jail—days, sometimes—alone, cold and soaked in her own urine.

She looked over at him—his eyes shut, his head lolling to one side. Had he been that pale a moment ago? "Are you still with me?"

She took a step toward him. "Rafe?" Stacy eyed his chest, looking for movement. Was he even breathing?

Dread filled her heart. She ran to his side, frantically trying to remember her CPR training. "Rafe?" She grabbed one of his hands and shook him as she pleaded. "Don't you fucking die on me."

* * *

STACY'S IMAGE SLANTED and blurred. Rafe blinked to clear the distortion, but it didn't help. When Stacy spoke, the movement of her lips didn't match her words, like he was watching a movie with an out-of-sync soundtrack.

"You'd better lie down."

He didn't remember changing his position, but the next time he opened his eyes, he was lying flat on the gym mat of a bed, staring up at the high ceiling, his body damp with sweat.

At the far edge of consciousness, he heard the wisp of material. Then felt a searing weight on his wound. His body jackknifed, his shoulders shooting off the mattress. "What the hell are you doing, woman?"

"Applying pressure. Relax."

How could he? She'd removed her blouse and was using it on him as a dressing. And her camisole? She'd wrapped it around his shoulder to hold the impromptu bandage in place. That left her naked from the waist up, except for a hardly-there lacy bra, breasts spilling over the top.

He wasn't dead yet, but he'd definitely gone to heaven. He reached up and cradled the weight of her. She slid out of his grasp, while keeping a hand on his shoulder.

"You're not willing to give a dying man his last wish?"

Her eyes rounded then crinkled at the sides as her mouth curved. "I'm going to assume you're delirious and forgive you for copping a feel."

No denying it. He *was* lightheaded. But he sure didn't regret touching her breast—the skin firm but soft, the tip hardening against his palm. Maybe he could talk her into letting him have a taste.

"A taste of what?"

He stared at her, confused. Had he actually spoken his request aloud? He focused on her wide, blue, trusting eyes…her full pink lips.

She must have managed to ease the bleeding. His senses were returning. Even his dick showed signs of life. He slipped his hand into her hair, twining the strands around his fingers, and gently pulled her down to him.

"I'd love a taste of *you*."

She came to him on a sigh, her sweet lips pressed against his feverish ones. Her mouth was smooth as silk, and shut tighter than the locked door she was afraid of. When she started to pull away, he cupped his hand on the back of her neck, holding her in place, coaxing her lips apart.

She opened to him, his groin tightening in response. He explored her mouth, circling her tongue with his. As if he had all the time in the world.

Time.

He ripped his mouth away, grabbed her wrist and twisted it, ignoring her cry of surprise as he checked her watch.

Shit. They had five seconds.

He clamped a hand on her shoulder. "Hit the dirt."

Rafe threw her to the ground and followed her down, using his body to shield her. A second later, the first blast hit.

CHAPTER SEVEN

SPRAWLED ON THE cement, Stacy spit out a mouthful of grit, as chunks of concrete and steel crashed down around her. A hard, naked body pinned her to the spot, shielding her from the falling debris.

And she'd thought his *kiss* was explosive.

The way he'd nibbled at her lips, and made love to her mouth, left her lady bits throbbing, while the rest of her fantasized about the oh, so noticeable part of him currently pressed against her hip. If the man was this impressive with a gaping hole in his shoulder, what would he be like at a hundred percent?

Except he wasn't a man. He was some kind of human-wolf cross.

Strange. Forbidden.

Stacy blinked, struggling to see past the veil of both dust and lust. Filtered sunlight bled in to the studio through a hole blasted in the roof. Screams cut through the walls like a chainsaw.

She caught a glimpse of their card-playing guards. No longer sitting at the table, they now peeked out from under it.

As they emerged from their shelter, the taller one grunted. When he looked down at the wide hole in his torso, his head kept falling, his body collapsing into itself until he was another pile of rubble on the floor. Before his buddy could dive back under the table, a chest shot spun him into a pirouette—a mini-tornado of smoke and fragments.

The warmth at her back vanished. A big hand reached down to help her up—the same hand that had caressed her breast moments ago. "Come on. Time to roll."

Rafe was still as pale as the snowy top of Mount Rainier and, like the stratovolcano, somehow found the energy to look dangerous. This was a man who'd been down for the count. How he even managed to stand was beyond her. Now, he was planning a prison break?

She hated to squelch his hopes, but the two of them weren't going anywhere. "We're still locked in."

"Not for long," a voice called from across the room.

Stacy turned to find a dark-skinned man approaching them—a smoking, high-tech rifle in his hand. His hair was streaked with gray but his muscular build could have belonged to someone much younger. His intelligent eyes matched Rafe's golden ones.

The new arrival stopped at the steel door and gave Rafe a quick inspection. "You look like shit."

Rafe leaned against the bars, naked save for the improvised bandage and a splash of blood, his jacket having slipped to the floor in their mad dash to take cover. "Rough day at the office."

The way the older man smirked gave Stacy the impression this was a familiar exchange. She almost expected him to provide a verbal rimshot as a topper, the classic *ba-dum-bum*. Instead, he holstered his weapon, pulled a different device from his belt, and aimed it at the lock. The metal smoldered and the door swung open.

A moment later, Rafe was at her side, his hand warming the small of her back. "Stacy, this is my team leader, Blaez. Blaez, this is Stacy."

It was a formal introduction, considering the speaker wore less than Adam. At least Eve's partner had a fig leaf. Which wouldn't have begun to cover Rafe. Stacy concentrated on keeping her gaze level but, with peripheral vision alone, she knew the man was exceptionally gifted.

Blaez gave her a nod as he entered the cell. He eyed the material around his colleague's wound, his mouth twitching. "You used to be able to talk a female out of her shirt without a scratch, Rafe. You're losing your touch."

Stacy crossed her arms over her chest. Before she had time to blush, Rafe retrieved his leather jacket and draped it over her shoulders. She hooked her arms into the sleeves, her hands swallowed by the excess material.

As she rolled up the cuffs, Blaez walked Rafe to the bed, pulled a knife from his belt, and began cutting away at the temporary dressing.

It was the perfect time to make a run for it. Blaez had his back to her and blocked Rafe from her view. And, therefore, Rafe's view of her.

She inched her way to the steel door, keeping a watch on the two men, though both were too preoccupied to notice her movements.

Nearby machine gun fire made her jump with each blast. But the greatest jolt came when her makeshift bandage hit the floor. She stared at the material, now saturated with blood.

Rafe's.

The older man shook his head and let out a hiss. "Jesus."

Fear spread through her insides, freezing the breath in her lungs. Was Rafe's wound even worse than he'd let on?

Now at the door, she could see past Blaez. Rafe's eyes were closed, his jaw slack. Then his lids fluttered and he looked at her. She tried to smile, to reassure him, but her lips quivered and her grin wavered.

Here she was, planning to run out on him, eager for a quick return to her normal life—far away from vampires, werewolves, and the maelstrom of violence that swirled around them. Self-preservation had to be her number one goal. Right?

Damn him for coming to rescue her. It made walking away now so much harder.

Just as she turned to leave the cell, Blaez pulled three items from his belt—a bottle, a sealed packet of capsules, and a mini version of the sci-fi gadget Rafe had used to mend her broken rib. He set them on the mattress beside Rafe.

"I gotta disinfect the wound before I close it." Blaez pulled the bottle's cap off with his teeth and spit it out on the floor. "It's gonna burn."

Rafe sighed. "Yeah, yeah. Just do it."

Right before Blaez let loose with the antiseptic, Stacy rushed over and slipped her hand into Rafe's. "Squeeze it, if you need to. It'll help."

* * *

RAFE RESTED HER hand on his thigh, afraid he'd bust it if he held on. "Thanks for staying."

She looked down, chagrinned. Of course he'd seen her creeping toward the door. He was a soldier, alert to his environs even when he was running on empty. Especially then.

"It saves me having to track you down later."

Her chin came up sharp, her eyes blazing. Good. A million things could go wrong before they made their escape, and anger would best fuel her survival instincts. If he could put that fire in her heart, so be it. Although he would have preferred doing it with another kiss.

Her taste lingered on his lips, hot and sweet. But there'd be no repeat performances. Crossing the line once was enough to skew his priorities, though not nearly enough to satisfy his needs.

He took a breath then glanced at Blaez. Through clenched teeth, he uttered one word. "Go."

Blaez dumped the contents of the bottle over Rafe's wound. It felt as if a hundred razor blades cut into him, followed by a chaser of acid. "Son of a bitch!"

"That I am." In spite of the flip delivery, Blaez's expression was grim. He tossed the empty bottle to one side, programmed the *heilen*, and held it over Rafe's shoulder.

Rafe watched Stacy. She stared transfixed as the flesh around his wound began to shift, fusing together, until it was smooth. Only a slight redness was left to show where the injury had once been, and even that would fade in a few days.

Blaez finished off his ministrations by handing him a couple of antibiotics and a stimulant. Rafe dry swallowed them, their bitterness finally obliterating the flavor of Stacy's kiss.

"That closes the wound." Blaez clipped the *heilen* back on his belt as he spoke. "But you've lost a lot of blood, Rafe."

"We'll be losing more, if we don't get out of here. Fast."

Rafe made it to his feet. He had to hang on for another twenty minutes, or so. His hatred of Andrion was enough to keep him going for a while. After that, he could take a break. But he was damn well going to ask for a raise if he made it back to their home turf. He reached for Stacy's arm and headed toward the cell door.

Blaez blocked their way. "I think we have enough time for you to put on your pants, Rafe. We wouldn't want you to come out of this battle half-cocked."

"*Fresch hound*," Rafe mumbled, as he snatched his jeans and stepped into them. "What's the situation?"

"Tala and Caleb are giving the vamps a workout at the other end of the building. Our blast took out a dozen."

"With the two guys you just dusted, that leaves at least fourteen more to go, by my count."

"Which we'll dispose of another day, when we aren't so outnumbered. I'll signal the others we're ready to leave." Blaez touched his communications device then tossed Rafe his toys.

Rafe secured the guns and gadgets to his waistband and wrapped an arm around Stacy, in case she tried to ditch him again. It also gave him an excuse to hold her, warm and curvy, at his side. He followed Blaez out of the cell, weaving around the wreckage in their path.

The sound of running feet pulled Rafe up short. He sidled in front of Stacy and drew his weapon.

He heard Caleb's familiar voice a split second before the pup came racing around the corner, with Tala on his heels. She smiled at Rafe when she saw him, her fangs visible. With the smell of blood in the air, she'd have little control over those canines, no matter how well she was able to manage her predatory nature.

Her gaze shifted to Stacy and the air chilled.

Vampires were hunters. Over the centuries, their senses had evolved to a level just shy of wolves. Vamps could hear their prey's heartbeat, smell their arousal. And Rafe was positive Tala could detect residual musk from the human. Almost as well as *he* could.

Jealousy blazed in her eyes. With a bit more blood circulating through his system, Rafe was sure his own response to Stacy's scent would have been a damn sight more obvious. Still, Stacy was well aware of Tala's feelings. She went rigid at his side, but held her ground. He gave her a squeeze, impressed that she hadn't caved under Tala's scrutiny, an intimidation tactic that could make grown males cry.

Blaez led the way to the nearest exit. The blast had collapsed part of the roof, putting extra weight on the door from above.

The team leader turned to Caleb. "Can you budge it?"

The kid's muscles bunched as he yanked on the handle. Caleb braced one foot on the wall and pulled again, grunting with the effort. "Nope."

Tala nudged him out of the way and gave it a try. With the same results.

Blaez frowned. "We'll have to backtrack. Go out through the same door I came in. Follow me."

As per their training, they arranged themselves in a diamond formation, with Stacy in the middle and Rafe pulling up the rear. It was the best way to protect her and cover their flanks as they ran back through the vampires' den.

Just as the other door came into view, two identical, half-naked women ran to them, screaming like sirens. One tripped over an upturned director's chair. The other tumbled over her downed twin.

They looked back the way they'd come, their legs doing a flutter kick on the floor, as they scrambled to flee from whatever was pursuing them.

Rafe shifted his position, joining Stacy to better shelter her from the new threat.

There were at least forty of them emerging around the corner—both male and female, eyes half-closed, mouths hanging open and drooling blood. They didn't move fast, but they moved as one, their halting shuffle and pale, greenish tinge reminding Rafe of an army of Frankensteins.

"What the hell are they?"

"Goltos." Tala's one-word answer hung in the air.

Rafe shot a look at his other teammates. He was about to ask Tala what the fuck that meant, when Stacy beat him to it.

"Care to explain that to the layperson here?"

Tala bristled at the question, her shoulders tensing.

"Go ahead, Tala," Blaez ordered, as he backed away from the mass. "And make it fast."

"They're what's left when a vampire uses extreme and extensive hypnosis on a human. I've never seen one before. Thought they were pure myth."

Rafe checked his back and looked around for an alternate escape route. "Sounds like you're talking about zombies."

"Only they're alive. And reduced to the basest of human impulses. To eat, kill, and fornicate." Tala's upper lip curled in distaste. "Sometimes in that order."

"Great." With their dark, vacant eyes, the goltos looked like a battery of barracudas. And Rafe didn't want to be around when the feeding frenzy began. "Can you un-hypnotize them?"

"I can try." Tala stepped forward, holding out her arms. The veins on her forehead bulged as she attempted to make mental contact with the goltos and stop them. Still, the things kept ambling toward the twins.

Rafe smelled Stacy's fear, a mix of damp soil and cedars. He held her close, felt her heartbeat against his ribs, strong and fast, as the goltos surrounded the two women—their high-pitched screams turning from panic to terror.

CHAPTER EIGHT

RAFE TUCKED STACY behind him and took aim at the nearest golto. He was a good shot, and the blank-eyed monsters were in such a tight group, he couldn't miss if he tried.

Before he fired off a round, an icy hand grabbed his forearm. With all her vampire strength, Tala forced the barrel of his gun downward until it pointed at the floor.

Rafe growled and jerked away. No one questioned his combat decisions, especially not the undead spawn of a desk-bound paper-juggler who'd never seen battle. If a male had pulled that same stunt, the guy would be lying on the floor, spitting out teeth.

"Your mind control isn't working, Tala. We have to shoot them."

"They're human, Rafe. And I have no idea if their condition is permanent or if they can be rehabilitated."

"So killing them would be a violation of our boss' code," Blaez concluded, then cocked his gun. "You've got ten seconds to come up with another alternative, Tala."

For once, Tala was speechless. Rafe might have gloated, but being correct in a hopeless situation wasn't a win. He didn't enjoy killing but, as a special op, sometimes it was necessary, whether the casualty was a piece of lowlife shit or the unlucky passerby who got in the way.

They were the ones that haunted him. Innocents caught in the crossfire.

He shook off the memories and sneaked a breath past the sudden tightness in his chest. The goltos were casualties of war. Regrettable, but they were set to eat two blue-haired women as an appetizer. Rafe figured his team would be the main course. And their mission took precedence over the lives of four dozen killing machines, human or not.

He was about to take aim again when Caleb pushed past them and wielded a punch at the closest golto. The blow bounced off its face as if it were rubber, and it kept right on walking. The pup then grabbed a huge, fallen board and swatted it across the crowd. Wood thwacked against heads, yielding a sound similar to a mallet crushing melons.

The goltos swarmed around their prey, obscuring them from Rafe's view. He couldn't fire into the horde. His bullets might just kill the people he was trying to save.

Rafe mopped the sweat from his brow with the back of his hand, out of ideas. But he couldn't stand by and do nothing while two women were ripped to pieces. He leapt forward. Without a better plan, he shouted, "Hey, you!"

Forty heads snapped in his direction. Their half-closed eyes shot open and fixed on the blood that still stained his arm and chest. En masse, they let out a wheezy gasp, then smiled. Forty purple tongues shot out to lick forty pairs of blackened lips. They changed direction and headed straight for Rafe, their speed increasing, along with his heart rate.

At least the two humans were free. Though scraped and bloodied from the golto attack, they managed to run away.

While Rafe was now officially fucked.

* * *

IN FRONT OF Stacy's eyes, Rafe's young colleague shed his clothes, transformed into a wolf, and took a bite out of the nearest golto.

She barely had time to register shock at the metamorphosis, before the young man was back to human. He slumped on the floor, naked and hacking.

Rafe left her side to pull his friend to safety. "What happened?"

"I couldn't maintain the transformation. They taste—" Caleb shuddered as he tugged on his clothes. "Really bad. Even worse than vampires." He shot a look at Tala, his cheeks matching the color of her hair. "Sorry."

Now Stacy understood why Caleb had surged forward and tried to defeat the goltos without bullets. Rafe's muscle-bound friend had a boyish face, a set of lips that would make any high school girl drool, and a big ol' crush on Tala. In his own way, he'd been defending the vampire's honor.

Tala touched Caleb's arm and Stacy could feel the electricity from where she stood. "It's okay," the vampire said. "Thanks for trying."

Stacy wondered if the redhead knew how Caleb felt about her. Or if any of them would live long enough to care.

Blaez pointed his weapon at the goltos. "We have to shoot them, Tala."

Tala nodded, looking defeated. Stacy sympathized, but not much. From what folklore she knew about vampires, Tala was already dead. She had the least to lose.

"Fire at will."

Hearing Rafe's order, Stacy clung to his back, covering her ears with her hands to block the deafening blast.

A half-minute later, the shooting stopped. She felt Rafe's already tense muscles bunch up even more. "No effect."

Stacy didn't want to see the mayhem. She peeked around him anyway. The goltos were riddled with bullet wounds but still shambled forward, blood speckling their faces. She forced in a breath and made it count, in case it was her last.

Blaez delivered what might be their epitaph. "We're running out of options."

Stacy remembered her earlier scheme, the one she'd intended to use against the vampires. She skidded away from the others and ran to the nearest spotlight, hefted the sandbags from the tripod on which it was mounted, and began rocking. When Rafe saw what she was doing, he joined her. Together, they built up enough momentum to tip it over.

"Get back," Rafe ordered, as the light toppled. It crashed, glass pieces imploding. The goltos *oohed* and *aahed*. They followed the light with their gaze, from upright to horizontal, some pointing as it made its way to the ground as if it were a falling star. When the light sputtered and went out the spell was broken and they advanced again, driven by their lust for blood.

Stacy and Rafe scurried to the next light and, instead of trashing it, swiveled it around. Physical pain and the threat of electrocution didn't deter the goltos, but Rafe's shouting had. The movement of the light sidetracked them, too. And that's all Stacy needed, a little diversion. With that, they could make their escape.

Rafe seemed to know what she was thinking. Together, they swung the light. The goltos watched the beam arc across the wall, mesmerized. They began moving toward it and away from the team.

"Good going, champ." Rafe grinned. He was proud of her. She could see it in his eyes, in the way his whole face lit up, and damned if that didn't make her insides turn to mush.

"We still need an exit plan," Blaez reminded them.

Stacy recalled the hole in the roof. "How about up? We could climb one of these tripods and—"

Before she could finish her sentence, Tala ran to the opening, pulled a grappling gun from a holster at her thigh, and shot it into the hole. The hook landed on the roof, secure. The vampire then bent her knees and leapt ten feet in the air. She grabbed the rope, wrapped her long legs around it, and pulled herself up the rest of the way. In the time it took Stacy to say, "Holy shit," Tala was on the roof, peering down at them through the jagged opening.

Rafe cupped Stacy's hands on the tripod, as he called out to the youngest member of his team. "Caleb, take over here. It'll be your turn to go up next, Stacy."

49

She stared at Rafe, as he led her to the opening. Did he really expect her to fly through the air? "If you're looking for an encore—"

"Don't worry." Rafe grabbed the rope and tied a loop in the bottom of it. "Just put your foot in here and hang on tight. Tala will pull you up."

Stacy wasn't sure she trusted Tala. The vampire hated her on sight. But it was better than being eaten alive by the goltos.

She rested her hands on Rafe's shoulders as he placed her foot in the stirrup. "You'll be right behind me, huh?"

He smiled but didn't answer. And in the silence, she knew what he was going to do—sacrifice himself to make sure everyone else got out safely.

Something inside her chest twisted, as if a giant hand had latched onto her heart and tried to rip it out. This guy kept getting better and better. Hot and compassionate men were hard to come by, and Rafe had just added bravery and selflessness to the list. As he began to holler up the command to lift her, Stacy flung her arms around his neck and pressed her lips to his.

* * *

WHAT WAS LEFT of Rafe's heart exploded, as Stacy slipped her tongue into his mouth.

For the past year, he'd functioned in about the same mental shape as the goltos, hoping that on his next mission, enemy fire would put him out of his misery.

But a kiss like this was worth living for.

Tala's voice, edged with impatience, intruded on the moment. "Are we ready to go, or what?"

Stacy pulled away, flushed and breathless. She grabbed hold of the rope. "Take care of yourself, cowboy."

He watched as she made her ascent, never breaking eye contact. Only when Stacy disappeared through the opening, did her magic over him weaken.

"Caleb, you go next." Rafe replaced him at the tripod and resumed its to and fro motion. But there was a difference in the goltos. The light no longer brought out sighs. They didn't shuffle back and forth to follow it anymore. They watched the light, but it held less interest for them.

He tried altering the pattern, which increased their curiosity for another minute. But that attempt too, died.

And worse, they'd fanned out, forming a semi-circle around him and Blaez. The only good thing was that five of the goltos they'd shot had finally keeled over. But they continued to crawl toward the smell of fresh flesh.

Rafe chanced a look up. Caleb was now on the roof and sent the rope floating back down. "Your turn," he told Blaez.

But his team leader grabbed the tripod and shouldered Rafe out of the way. "You go first."

The words stole Rafe's breath and muddled his thoughts. "I-I always bring up the rear."

"Not this time. I'm the captain. It's my job to go down with the ship. It's your job to carry on in my place."

"But—"

"That's an order, soldier."

Rafe locked his jaw and swallowed hard. Blaez was the closest thing he had to a friend, a father. He wrapped his arms around the male, around the wolf.

His alpha, his mentor.

Stacy's voice shouted down to them. "We hate to interrupt your bonding moment, but you boys need to move it."

Blaez smiled. "You heard the lady. And don't worry. I'll be right behind you."

Chest tight with worry, Rafe shoved his foot in the loop and hollered his one-word command. "Go." Caleb and Tala lifted him, while Stacy's eager face looked over the edge.

Halfway up, Rafe saw the goltos advance on Blaez. "Lower me. Fast."

But he couldn't wait. Rafe supported his weight with his arms and pulled his foot out of the stirrup. He shouted a warning to his team members that he was about to jump, then let go of the rope.

Freefalling, he bent his knees, readying himself for the impact. He landed dead center in the mass of bodies, Stacy screaming his name.

CHAPTER NINE

THE BODIES OF three goltos broke Rafe's fall. They slammed to the ground under him, bones crunching.

He caught a glimpse of Blaez through the tangle of legs. The team leader lay on the ground bleeding, huge chunks ripped out of his flesh.

Cold rage surged through Rafe's veins and gripped his heart in a stranglehold. Fueled by desperation and anger, he dove for the pole on which the nearest spotlight was mounted and heaved it up. Holding it horizontally, he spun around, gathering up the goltos in a straight line, howling as he whirled.

With all his might, he pushed the fiends back—far enough, he hoped, to buy escape time for him and Blaez. On wobbling legs, he ran to his team leader. But Rafe's touch brought only cries of agony.

Blaez panted through clenched teeth. "I'm finished, Rafe. Save yourself and the others."

Rafe grabbed the lapels of Blaez's jacket—afraid to move him, afraid not to. He looked into his friend's eyes, calm and clear, in spite of the pain.

A sob crawled up Rafe's throat. He rammed it back down and pounded his fist on the floor. He knew Blaez wasn't afraid of dying, but Rafe sure as hell wasn't ready to let him go. "I'm not leaving without you."

Summoning the last of his energy, he hoisted Blaez over his shoulder with an audible grunt. He grabbed the end of the rope, put his foot in the stirrup, and signaled for his teammates to lift them, praying for ten more minutes of strength so he could get them all out of danger.

As they made their slow ascent, the goltos gathered below. They held out their tongues, lapping up droplets of Blaez's blood, like kids catching snowflakes. Sickened by the sight, Rafe looked up.

Stacy waited above him, her arms outstretched, ready to help lift Blaez through the hole in the roof. That she'd be so willing to give of herself, after she'd been dragged into his fucked-up world, squeezed at his chest, making it ache.

Until a bullet whizzed by him, threatening a very different kind of hurt.

Rafe looked around and saw Andrion enter the room below, a pack of vampires clumped around him. As sitting ducks went, he and Blaez made for a big target, and he knew Andrion was a decent marksman. Which the vamp proved with his next shot.

Fire laced through Rafe's leg as a bullet grazed his thigh. He almost lost his balance but hung on, as his teammates pulled Blaez and him onto the roof.

He slumped against the asphalt shingles. While Caleb and Tala saw to Blaez's injuries, Stacy ripped off a strip of her skirt and fashioned a tourniquet for Rafe. Given his rate of injury, he'd have her naked before the day was done.

"I'm so glad you got away," she whispered to him, her lips caressing his ear, her breath sending warmth from his neck to his toes.

He hated to ruin the moment, but lingering to enjoy it wasn't an option. "We're not off the roof, yet."

* * *

STACY GLANCED AT Rafe's blood-soaked jeans, panic skittering around her insides. Then Rafe wove his fingers through her hair, his touch as reassuring as his voice.

"It'll be okay. Tala will help you down to street level."

The vampire was currently in the process of lowering Caleb and Blaez with the same rope that had pulled them up. Stacy clutched Rafe and forced a smile.

"Are you going to be *right* behind me this time?"

His eyes crinkled. "Oh, yeah. I like the view of that behind."

Fear retreated as a sexual heat spread over Stacy's skin. Covered in blood and grime and looking as if he were about to keel over, Rafe could still make her heart flutter.

"I'll hold you to that, cowboy."

Tala *ahemed* at their side. "Unless the two of you plan to stay up here and greet Andrion—"

"Take Stacy first."

The vampire popped a hand on each hip. "I can take you both at once. You forget, Rafe—I'm stronger than you. In more ways than one."

The saucy tilt of Tala's head left Stacy mouthing a silent, "Ouch." She'd obviously stepped right in the middle of whatever was going on between Rafe and the redhead.

He sneered at the vampire and thrust his foot into the loop. Rafe held onto Stacy tight as they made their descent, using his muscled body to shield her from their foes, who could attack again from any direction. When the two of them touched the ground, Tala leapt from the roof and landed a foot away, the rope coiled in her hand.

Caleb's voice called out to them, louder than the approaching emergency sirens. "Look what I found." The young man stood beside a shiny, black convertible—someone's cure for either a mid-life crisis, or a teeny weenie. Caleb already had Blaez slouched in the middle of the backseat, and the doors to the vehicle open. "Our chariot awaits."

Stacy shot a look at Rafe. "Can you hotwire one of *these?*"

"Even better." He pulled a gadget from his belt and aimed it at the car, which roared to life. Along with the radio. It blared with an overtly sexual ditty, banned by commercial stations and most dance clubs.

Rafe shouted over it. "Takes out the Stolen Vehicle Tracking device, too." With that guarantee, he limped over to the far side and slipped behind the wheel.

Stacy nudged Caleb. "He's hurt. He shouldn't be driving."

"He's the only one of us who can."

She stared in amazement. Of his four adult friends, Rafe was the only one who knew how to operate a vehicle? "Maybe *I* should drive then."

Tala retrieved a pair of sunglasses from an inner pocket of her floor-length trench coat. "Ever engage in a high-speed chase?"

Stacy reached for the handle on the car's door. "There's a first time for everything."

The vampire clicked her tongue. "Leave it to the master," she said and shoved Stacy away from Rafe and into the backseat.

Tala jumped in with her, on the other side of the unconscious Blaez, while Caleb took his position in the front, riding shotgun. The car lurched forward and they were off, speeding down the street, the beat from the speakers matching the slow thrust of lovers just getting things underway, the raw lyrics reminding Stacy of Andrion's encounter with the twins.

She blinked away the images. She didn't want to think about him. Or worry about the two women. Or what her father would say if he knew she was riding in a stolen vehicle. Instead, Stacy made herself busy. She found a box of Kleenex on the floor at her feet and used the tissues to mop Blaez's brow.

"I already gave him a shot of Dormidryl," Caleb hollered over the music and the rush of wind.

Stacy dragged a clump of hair from her mouth. "Dormidryl?"

"For the pain," Tala answered, pulling a healing device from her belt.

Stacy inched forward. "What can I do?"

The vampire shook her head. "I'm not sure there's much anyone can do." She shrugged out of her coat and, with Stacy's help, used it to keep Blaez warm, then fiddled with her gizmo. "Hey, Caleb. Can you turn down that—"

A heavy thud demolished the rest of Tala's sentence. The vehicle jolted, hit from behind. Stacy swiveled around and bit back a scream, her lips quivering against her teeth. Andrion had latched onto the car, lying on his belly across the trunk. His fingers gripped their headrests, his bared fangs only inches away.

"Give... me... back... my...*caaaaaaar*!"

"Ladies...duck!" Caleb pounded a round of bullets into their excess baggage. Stacy kept her head down, her hands splayed over her skull, shell casings tumbling onto her flesh like hot coals. Peeking between her fingers, she saw Andrion convulse which each shot, but he held on fast.

Rafe cranked the wheel and poured on the gas. "Fasten your seatbelts."

Stacy's heart crammed into her throat as he made a sharp left and climbed onto the sidewalk to avoid a pedestrian crossing the intersection. They passed a busker playing *Scotland the Brave* on the bagpipes. The mouthpiece slipped from the musician's lips, the air deflating from his instrument like a noisy balloon. His kilt flapped in the breeze as the car plowed by.

Tires squealing, the vehicle swayed down the street, back and forth over the white line. The vampire's legs swung out at forty-five degree angles with each turn, but the maneuver didn't shake him.

Tala punched him in the face. He sneered back at her. "Baby, you know I like it rough." Tala spat at him, then redoubled her efforts, using his face as a punching bag, her hands a blur of motion.

Stacy drew strength from her. Truthfully, she wanted to leap in the front seat beside Rafe, desperate for his protection. But she refused to be the only wuss in the car. She grabbed the fallen healing machine and used it to hammer Andrion's fingers, hoping to loosen his grip.

Up ahead, the light was amber, and Stacy whispered a silent prayer. She braced her feet on the floor and held on to the driver's seat as Rafe sped through the now red light. He swerved but still clipped the front end of a car coming at them from the opposite direction—chrome buckling, headlights crashing.

Andrion hung on with one hand, so he could shake his fist with the other. "I'm going to kill you, dog breath."

At the next intersection, Rafe pulled a one-eighty and raced back the way he'd come. The smell of searing meat from a passing fast-food restaurant, burnt rubber, and the rollercoaster motion of the car, sent Stacy's stomach churning.

A police siren wailed. Stacy twisted her neck and saw the red and blue flashing lights of a squad car.

"This is so not my day," Rafe muttered, his raspy voice echoing the radio's lead singer.

"Get us out of here," Tala yelled.

Pain shot across the right side of Stacy's head. Andrion held a fistful of her hair and was using it as a rope to pull himself into the car. Tala fired at him, point blank, but it only annoyed him more.

Through her tears and terror, Stacy caught Rafe's expression in the rearview mirror, his eyes intense, his brows knitted with alarm. Nice that he was concerned about her, but…

"Keep your eyes on the road, cowboy!"

Rafe wheeled into another turn and ran straight into the afternoon's rush hour traffic. He whizzed down the wrong side of the road to avoid the jam, then pulled back into his proper lane. His hard right turn knocked Stacy to one side, crushing her shoulder. Andrion's hand was ripped away from her, along with a hunk of her hair, though it felt as if half her head went with it. She out-wailed the cries of bullets, and the police siren, as Caleb fired another round into the vampire.

The beat of the music accelerated, matching the frantic speed of the car—faster, surging, techno-throbbing, the frenzy of a couple out of control.

Tala bared her fangs and sank them into Andrion's other hand, while Stacy smashed his fingers with the healing machine. His grip loosened and he hit the pavement behind them with a sick thud. He rolled across the asphalt and under the wheels of the police car, blood splattering across the front fender.

Tala gave a satisfied smirk. "That should slow him down."

Stacy stared at her, open-mouthed. "*Slow* him down?"

Rafe steered the car through several side streets, changing direction every block, sticking to the speed limit. Holding her aching head, Stacy looked to their rear. No one was following them.

Tala let out a huge sigh. "Hey, Caleb. Do me a favor and kill the music."

Using the butt end of his gun, Caleb bashed the console and the sound died.

Rafe grunted. "You could have used the OFF switch."

Caleb shrugged and turned his attention to Blaez.

He was barely breathing, his face as pale as the vampire's beside him. Stacy mopped the sweat on his forehead and finally exhaled, as Rafe piloted them away from the city.

To God knows where.

CHAPTER TEN

RAFE DITCHED THE car on a side street, as close to Discovery Park as they could get without drawing attention. Even though the tracking device in the convertible was deactivated, Andrion would still be looking for them, bent on revenge.

Just northwest of the city center, Discovery Park boasted more than five hundred acres of forests, meadows and streams, all framed by Shilshole and Elliott Bay. It was the perfect place for Rafe's team to hide out and lick their wounds.

And one of Blaez's favorite spots.

Caleb ran up ahead, carrying their team leader toward the orange glow of a beautiful sunset. Rafe would have liked to do the honors, but he was in no shape for it. His leg throbbed and he felt as weak as watered-down beer. He dragged himself along, between the two females, doing his best to keep up to their pace.

He cupped the back of Stacy's neck, careful to keep his hand away from the injuries Andrion had inflicted on her scalp. It tore him up to see her ruined hair, to know the pain she'd endured.

When the vampire had grabbed her, Rafe had just about lost it. His first impulse was to vault over the car's seats and rip out the bloodsucker's throat with his teeth. It was all he could do to stay behind the wheel and drive hard enough to shake Andrion from the vehicle.

"You okay, champ?"

"*I* didn't get hit with a bullet, cowboy."

"I'll be fine." He looked at his stained jeans. Was the blood his? Blaez's? He was starting to hate the color red.

Up ahead, Caleb glanced back to check for them, then disappeared into the woods. A second later, Rafe nearly fell headlong into Tala, who'd stepped out in front of him, blocking his way.

"It would be faster, if I carried you."

He pushed past her, jarring his leg in the process. "No thanks."

"*Were*chismo bullshit," she muttered behind him.

He could pretend he hadn't heard it. There were more important things on his mind—Blaez for one, their balled-up mission for another. But he couldn't let it go. He stopped and turned on her.

"Insubordination, soldier. I still outrank you."

Tala kept her gaze steady, challenging him to a staring match, one he was determined to win. After half a minute, she blinked and looked away. "May I offer you a shoulder to lean on then... *sir*?"

Reacting to the suggestion, Stacy slipped under his arm. There was no use putting his weight on her, though. He was twice her size. He would have knocked her over.

He didn't want to lean against Tala, either, but he wasn't going to make it much further without her help. It felt good to take some of the pressure off his bum leg. "Thanks, ladies."

Though supported by his two female companions, Rafe was the one who led the way, following Caleb's scent. They caught up to the pup in a secluded clump of trees. Large rocks and a few fallen logs produced the best chairs they were going to see that night.

Caleb had made a bed for Blaez near a cluster of bushes where the ground was soft, and draped Tala's long coat over top of him.

Rafe stopped short. Seeing Blaez like this—his slack mouth, his half-closed unseeing eyes—was more than Rafe could bear.

He felt helpless. Useless.

Normally, he would have acted as blood donor, since they were the same type. But Rafe couldn't even do that. He'd lost too much himself.

"I gave him another shot of Dormidryl," Caleb reported, looking as forlorn as the day Rafe first met him, two years earlier.

Rafe clutched the lad's forearm, hoping to give him some reassurance. "Stay with him."

Caleb knelt by the team leader's side. Rafe took a last look at Blaez then walked back to the females. Both remained at a distance. He didn't blame Stacy—she wasn't part of their team. But Tala was a different matter.

As he approached, Stacy intercepted him. She spoke in a soft whisper. "Is there anything we can do?" She held herself stiff, shivering. From fear or anxiety, he guessed, since it wasn't that cold.

He rubbed her arms to comfort her. "Tala can help him."

"How?"

He expected the vampire to explain, but she was looking past him, over the bluffs to the bay beyond. "By giving him her blood."

Again, he waited for Tala to speak. When she didn't, he continued. "Vampires are universal donors." He made his way over to her, close enough to feel her breath on his cheek. "You can save him. Right, Tala?"

She met his eye. The brown contacts warmed a face that could have been carved from stone. "It isn't as simple as that."

"What's hard about it? Is it because he's different from you?"

Rafe didn't see the blow coming. He stumbled backward as Tala struck his chest with both fists.

"You are so thick sometimes. This isn't a simple broken bone or a laceration the *heilen* can repair. Parts of him have been ripped away. And there's internal damage. I can give him all the blood in my body, but it's not going to save him. Only prolong his agony."

Rafe felt his world give way. He knew it was the truth—knew it back when he'd picked Blaez off the floor and away from the goltos. But he'd denied it to himself. Now, he'd caused his friend extra pain, extra suffering. Because he'd been too bullheaded to listen.

Still, Tala could have tried. He was willing to do anything to save Blaez. Wasn't she?

When he felt Stacy's hand in his, he brushed her off. Rafe didn't want her condolences. He wanted to be alone with his grief.

He ordered his feet to move, misery and regret weighing him down. He stumbled back to Blaez, wishing he could go deep into the woods and howl out his pain in private. But that would make him even more of a coward.

He'd sit with his friend. Hold Blaez as he slipped away. Just as he had with Daciana.

Rafe took up his place on the opposite side of Caleb, and concentrated on Blaez's chest—willing it to rise, praying it stilled—hoping for an end to his friend's suffering. Tala stood nearby, tears glistening her cheeks. Caleb's shoulders quaked with silent sobs, his eyes misting. Or maybe it was the haze through which Rafe viewed him.

He felt Stacy's presence, smelled her scent. She knelt beside him. That she chose to be there, to include herself in their death vigil—after all they'd put her through, and even after he'd pushed her away—meant more to Rafe than she could know. It gave him the strength to force another breath into his own lungs, past the tightness that spread across his chest like a steel band.

He took her hand in his as they formed a close circle around Blaez. In the custom of their kind, they howled out their anguish into the night sky as their team leader's body dissolved in a twinkling of lights.

* * *

STACY STARED AT the spot where Blaez's body had rested. The grass was crushed, the earth slightly warm, but the man was gone, vanished along with his last breath.

It was different from the way the vampires met their end. They were reduced to dust. They didn't go anywhere. This guy had disappeared, amidst a light show that made the aurora borealis look like the glitter off a cheap disco ball.

As the boys moved away to deal with Rafe's leg wound, Stacy confronted Tala. "What the hell just happened? Did he get beamed somewhere?"

59

Tala's eyes widened. "Beamed?"

"Like on Star Trek."

The vampire cocked her head to one side, as if she'd never heard of the series, or its many spin-offs and movies. Tala collected her coat from the ground and slipped into it with a sigh. "I'll let Rafe explain it to you. In the meantime, I'll see to your injury."

She pointed to a fallen log. Stacy got the message and took a seat, as Tala drew a healing machine from her belt.

"At least the *heilen* can fix this. It doesn't replace the hair, but will help it grow in naturally." She hummed as she waved the device over Stacy's head. "Just a small patch, really. Hardly noticeable."

Like magic, the pain was gone. Stacy reached up and patted the area. "Thanks."

The vampire pulled a bottle and what looked like a protein bar from her medical pack. "Here, eat this. I'm told they're tasty. And the water swells in volume as soon as you pop the cap."

Water that expands? Were these otherworldly people from NASA? Or maybe another planet? It would certainly explain all their cool gadgets.

No. That would be too fantastical. Werewolves and vampires were enough for Stacy to digest. Besides, if Rafe did have a spaceship, they would have teleported to the safety of it as soon as the goltos attacked.

If teleportals actually existed.

From an inner pocket Tala revealed a plain, old-fashioned handkerchief. "Use some of that water to wash your face. Rafe won't want to be reminded of tears."

Stacy touched her cheeks. The skin was tight where her tears had fallen. Caught up in the drama surrounding Blaez's vanishing act, she'd forgotten she'd wept. She'd only just met the man, but he struck her as decent and loyal. She'd experienced the bond he shared with Rafe, felt it, along with his wicked sense of humor.

And now, he was dead.

She'd never seen anyone pass before, the light fade from them, the candle's flame burn out. When Rafe and Caleb had howled up at the moon, the sheer pain and anguish in their soulful cries had sent tremors through Stacy. Her tears had fallen to the ground, mingling with Blaez's blood.

She forced away the memories and cleaned herself up, then tore off the wrapper and bit into the bar. It was good, a chocolate-oatmeal combination with a big dollop of spices she didn't recognize. She finished it fast, not realizing how hungry she was until it was gone.

Stacy was about to slip the wrapper into her skirt pocket to dispose of later, when Tala reached out to take it. The vampire rolled it between her palms till only particles remained, like bits of dried leaves. She blew the remnants onto the ground. "Makes good fertilizer."

Tala's gaze then shifted to Rafe. Stacy's unconventional nurse squared her shoulders. "Now, if you'll excuse me, I have some other shit to deal with."

* * *

SPRAWLED UNDER A tree, his back against it for support, Rafe watched Tala's approach.

Why couldn't she leave well enough alone? Give him five minutes of peace? He braced himself for another fight.

"We need to get you taken care of, Rafe."

He checked out the scuffmarks on his boots. He couldn't even look at her, couldn't see *who* she was without seeing *what* she was.

A vampire. Like the one who'd taken Daciana, the one who'd hastened Blaez's death. He tightened the lid on his anger until his head pounded.

"Caleb's seen to my leg. I'm good."

"You're still weak. I can help you with that."

"By giving me your blood? Blood you withheld from Blaez?"

She lowered her chin, but held her ground. "I explained why."

"Fuck your explanation." The words were out before he could stop them. All the hatred he'd been storing up for the past year, spewed from his mouth like poison.

And he wasn't done. Wouldn't be until that façade of hers cracked. Until he'd hurt her. The way he'd been hurt, by her kind.

He'd rather have traded places with Blaez, or had his heart ripped out and be done with it, than live with the pain he'd been carrying, the type that ate away at his soul.

Now he was going to show her just how little of that soul he had left, as he aimed his parting shot.

"And fuck you."

CHAPTER ELEVEN

RAFE GOT HIS wish. Tala's face crumpled, her eyes glazed with tears. Self-loathing brewed in his belly. Hurting her hadn't brought him any kind of joy. How could he have thought it might?

He called to her, but she'd already dashed to the far edge of the bluff, her back to him, rigid as though she might break. And Caleb was eying him as if he'd just killed Bambi's mom.

Rafe was used to seeing adulation in the kid's eyes. That hero worship had helped Rafe through more dark days than he cared to remember. Now, he'd blown it with his buddy, too.

"I'm going hunting," the young wolf announced, filling the awkward pause. "Anyone want me to bring something back?" When no one replied, he stripped out of his clothes and scampered off on all fours.

The coolness of the coming night crept into Rafe's bones and chilled his flesh. *Weres* burned hotter than humans—he was rarely cold. But loss, of both blood and kin, had taken their toll.

Blaez was gone. That placed Rafe in the position of team leader. It was time he started acting like one. Put his differences aside, and do what was right for the mission, for his people—regardless of their species.

And it looked like his first shift as boss would start with an apology.

Before he could lift himself off the ground, Stacy strode toward him like a general on a campaign and plunked herself at his side. "You're being an asshole."

He shook his head. Whereas Tala and Caleb had retreated, Stacy went on the attack. Why had he thought she was too delicate for him to lean on? She was braver than all three of them combined.

"I'm the same asshole who came to your rescue today. *Twice.*"

"And, if you hadn't come for me at Andrion's, Blaez would still be alive. Is that what you're thinking?"

It had crossed Rafe's mind. But going back for her had been his decision, his plan. *He* was ultimately responsible for Blaez's loss.

The pitch of her voice kicked up a note. "If you're looking for someone to blame, take your anger out on me. Not Tala. It's not her fault Blaez died."

He nodded, realizing why he'd lashed out at the vampire. He'd been angry at himself—frustrated by his own helplessness. For losing Blaez. And Daciana.

He lowered his head. "I know."

Stacy put her hand on his arm, warm and consoling. "We're all here trying to help each other. And Tala's right. If she can make you stronger, you should let her. You're already one team member down. If you're functioning at less than a hundred percent, where does that leave your mission? Whatever the hell it is."

She was right, again. His condition put their assignment in serious jeopardy. But the thought of drinking vampire blood turned his stomach. "I'll be fine by tomorrow."

"Bullshit. And I can prove it." She pulled up her leather sleeve. "With an arm wrestle. If you win, you can sit here all night and wallow. If I win, you accept Tala's blood. Deal?"

He almost laughed. For a tiny thing, she sure had pluck. And he didn't trivialize her challenge. She was so pumped in her intermediary role, she just might best him. "That won't be necessary." He tugged the cuff of her sleeve back down to her wrist. "You're right. About everything. And I'm sorry."

"It's not me who's owed an apology."

He scrubbed a hand down his face. He needed to walk right over to Tala and admit he was wrong. He just hoped he could make the trip without falling butt first in the dirt.

Rafe hauled himself onto his knees, but Stacy pressed against his shoulders, easing him back.

"Sit tight, cowboy. I'll ask her to come to you."

"Thanks, Stacy.

As she started to move away, he grasped her hand and held it to his chest. She filled a spot there he'd thought would be empty forever. Being around her made him feel good. It was something about those big, blue eyes. That trusting, open face. And a heart full of compassion, of courage.

He wanted nothing more than to take her in his arms and curl up with her under the tree—smell her hair, feel her curves, and lose himself in her softness.

But he had no right to her. She was human and a civilian. Totally off limits. He pushed his own needs aside and released her hand.

* * *

TALA WATCHED THE exchange from her seat on the rock, seething.

Bad enough Rafe told her to fuck herself. Now he was showing her, in no uncertain terms, how little he cared. With every heated glance, every longing touch he bestowed on the human.

This was the first interest Tala had seen him take in a female since Daciana. Sure, he'd had a couple of one night stands in the past year, if you believed the office gossip. But this was different. Around Stacy, Rafe's demeanor changed, his hard edges softened. Tala had half a mind to pop the top off the woman and drink her like a soda.

Then, as if responding to her thoughts, the human stood and approached. She could see fear in Stacy's eyes, but still she came, and was close enough for Tala to hear the blood flowing through her veins when she finally spoke.

"Rafe's rehearsing his apology... if you're willing to accept it."

A fine howdy-do. The big wolf was getting the tiny female to run interference. As much as Tala resented Stacy, she had to admire the woman for her courage.

Tala stood, easily towering over her, but the human didn't back down. "I don't need you to defend me."

Stacy jolted. "You heard?"

"I can discern a human heartbeat at ten paces. Voices carry farther." It was a maddening ability. Tala heard too much. People thought that, because she was dead, she didn't have any feelings. She faced the water, bent her head, and spoke to the waves below. "Especially Rafe's."

"I'm right here," he said.

She swiveled around to find him standing a few feet away. Make that leaning. Against a tree. Looking ready to pass out.

Tala took a half step toward him, before forcing herself to stop. When Stacy approached him, he waved her away.

"Tala... I was out of line. I'm sorry. It won't happen again."

Her traitorous heart clattered against her ribcage. There was nothing like an unobtainable man to get her juices flowing. She trained her features into a neutral mask.

"You don't need to apologize to get my blood. I'm willing to give it, for the sake of the team."

"Your loyalty to the mission has never been in question. I'm apologizing because I was wrong."

It wasn't an 'I love you' but she heard it that way. Tala rushed to his side and eased him into a sitting position on the ground, trying to think of a funny quip to cover the fact that she'd practically skipped over to him.

"Stubborn wolf."

She flipped back the collar of her coat and raked the nail of her index finger across her jugular vein—felt the sudden sting, the growing burn. She leaned in to Rafe. He hesitated, and she almost fell to pieces. Was he going to humiliate her again? Refuse her gift?

When she inched closer, he latched on and sucked.

The sensation of his mouth on her neck, his tongue against her skin, sent a hot message right to her core, her inner muscles tightening, longing to grip him. Rafe clasped her waist, his arm brushing the underside of her breast, and her fangs grew along with her arousal.

"I thought it was going to be a transfusion."

She'd forgotten Stacy was there until the human spoke.

"That would be more effective, but less practical." Tala's voice betrayed her. It came out deep, dreamy—her breath, rapid and shallow. She forced herself to focus. "Vampire blood isn't like human's. Ours is immediately absorbed into the circulation, even when ingested."

Odd pillow talk, but it answered Stacy's question. And drew an end to Rafe's *treatment*. He broke away and wiped his mouth.

The incision on Tala's neck instantly healed. She made another slash with her nail. Blood spilled from the second wound, oozing down her skin.

Use me, need me, love me. "You can take more."

Rafe lay back. "I'm good. Thanks."

Another rejection. Tala smiled to cover the hurt. She touched his forehead, at the center and on each temple. "Then sleep. Sleep deep. Everything will look better in the morning." He closed his eyes and within seconds, Rafe was breathing evenly.

"Did you use your hypnosis on him?"

Damn, the human was tiresome. Always with the questions. "Rafe's not usually such an obedient subject. He must be exhausted." Tala made sure he was resting comfortably, soothed a willful curl from his forehead, then sat back on her heels, soaking up his nearness.

What would it be like to lie beside him? To rest her head on his shoulder? To believe he wanted her there?

She heard Stacy stir, felt the human draw closer. "You're in love with him, aren't you?"

Tala whipped her head around and followed the line of Stacy's gaze. Without realizing it, Tala had twined her fingers in Rafe's hair.

She didn't answer. Didn't have to. The human knew the truth.

It was difficult for her kind to blush, but Tala managed all the same, the heat of her heart's confession burning up her cheeks.

One more reason to hate the blonde.

* * *

TALA LOOKED LIKE a kid with her hand caught in the cookie jar.

Strike that. The vampire was sending out too many pheromones for Stacy to mistake her for anything but a woman with a raging need for a man.

"It's in your eyes. Every time you look at him."

Tala withdrew her hand and slipped it between her knees, as if holding it captive. "Sure doesn't help that he's always running around naked. Way too much eye candy for a girl with a sweet tooth." She sobered and placed her long coat over him. "But there'll be no sugar for me. Rafe is the most off-limits guy on the planet."

"Does he know how you feel?"

Tala raised a brow. "Apparently, I haven't been subtle. But he doesn't want me. He's still in love with his wife."

"Rafe's *married?*" Stacy's stomach plummeted seven floors, while the rest of her stayed in the same spot. Had she been lusting after a married man?

"Was." Tala dipped her chin low. "She was murdered. By Andrion. Along with their unborn child."

Stacy replayed Andrion's remarks in her mind. When he'd taunted Rafe, the vampire said something about a woman tasting especially delicious because she was packing an extra ingredient. What a sick bastard.

Tala tucked her coat around Rafe. She placed her hand on his chest. It rose and fell several times before she spoke again, her voice soft.

"What he said to me earlier, I wouldn't take from anyone else. That doesn't mean I condone his behavior. But I understand it."

Stacy remembered her parents fighting, dishes flying along with the insults. Her shoulders tensed at the thought. She'd made a promise to herself, never to fall for someone who could hurt her that badly. People accepted far too much in the name of love.

"When was his wife killed?"

"A year ago."

"And she was human?"

"A *were*, like Rafe. Most wolves frown on mixed unions, especially the members of the First Pack. There's not that many purebreds left—about a hundred thousand worldwide. So an untainted line has become increasingly important to them. Especially to Rafe's mother."

Stacy blinked. "I can't picture him with a mom."

"He's got one, all right. And two sisters. All trying to set him up with another mate. Difficult, because he's half-assed royalty among the werewolves." Tala sat back on her haunches, mirroring Stacy's posture. "Another reason I'm a fool to want him. They'd never approve of me."

Half-assed royalty? And they let him run around dodging bullets? "Rafe's dad's out of the picture?"

"He died when Rafe was a kid. Luckily, Blaez took him under his wing. As role models go, Rafe picked a good one. It makes Blaez's death doubly hard for Rafe, though." Tala lowered her head. "Daciana bled out, too."

A breeze shivered through the long grass around them, making Stacy shudder. Tala straightened, as if sensing a presence.

The vampire called over her shoulder. "It's safe, Caleb—you can come back. Rafe and I made up."

Stacy looked around to see Caleb, fully dressed, emerging from the trees, a large fish in his hand. He opened his mouth, ready to take a bite out of the middle.

Stacy cringed. "Aren't you going to cook it?"

"A fire will attract attention. And I love sushi." As Caleb bit down, Stacy looked away. She'd seen enough exotic feeding for one day.

"Not much out there for you, Tala," the young man continued between chomps. "Squirrels, rabbits…"

"I'll pass, and stand guard while the rest of you sleep."

"You sure?" Caleb shuffled his feet. "'Cause... if you need to... you can bite me."

Tala jumped up and kissed him on the cheek, leaving Caleb blushing as if she'd Frenched him in a church. "You're a sweetie," she said. And he was. Especially for a guy who looked like he could put you in a body cast without breaking a sweat. He found a quiet place to sit and finish his meal, while Tala rejoined Stacy, once again kneeling beside Rafe.

Stacy took advantage of their newfound bond. "Could I borrow your cell? I want to let my dad know I'm okay."

"My cell?" Tala's brow furrowed. "Sorry, we don't have cells. I'll talk to Rafe tomorrow. See if we can find you one."

Who were these people with gadgets that could heal broken bones but didn't carry cell phones? Stacy wanted to learn all she could. She'd landed smack-dab in the middle of a deadly war, and knowledge of the players might give her the edge she needed to survive.

"How is it that you fight against your own people?"

Tala twitched inside her clothes, as if they'd grown uncomfortable. "I hate bringing my kind to their final death. But the ones like Andrion are so blinded by wealth and power, they don't care about anything else. I mean, I like cute shoes as well as the next girl, but how many pairs can you own?"

A hint of fang shone as she smiled, a grin that was gone in an instant. "That's why it's hopeless for me to want more from Rafe. I'm a vampire. He's always going to look at me as the enemy. And he's not the kind of male who dates the boss' daughter to get ahead."

Her eyes shone in the darkness. "But there's something about Rafe— his daring, his loyalty—that reaches out and grabs me. I know you've felt it."

Had she ever. And a million other things Tala hadn't named.

Curious, though, that the vampire had turned the discussion back to the werewolf. Stacy was reminded of a Shakespearean quote she'd learned in high school: 'The lady doth protest too much, methinks.' Was Tala trying to convince herself to move on? To forget about Rafe?

Stacy felt a cold grip on her arm. The vampire leaned closer. "I need a favor."

After their heart to heart, Stacy didn't fear Tala as much as she once did. She wasn't ready to book a girls' mani-pedi date with her new ally, but a favor was certainly doable. "Name it."

Tala paused, as if caught in an inner debate. She lowered her voice to a whisper. "Sleep with Rafe tonight."

Stacy's cheeks heated. Apparently, they were all suffering from a blushing disease. "You want me to—"

"He's still vulnerable to shock. He needs to be kept warm, especially when the temperature dips. I can't do that. I have no warmth to give. And I'm afraid Caleb, as much as he idolizes Rafe, is a tad homophobic." Tala shrugged. "It's a werewolf thing."

The vampire raised her gaze to Stacy's, all levity gone. "If you could sleep next to Rafe, keep him—"

Stacy tried not to sound too eager. "I understand."

Tala stood, hovering there, clearly reluctant to move. She stared out at the night sky. Stacy followed her line of vision to the moon, hanging like a big white dish with a wedge broken off one side. When Stacy looked back, Tala was eyeing her.

"Be careful, tonight. There's a full moon approaching, and Rafe's not a male who's built for celibacy." The vampire took a last look at him, her eyes shimmering, and then she walked away.

Stacy watched her go, unsure if her last words were a warning or a promise. Or how she felt about a man being offered up to her on a platter. But the thought of bedding down with Rafe made her as woozy as if she'd binged on red wine. Barely beneath that was a bottled-up energy that had her tingling all over.

When he'd fed on Tala, Stacy had felt like a voyeur hovering over them, but couldn't look away. Their joining was erotic, carnal, more intimate than sex and, though she had no claims on Rafe, it bothered Stacy that he and Tala were so totally connected. That Tala could give him something she couldn't.

Now, the tables were turned and, with the change, Stacy realized why she'd felt such ongoing animosity from Tala—the icy looks, the weighty frowns. They were both attracted to the same man.

Actually, in Tala's case, it went far beyond that. The redhead was crazy in love. And it struck Stacy that the vampire hadn't been confiding in her so much as marking her territory, making sure Stacy knew her chances with Rafe were nonexistent.

Before asking her to be his hot water bottle.

Nice play. But Stacy had her own reason for wanting to be near Rafe. Ever since they'd escaped from Andrion's studio, she'd been dying for an excuse to touch him, to convince herself he was okay. So she slipped under Tala's coat and cuddled up against Rafe's side, flattening her palm against the velvety skin of his chest.

She lay awake for hours, listening to him breathe and feeling the hardness of his body. Even in sleep.

CHAPTER TWELVE

RAFE WOKE IN the pre-dawn with a killer erection—testicles tight, dick rock hard.

His dreams had been all over the place. A prison cell... a deadly battle... and a warm, curvy body pressed up against him.

All true. But the first two were in the past. Stacy—curled around him, her arm over his, her hand on his chest—was very much in the present. And way too much temptation for him to handle.

He slipped away from her, then rolled onto his feet, muscles stiff. He sniffed the air and scanned his surroundings.

There wasn't a cloud in the sky. Bad news for Tala. He'd have to find a safe place for her before daybreak. The vampire's sunscreen wouldn't protect her from direct light. Or Rafe from her accusations if she saw his present condition.

A morning dip in the frigid bay was just what he needed. He could even catch a fish for breakfast, while he was at it. As long as he got his boner down before the sun rose.

And to do that, he'd have to get as far away as he could from the luscious blonde that had raised Lazarus from the dead.

* * *

STACY WOKE, SHIVERING and desperate to pee.

She felt beside her. The body that kept her awake half the night, and filled her with lusty dreams the rest of the time, was gone.

She looked around for him in the twilight. Caleb was slumped in the shadow of a nearby tree, growling in his sleep. At first, she couldn't see Tala. Then Stacy spotted the vampire slinking through the forest, still on guard duty.

Rafe was nowhere to be found.

Dealing with her most urgent need first, Stacy scouted around and discovered a clump of shrubs that promised some privacy. She made her way to them, hiked up her skirt, pulled her undies down to her knees and squatted.

Thank goodness for those camping trips with her father. At least she knew how to pee in the woods.

Business done, she stood and gazed beyond her outdoor lavatory. The bay beckoned, the salty smell of it guiding her better than a map. She could freshen up there—splash some water on herself. If she was going to escape, it would be easier to solicit help if she didn't look like a homeless person.

Except, a getaway wasn't at the top of her To-Do List anymore.

Rafe *was*.

She didn't want to leave him. Not after what they'd been through together—what he'd sacrificed to save her. She couldn't take off without thanking him, at least.

And... she wanted an excuse to kiss him again.

She'd never reacted to a man so quickly, so completely. Was it the beast in him that spoke to her on some primal level? Made her want him as much as her next breath? Even though the chances of building any kind of permanent relationship with him were slim to nil?

She'd been horrified by the violence that surrounded Rafe, and should have been equally repelled by his transformation into a wolf. But she wasn't. Discovering his special talent had only made her more intrigued. And, God help her...*aroused*.

Lust aside, there was also her safety to consider. If Andrion was still after her, sticking with Rafe and his friends was her best option. Going to the police with her story would guarantee her a psychiatric evaluation. And she doubted they could protect her half as well as Rafe.

Stacy couldn't hide out in her apartment, either. The bad vampires had her purse. They knew her name, her address, and could be draining her bank account at this very minute, for all she knew.

She needed a phone—to cancel her credit cards and to let her father know she was okay. Cleaning up would be a good start.

She made her way down to the dim rocky shore, thankful she'd worn practical shoes. She cupped the water, cold as a slushy drink, and splashed it on her face.

The hairs on her body jumped to attention—goosebumps on top of goosebumps. She rubbed under her arms and down her legs. She might not be any cleaner but she was now totally awake, and feeling like a Freezie.

That's when she saw him, through the branches of a fallen tree—a figure, emerging from the water like a Greek god. She'd already seen Rafe naked. But not like this. Not with time to gaze and appreciate him at her leisure.

As he waded to the shore, he threw back his hair, droplets cascading off his tanned body. The man was packing enough junk for a feast and Stacy was hungry for the all-you-can-eat buffet. She groaned with disappointment when he pulled on his jeans, obscuring her view of his tight butt.

Stacy remained concealed behind the tree stump, mesmerized. She didn't feel right about spying. But she didn't feel right about making her presence known, either. That would just embarrass both of them. She hunkered down in her hiding spot, holding her breath, waiting for him to pass.

When she was sure he'd gone, she rose, headed away from the water, and slammed into a hard chest.

Rafe caught her in his arms—his grasp firm, his mouth rigid, danger in his eyes. "Something I can do for you?"

She could think of lots. All X-rated. And he was on the same wavelength, if that bulge in his pants meant anything.

The blood and grime from the past day were gone. His hair, still wet, was tousled and wild, styled with a quick swipe of his fingers.

"You clean up nice."

He raised a brow. "Nice?"

An innocuous word. One that didn't describe him at all. "Stallion-esque, then."

His lips twitched, but he still managed to look stern. "You need to be careful. Sneaking around could get you killed. I knew it was you in the bushes from your scent. But if Tala had found you, she'd have shot first and asked questions later."

"Sorry. I had to...*you know*." When his eyes narrowed, she threw out another euphemism. "Freshen up."

His gaze traveled over her, settling on her exposed bra, before drifting back up to her lips. His attempt at anger faded. Now, he looked hungry. But not for food.

The expression vanished in an instant, making her wonder if she'd imagined it. Did he want to kiss her? As much as she wanted him to?

If so, he was doing a better job of denying himself than she was. Stacy knew, if he so much as touched her, she wouldn't be able to hold back. She'd fall willingly, anxiously, recklessly into his arms.

"Are you finished chastising me? Can we kiss and make up?"

Her name rumbled in his throat, the vibrations humming over her flesh. "A kiss... is not a good idea."

His nearness left her jittery and incredibly turned on, at the same time. She took a step closer. "What's the matter? Don't you trust yourself?"

"Stop."

She gave him her innocent look. "Stop what?"

"Pouting like that."

"Am I pouting?"

"Yes. And with those lips..." He exhaled, his breath warming her skin. "You don't play fair."

"You kissed me first, cowboy." And she was hoping for a repeat performance. A second later, she got her wish.

His touch wiped every other man from her mind. She'd never been kissed before—not like this—intensely, thoroughly, as if he were worshiping her with his mouth.

His tongue traced her lips. She opened them, inviting him in. He groaned his approval, his hands tangling in her hair, angling her head for the best position.

He retreated slightly, no doubt giving her a chance to change her mind. In reply, she wrapped her arms tight around his neck, his kisses as glorious as the coming sunrise.

When his teeth grazed her bottom lip, the air vanished. Light-headed, she could no longer think, only feel—his mouth, his hands, and the sweet ache between her thighs.

Stacy wanted... *needed* him to touch her there. She parted her legs, as far as her skirt would allow, and pulled him closer, arching her back and grinding herself against him.

It didn't help ease the pressure. Only made it worse.

Deliciously worse.

He ripped his mouth from hers, grabbed a breath, then trailed his lips down her neck, kissing and nibbling. He cupped her bottom and lifted her, settling her hot core at his hips.

Stacy wrapped her legs around his waist. She eased herself back, wanting his mouth to stray lower.

He obliged. Through her bra, he caressed one erect nipple—then gave it a tug with his teeth, making her gasp. Her few clothes felt restrictive. She wanted—needed—to feel his skin against hers.

She'd never done casual sex before. Always waited for the third date before shedding so much as a sock. If she hadn't known better, she would have sworn he'd given her a love potion of some kind. But he hadn't. She was drunk on his presence.

"Please, Rafe. Make love to me."

Not that he'd need an invitation. This was a man who didn't wait for permission. He was built to take what he wanted—tall, muscular and edgy. But with a touch so caring, her insides melted.

Yet, that sweetness curdled with his next move. He unwrapped her legs and planted her back on the ground, holding her at arm's length. The change was so abrupt, her head spun, still half-clouded with a sexual fog.

"You don't even know me, Stacy—don't know what you're asking for. I've seen and done things most people wouldn't be able to live with. You wanna fuck? I'm game. You want true love? Find yourself a nice, human boy."

She looked into his eyes—the piercing eyes of a wolf. He wanted to scare her. Of that, she was certain. But she didn't know why, only knew that she'd entered into a risky situation. And, if she were smart, she'd back the hell away.

"Okay," she said. But when he turned to go, she caught his arm. "I want to fuck."

CHAPTER THIRTEEN

DEFINITELY NOT THE answer he'd expected. He'd hoped to scare her off by being crude, by showing her the beast inside the man. Her reaction left Rafe scrambling—the desire to mate and his duty to protect her battling it out, making his chest tight and breathing damn near impossible.

He'd never had sex with a human before. Never wanted to. They were delicate. Easily broken. Or so he'd heard.

Weres liked it rough.

"Take off your clothes."

Her blue eyes opened wide. "Don't you want to undress me?"

God help him if he touched her. He'd lose all ability to control himself, so close to a full moon. Knowing that she had so little on under that jacket was torture enough. The tops of her breasts peeked out from her skimpy bra, making him forget about everything else. Except wanting her. And burying himself in her, balls deep.

"No. I want to watch."

And make her run away. Even though it was still half-dark, and a light mist hung above the water, they were in a public place. Doing the wild thing, *in the wild*, suited him best—but he couldn't imagine this mom's-apple-pie-type was a closet exhibitionist.

To make sure she was thoroughly disgusted with him, he reached down, unzipped his fly, and cupped himself. He didn't need the extra friction to get aroused. Looking at Stacy was enough to put a rise in his Levis.

Especially when she tossed the leather jacket to the ground and reached behind to unclasp her bra—a move that accentuated her collarbone and that sexy dip at the base of her throat. She let the straps fall from her shoulders, before pulling the rest of the material away to reveal her breasts. Pale, pert mounds—the nipples long and hard—made for sucking.

So much for calling her bluff. He struggled to remember why having sex with her was such a bad idea.

"And your skirt."

He freed his dick—there was no longer enough room for it in his pants, anyway—hoping she'd see him for the animal he was and get cold feet. But she reached for the waistband of her skirt and wriggled out of it before another wave lapped against the shore.

Air caught in his lungs, sticking to his ribs. When he managed to exhale, the breath came out with a groan. A growl.

He'd always liked athletic women—ones with a runner's build—sleek and taut. Man, what he'd been missing. Stacy was toned, but shapely. He loved the swell of her breasts, the curve of her belly, the edgy look of her pierced navel, its sparkling diamond winking at him.

He could smell her musky desire. He had to stop himself from howling out with lust and diving into her. There were rules against impregnating civilians. But the handbook didn't say anything about tasting one.

Rafe fell to his knees at her feet, just looking at her for a moment, before he licked one nipple. He let it dry in the cool air—watching it contract even more, the delicate skin forming ridges. Then he sucked it into his mouth.

Stacy closed her eyes and let her head fall back, too overcome with sensation to think. The air kissed her skin, even as Rafe did—his mouth on her breasts, her core pulsing with every flick of his tongue.

With his elbows, he nudged her legs apart. Not that she needed any coaxing.

She wanted this. Wanted him.

He made short work of her thong, ripping it from her body. Her cry of shock ended on a sigh as he parted her folds and kissed her. Stacy tumbled against the fallen tree behind her, unable to stand on her own.

Now seated on her perch, Rafe draped her right knee over his shoulder, leaving her fully open to him. He lapped at her clit, then dragged his teeth over it. Each move sent a sizzling current through her, bringing her closer to the brink. Then he slipped his hands under her hips, raising her to him, and sank his tongue deep inside her.

She came, panting—her breath making clouds in the cold morning air, sweat trickling down between her breasts.

He brought his head up, a big grin on his lips, clearly proud of himself.

At the risk of turning him into a complete egotist, she blurted out the truth. "I've never had a man do that to me."

He drew his brows together, puzzled. "Make you come with his mouth?"

"Make me come at all."

He cocked his head, like a playful pup. "Guess I'll have to prove it wasn't a fluke."

His breath on her still sensitive parts made her tingle all over. He slid a finger into her, with agonizing slowness—stretching her, making her beg for more. Her muscles clenched around him.

"So tight. So beautiful."

He withdrew. Then a second finger joined the first.

He gained speed, pumping her—in and out—driving her wild. Just when she thought she couldn't get any more excited, the heat of Rafe's tongue flicked over her.

She grabbed his shoulders, dug her nails into his flesh, and bucked against the searing friction—desperate for release.

"Oh... God... Rafe."

She came again. Harder than the first time. The world fragmented around her, exploding into tiny pieces.

When she finally opened her eyes, he flashed her a devastating smile. Dear God, the man was happy, even though she'd left him unfulfilled.

"Your turn, cowboy."

She ran her hands across his chest and down his belly, relishing every hard inch of him. "I want you inside me. And not just your fingers." She gazed down at his erection and drew in a breath. "I just don't know if it'll fit."

"It will," he said, low and raspy. "But we can't. I don't have any protection with me."

Her heart sagged. Even if she'd taken him home to her condo, she hadn't gone far enough with her last boyfriend to invest in condoms. "Then I'll improvise."

She knew what she wanted to do to him. *For* him. He'd shown her, when he stroked himself. An unexpected turn-on. It was as if the need to be touched had overwhelmed him—a need she'd created.

Still, he'd held back and pleasured her first. Put her desires ahead of his own.

Now, it was all about him.

Stacy kissed his neck, making her way down his chest. She swirled her tongue around one nipple, then grazed her teeth over it, just as he'd done to her. She smiled when she felt a shiver go through him, when his fingers tangled in her hair, holding her in place.

She slipped away, switching positions with him, so that his back was against the fallen tree and she was free to maneuver. Stacy continued her descent, running her tongue over those rippled obliques she'd fantasized about.

And moved lower still.

She'd attended a Catholic boarding school for a few years. While the nuns had praised chastity and taught her that holding hands was a sin, because it led to 'other things'—the older, racier girls had shown her how to perform fellatio on a banana, and how to caress a man's testicles with a couple of peaches.

Stacy had never looked at a bowl of fruit the same way.

She'd used her techniques on a few boyfriends—giving pleasure in the hopes of getting some. Generally, a wasted effort. But with Rafe, she'd already received. She wanted to return the favor. Wanted to thrill him as he'd thrilled her. Wanted to bring the big man to his knees. To undo him with the power of her touch.

She chucked his jeans down to his ankles and sighed with appreciation—so much there to love. She smoothed her hands over him, feeling the weight of him—heavy with need.

He tensed. Semen glistened from the tip of his penis. She ran her tongue over the slit and licked it up, tasting the sweet, saltiness of him— enjoying his moans of pleasure, of the control she had over her brave warrior.

Turning Rafe on made her hot for him. All over again.

As she swirled her tongue over the head of his cock, she stretched her arm around and grabbed his butt. With her other hand, she reached in between his legs and massaged his sack, stroking the flesh between his balls with firm strokes.

He clasped her shoulders and pushed her back. "I'm going to come right away, if you do that."

She smiled. "Go ahead. Make my day."

Before he could protest, she covered him with her mouth, relaxing the muscles at the back of her throat to accommodate the size of him. She moved her lips down his shaft, the light dusting of hair on his belly tickling her nose. She took in as much of him as she could and used her hand to massage the rest. Milking him, drawing him closer.

His butt tensed with every thrust of his hips. His testicles contracted. It would be soon—very, very soon. She reached up to tweak his nipple, as she pulled him deeper into her mouth.

Rafe came, his climax so intense he cried out. He sat back on the tree trunk, gulping air, sure his legs would give way.

He'd had his share of partners before he'd picked a mate. But he'd never had a female go down on him as well as Stacy—make him fall apart like that. And what she'd done to his chest? She'd found an erogenous zone he didn't even know existed.

The taste of her was like nothing he'd ever experienced before, either. He loved to give pleasure with his mouth. And Stacy was sweeter than any *were* female he'd ever known. Instead of sating him, sex with her had only made him want more. Too bad he was out of luck.

He sniffed the air. He was able to lunge for Stacy's clothes and hand them to her moments before Caleb emerged from the trees. The young wolf eyed them both, let out a howl, and pawed at the air, giving Rafe a *were* high-five.

Stepping in front of Stacy while she dressed, Rafe acted as a privacy screen. Behind him, he heard her chuckle. "Looks like we've got a cheering section."

Rafe felt as if he'd been struck in the chest with friendly fire. He couldn't lead her on. In less than a week, he'd be gone and out of her life.

Even if he wanted to care for her, he couldn't. It was too risky. She was a weakness too easily exploited. If Andrion sensed anything between them, he'd use it to their detriment. And Stacy would wind up dead, just like his wife.

Rafe had to shut her down, freeze her out.

"Don't be getting big ideas. You're a nice piece of tail, babe—but that's all you are for me."

He couldn't look at her—afraid she'd see through him if he did. He exhaled, imagining his breath as a door—closing off his feelings and locking them away as he zipped up his fly.

CHAPTER FOURTEEN

ICE CRYSTALS SEEMED to form in the air between her and Rafe.

What the hell?

Okay, they'd fooled around. It's not like she'd expected a diamond ring. Or even a repeat performance. But the physical closeness, the intimacy—it had meant something to Stacy. Had it truly meant nothing to him? Nothing at all?

On the cliff above her, Caleb morphed back to human. (Would she ever get used to that sight?) As he wriggled into his pants, Rafe approached him. Her recent sex partner kept his back to her—as if she were already part of his distant past. A clear rejection.

You'd think she'd be used to it by now. She could fill a busload with guys who'd tried to get close, just they could gain access to her father. She'd learned to recognize users, protect herself from them. Then along came Rafe, packing enough raw magnetism to make her weak in the knees, and enough sorrow to trigger the Florence Nightingale in her—the part longing to cure an emotionally wounded man with a kiss. She'd been a fool to let him slip past her guard.

Fuck him. Fuck 'em all.

Stacy pulled up the zipper on her borrowed leather jacket—the warmth of Rafe's scent on the material and her skin.

Damn. She couldn't escape him. The man enveloped her.

She thought about pitching the coat, but that would leave her running around in a bra. Not the best attire for a lone woman fleeing from supernatural baddies at six a.m.

She kept her head down and followed the shoreline. She'd walk all the way back to the city, if she had to. Gladly. As long as she didn't have to face Rafe again.

Her footsteps clattered along the stony beach. Soon, another set joined hers, crunching in synchronization. She felt Caleb's hand on her arm. Stacy shook him off and kept walking.

"I'll help you back up the hill." His youthful voice was sweet, coaxing.

She stuck her hands in her pockets and hunched her shoulders. "I'm not going that way."

"Whadda ya mean?"

Stacy turned on him. "I mean, I'm done. I've had enough. Of vampires, werewolves, and the whole fucking drama that surrounds you people."

He looked hurt, his amber eyes brimming with innocence. In spite of his superior strength and ability to change form, he was a teenager. Stacy remembered herself at that age—filled with insecurities, craving approval.

Had anything really changed?

She sighed. As much as she'd like to console him, he wasn't her problem. None of this was her problem.

"I'm sorry, Caleb. You seem like a really nice young..." She paused, searching for the right word. *Man? Wolf?* "*Guy*. But I've had enough for one day. For the rest of my life. I'm going home." She picked up her pace, slipping over the slimy rocks.

He stuck to her side. "Rafe won't like that."

"Frankly, I don't give a shit what Rafe likes."

"He thought you might say that. He told me to bring you, even if I had to chuck you over my shoulder and carry you."

Stacy stopped short. If she hadn't already seen Caleb in action—and that amazing right hook—she might have let him try. But there was no point. He could easily subdue her. Even with all her self-defense training, the teenager was like an adult to her child.

And run? She wouldn't have a chance. She was stuck, back to playing a waiting game—looking for an opportunity when they weren't watching her, when she could sneak away and make her escape.

"Fine. Lead on."

He smiled, managing to look bashful. Even though he was acting as her current jailer, she couldn't find it in her heart to resent him. The kid had 'adorable' down pat.

Stacy began her climb up the cliff. Halfway to the apex, she was huffing and puffing. "Has Rafe always been insufferable?"

Caleb frowned, not even winded. "I'm not sure what that means."

At the top of the slope, Stacy doubled over, her hands on her knees as she gulped in air. "It's a polite way of saying your friend's a jerk."

He straightened, as if someone had goosed him with an electric prod. "No way. Rafe's the best. He took me in. Even after I stole from him."

Caleb reached for a thin, dead branch on a tree and started snapping it off in bits. "I was hungry—broke into his house, raided his kitchen and grabbed some cash. Rafe tracked me down. I thought he was going to kill me. He says he'd planned to, or at least kick the shit outta me. But when he saw the shape I was in..." Caleb let the busted segments of the tree fall to the ground. "Let's just say he has a big heart. Daciana did, too."

The name stung her. It was ridiculous to think of a dead woman as her rival. There was no competition. Tala had stressed that Rafe's late wife had no contenders.

As they trudged to their base camp, Stacy flipped the conversation back to her escort. "What happened to you? Where were your parents?"

"They died when I was nine. Shot by poachers."

She stopped and clutched his hand. "Oh, Caleb—I'm so sorry."

He nodded a thank you, as if unable to speak. Stacy sandwiched his hand between hers and gave it a squeeze. "So Rafe took you in when you were nine?"

"Fourteen. I was living wild till then—on the streets, in the woods. That was three years ago." His face brightened. "Rafe's helping me study for my high school diploma."

Stacy smiled back. Nice to know education was important, even among werewolves.

She should have left it alone. But, after her late night chat with Tala, curiosity prickled. She slipped her hands from Caleb's as they resumed their walk.

"Tell me about Daciana. Was she part of your team?"

"Daciana?" He giggled—a high-pitched boyish squeak that didn't suit his muscled build. "She was a *wolf-amme.*"

"Which means?"

Caleb hummed, his forehead creased in thought. "I forget what humans call it. She delivered babies."

"An obstetrician? A vet? A midwife?"

"Yeah, *that.* She brought a lot of *weres* into the world. That's why she and Rafe were so excited about having a child of their own."

Stacy blinked. A badass fighting machine and a... *midwife?* "Sounds like the original odd couple."

"Nah, they were great together. Met when Rafe took his first aid training."

"Why did Andrion kill her?"

Caleb's expression hardened. His hands fisted. "Our missions are dangerous. Rafe resigned so he and Daciana could start a family. He didn't want to bring any of that stuff home."

"But he did."

The young man stiffened. "The last thing he had to do was testify at Andrion's racketeering trial. But the vamp bribed the jury. As soon as he was free, he came after Rafe. Figured he'd hurt him more by killing Daciana." Caleb bowed his head. "Andrion was right about that. A piece of Rafe died along with her."

Stacy's heart gave a tug. She'd seen how choked up Rafe had been over Blaez. Holding his wife while she died in his arms must have been a million times worse. Stacy could only imagine the pain. So far in life, she'd been spared that sorrow. She'd never lost anyone close to her. Not really. Sadly, her mother's passing had almost qualified as a blessing. It freed Stacy. Made her feel safer.

And that set her wondering. Had Rafe acted like a jerk in order to, somehow, keep her safe? Had he tried to protect her by pushing her away?

Stacy shook her head. She was probably reading more into his actions than she should. Believing he cared for her, even a little, was wishful thinking on her part and would only lead to further heartache. Still, she felt as if she'd just completed a jigsaw puzzle, the last piece falling into place. She might not be able to forgive Rafe, but at least she understood him better.

"Oh, shit." Caleb stepped in front of her, blocking her way. "Please don't tell Rafe I talked about this. He doesn't like loose lips."

Stacy chucked Caleb under his dimpled chin. "Don't worry. Mine are sealed."

Up ahead, she saw Rafe waiting for them—hands on hips, his stance wide, his broad chest glistening in the early morning light. In spite of his rejection, her blood surged at the sight of him.

"We need a hide-out before sunup," Rafe announced.

Caleb brightened. "The zoo?"

"Sometimes we hang with the wolves there and blend in," Rafe explained, avoiding eye contact with her. "Caleb's shy around female *weres*. But wolf-girls are easy."

Caleb gave him a playful punch on the arm. In retaliation, Rafe grabbed the teen in a headlock and rubbed his knuckles against the top of Caleb's skull—a couple of frat boys at play.

It came off forced, as if Rafe was trying too hard to act casual. But Tala, who'd joined them, rolled her eyes as if she'd seen the same exchange dozens of times. "You two are so sophomoric."

"It's called male bonding," Rafe countered.

"Can't you just go shopping?"

"Our way's cheaper."

Tala shrugged in defeat. Wordlessly, she handed Stacy another protein bar and a bottle of water. Stacy felt the vampire's cold gaze travel up and down her body. She swallowed and tried to ignore it.

Instead, she focused on Rafe as he checked a device on his wrist. "We need to get Tala to a safe place for the day. Sun's up in fifteen minutes. We'll have to run."

"Where?" Stacy asked between bites, indigestion brewing.

"Back to the city." He finally looked at her, those amber eyes of his knocking the breath from her lungs and making her heart flap around in her chest. If he held out his arms to her, was she fool enough to rush into them?

Stacy didn't get the chance to find out. Tala chose that moment to step between them, her shoulders squared, her back ramrod straight. When the vampire spoke to Rafe, her voice was tight, hurt and anger packed into every word.

"I can smell her on you."

* * *

RAFE HEARD THE contempt in the vampire's tone—saw it in the defiant lift of her chin, felt it in her stare.

If Tala was expecting another apology from him, she was going to be very disappointed. Her jealousy was showing, and her interest in him was seriously clouding her judgment.

As his groin muscles tensed, he realized he had the same problem. He'd had no business enjoying a sexual encounter with Stacy. Lives, the country—hell, the whole world—hung on the outcome of his assignment. And he couldn't resist tasting a human?

Damn. If he'd had some condoms, he would have gone a lot further than that with Stacy—licking, stroking, making her wet, and driving her to the edge. Again and again. He wouldn't have stopped until he was deep inside her—her softness surrounding him, her body writhing beneath his—until she screamed his name and begged for more.

He ran a hand down his face. Man, he was still hard. And getting harder just thinking about her, and everything he wanted to do to her. Wanted her to do to him.

That was the problem. Where Stacy was concerned, he let his dick do all the thinking, and it had a one-track mind.

He faced Tala full on. "You got a problem with me, take it up with your daddy. He's my boss, not you. In the meantime, fall in soldier. We're heading out."

Rafe marched away and made a last sweep of their camp, pausing at a section of crushed grass—the spot where Blaez died.

He had to make the right decisions, now. Had to think of what Blaez would do in each situation. But dammed if he was going to forget about Andrion. Before the mission was over, he planned to kill the bastard.

He felt Stacy at his side, running to keep up with him as he moved out in front of the others. The scent of her was enough to knock everything out of his mind. Even his thoughts of revenge.

"Look, tell me where you're headed and I'll grab a cab and meet you there."

Grab a cab? As if he'd let her out of his sight. "You're sticking with us."

"Not if you run. I'm not fast enough to keep up with you. Unless you plan to steal another car."

Rafe stopped and searched her eyes. He'd like to trust her. But he still hadn't figured out what she'd been doing in that alley, or how she fit into the vampires' plans. And, instead of using their time alone together to explore her motives, he'd used it to explore her body—to satisfy his needs.

Not that she'd quenched him. She'd only made him crave her more.

Good thing Tala was happy to play watchdog over his libido. Though the idea sounded about as appealing as stuffing his junk into an iron maiden, spikes included.

"I'll be giving you a lift," he told Stacy at last. "There's just one catch."

Her brows rose and hid beneath her wispy bangs. He fought the urge to brush the hair from her eyes and grinned at her instead. "You'll have to carry my clothes."

* * *

BEFORE STACY COULD protest, Rafe kicked off his jeans and transformed into a wolf.

"You want me to ride... *you?*"

Well, sure. Why not? She'd already taken a jaunt on his face, twice that morning. "Been there, done that."

The wolf grabbed the cuff of her jacket with his teeth and gave it a tug, throwing her off balance so that she almost landed on top of him.

Caleb steadied her. "Ever ridden a horse bareback? It's like that. Just dig your hands into the fur at his shoulders and hang on tight."

"Won't I hurt him?" After his behavior in those last minutes on the beach, the idea was tempting.

"Naw, Rafe's tough. You should see him when we go surfing."

"Surfing?"

"You get two wolves, side by side. Another person rides on top—a foot on each *were*, straddling them. Then we race. It's awesome." With that pronouncement, the teen stripped and morphed, leaving his clothes scattered on the ground.

Tala picked up all the fallen articles, folded them neatly, and handed them to Stacy.

"Don't keep Rafe waiting. Get on."

Rafe took the initiative and poked his head between her knees, coaxing her legs apart. Stacy eased herself down on his back, feeling the heat of him at her core before she was even fully seated. His backbone nestled her still sensitive parts from their morning sex-play. As he started to move forward, the friction made her hot for him all over again.

She prayed she didn't lose control in front of Tala. The vampire's stare was as cold as her touch. Their girl-bonding from the night before was over, dead and done. Having an orgasm while riding Tala's dream lover, might just put Stacy at the top of the vampire's blood donor list.

Fighting to keep her mind off all things sexual, Stacy tucked the men's clothes between her legs, tying two sets of boots together by their shoelaces, and flinging them over each shoulder. Then she grabbed two handfuls of Rafe's thick fur. She held on tight as he increased his speed to a trot—then dug her knees into his sides as he hit a run. In the time it took her to get her rhythm, they were out of the park and racing down a residential street—Caleb running beside Rafe and Tala pulling up the rear, the vampire easily keeping pace with her four-legged colleagues.

Stacy almost let go with a, "Yahoo!" as the breeze streamed through her hair. The speed, the adrenaline rush—it was like being a kid again, taking her turn on Splash Mountain at Disneyland.

An older woman, her hair in curlers and obviously half-asleep, dropped the trash bag she was holding, her mouth opening in surprise as Stacy rode along.

Stacy shrugged, hollered a breathless, "Good morning," and rounded herself over Rafe, clinging to him as he increased his speed even more.

She chanced a look ahead—a cold, uneasy feeling sinking into her bones. They were coming up on the inner city fast. Back to civilization.

And Andrion.

CHAPTER FIFTEEN

RAFE KEPT UP his pace until he spotted the big totem pole in Pioneer Square. He didn't need to be reminded of large erections. Not while he was running.

He made a sharp turn and headed for the entrance of a brick building. There, he switched back to human form and grabbed his pants from Stacy.

As she handed Caleb his clothes, she eyed the locked door and frowned. "Isn't this an entry for the Underground Tours?"

"You bet." In fact, he'd taken the tour a couple of times in his own century. "Tala needs to rest—away from sunlight. No better place than here."

As Rafe laced up his boots, he filtered through the facts he knew about the Great Seattle Fire, which destroyed twenty-five blocks of the downtown area in the late 1880s. New buildings were constructed on top of the old ones, making them a story higher. That created a chain of underground passages and a brand new tourist attraction. Seattleites were nothing if not enterprising.

Rafe edged around the corner to make sure the area was clear. It wasn't. An early-bird panhandler was close enough to catch their break-and-entry.

Hoping the guy would move on, Rafe waited. After two minutes, delaying was no longer an option. The sun was coming up fast. "If we could just get him to face the other way..."

"Allow me," Stacy said, as she sauntered by.

Rafe watched as she approached the man and engaged him in conversation. It looked like Stacy was asking directions, pointing up the street, effectively turning the panhandler around until his back was to the team. Rafe took the opportunity to sneak up on the man and put him in a sleeper hold.

"Good work," Rafe muttered to Stacy as he lowered the unconscious panhandler to the pavement. He grasped her elbow and together they ran back to the locked door.

Rafe reached for the *schlu-locke* on his belt—the same device that had started Andrion's car—and pointed it at the door. It swung open with a squeak, as if protesting the rude entry. Rafe ushered Tala and Caleb in first, then closed the door behind himself and Stacy.

Weres had excellent night vision. Without it, Rafe wouldn't have been able to see squat, just waves of never-ending blackness. As it was, he could make out shadows—Caleb moving down the stairs in front of him and Tala beyond that.

Behind him, Rafe heard Stacy's pinched voice. "I can't find the light switch."

"No lights. We don't want to attract attention." He clasped her wrist and took a step. But Stacy remained frozen to the spot, clinging to the wall at her side.

"I'll wait here. Someone should stay and guard the door."

"I'm not letting you out of my sight, remember?"

She trembled, as if a mini-earthquake passed through her. "I can't, Rafe," she whispered. "Please, don't make me."

Rafe tightened his grip. This was the same brave woman who'd taken on vampires and goltos alike. But, when it came to locked doors and dark places, Stacy was like a frightened child. What the hell had happened to her?

He gritted his teeth as rage lashed through him. Someone had created this dread in her. And, whoever that person was, Rafe wanted to crush him.

"Go on ahead," he barked to his team. Caleb nodded, while Tala harrumphed. Their footsteps faded into the pitchy depths as they made their descent.

Rafe climbed the step that separated him from Stacy and softened his voice. "You have to trust me. I won't let anything happen to you."

He wanted to hold her and melt her fears away. But he didn't think he could stop at that. And anything more would get them both in trouble. "Take my hand, and close your eyes. I'll guide you."

Stacy's fingers were cold. He brought them to his mouth, breathing warm air on her flesh. He let his lips draw closer, close enough to kiss her soft skin.

He felt another shudder go through her, but not from the cold. Not from fear.

The soldier in him wanted to leap on the opportunity and interrogate her while she was vulnerable—to find out what connection, if any, she had to the vamps. The man in him just wanted to pull her into his arms and kiss her senseless.

But he had a job to do. And she still hadn't closed her eyes. They shone in the dark, large and luminous.

"Your eyes are still open."

She touched his face. "I wish I could see you."

He grinned. "I bet you'd like to see anything right now."

"No. Just you," she said, her hand smoothing his stubbled jaw—silk on sandpaper. "I like the way you look."

That she found him attractive, even after he'd insulted her on the beach, made him happy as a lovesick teen.

"Backatcha. But right now, you need to close 'em. It'll be less scary that way. Once we're down the steps, there'll be more headroom. Then I'll piggyback you."

With her free hand resting on his shoulder, they started their slow descent. He called out each step to her, and kept talking in between, telling her she was doing great, and that they were almost there. As soon as he hit the floor, he ordered her to stop.

"Wrap your arms around my shoulders and your legs around my waist." He would have preferred the same move with her facing him, but walking would have been impossible. He'd be too busy taking her up against the wall.

He crossed her ankles in front of him and reached back to cup her thighs, giving her support. It was torture to feel her breasts crushed against his shoulders, her heat nestled into the small of his back—a completely different sensation from when she'd ridden him in wolf form. Then his thick fur and her skirt separated them. Even so, she'd made his blood stir.

Now, with her panties gone and her bare legs wrapped around his middle, nothing separated him from her sweetness.

"Keep your head tucked near mine." His words came out raspy, choked. Her breath fluttered against his cheek. Close enough for another kiss.

He swallowed hard, trampled down his lust, and started walking instead. Rafe moved forward, following the round dot of Tala's penlight.

"This is far enough," he called out. "Hit the flares."

He knew the illumination would help calm Stacy's fears but, at the same time, he sure didn't want to let her go. He savored his last moments with her in the dark, feeling the warmth of her body draped around his.

With a soft whoosh, then a crackle, the first flare lit up with a ruddy-orange glow. Caleb impaled the handle of his flare into the earth as Tala lit hers.

They each fired up a second. The four lights flooded the area, revealing the dirt floor beyond the tourists' path, brick foundations, and a variety of debris—a broken chair, an abandoned ladder, and busted pipes—all framed between the wooden beams that kept the roof from caving in.

The air was cooler here, as if they'd just walked over someone's grave. Rafe hoped it wasn't his. Not just yet.

He wasn't looking forward to rats, either. Gun battles he could handle. Hand-to-hand combat with vamps, *no problem*. Furry, cat-sized rodents streaking out at him from the shadows—even the thought of them made

Rafe squeamish. Thankfully, they wouldn't snack on Tala. Vampires were too dead, even for scavengers.

Rafe scanned the area, making sure it was clear of critters before he bent his knees and lowered Stacy to the ground. "Ride's over. Open your eyes."

She kept her hands on his shoulders, steadying herself as she swung her legs onto the ground. When she tugged on his arm, he leaned down to her.

"Sorry I was such a baby," she whispered.

"You felt very grownup, to me. Very womanly."

Her skin flushed and a smile touched her lips. Did she have any idea how much he wanted her? How difficult it was for him to hold back?

He forced himself away and surveyed their makeshift base. It looked like the perfect place for Tala to rest. Not a crack anywhere that would let in light.

He and Caleb had several hours before the tours started for the day. They could question Stacy, review Blaez's mission notes, and come up with a plan of attack. Maybe get some decent food and a change of clothes. Shirtless, there weren't many places Rafe could go without attracting attention.

"I'll find a slumber place under the scaffolding," the vampire announced as she approached him. "Away from the tourists."

She paused, as if waiting for him to say something. Small talk wasn't his forte, so his attempt at it was lame. "Hope it's not too noisy for you."

"I can sleep through almost anything."

He nodded, dismissing her, but she remained in place. If he were the kind of guy who could read a female's mind, he'd be making a hellavalot more money than he was in his present position, and be declared some kind of patron saint. Unfortunately, he had no such aptitude. So he stepped away.

Tala grabbed his arm. "Promise me you won't do anything until I'm awake."

Rafe sighed. Another reason why having a vampire on the team was a bad idea. *Weres* could go day and night, functioning without sleep for long stretches, if they had to. Not vampires. Even in cloudy Seattle, and equipped with special sunscreen, there were days when all Tala could do was hide. Rafe stopped himself before he voiced his thoughts and insulted her again.

"I can't predict the future, Tala. I don't know what Andrion is planning for us. We'll just have to get along without you until sundown."

The vampire's laugh carried a cruel edge. "You and the renegades have a lot in common."

The spike in his shoulder had hurt less than her slur. He was nothing like the renegades. The comparison was so ludicrous, he should have been able to shrug it off and walk away. But he couldn't. He stood there staring her down, his blood simmering, as he waited for her to finish the insult she'd started.

"You're the only people who make me feel ashamed of what I am." Tala's eyes glazed, then she disappeared into the darkness.

Rafe felt like Blaez must have at the end, as if someone had torn a chunk out of him.

He knew he was hard on Tala, always on her case, always finding fault. No matter how much he promised himself he'd be professional and treat her like an equal, having a vampire around raised his ire.

Sure, a part of him admired her. Fighting her own kind, no matter how despicable the renegades were, had to be tough. Now that he was in command, he had to force himself to be more diplomatic with her. At least until the mission was over. He wasn't planning on anything after that. Because his main goal in this time period was to kill the vampire that murdered his wife. And Rafe figured he wouldn't make it back alive.

"You and Tala need a full-time referee."

He felt Stacy at his side before she'd spoken—could sense her, as if he'd known her a decade, instead of a day. "We don't see eye to eye."

"Ya think?"

Her expression wasn't accusatory, more conciliatory, as if totally understanding where he was coming from and only wishing to make it better.

Before Rafe could suggest how she could make him feel *really* good, Caleb moseyed over to them.

"Whadda we do now, Rafe?"

"Figure out a plan. The portable *heilen* is running out of juice and, after abandoning the warehouse, we don't have quick access to a power source." Rafe consulted his *zeitmeter* as he mulled over the options. "Our auxiliary base is three hours away, and hasn't been used for a while. I don't know if it's still secure, or if we'll find working equipment there. But we can give it a shot. It'll put some distance between us and the vamps, and give us some breathing room to anticipate their next move."

Speak of the devil.

Rafe smelled them before he saw them. He pulled the gun from his belt and stepped in front of Stacy, protecting her from whatever threat was coming their way.

From the shadows, they emerged, a group of about twenty. The females were as tall as Rafe. The males towered above that, big and shaggy.

All were armed to the teeth—teeth that were bared and ready to feed.

CHAPTER SIXTEEN

BEFORE RAFE COULD stop him, Caleb morphed and took a running leap at the biggest vamp. The bloodsucker flung Caleb to the ground, as if he were a newborn pup instead of an oversized werewolf. The teen hit the dirt hard, bones breaking with a sickening crunch.

Then he went still.

Rafe's heart boomed. His first instinct was to go to Caleb's side. But the vamps had already turned on Rafe, hissing.

Outnumbered, and at such close quarters, Rafe didn't have a lot of choices. He thought fast and hard, sweat beading on his forehead as he weighed his options.

He didn't have a chance in hand-to-hand combat. He'd meet the same fate as Caleb, busted and bloodied. If he fired his weapon, they'd shoot back, and he'd be dead in seconds. And, while they were pumping him full of silver bullets, making him spin around on the dirt floor, Stacy would be caught in the crossfire.

But he couldn't just stand there.

Rafe dropped his weapon on the ground and held up his hands in surrender. He still had a couple of stakes in his belt. He might be able to take one or two of the vamps out at close range before he fell, and buy Stacy some escape time with the diversion. These vampires were enormous and strong but, judging from their halting steps, slow. He hoped to use that to his advantage.

Oddly, he wasn't afraid. Pumped and high on adrenaline, yes, but not frightened. He'd trained for this moment, for the inevitability of death.

He was, however, pissed. He'd finally located Andrion and was so close to getting his revenge he could almost feel the scum's flesh between his teeth. Instead, Rafe was going to end up as a snack for a bunch of subterranean bottom-feeders. Where the hell was the justice in that?

He took a slow step toward them. And another.

Stacy grabbed his arm. "Rafe, don't."

He brushed her off and pushed her away. He hoped she got the message—that she'd know to run as soon as the vampires fell on him.

But they'd stopped their approach and held their ground, guns ready. Waiting.

As Rafe advanced, he scrambled to take in as much information about them as he could, looking for any clues that would help him in his final battle.

These vamps were unlike any others he'd seen—clad in tattered, black clothes and silver jewelry. But the charms didn't burn their flesh, a phenomenon that bordered on miraculous. They were pale but, even in the soft glow of the flares, he could tell they weren't as light as regular vamps. Their skin resembled a human's, one that had been ill, or shut away from the daylight for a long time.

Most startling, their eyes weren't red, but yellow. Like his own. And they smelled very much alive.

With Rafe's next step, three of the vamps started to morph. Their jaws elongated, their hair turned to fur and covered their faces. They had the heads and claws of werewolves, but remained standing and clothed in their vampire bodies.

Rafe froze, mesmerized. He'd never seen anything like it. Had a vampire and werewolf mated to create this new species? It was too weird to believe.

Apart from the fact that vampires were dead, werewolves didn't approve of interracial bonding. Sure, some had married humans and produced offspring, but they were usually rejected by the pack, and their children ostracized as half-breeds. Even humans who'd been turned *were* weren't entirely accepted, if they survived the ordeal.

But *weres* mixed with vamps? He struggled to control his disgust. Somehow, he shared a common gene with these creatures. On some level, they were the same. And that gave him a way to reach them.

"My name's Rafe... and I'm a werewolf." Inside, he cringed. He sounded like a participant in a twelve-step program. "Who are you?"

The largest one, the creature who'd thrown Caleb, moved forward, sniffing at Rafe. "We're vampweres. And you've invaded our home. We will defend it and ourselves, if necessary."

The speaker's voice was deep and rich, like the bass singer in an opera. In spite of his ragged clothes and imposing size, his manner was refined, almost gentlemanly.

"You're the leader?"

"Unofficially. As are you, I take it." The stranger handed his gun to his nearest follower and took another step toward Rafe, a tentative one. "Leander is my name."

With imminent death on hold, Rafe shot a glance back at Stacy to satisfy himself she was okay. She looked scared, but mostly curious. Damn, the woman had guts.

Then Rafe spread out his hands to Leander, to show he was unarmed. "We didn't know this place was occupied, and we needed somewhere to hide."

The group stirred, their whispered gasps sounding like a tank full of snakes. Leander reached out and grasped Rafe's shoulder, a gesture of *were* brotherhood. "Are you running from Nikolas?"

Rafe jolted. Nikolas was a legend, one of the vampires who developed time travel. A dark, brooding genius, he'd disappeared from Rafe's century shortly after Daciana was killed. No one knew if he'd been abducted, up and left to pursue other challenges, or if he'd finally decided to end his thousand-year existence and face the sun.

Rafe had never met the vamp and didn't know much about him—except for one, well documented truth. Nikolas was Andrion's creator. It made sense that the two of them had ended up in the same time period together.

But had Nikolas come willingly? Rafe didn't think so. It seemed unlikely that the legendary vampire was behind the history tampering. Nikolas knew what was at stake, more than anyone. Still, if Rafe could find him and put a stop to the sabotage...

He returned Leander's brotherhood salute, playing nice. "Is that who you're hiding from?"

"He created us, such as we are." Leander's voice filled with bitterness. "We're part vampire, part werewolf, complete misfits. We need to consume blood to survive, but eat human food, as well. We can walk in the sunshine, but we're too conspicuous. So we stay in the shadows. The Underground is our place. We live on rats. Live like them."

Rafe swung his gaze over Leander's followers. "I don't understand. Why did Nikolas make you?"

"To act as guards" Leander signaled to the males at the front of the pack. The vampweres lowered their weapons and holstered them.

"We were an experiment," their leader continued. "One that failed. Now, there's a new army—humans hypnotized past the point of feeling pain, past any kind of remorse for their crimes. Relentless and unstoppable."

Rafe nodded. "The goltos. I've met them."

"And lived?" Leander smiled. "Then you're very lucky."

It was hard not to like the vampwere leader, although Rafe was giving it his best try. There was a nobility about him, a gentleness in spite of his imposing size. It was even harder not to feel sympathy for Leander and his people. They hadn't asked for their fate. But Rafe had his own team to worry about.

"I need to go to my friend."

Leander bowed his head and stepped aside. Rafe motioned for Stacy to join him. She picked up Caleb's clothes and, together, they went to the teen's side.

He was still unconscious, his body twisted. Rafe felt Leander's presence, hovering behind him.

"I wasn't prepared for his attack. I am sorry."

"Not your fault. You were only defending yourself. And Caleb didn't wait for orders. Once he's better, I plan to kick his ass."

As Leander's chuckle bounded off the walls, Rafe grabbed the *heilen* from Tala's pack. He noted the low reading on the power bar, and willed it to work. Within a few minutes, Caleb was sitting up, sipping on the water one of the female vampweres had passed him, and beaming from Stacy's attention.

The ass-kicking could wait until later. Rafe was just thankful the kid was okay. And, with Stacy stroking Caleb's forehead, more than a little envious. Rafe would have liked to be the one on the receiving end of her physical attentions. He started to put the *heilen* away, when Leander clutched his arm.

"Does that work on all life forms?"

"It's pre-programmed for werewolves and humans. Why?"

"One of us... is ill." Deep lines of sorrow ran across Leander's forehead.

"I can give it a try, but the power is almost gone." As soon as Rafe stood, Stacy was at his side. "You should stay with Caleb."

"He's fine. Besides, you promised not to let me out of your sight, remember?"

"I thought you didn't like that plan."

She tilted her head, a saucy smirk on her lips. "I'm getting used to it."

And he was getting used to her. Of her being there with him, always, glued to his side as if that was where she was meant to be.

He leaned in for a kiss then remembered where he was. *What* he was. He turned back to Leander. "Where's the patient?"

The head vampwere led the way, his followers parting to let Rafe and Stacy pass. At the back of the group, a female was huddled on the ground. She cradled a small bundle.

"Like other hybrids—donkeys, mules—we beasts of burden are mostly sterile," Leander stated. "Milan is the only offspring we've been able to produce."

From the bundle, he peeled back a flap of material to reveal a child, not more than six months old. Though her large, golden eyes hinted at an intelligence well beyond her age. Her face was serene, ethereal—as if she'd been touched by some mystical being.

Leander picked up the girl, balancing her in his giant hands. "Milan, this is Rafe." As he smiled down at her, the child reached up to pat Leander's cheek. "Rafe... this is my daughter."

Before Rafe could protest, Leander placed the babe in his arms. She was so tiny, Rafe was afraid he'd hurt her. He felt awkward at first, but soon remembered what Daciana had taught him. He held the child close to his body, her head in the crook of his left arm, while he supported the small of her back with his other hand.

His chest ached as he held her. Then the ache became an open wound, as Leander pulled back the baby's blanket and Rafe saw the horror that lay beneath.

The girl was covered in sores—round welts, red and weeping. But the child never complained. Didn't cry, didn't whimper.

"We're extremely susceptible to cell degeneration," Leander said, tears glazing his eyes. "It's not contagious, but it's painful and deadly."

The father covered his child's body and kissed her forehead. Then he touched Rafe's arm. "You have a daughter, too. I can tell."

Rafe shook his head, his throat so thick he didn't trust himself to speak. Instead, he handed Milan back to Leander.

The pain in his chest intensified, becoming as bad as those first weeks after Daciana was murdered. Sometimes, it stabbed him so hard he thought he was having a heart attack, and he found himself wishing for the end.

"No. I don't have a daughter. Not anymore."

He choked up again. Then he felt Stacy's hand slip into his. He didn't look at her, didn't think he could hold it together if he did. But her warmth buffered the pain, protecting him like a shield. Somehow, her touch softened the ache and made it more bearable, until he was finally able to speak.

"She was murdered. Along with my wife. By Andrion."

* * *

STACY SHUDDERED AS the stale air filled with the sound of hissing, even louder and more venomous than before. These vampweres clearly hated Andrion. Almost as much as Rafe did.

She'd felt his pain when he'd held Milan, saw it in his eyes, in the way his jaw clenched as he fought back tears. She'd known he was reliving his own loss. And seeing how it tore him apart made her hate Andrion even more.

She hadn't realized Rafe's wife had been far enough along in her pregnancy to know their child's gender. Perhaps they'd even picked a name. Stacy couldn't imagine the devastation Rafe felt at losing his entire family with one deadly stroke.

That she was able to bring him any level of comfort through her touch was the very least she could do. The man had been willing to sacrifice his life to save her. She owed him a hell of a lot more.

Stacy let go of his hand so he could fiddle with the medical gadget. He mumbled as he worked, something about vampires healing on their own and having to make manual alterations to accommodate the vampweres. When he was satisfied, he waved the device over the child's arm.

Nothing happened. The sores remained.

Leander's massive shoulders sagged. The girl's mother began to cry. Rafe reached out to them and in a quiet voice said, "I'm sorry."

Stacy smoothed Milan's cheek. She could tell the baby was sensitive, aware of her surroundings. With so much sadness in the room, Stacy didn't want her to be fearful.

Milan's little hand curled around Stacy's index finger. She looked into the child's eyes, losing herself in their depths. Then the girl, who'd yet to make a sound, cooed.

The noise so startled Stacy, she drew back. When the child's grip on her hand tightened, Stacy looked down. The lesions on Milan's skin were fading. By the time Stacy recovered from her shock and said, "Look," the sores on the girl's arm were completely healed.

A roar of excitement filled the room—vampweres, werewolves, and human alike, rejoiced. Rafe waved his healing gadget over the child again just as the light on the machine flashed red and faded.

"Shit." Rafe hit a couple of buttons then shook his head. "It's out of power."

The feeling of euphoria died, replaced by a wave of hopelessness Stacy couldn't understand. "Can't you recharge it?"

"We had to abandon our base camp after the vamps ambushed us," Rafe explained to her. "We destroyed everything we couldn't carry."

His expression was dire. From the moment she'd met him, he'd been a man of action, dealing with whatever crisis came his way without hesitation, without compromise. So what was the big problem now?

"Can't you just plug it in somewhere?"

"The human's right," Leander said, raising his head. "We can tap Nikolas' power source."

Stacy had an even better idea. Just boogie on down to the nearest Starbucks and use one of their sockets. She opened her mouth to speak but realized no one was paying attention to her. Leander was already forming a plan and Rafe was listening, his eyes bright with interest.

"We can break into Nikolas' compound, steal his power, and save my child. And we can help you put an end to Andrion."

She saw the hunger in Rafe's steely features, the bloodlust. It scared her. She'd seen him fight, but it had always been to defend her. Until this moment, she hadn't viewed him as a predator. One who'd be willing to sacrifice everything to repay the vampire who killed his wife and child.

She tried to put herself in his shoes. Maybe she'd feel the same way if someone she loved had been murdered, driven to revenge no matter what the consequences. She'd never thought of herself as a vigilante. Or a killer. But, only yesterday, she'd staked a vampire. Perhaps she merely needed the right circumstances to release her own inner marauder.

As she thought through it, she realized that her fear wasn't *of* Rafe but *for* him, for his safety. Leander's plan sounded like a suicide mission. Stacy wanted—needed—to know just how committed these vampweres would be to Rafe's cause. "What beef do you have with Andrion?"

"He's the one who forced Nikolas to make us."

Stacy felt a prickle at the base of her neck, her instincts sending out a warning flash. They were going after Andrion and his goltos? Why didn't the boys simply dive off the Space Needle? The results would be the same. Even with Leander and his people on board, the plan reeked of danger. But when she saw Rafe's expression, the prickles reduced to a buzz. Even Mr. Reckless looked skeptical.

"Nikolas is older than Andrion, and is his creator. What power does Andrion have over him?"

The vampwere shrugged. "I don't know. But when Andrion took the leap back to this time, Nikolas followed him."

Stacy felt as if all the air had been sucked out of the room. Her ears roared as she struggled to take in a breath. "What do you mean, back to this time?"

Leander flinched like a third grader caught talking in class. He turned to Rafe. "Did she not come with you?"

"No, she did not come with him," Stacy shot back, her body trembling from both fear and rage. With lightning speed, she mentally reviewed the evidence—the gadgets, the weapons, the way Blaez had disappeared, the fact that Rafe was the only one of his friends who could drive a car. She'd always assumed they were part of a top secret band of the armed forces., and didn't like where her mind was taking her now—on a tightrope walk to the far edge of sanity.

She struggled to gain control of her breathing. "Where are you from?"

Rafe pressed in close to her, his voice low and steady. "I told you. I'm from Seattle."

She struck him, punching his chest as hard as she could. "Don't fuck with me."

They'd been locked up in Andrion's cage together, faced death together, experienced pleasure together—and, all the while, he'd kept her in the dark about this?

"*When...* are you from?"

His Adam's apple bobbed. He clasped the hand that had hit him, the one that throbbed, and gave it a gentle rub. "The twenty-third century."

This man, the one she'd shared so much with, was from…*the future?*

Stacy's legs went limp, as if someone had whipped them out from under her. She stumbled and fell against the wall, but managed to stay upright.

"Damn. I was just getting used to you being a werewolf."

CHAPTER SEVENTEEN

AFTER EVERYTHING SHE'D been through, Rafe had expected her to faint. Not his champ. She'd come back with a right hook and a smart-ass jab.

Still, he could see she was confused, disoriented.

He looped an arm around Stacy and led her to the opposite side of a brick wall—a private spot away from the others. "Relax. Everything's fine."

"Easy for you to say," she murmured. "You won't be born for another two hundred years." She rested her head on the rock behind her and closed her eyes, her long lashes partially obscuring the dusky smudge below each lid. "Or maybe I'm losing my mind."

Rafe squeezed her hand, wishing he could erase all the pain he'd caused her. "You're not."

She'd been going full out and nonstop since they'd met, rolling with the punches. And on what fuel? A protein bar and a couple hours sleep?

Then he'd dragged her into the Underground, into the dark she feared. He'd forced her up against the ropes, even though she'd begged him not to. Admitting he was from the future was another blow in a combination of hits.

And she still hung in there.

He reached out to her, an invitation for a hug, and was pleasantly surprised when she came to him willingly. He held her for a while—just held her—until her breathing steadied, until most of her tension eased. Slowly, he lowered them both to the ground and cradled her in his lap.

Rafe smoothed the hair from her face. "I'm sorry about bringing you into this."

"It's not your fault. It's just a lot to digest," she said, interlacing her fingers with his. "I've seen vampires and shape shifters in movies and on TV. Only they're actors playing parts."

Spoken like a true twenty-first century human. They weren't ready for such creatures to be anything but special effects magic. Still, Stacy had adapted to her new surroundings. Fought the enemy at his side. He owed her something of an explanation for her courage.

"Who do you think is writing and producing most of those shows? It's all in preparation, so that when we reveal ourselves to humans, it won't be so frightening." Rafe slid his fingers along hers, following the contours of her hand, memorizing her by touch—an unhurried, sensual journey.

"How long have werewolves been living among humans?" she asked, cooling his thoughts.

"Did you study ancient Rome in school?" His chest puffed with pride. "Remember the defeat of Caesar's army in the Teutoburg Forest?"

Her eyes widened. "Werewolves did that?"

"My ancestors. Their home was invaded so they defended themselves... and their families."

"Sounds like you've inherited their protective ways."

They could have been sitting at a plush resort instead of on a dirt floor, the way her smile made him feel. And talking about the past? It damn well beat a discussion of the future. Because they sure as hell weren't going to get one together.

"What about the vampires?"

"They've been around longer than us. For centuries, we were at war with them. Then, a couple hundred years ago, a group of vamps developed a conscience. They sought to isolate the original virus or curse that caused their condition."

"Why?"

"To find a remedy, for those who wanted it, and to police the dangerous ones who lived outside their laws. They were hoping the answer was in one of the papyrus manuscripts burned at the library in Alexandria."

"Hold on." Stacy waved her hands, signaling a time-out. "Are you talking about ancient Egypt? Vampires have been around as long as that? And in the Middle East?"

"That's where everything started. Although the original vamps from those days are long gone——destroyed by infighting, religious zealots, or fried by the sun. So we can't ask them how they came to be. Or take tissue samples."

She pursed her lips as she mulled over the facts—lips that were full, pink and entirely kissable. "Okay... but that library you mentioned was burned in ancient times, wasn't it? Even before Christ."

He wiped his forehead on the crook of his arm. The next part of his explanation would be the toughest for her to swallow. "That's why the vampires developed a way to journey into the past."

Stacy stared at him, unblinking. "Well, why not. As immortals, they must have a lot of time on their hands."

He stared back. "Did you understand what I—?"

"Got it. We're talking *Back to the Future* and all that jazz. I like Michael J. Fox, too."

Rafe wasn't sure who this Fox guy was, but he knew from the upsweep of Stacy's mouth that she'd just cracked a joke. "You're handling this well."

She lowered her chin, holding his gaze. "If I'm buying the existence of vampires and werewolves—and I have to because I've seen you with my own eyes—then time travel isn't that far out. I'd already dismissed the idea that you're from another planet, because you sure don't look like E.T." She smiled again. "Too tall."

Rafe huffed out a breath, flabbergasted. Earlier, he'd thought the woman was amazing. But he'd been wrong. She was nothing short of incredible—her adaptability, her willingness to accept the extraordinary.

The black of her pupils encroached onto the blue of her iris, revealing her hunger for information. It reminded Rafe of all the times he'd sat by the pack leader, listening and learning. Now, it was Rafe's turn to be the teacher, to answer what questions he could.

"I'm telling you all this because—"

"You can't erase my memory."

"Exactly. And, if you reported what you saw—"

"It could jeopardize your mission. Not to mention, land me in a psych ward."

Shit. He couldn't bear to think of her suffering more because of him. "I need you to understand how important this is. I need you to—"

"Keep my mouth shut. I get it."

"And to stop guessing what I'm going to say before I figure it out myself."

She grimaced. "Sorry. I'll let you answer this next question all on your own. Are the vampires still looking for a cure? Didn't they find it at Alexandria?"

"That's two questions." Rafe shook his head. "We haven't been able to travel back that far, yet. Our scientists are still working on it."

"How do the werewolves fit in?"

"We do the *tripping*."

"*Tripping?*"

"That's what we call jumping back in time."

Her brows sandwiched a faint line. "Why don't the vampires do it themselves? Why involve *weres* at all?"

"Our DNA's unique, so we're easier to pick up. The time portal is programmed to look for our genes."

"What about Tala?"

Rafe flinched at the mention of her name. He remembered her last words to him, the way she'd compared him to the renegades and her accusation that he'd shamed her. He knew he was hard on Tala, and that he shouldn't judge every bloodsucker on the weight of one's actions. But some days, it was damned hard.

"She has to travel back with us. We have to stand right beside her so our control base can locate her coordinates. Otherwise, she could get trapped here."

"And if you die?"

"Then we're immediately transported to our time; that way there's no werewolf bodies to explain."

"Like Blaez."

He lowered his head and nodded. "Another reason why vamps don't usually take the leap. Low heartbeat." Rafe felt her hand on his chest, her touch making his own heart leap.

"Sounds like a good system. So what's the problem?"

"There wouldn't be one, except for a group of renegade vampires who've escaped justice in my time by *tripping* into the past. Because of them, our missions have altered. Instead of looking for a cure, we get stuck straightening out the glitches they create."

Ironic really. Werewolves had always been considered the beasts. Now, it was up to them to save the human race. And their own.

"So you're the underdogs?"

"No pun intended."

Her mouth twitched then she sobered. "If the renegades know the consequences of their actions, why do they do it?"

"Because their thirst for power and wealth overrides everything. They use their knowledge of the future for their personal gain. To hell with anyone else."

"That describes Andrion. What about Nikolas?"

Rafe frowned. "He was already wealthy, and he's one of the engineers who developed time travel. Nikolas, more than anyone, understands the dangers of altering the past. I can't believe he's behind the tampering."

"So what happened to bring you here? It has something to do with the dead man in the alley, doesn't it? The vampires killed him before he could do... whatever it was that changed history. Is that it?"

"Yes. We were sent to protect him."

"But you said he was an assassin."

Crap. She remembered that? "Have you been taking notes?"

"I was always a good student."

"Maybe I should have my lips sewn shut."

She traced a finger over his mouth. "That would be a huge loss."

He kissed that finger, then her palm. He brushed his lips over hers— soft and sweet.

"If you keep doing that, I'll forget all the questions I want to ask you."

103

"Good." Though distracting her hadn't been his motive. At least, not his main one.

"I want to know about that man in the alley. He was supposed to kill someone, wasn't he? Someone important, I take it. A modern-day JFK?"

Rafe knew she'd keep questioning him until he said something. He chose his words, hoping they would be enough to satisfy her. "Sometimes good people have to die to bring about change."

"And you're not going to tell me who?"

"Nope. No matter how much you kiss me."

"Too bad. I like kissing you."

He liked it, too. And he liked her. In the space of a day, he'd stopped thinking of her as a bit of fun on the side. He wouldn't be able to discard her so easily.

"Can't you just start the mission again? Go back farther in time and catch the renegades before they act?"

"It's an option. But a dangerous one."

"Why?"

"Imagine pouring a cup of water into a plastic bag."

"You mean the kind of bag you'd use to pack a sandwich?"

"That'll do. Now, imagine the water as time. *Tripping* to the past causes a stretch in the fabric of time. Or, in our analogy, a stretch in that plastic. We don't want that stretch to become a tear. According to our scientists, that would bring about Armageddon."

She licked her lips, leaving them glistening. "I thought, if you stepped on a butterfly, you changed everything."

Ray Bradbury and his dinosaur hunt—Rafe remembered the short story. He'd read it, too. "An exaggeration. It's more about key events, key people. Think of a river when it overflows. Small tributaries may emerge, only to dry up later. It's the original river that keeps flowing, keeps moving forward, bringing the main players together."

Stacy leaned close to his ear, her breath warm on his neck. "If you save Milan, won't that change the future?"

"I don't think so." As far as Rafe knew, there weren't any vampweres in his time. He guessed they didn't survive as a species. Saving this child wouldn't help the race. But it might give one father some peace.

"I used to think I was special. Now I feel like just another cog in the wheel."

He slipped his hands to her waist. "You are special. A human, without training, who staked a vampire on her first try. A woman who's faced every kind of danger in the last thirty-six hours and survived. You're the bravest person I've ever met."

"Not brave enough for the dose of fear you and the others live with daily. How 'bout I just meet you at the pub after it's all over?"

He'd like that. Except there wasn't going to be any congratulatory toasts with her at the end of his mission.

"Our stay here is limited, Stacy. We'll try to right whatever we can before Zero Time. Then we're automatically transported back home to see if we've achieved our goals."

"When's Zero Time?"

"At the end of the week."

Her mouth went slack, the color in her face faded.

"I'm sorry. I didn't know I'd be meeting you. That we'd—" He stopped himself before he blurted out some romantic garbage about wishing he could stay longer and get to know her better. He wasn't going to make promises he couldn't keep. If she still wanted his kisses after knowing the truth, he'd make it worth her while. If not... he'd stay away from her, no matter how much it ripped at his insides.

"My mission is over in four days, Stacy. Then I'll be gone. Forever."

CHAPTER EIGHTEEN

STACY TRIED TO breathe. She stared at Rafe, her jaw slack, her brain fighting to wrap its way around this new revelation.

Four days?

She hadn't bargained on a lifetime commitment from him, or even a glib declaration of love. He'd been straight up with her. No hints at a future. No promises.

But she'd expected him to be in her life for more than four days.

He'd entered her world in such a huge way. From the moment they'd met, they'd been in danger and on the run. That had fused them together, bound them to one another. It didn't hurt that he was built like an Adonis on steroids, came equipped with a movie stud smile, and packed a heavy dose of bravado that made her knees weak. Whatever crazy pheromones this werewolf was sending out, her libido was receiving loud and clear.

But, in truth, Rafe was a stranger. He hadn't even shared his last name with her. If he had one.

She dropped her gaze to avoid his eyes and the guilt that needled her—a result of her own subterfuge. She hadn't disclosed her identity, either, hadn't divulged her secrets to Rafe. Even though they'd been intimate in other ways.

And how weird was that? She trusted Rafe with her body, with her life, but had held back the truth about who she was at Andrion's urging. Whatever the reason behind his advice, it worked with her own life experience. Because she'd never had a man who wanted her just for her. It had always been about her father.

Truthfully, Rafe had revealed far more of himself to her. She knew when he was born and his heritage. He'd also been honest about his feelings back at the park. He was game for some recreational sex, but that was all. And, with him, the foreplay was mind-blowing enough that Stacy shouldn't have wanted more.

But she did.

Not that it was going to get her anywhere. No matter how strong their connection, he would be out of reach before the week was through. And there wasn't a damned thing she could do about it.

Her lungs froze and wrapped a chill around her heart. It was past time to protect herself, lock up her feelings and block any romantic thoughts from her mind. She could share her body with Rafe, and enjoy him while he was with her, but any kind of relationship was over—finished before it was half-begun. All she could do now was follow him, and trudge her way around the corner that led them to the others.

As soon as Caleb saw them, he sprang up from his seated position and trotted over. "You okay?"

His face was so full of concern, Stacy smiled in spite of the pain constricting her chest. She gave him a peck on the cheek and squeezed his hand. "I'm fine. Thanks."

"What have you learned from our new friends?" Rafe asked his teammate, his voice low.

"The vampweres have spent their nights digging a tunnel. Leander says it'll be finished soon. Maybe by tomorrow, if we help."

"Where does the tunnel go?"

"Right under Andrion's downtown office."

Stacy wondered why the wannabe movie mogul needed a second hangout. "Is that where he auditions new talent?"

"Nope. T.J. runs his stock market deals from there."

Rafe's golden eyes narrowed. "Sounds like the vamps have their fangs in several pies. And, using their future knowledge of when to buy and sell, that trading business is gonna be plenty sweet."

"Yeah, that's what Leander says. The money T.J. makes on Andrion's behalf pays for Nikolas' experiments."

The way Caleb said 'experiments' had Stacy thinking about monsters like Josef Mengele, the Angel of Death at Auschwitz. The poor vampweres were already paying the price for Nikolas' projects—living a marginal existence while battling a fatal, genetic disease. Stacy was reminded of that age-old argument posed to medical science—just because you can, *should* you?

Still unwilling to make eye contact with Rafe, she questioned Caleb. "Leander said Nikolas created the vampweres as an army for Andrion. Why does he need one?"

She may have asked Caleb, but it was Rafe who answered. "To protect himself from anyone who interferes with his plans. The renegades' lust for money and power is almost as strong as their need for blood. They'll risk everything for it."

A shiver went through Stacy. If T.J. was manipulating the stock market, the results could be disastrous—an economic crash greater than anyone had ever seen. "Does he understand what he's doing?"

"Oh, yeah. And it gets worse." Caleb took a step toward Rafe, his expression grave. "Nikolas is making a *tripping* portal. Here... in this time."

Rafe snarled. Stacy hardly recognized the man who'd treated her wounds, who'd kissed her with such tenderness, with such passion. Now, all she could feel was the raw hatred that surged through him—saw it in the way his muscles tensed, from his jaw to his clenched fists. His eyes were lit with a deadly fire, and when he spoke, his tone was flat. Lethal.

"Which means Andrion can escape justice by going farther back into the past."

* * *

THE DESIRE FOR revenge burned hot in Rafe's veins. "How close is he to completion?"

"Leander doesn't know."

Rafe sensed fear in the young lycan. Not that the boy had ever run from a fight. His alarm was born out of concern, and Rafe regretted that he was at the crux of it.

He looked around the room, taking in all the faces and the alarm that showed on them. Especially Stacy's. She'd seen the animal in him, the killer.

He clutched Caleb's arm and used a more casual tone, as much to console Stacy as the lad. "It's okay. I'll keep a cool head."

Caleb looked relieved, and Rafe heard a collective sigh as everyone let out the breath they'd been holding. Tension melted from the vampweres, but Stacy's shoulders remained tight, and on a collision course with her ears.

"Give me a few minutes with Stacy. Then I'll take a look at Leander's tunnel."

"Me, too. Right? I'm coming with you."

Rafe caught Caleb's eagerness—saw it in his expression, heard it in his voice. He hated to disappoint the kid, but didn't have an alternative.

"Tala watched over us while we slept. I need you to stay here and do that for her now. And protect Stacy." Because Rafe sure as hell wasn't dragging her into the dark, confined space of an underground tunnel. He'd already subjected her to enough for one day.

Still, he could tell Caleb was disappointed, so he laid it on thicker. "I need someone I can count on. Someone I can trust."

The pup looked up, a shy grin on his lips. "I won't let you down."

Rafe sent him over to the vampweres with a clap on the back, and turned his attention to the woman at his side.

"Tala's in love with you."

He blinked. He'd expected Stacy to ask about Nikolas, and how this new development would affect her chances of going home. Talk about left field. "Love has nothing to do with it. Tala wants what she can't have."

"Then why don't you sleep with her and get it out of her system?"

Was Stacy really trying to pair him up with another female? "Sex with a coworker is never a good idea. Besides, I'm not interested in dead girls."

"No. You're fixated on revenge. For Daciana."

"Who told you about her?" A stupid question. The answer was obvious.

"Caleb... and Tala."

They had no right to reveal his personal life to an outsider. Or to remind Rafe of what he'd lost.

He used to dream about his wife every night. Used to be able to close his eyes and form a vivid picture of her in his mind. He still remembered her hands, those long, tapered fingers moving with confidence and grace. He could recall how she smiled, as if she had a secret no one else knew. And her eyes—the joy in them, the way she could make him hard with just a look. But her other features had begun to blur, distorted by the horror of her murder—her skin turning gray and waxy, her body growing cold and stiff. If Caleb hadn't pulled him away, Rafe might still be cradling Daciana on the kitchen floor, stroking her face and begging her to stay with him.

"What do you want from me, Stacy?"

"I'm sorry about what happened to your wife. But playing vigilante isn't going to bring her back. Or give you peace. It's going to get you killed."

"You're being dramatic." And perceptive. How many times had he wished for death, for an end to the pain eating away at him? "I'm going after Andrion for the sake of the mission."

Stacy grasped his hand. "Then let me help you."

Her touch—warm and alive—made his heart thunder. A part of him wanted to abandon the revenge he sought, abort the mission, and steal away with her to a little cabin somewhere in the woods. But they were from two different times, two different species. Being with her wasn't an option. The only choice he had was to continue on the course he'd set for himself a year ago, as he embraced his wife that last time. He couldn't hold Daciana anymore, so he clung to the hatred that had sustained him for so long.

"Help how?"

"If Andrion and T.J. are trading, they must have computers. Maybe a room full of them."

"So?"

"If those computers are hit with a virus, Andrion and his thugs will be so busy dealing with that, they won't notice if you enter the building."

A distraction? It sure wouldn't hurt. "But we don't have a virus."

"I'm a computer geek, remember? A friend and I created one back in college as a project."

A red alert jangled up Rafe's spine. He didn't like where this idea was heading. "We can't risk going to your home. The vamps might have someone watching your place."

Stacy's big, blue eyes sparkled. With excitement? With fear? "It's not at home. My friend has it. He runs a comic shop at Pike Place Market. We can walk there."

"And how does this virus get into Andrion's computers?"

"I can search his IP address and deliver it remotely."

Rafe crossed his arms over his chest and rocked back on his heels. If he'd ever thought of Stacy as just a pretty face, he'd been dead wrong. She was smart, resourceful—and, God knew, resilient. Now, she was even thinking like a team member.

His smile withered as he remembered his fallen comrade. Blaez had told him to look for the brains behind the history sabotage. Was that Nikolas? Or was Andrion somehow manipulating the scientist? Holding him hostage?

It made sense to learn the truth about Nikolas' involvement. To rescue him, if possible. And Stacy's plan sounded like a step in the right direction.

"We're gonna have to start paying you a salary."

"Stay safe. That's all the payment I need."

He wished he could promise her that, but Rafe wasn't about to let Andrion off the hook. He'd spent the better part of the year looking for his wife's killer and vowed, with everything in his being, to stop the bastard, before the vamp eluded him again, by disappearing into history.

CHAPTER NINETEEN

STACY WAITED FOR Rafe while he checked out the vampweres' tunnel. She had little choice. Caleb's eyes worked as well as a pair of handcuffs, locking her to him. He grinned at her and made a few jokes, as boyish and disarming as usual. But every time she took a step away, he was right there at her side—tracking her, keeping watch.

When Rafe returned, he gave Caleb a quick nod, which Stacy interpreted as his seal of approval on the tunnel. Now, it was up to her to deliver the computer virus.

Although her inner-anarchist wanted an excuse to use it, the rest of her wanted to run from the vampires, to hide in bed with the covers pulled up to her chin. But as soon as she pictured herself under the sheets, she thought of Rafe beside her.

Which was an utterly useless fantasy. They didn't even live in the same century. She'd never spent time mooning over a man before. Pining for an unobtainable werewolf would be a lesson in heartbreak.

Still, when Rafe cocked his head in a come-hither gesture, she jumped to her feet, ready to follow him. Wherever.

Surely, she hadn't turned into some Rapunzel-haired, castle-bound princess overnight. Stacy wanted—needed—a say in her own destiny. Because there was far more at play here than her attraction to a certain charismatic shape shifter, who packed so much sexual heat he should come with a warning label.

If the diversion she planned worked, it would save lives—Rafe's included. She'd feel useful, vital. And, God help her, she was desperate to be out of the Underground, to feel sunlight on her face.

It would be good to see Perry, too. He'd be thrilled the virus they'd created together in college would finally get its moment in the spotlight. And Stacy was hungry to see another human. To reassure herself she wasn't losing her mind. To know that there was, indeed, a world beyond vampires, time travel, and *weres*—oh, my!

When Rafe took her hand and led her toward the stairs, tingles coursed up her arm and settled in her stomach. Not only because she'd be moving from the darkness she feared, but because of his touch. *Damnit*, no matter how often he pushed her away, she still felt a connection to him. Craved it.

But, as they moved from the orange glow of the flare lights and into the darkness, her anxiety level spiked, fear crushing her chest until she couldn't squeeze in a breath. She closed her eyes tight.

"Talk to me. Please." Even though he was guiding her by touch, she needed to hear his voice—a beacon in the night.

"Sure. Have I mentioned how beautiful you are?"

"In the dark? Cute." So much for an attempt at humor to mask her fear. Her shaking voice betrayed her. "Talk to me about your kind. When will you reveal yourselves?"

"I've told you too much already."

"Please." *Great*. Now, she was whimpering. And she'd used up all the air in her lungs. Light-headed, she shuffled forward, her feet as awkward and sluggish as if she were wearing giant flippers. And she could barely feel Rafe's hand through the panic.

Then he started to talk.

At first, she couldn't focus long enough to make out the words. But it was good to hear the low rumble of his voice. It calmed her to the point where she was able to take in a breath. And another. Slowly, the fog in her brain lifted and she could understand what he was saying.

"...soon. The shape shifters come out first—*weres* and the like. They gain acceptance by entering the military... and help end what humans will think is an unwinnable war."

Stacy shook her head, clearing the last of the cobwebs. Did he mean the war raging now? Were they doomed to fight that battle for years to come? Or did he mean another, deadlier conflict?

"And the person that assassin was supposed to kill—without that murder, this war continues?"

"Yes. Millions more die and the country collapses."

The gravity of his mission broadsided her. No wonder he was so protective of it. "What about—"

"No more questions. The stairs are right in front of you."

He helped her climb the first two steps—her back pressed against his chest, his arms enfolding her. When he bent one knee to climb higher, she was obliged to do the same. It sure wasn't a fast way to navigate the stairs, but having him tight against her was certainly reassuring. She could feel his muscles ripple around her as they climbed, feel his steady heartbeat echoing within her own body, and knew she'd never be safer than when he was with her.

She heard him open the door, and the glare of the morning light flared across her closed lids. She gulped in the ocean breeze, her lungs greedy for the fresh air. Her ears filled with the sound of a city coming alive—the whoosh of traffic, the deep blast of a ship's horn.

Although she was perfectly content to stay by Rafe, Stacy knew she couldn't cling to him forever. She stepped away and opened her eyes, only to find him towering over her—his hair mussed, his bedroom smile making her mouth water.

Stacy licked her lips, hoping for a kiss. But Rafe shifted into business mode. He glanced at the watch-like device on his wrist.

"The Market doesn't open for a while, but better that we appear before the foot traffic's heavy. I don't want to get caught sneaking out of what should be a locked tourist attraction." Rafe lifted his head, gesturing to the north-east with his chin. "We can saunter down toward Pike Street... watch the boats, grab a coffee."

"I was anticipating a different kind of morning stimulant."

His eyes darkened so that only a thin strip of gold showed around the pupil. "You're killing me."

"Are you so susceptible to a kiss?"

As he moved in, Stacy closed her eyes. She could feel him, hovering above her, but their lips didn't touch. Instead, he took her hand—weaving his fingers between hers, sending shockwaves over her flesh.

When he gave her a gentle tug, she opened her eyes. His smile was gone, his expression serious. Clearly, she'd have to wait for that kiss.

They started walking along city streets that were just waking. And something in Stacy was waking, too. The touch of Rafe's hand, somehow more intimate than the kiss she'd wanted, made her realize the importance of the moment. Whatever battles they had to face, whatever would ultimately tear them apart, she'd always have this time with him to remember.

"Can I ask you something?" His voice was gentle, hesitant. From his tone, Stacy was pretty sure she wasn't going to like his question. So much for their quiet walk.

"Go ahead."

"What's with the locked doors and dark places? If I'm getting too personal, tell me to back off."

Too personal? He'd brought her to climax. Twice. With his mouth. What could be more personal?

Except for divulging her secrets. She'd never shared them with anyone. Apart from the counselor she'd spent a year and a half with as a child. Everyone around her knew the sanitized version of the story, the one she'd constructed over time.

Time... which would take Rafe from her in a matter of days.

If she wanted to unburden herself, he was the best ear for it. She'd already been far more intimate with him than anyone else. And he had no idea who she really was. When he disappeared at the end of the week, her anonymity would remain intact.

"My mother was an alcoholic. When I was a kid, she'd lock me in my bedroom closet and go on a binge."

Their rhythmic footsteps pounded the sidewalk, counting out the seconds of silence. For a moment, she wondered if he'd heard her.

She glanced over at him. His face was slack with shock. "Jesus. Why didn't you tell me?"

"Would it have made a difference?"

"Hell, yes. I wouldn't have dragged you into the Underground if I'd known."

"Even for the sake of your mission?"

He ripped his hand away from hers, tearing out a piece of her heart at the same time. She should have gone with her standard answer—a bullshit story involving a violent thunderstorm, a power outage, and a mother racing home to be at her daughter's side. Bullshit, because Stacy's mom only ever raced to the liquor store.

She swatted the air between them, ready to pass the whole conversation off as a joke. But Rafe enfolded her in his arms, pulled her tight against his chest, and into an alcove between the buildings.

"Mission be damned. I would have found a way to protect you."

Stacy melted into him, the pain and anger in her body easing away as he held her. She buried her face in his chest, surprised to find it wet with her own tears. Embarrassed, she struggled to get away, to gain control. But Rafe just held her closer, rubbing her back as she cried.

It felt good to let go, to let those past hurts drain out of her. She cried until there was no moisture left in her body. Then she swiped her eyes with her hands. When her vision cleared, she tilted her head and looked up at Rafe.

"Sorry about that."

"You have nothing to apologize for. No child should have to endure that." He smoothed the hair back from her face and kissed her brow. "Where was your father?"

"He was out of town a lot. My mother made me promise not to tell him anything. Said my dad would abandon us if he knew, and I'd never see him again."

"Did he ever find out?"

Stacy nodded. "He came home early one day... heard me crying... and found me in the closet. I'd been in there overnight."

Rafe winced, as if feeling her pain. "Sweet Jesus."

"Don't worry. This is when the story gets better. The next day, my dad filed for divorce and sole custody. He's been my number one hero ever since." She lowered her chin and looked up at Rafe through her lashes. "Until you came along."

His lips twitched and spread into a bashful smile. "Sounds like I'm in very good company."

"If I could call him today, let him know I'm okay—"

"I'll make sure you get to a phone." He slipped his arm around her and motioned her back onto the sidewalk. They traveled a block in silence before he spoke again. "Where's your mother now?"

Stacy hung her head, mourning the wasted years. "She went on a binge when she found out my dad was leaving her and wrapped her car around a tree. She died instantly. It was a miracle she didn't kill anyone else."

Rafe tucked Stacy against his side. "I wish I could have been there for you."

As she looked up at him, a new memory came into her mind—Rafe speaking to her from the other side of that closet door—his deep, comforting voice, reassuring her, helping her through the fear.

"I think you were... somehow. Is it possible you—"

But that's all she managed to say. Rafe cut her off with a loud, "We're here."

They'd arrived at Pike Place Market on a trail of her tears. And, if all went well, Andrion would be the next one to cry.

CHAPTER TWENTY

RAFE HAD NEVER been happier to see Rachel, the giant, brass piggy bank that acted as a sentinel at the main entrance of The Market. He needed a moment to work his head around Stacy's childhood trauma, and squelch the desire to pound his fist into something.

Passing judgment on Stacy's mother would have been easy. But he'd been in that dark place, too—knew what it was to lose oneself in a bottle, to medicate for the pain.

The day after Daciana's murder, he'd started drinking. And hadn't stopped until her funeral. He'd been sober enough for the service to realize he couldn't go on dishonoring his wife's memory with alcohol. He was a better male for knowing her and, if she'd seen him wallowing in self-pity at the bottom of a whiskey glass, she'd have kicked his sorry ass from here to Kansas.

That's when he'd decided to do something positive with his rage and grief—to avenge her murder. If he died in the process, so be it. Far better than drowning in an endless sea of booze.

Rafe wondered what had so destroyed Stacy's mother that she took to drink and, in turn, devastated her own daughter. When Stacy told him the cause of her fears, his first impulse was to travel back in time to rescue her. A clear breach of protocol. Unauthorized *tripping* would snag him a court martial. And for Rafe to save Stacy as a child was like going AWOL to prevent Helen Keller from contracting the illness that left her deaf and blind. A humanistic gesture…and a Pandora's box. The number of lives Keller touched with her story would be impossible to determine. Or recreate.

Even though it tore Rafe up to imagine Stacy locked in a closet, he knew he couldn't rescue her from the past. The experience formed her, led her father to seek a divorce, brought about her mother's death... and God only knew what else. Screwing around with that kind of powder keg would definitely blow up in his face.

Still, he wanted to befriend that terrified child, to ease her burden. Had he? Did he sneak back on his own to help her after he completed his assignment? The possibility troubled him far more than a mere court martial.

While it gave him hope he would survive this mission, that very optimism could be his undoing. Too many *trippers*, who thought they were home free, got sloppy and ended up in the morgue.

Rafe didn't want to die. Not before he tasted Andrion's blood.

And, now that he'd met Stacy, hara-kiri didn't have the same allure it used to. He'd spent the last year feeling crushed, as if someone had ripped open his chest and trampled his insides with cleated boots. Already, Stacy had eased that raw ache—with her humor, her courage, her touch.

But was he that into her that he'd risk it all? For a woman who'd be out of his reach in a matter of days?

Rafe wasn't superstitious, but he patted Rachel for luck as he passed. Pigs symbolized sacrifice, sensuality, unbridled passion... *bacon*. And he could eat a couple of pounds of it right now.

As he scanned the already busy market, he caught several shoppers staring at him. Not only was he bare-chested, his eye color was startling enough that people wouldn't pass it off as a new shade of contacts. In the twenty-third century, *weres* walked the city freely but, for now, he'd have to blend in, which meant buying a shirt and a pair of sunglasses. Team members always carried some century-appropriate cash for such occasions.

Rafe guided Stacy past the Fish Company kiosk—the clerks tossing their finned merchandise overhead to one another, a juggling act still popular in his day—and headed into the first store that sold shades and T's. He picked up three shirts—slipping into one right away—and two pairs of jeans. He and Caleb would need a change of clothes after the night ahead.

He invited Stacy to pick up something, but every garment was huge on her small frame. Amazingly, the thought of her body revved his engine no matter what she wore. He did buy her a pair of glasses, along with his own, and the Mariners baseball cap she modeled for him.

Purchases made, Stacy led the way to the lower level of the 'Soul of Seattle.' Rafe followed her down the staircase, and across pine-colored wooden floors, to a shop tucked into a corner by a red emergency door. A handy escape route, should they need one. While Stacy went to the counter to ask for her friend, Rafe examined the store—from its blue neon overhead sign to its jam-packed shelves beyond.

The place definitely sold comic books, hundreds of them, as well as lunchboxes, stuffed animals, posters, action figures, and the trio of life-size cardboard cutouts that greeted him at the door. He recognized Marilyn Monroe and Elvis Presley, but there was a yellow cartoon dude holding a beer can that was a complete mystery.

Before he could ask Stacy about it, her friend appeared. Rafe expected a computer nerd—skinny, bespectacled and awkward. He wasn't prepared for a good-looking guy with a ready smile.

The man was an inch or two shorter than Rafe, his surfer's build tucked into a pair of loose-fitting khakis and a red shirt so tight it could have been the top half of a wetsuit. He had a Shake & Bake tan, his hair shimmered with gold, and he smelled better than most females—a spicy, citrus combo—part grapefruit, part cayenne pepper.

Rafe's immediate dislike of him grew when Surfer Boy wrapped an arm around Stacy and gave her a kiss.

She giggled—a rich, throaty sound Rafe had never heard from her before. There hadn't been much reason for her to laugh in the last day and a half.

As Stacy cuddled into Surfer Boy she turned, looking surprised when Rafe's gaze locked with hers, as if she'd forgotten he was standing there.

"Oh, Rafe—this is Perry Davidson. Perry, this is Rafe..." Her introductions trailed off with an, "Uhhhhh."

"And does Rafe have a last name?"

Rafe felt two sets of eyes on him, both waiting for an answer. Team members went by first names only. It was harder for their enemies to find them that way. And Rafe well knew how vulnerable he was to attack. When he'd testified at Andrion's trial, he gave his full name on the stand. That nugget led the vamp straight to Rafe's house. And Daciana.

He had nothing left to lose, now. No reason to create an alias.

"Garrett. Rafe Garrett." He extended his hand for Perry to shake. It was a good excuse to get the man's paw off Stacy's waist.

She stood on tiptoes and whispered to her friend. "Can we talk in the office?"

Perry's smile disappeared. "Sounds serious."

Surfer Boy shot Rafe an accusatory glance before jerking his head toward the back of the store. "Anything for the girl I love."

Stacy gave the guy a squeeze. "Thanks, Perr. I love you, too."

Rafe's heart shattered a little. He hadn't pictured Stacy as the promiscuous type, letting him go down on her while poor 'Perr' kept the home fires burning. Then again, Rafe didn't keep his fly zipped up with a padlock. He'd been more than willing to touch her, taste her, bury himself inside her. He had no problem going after what he wanted, but drew the line at running off with another male's mate.

Perry told the cashier he was leaving the floor and asked her to take messages. He led the way through a door in the back to a small office, no bigger than your average bathroom. The cramped space held a small built-in desk and a filing cabinet. All around were shelves, extending up to the ceiling and overflowing with extra stock.

As soon as Rafe stepped through the door, Perry reached around him to close it and gave Stacy the once-over. "What the hell happened to you?"

The man slipped another notch on Rafe's scale. So what if Stacy had matted hair and a soiled skirt? She was still gorgeous. And alive. Rafe doubted Surfer Boy could have survived what they'd been through.

"It's a long story. I'll fill you in over a glass of wine sometime."

"Tease." Perry pursed his lips, showing off a pair of dimples. "I called you last night. Where were you?"

"I didn't go home."

"Girlfriend, you are always home. Haven't I said you need a little adventure in your life?" He looked past Stacy and focused on Rafe. "And I spy some standing right behind you."

Rafe gathered he was the adventure in question, an odd way for one male to refer to another. And he didn't much care for the way the human was staring at him, with a covetous glint in his eye.

"I'm sure Rafe can supply you with everything a girl could want... so how can I help you?"

Stacy blushed and removed her sunglasses. "I've come for the virus."

Her friend made a fist and pulled it into his body. "Yes!" He performed a jazzy twirl, quite a feat given the limited space. "I don't even want to know who pissed you off, but I've been dying to unleash our baby on the world."

Perry crouched beside a safe and pressed four numbers on the digital keypad. After it clicked, he grabbed the handle, swung the door open and reached inside. Before kicking the safe shut, he passed Stacy a small, rectangular doodad. From Rafe's limited knowledge of twenty-first century computers, he assumed it was a flash drive of some sort and used for storing data.

Stacy palmed it. "You'll cover my butt if I get in trouble? Bail me out of jail?"

"Even if I have to sell my body to Payday Loans."

She patted her friend's cheek. "You're a doll. Can I use your computer for a minute?"

"Oh, baby—I'd love to stay and watch, but it'll be easier for me to plead ignorance if I'm not around for this part." Then Perry kissed her again. Rafe's knuckles itched and he figured Surfer Boy's jaw would be the perfect scratching post. But Perry hurried from the office before Rafe could deck him.

Stacy sat at the computer, Rafe saddling up behind her as she maneuvered a palm-sized device—was it called a *mouse*? When the internet came up, Stacy pecked at the keyboard, one screen replacing the other in rapid succession.

"What are you doing?"

She swiveled around and gave him a saucy smile. "Don't tell me you haven't seen a computer before."

"Sure. But ours respond to voice commands."

"Aren't you fully versed in twenty-first century technology for your missions?"

"Each group member has their own specialties." Rafe swallowed. "Blaez was our computer guy."

Stacy clutched his hand. "Sorry."

Blaez's death was still too close to the surface for Rafe to hide his emotions. Still, he hadn't expected her to pick up on his sorrow. Or feel guilty for reviving it.

"It's okay." He raised her chin with his index finger, then ran it down her neck, enjoying the silky feel of her skin.

She closed her eyes and purred in contentment as he stroked her. A bigger reaction than ol' Perry got. If Surfer Boy couldn't satisfy her—

No. They'd all be better off if Rafe kept his distance. He clasped his hands behind his back to save himself from temptation. "So... are you going to answer my question?"

Stacy blinked, as if coming out of a daze. "Right." She faced the computer again and clacked away on the keyboard. "I'm pinging— searching for an IP address, based on the information Leander gave me." She sat forward in her seat. "There, that's it."

"So now what?"

"Just as Andrion took over humans and turned them into goltos, we'll take over his computers and turn them into zombies. It's poetry." Stacy bent down and shoved the flash drive into a slot located in the rectangular section of the computer stored beneath the desk—the *tower*, if Rafe remembered correctly.

"Cross your fingers." She hit more keys, frowned and then squinted at the screen. After several minutes of typing, squinting, and frowning, Stacy leaned back in the chair and sighed.

"Is there a problem?"

"They've got a really good firewall. I can't break through it."

"Where does that leave us?"

She retrieved the flash drive, stood and faced him. With the limited space in the office, they were toe to toe. It was the perfect opportunity to give Perry a run for his money in the kissing department, but Rafe held back when he saw Stacy's bleak expression. He settled for resting his hands on her hips and waited until she was ready to speak.

When she did, it was with the gravity of a physician handing out a death sentence. "We'll have to deploy the virus in person."

CHAPTER TWENTY-ONE

STACY FOUND THE ladies' room and stared at herself in the mirror above the sink, cringing. No wonder Perry commented on her appearance. She looked as if she'd been on the losing end of a catfight. Her clothes were grimy and fit for the garbage, while her hair was a bird's nest of tangles. She adjusted her cap, slipped on her sunglasses and focused on her next move.

First, she needed to call her dad. Rafe had promised to find her a phone and she was damned well going to hold him to it. The one at Perry's store had been ringing off the hook, so she hadn't had the opportunity to use it. After her call, she'd see about food. That pre-dawn power bar Tala gave her was wearing off fast.

Stacy pulled back the heavy washroom door and spied Rafe leaning against a pillar near a silversmith's kiosk, looking even more tempting than the big Starbucks bag he held in his hand.

She salivated as she approached him. "Tell me you have food in there."

He smiled. "And coffee. Let's head back. It's getting too crowded for me here. We can find a place to sit down along the way."

Stacy looked around. The number of patrons had increased, but the two-hundred-plus businesses were nowhere near the sardines-in-a-can state they'd be in by the afternoon. And Rafe was as conspicuous as hell—a head taller than anyone, shoulders wide as a door and testosterone radiating off him like expensive cologne.

"What about my phone call?" A convicted felon had more rights than she did.

"Later. We'll go somewhere quiet. Private."

"It's not private if you're going to eavesdrop. You still don't trust me, do you?"

He rested a hand between her shoulder blades, guiding her. "It's not personal. I don't trust anyone."

His touch sizzled down her spine, short-circuiting her anger. "I know, I know. Your mission comes first. Are you going to explain to me what it's all about?"

His silence provided a resounding *no*.

They left the Market, passing a couple of buskers—one playing the banjo, the other strumming a guitar while step dancing on a piece of plywood. Rafe tossed a handful of change into their open instrument cases as he passed.

Stacy's stomach rumbled along with the traffic on 1st Avenue. Thankfully, Rafe found an empty park bench and reached into the Starbucks bag. He handed her a cup.

"I figured you for a cream and sugar girl."

"You figured right."

The caffeine jolt was heaven, the coffee creamy and rich. He'd purchased a breakfast sandwich for her, a fluffy frittata in an artisan bun with roasted veggies and gooey cheese. She needed both hands to eat it, so she held her drink between her knees. The liquid was still hot, but a far cry from lawsuit-scalding. Even the sandwich had cooled, which was a blessing. She was so intent on getting it into her mouth she would have burned her tongue otherwise.

"Take your time. We're going to be here for a while."

"You like this particular bench?"

"I like the view."

Stacy was about to thank him for the compliment, but he wasn't looking at her. She followed his gaze to the street. There were buildings, pedestrians and cars—none of which looked remarkable.

"You're a big fan of concrete?"

"I'm checking out the enemy."

"Andrion? You see him?" She ducked her head, tipped her hat down over her eyes, and wriggled closer to her protector.

"No. His office building. According to Leander, it's up that street and on the left—the place with the blackened windows." Rafe pointed to it with his nose. "I want to see who goes in and out," he said, and then bit into his sandwich.

"Has there been anyone?" Stacy had no idea why she was whispering. It wasn't as if the renegades could hear her from this distance. She hoped.

"Two humans, so far. A male and a female. Both had briefcases. The guy went in, the woman came out."

"Was the woman running?" As in, *for her life*?

"Nope. It looked as if she was just going about her day."

"No vamps?"

"Not so far. But I can smell 'em." Rafe leaned back, his face lifted up to the clear, turquoise sky. "They're inside somewhere... hiding from the sun."

Thank God. Stacy wanted to finish her breakfast, not *be* breakfast. She popped the last bit into her mouth and wiped her lips on a paper napkin. "How's your sandwich?"

"Good. Wanna bite?"

Why not? Since he offered. Rafe passed his panini to her—crusty on the outside, warm and soft in the middle, with juicy chicken, sweet peppers, and more tangy cheese. Before she knew it, she'd eaten half.

When she handed back the remains, he grinned and waved it away. "Go ahead. Finish it."

She felt bad about eating his food. But not bad enough to disobey his direct order. After all, he was the team's commanding officer. Rank may have its privileges, but it certainly had its disadvantages. She gobbled up the sandwich in record time, and licked her fingertips afterward.

Rafe gathered the empty wrappers and chucked them into a nearby trash can without leaving his seat, dunking them like a professional basketball player. They sat back on the bench, sipping their coffee and staring at Andrion's building.

"How long have you known Perry?"

His question took Stacy by surprise. Rafe had been quiet for so long, she'd assumed he was completely absorbed in his stake-out.

"Since college."

"You see him a lot?"

"All the time. He's my best friend."

Rafe jerked his head around and locked eyes with her. "Your best friend is *male*?"

"Sure. Don't you have female friends?"

He screwed up his forehead, as if he'd never heard of anything so absurd. "No."

"What about your sisters?"

His features turned to granite. "Sounds like one of my colleagues has a loose tongue? Who was it?"

Stacy didn't want to get either Caleb or Tala in trouble. Her life might well depend on their allegiance. "A lucky guess on my part. Let me make another. You're the oldest. You have that forceful, driven way about you."

He stared her down, and she was sure he'd call her out for dodging his question. But he returned his gaze to the street and took another sip from his cup. "I'm second-born."

"*Ahhhh.* Middle-child syndrome."

"What's that?"

She scrunched up her nose, trying to remember the particulars. "I'm not entirely sure, but I hear it's bad."

"And you?"

Stacy shrugged. "An only child. Critical, self-absorbed, pushy."

Rafe shifted closer and ran a finger along her jaw. "Beautiful, intelligent, compassionate."

His words and touch made her skin hum. "Aren't you sweet," she managed to say. She swallowed, hoping to rid her voice of the sexy contralto purr. "I take it you don't think a man and a woman can have a meaningful, platonic relationship."

He dropped his hand lower and drew a lazy line across her bust, right along the edge of the leather jacket. Beneath her bra, her nipples tightened, scraping against the lace with every breath.

"Is that what you want from me, Stacy? A platonic relationship?"

"No." *Hell* no. What a waste that would be. "I was just hoping for a more progressive future. Sounds like you guys have taken a step backward."

"*Weres* are territorial. We don't like other males around our mates."

Is that how he viewed her? As his mate? "Are you jealous? Of Perry?"

"Of course not." He downed the rest of his coffee and aimed the paper cup at the waste basket. It bounced off the rim and fell onto the sidewalk at his feet. "But if we go back there, warn me when you're going to kiss him, so I can look the other way." As Stacy laughed, Rafe reached for her cup and hurled it into the trash.

"I can assure you, Perry's not interested in me."

"He's male and you're very attractive. Of course, he's interested."

"Not like that, Rafe. Not sexually."

"How do you know for sure?"

"Because... I'm nothing like his boyfriend." Stacy wished she had a camera to capture Rafe's changing expressions—first blank, then brows raised in question. After several seconds, he nodded. One slow downward thrust, as if the penny finally dropped.

Rafe cleared his throat. "His boyfriend?"

"Yes. His name's Carey."

"Perry... and *Carey*? Is the other guy a poet?"

"Hairdresser. How cliché is that?" Stacy giggled. "Hey, I know two Michaels who are a couple."

"Must get confusing."

"No more confusing than a man who turns into a wolf."

"Touché."

A chill settled between them. She'd said the wrong thing, pushed a hot button. Time to backpeddle, to recapture the lightness of their conversation—the playfulness, the fun. "You honestly didn't know about Perry? He set off my *gaydar* the first time I met him."

"Gaydar?"

"My gay radar," she explained. "I mean, with some guys, you can't tell. Maybe they're metrosexual, or whatever they're calling it now. But Perry is so out there. He was seriously checking you over. Heck, *I* was almost jealous."

Rafe shifted his weight, as if the topic was a snarling vampire and he was getting ready to run. "Why was he looking at me, if he already has a mate?"

"As Perry puts it, even those on a diet can still peruse the menu. Don't you notice women?"

He tilted his head in her direction. The grin on his face made her tingle. "Only certain ones."

Why did everything out of his mouth sound like a come-on? And why did that mouth have to look so enticing? "People notice *you*. Both men and women. When it comes to scrumptious, you've got the market cornered."

Rafe turned his attention back to the building. His cheeks reddened. Was the man embarrassed?

"Has no one ever told you that before?"

"What?"

"That you're totally hot."

"Not while we're sitting in the shade."

"*Hot* as in gorgeous. Don't they use that word in your time?"

He faced her again, his mouth a whisper away, but he stuck to his side of the bench. "You're torturing me, Stacy."

Good. It made things even. "You didn't like it when Perry kissed me, did you?"

"How could you tell?"

"There was smoke coming out of your ears."

"That's because I'm hot...*for you*." He tore off his glasses and bent his head to take her mouth.

Breathing wasn't an option. Thinking was on its way out the door. And she wanted more. Faster. Deeper. She slid her tongue past his lips.

When she heard his sexy growl, she moved closer, gluing herself to him, rubbing her breasts against his chest to find relief. She tasted the sweet coffee on his tongue, ran her hands up his sides and down his back, all the time wondering where the nearest hotel was, so she could drag him there for the afternoon and chain him to the bed.

Somehow, through her lust, she heard a voice. "Get a room," it said.

Rafe broke off the kiss. As they each gasped for air, Stacy saw an older couple walking away, their silver-streaked heads swiveling around to take in the park bench as if their necks were made of rubber. The woman was scowling, the man smiling.

"I think that fellow would like to trade places with me."

"Or maybe with *me*," Stacy joked.

Rafe shuddered. "Sorry. He's not my type."

"Tala was right. You *weres* are homophobic."

He wrapped a strand of her hair around his finger, the move sending shivers across her scalp and down her neck. "I have nothing against two men forming a couple. I just don't understand it."

"Aren't there any gay werewolves?"

"Not that I've met. But apparently I'm naïve in that department."

"It's okay. You make up for it by being extremely skilled in the areas that matter to me."

She leaned forward and kissed him again. Lightly this time, so she wouldn't get carried away. As she retreated, she noticed a cheap clothing shop across the street. Stacy pointed it out to him. "I should pop in and grab some better clothes. I'll be quick."

His big hand clamped around her wrist, locking her in place. "Why were you in that alley, Stacy?"

The abrupt question, and the harshness of his tone, sent her heart skittering. "I-I-I told you. I was supposed to meet a client."

"Who didn't show. Is that all? Really?"

She tried to pull away——an exercise in futility. "You think I'm lying?"

"I think you might be withholding something. Information I need to keep you safe."

She thought back to Andrion's warning. What would happen if she told Rafe who she really was? When guys heard about her father, they either came running, or bid a hasty retreat. Was it so wrong to want Rafe to like her for herself?

"That's all, Rafe. Honest. I was in the wrong place at the wrong time."

He loosened his iron grip, stroking her wrist with his fingers. "Okay. Go find yourself something to wear. Do you need money?"

She patted the credit card in her skirt pocket. "No. I'm good. Aren't you coming in?"

"I'll stay out here. The vamps will have to go through me to get to you—guaranteed. As soon as you're done, we'll find you a phone."

Stacy nodded and pulled the cap lower to conceal her eyes. As she reached the store's entrance, she froze. At the back of the shop, she spied another door—a rear exit. From what she could see, it opened onto a small shipping dock, where trucks stopped to unload stock.

Her throat closed up. Fight or flight tremors seized her, making her hands shake.

She glanced back at Rafe, engrossed in his surveillance, fiddling with one of his gadgets. She'd have a ten, maybe fifteen minute head start, before he wondered about her. Possibly twenty minutes, until he came after her.

Stacy took a breath and stepped into the store, letting the door shut behind her—blocking out the world of vampires, werewolves, and the searing memory of Rafe's kiss.

This was it. Her chance to get away from them all.

CHAPTER TWENTY-TWO

RAFE SHIFTED HIS hips on the bench. It didn't ease the major wood slamming against his zipper. If he spent any more time lusting without release, he'd end up with a serious case of blue balls.

It had been years—since high school—when just kissing a female got him hard. Then he'd met Stacy, and lost all control over his dick.

Crossing his legs only made it worse. Time to think about baseball.

First base, second base, third—

He groaned. Imagining bats and balls didn't help either.

Rafe visualized Stacy's blue Mariners' cap, instead. He'd been eyeing it and her until she'd disappeared into the clothing store. Since then, he'd stepped up his watch on Andrion's office. No one had gone in or out of the vamp's lair. Not through the front door, at least. So Rafe spent some time conferring with his *zeitmeter*, confirming Leander's specs on the tunnel, and reviewing the timeline of their assignment.

Again, he wondered what role Stacy had in it. He'd asked her pointblank and she'd told him squat. Rafe knew she was hiding something. She'd blushed, stuttered, and tried to pull away from him when he'd pressed for answers.

She'd already shared her dark childhood with him. What the hell else was locked inside that beautiful exterior? And, more important, would her secret jeopardize his mission?

He needed to find out. And fast. Through sweet-talk, intimidation, even force—if necessary. Though, the thought of hurting Stacy was enough to put his cock on ice.

One problem solved.

The next involved his stomach. It growled as the smell of Chinese food drifted by—a nose-twitching combination of sesame oil, ginger, and soy sauce, mingled with duck and spare ribs.

He hadn't begrudged Stacy his sandwich. Anything she needed, he was more than happy to give. But he bet Caleb, a growing boy, was just about ready to chomp on his shoelaces and call it linguini.

And the vampweres? When did they last eat?

Rafe checked his money supply. Chinese take-out would stretch a long way. As soon as he reunited with Stacy, he'd place an order.

He consulted his *zeitmeter* again. He knew women liked shopping—but how long did it take to pick out a new set of threads?

Then the weight of the delay crashed in on him. Most stores had shipping doors. Had she given him the slip? Gone out the back and escaped? Or had one of the vampires used the alternate access to attack her?

Rafe catapulted off the bench, heart pounding to the beat of some techno crap thumping from the open windows of the pink Hummer that passed him. As he reached the door of the shop, Stacy's baseball cap appeared. She emerged from the store wearing dark jeans, a navy T-shirt, and a thin denim jacket under his leather one.

She carried shopping bags. Two of them. *Big* ones. Jam-packed.

His mouth hung open. "What's all this?"

She sighed and dropped the parcels at his feet. "I'm glad you're here. There's more stuff at the cash desk."

He caught her arm before she could disappear into the store again. "I thought you were getting a shirt and pants."

"I did." She slid out of his jacket and passed it to him. "Here, you can have this back."

He eyed the black leather dangling from her outstretched hand—the jacket he loved, from the female he loved. "Keep it. I like the way it looks on you."

She slipped her arms into the sleeves. "Thanks. I like it, too. It smells like you."

Her shy smile curled around his heart. He wanted to be angry with her for making him sweat, but found himself grinning. She was safe, hadn't ditched him... and she liked the way he smelled.

He was losing it. Big time. An assassin turned soft.

He forced his features into a hard mask and stooped to gather the bags. "Looks like you bought a whole wardrobe."

"Just a few things for the vampweres."

Sucker punched again. He didn't know how much money she made as a website designer, but she'd just spent a big chunk of it on creatures she barely knew. Another Mother Teresa but with a sexed-up chassis.

Why did she have to come into his life, now—with his mission in the toilet, his baggage piled high, and the roadblock of a couple of centuries smack dab in between them?

"You a bleeding-heart?"

Her smile disappeared. Her blue eyes burned bright. "They've been abandoned by a parent. I know how that feels."

He wanted to hug her, chuck the bags and lock her in his arms—but how would he ever let her go? He settled for giving her a kiss on the tip of her nose.

129

Stacy retreated into the store for a moment, coming out to join him with another two bags in tow. "Shall we head back?"

"After we stop in next door."

She looked up at the shop's sign. "Chinese food?" Her skin flushed, from her neck to her cheeks. "Sorry I ate your sandwich."

"That's okay. I offered. And the take-out isn't for me."

"Caleb?"

"And the vampweres."

She angled her head and met his eyes, her mouth pursed—saucy and kissable. "Who's the bleeding-heart here?"

Now, *his* cheeks heated. "Maybe you've renewed my faith."

Rafe switched as many of the bags as he could to one hand, so he could grasp the restaurant door with the other. But he didn't open it. He leaned against the handle and turned to her. "I thought you'd try to ditch me."

She lifted her chin, her gaze unwavering. "It crossed my mind."

"You couldn't, you know. I'd track you down."

"That's why I didn't bother. Besides, we have some unfinished business to settle. Which involves a trip to the pharmacy and a pack of Trojans." She flashed a set of bedroom eyes at him, her lids half-closed. "I'm thinkin' ribbed... extra large."

Again, Rafe's dick stirred. Did the damned thing have ears? One case of blue balls coming right up.

* * *

WHILE RAFE ORDERED the food, Stacy asked the Asian woman behind the counter if she could use the telephone to make a quick, local call.

She dialed her father's personal line. Usually, she left him a message and he got back to her. This time, it barely rang before she heard him on the other end.

"Hello?"

"Dad. It's me."

"Where have you been? I've been worried sick—"

His pinched voice fed her guilt. "Dad... it's only been a day or so and—"

"Someone broke into your condo."

The clamor of the busy restaurant—the cashier hollering orders in Cantonese, pots and pans crashing together—it all faded into the background, drowned out by the mad thrum of Stacy's heart.

"When?"

"Last night. Your place was ransacked."

The air around her grew thin, sucked out of the shop along with the sounds.

The vamps had come after her. They'd kept her purse, her driver's license—of course they knew where she lived. Thank God, Rafe hadn't taken her home. She braced herself against the high counter and hoped her knees didn't give way.

"I thought you'd been kidnapped."

"I'm fine. I'm with—" How could she describe her muscled companion? As her bodyguard? Her werewolf lover? "—a friend. I'm okay." She kept her voice steady, though her hands were shaking.

"Come to the house. Right now. I'll meet you there in—"

"No, Dad. Like I said—I'm fine. Really."

"But the police need to question you. Find out if anything was stolen—"

"I'll take care of it. Later."

The woman behind the cash desk lined up Rafe's order, while shooting impatient glances at the phone. "I'll call you again. As soon as I can. Promise. And I'll be there Saturday." She hoped that part wasn't a lie. Though she doubted she'd have the new website up and running by then.

"You're sure you're okay?"

She finally clued in as to why he kept asking. "Pettifogger," she whispered, recalling the code word they'd agreed upon when she was a girl, to signal that all was well—though she couldn't remember now what it meant. "I'm good. Honest. I just need time to collect myself."

"Okay, honey," he said, but didn't sound reassured. "I love you."

She turned away from Rafe and the woman, blinking as she teared up. "I love you, too, Dad. Bye."

Stacy returned the receiver to its cradle. She knew Rafe was standing beside her, could feel his presence—big and strong, ready to battle her demons.

"Everything all right?"

"Yeah."

"Doesn't look that way."

If she told him about the break-in, what would he do? Risk his life to hunt the vampires? Just as he'd sacrificed himself to save her from Andrion's studio? The thought of him dying—all the life draining from his beautiful eyes, left her cold and hollow inside.

She wiped her damp cheeks before facing him. "Water damage in my condo. From a faulty dishwasher in the apartment above, but my dad took care of it."

She wasn't sure if Rafe believed the lie. He kept looking at her, as if waiting for her to say more. "Thanks for letting me call."

"It's not like you're my hostage, Stacy."

"I'm just not allowed to go anywhere on my own."

He smoothed his hand alongside her cheek, held it there. "Think of it as protection."

She was thankful he offered it. Because, if the vamps had totaled her place looking for her, she needed all the protection she could get.

CHAPTER TWENTY-THREE

OUT ON THE street again, Stacy shoved her father's newsflash to the back of her mind. "Are you going to steal another car?" she asked Rafe.

She kept her voice playful, teasing, pulling a Pagliacci and laughing on the outside. Inside, she felt brittle, held together with too little glue and ready to crack.

She swept her arm over the mountain of packages—bags of clothes, food, and a small box from the pharmacy tucked into her jacket pocket—more parcels than she and Rafe could carry in one trip.

Mid-swing, her hand trembled, the aftershocks traveling along her arm. She dropped her hand to her side, hoping he hadn't noticed.

But Rafe was looking past her, farther up the street. "Thought I'd treat you to what the future offers in the way of transportation."

Stacy wasn't sure she could handle any more surprises. Were they going to dematerialize from the sidewalk and reappear in another country? Would a spaceship swoop by to pick them up? Leaving the planet sounded like a good idea, right about now. Then she wouldn't need to spend the rest of her life watching her back, waiting for an unseen enemy to creep up behind her.

But no flying saucers came her way. With a funny smirk, Rafe hailed a cab—your regular four-wheeled, twenty-first century variety. "You were expecting the space shuttle?"

After he tossed their purchases in the trunk, they piled into the backseat.

During their short ride, Stacy watched pedestrians amble along, checked out storefronts, and played a lone game of Punch Buggy—anything to keep her mind off the vampires who'd raided her condo, and thoughts of what they would have done to her if she'd been home.

Or was she jumping to conclusions? With the timing of the break-in, it made sense to blame the vamps. Maybe it was a random crime, a group of thugs waiting for the one night when she wasn't home.

Her thoughts volleyed between the vampires and the mystery gang, until her brain got whiplash. When Rafe started fiddling with the device clipped to his belt, Stacy was happy for the diversion, and raised her brows in question.

"I'm getting Caleb to meet us on the street," Rafe told her.

Sure enough, when they got to the Underground entrance, the young man was waiting for them. Rafe handed him an armload. "Anyone see you?"

"Naw. I joined the tail end of a tour and followed them until I got to the stairs. When they moved on, I ditched 'em. The timing's tricky, but doable."

Rafe hummed his approval, gave the driver a crisp bill and, with Stacy's help, grabbed the rest of the packages from the trunk. "Anything else to report?"

"Tala's up, and wondering where the hell you've been."

"Getting food. Though not her kind."

"That's okay. I let her bite me." Caleb lifted his chin to reveal two puncture wounds on his neck, treating them with the same shy pride as a new tattoo—a sappy one, with his lover's name encased in a heart.

Stacy saw Rafe's tension rise, like steam off the bay. "Don't get too fond of that. Being a vamp cocktail is addictive, I hear. You gonna be okay for tonight's dig?"

"Sure. Once I eat something. All this for me?"

There were more than a dozen large paper bags full of Chinese food, but Stacy had no doubt the bulked-up teen could have worked his way through much of the feast.

The kid's question wasn't especially funny, but with all the pressure she'd been under, Stacy gave into a laugh. She covered her mouth to muffle the sound that exploded from her—too loud, too shrill. With it, most of her residual fear found an escape.

Thank God neither of her male companions noticed. They busied themselves roughhousing, Rafe giving his friend an elbow jab to the ribs.

"The food's for the hybrids, too. The clothes are from Stacy."

Caleb smiled at her, his yellow eyes glowing. "Prime. I know they'll appreciate it."

Stacy accepted the compliment, assuming 'prime' referred to her donations and not a side of beef. But her generosity hadn't been entirely selfless. Aiding her fellow man—or in this case, her fellow non-human waifs—worked like a bandage for Stacy, covering her childhood issues and helping her heal.

"Take as much of the food as you can down with you now, Caleb. I'll bring the rest. And tell Tala to slather on her sunscreen and come topside. There's some cloud cover now, so she should be fine."

Caleb complied with Rafe's order, a couple of bags stashed under each arm, the rest in his hands. As Stacy watched him disappear into the dimness below, a new wave of anxiety hit her, knocking the breath from her lungs and turning her blood to ice water.

She couldn't face the Underground again. While the tours were on, at least there'd be some light. But later, when Rafe and his team were busy digging, she'd be alone, in the dark, shaking and quivering like a coward. Without Rafe at her side, she didn't know if she could get through it.

Maybe she could volunteer for the dig, too. At least, she'd be with him. But the thought of going down a darkened tunnel was enough to make her breakfast sandwich play loop de loop in her stomach.

She sagged against the brick exterior, with eyes closed, and took deep breaths. She wanted to drink in as much fresh air and sunshine as she could, hoping they'd fuel her courage through the night ahead.

Rafe touched her hand, his warm fingers curling around her cold ones, his touch zinging over her skin. She wondered if he'd anticipated her fears, if he'd sent Caleb down with the first load as a stalling tactic, waiting for the last possible minute to take her underground. She squeezed back to show her gratitude.

"I have something for you."

As she opened her eyes, Rafe lifted the hand he'd been holding and placed a small, blue box into her palm.

Her lips sprang apart. "You bought me a present?" The lid's label gave the name of a silversmith at Pike's Market—the place he'd been standing in front of when she'd emerged from the ladies' room.

"Open it."

She peeled back the lid to reveal a Celtic cross pendant, the moonstone at its center a milky white, and all of it floating in a fluffy sea of cotton batting. The design was intricate, the piece hauntingly beautiful. The ice in her veins turned to melted chocolate.

"Rafe—it's gorgeous."

He smiled and positioned himself behind her. From there, he fastened the chain around her neck. "It won't protect you from a hungry vamp, but it will slow the bloodsucker down for a few seconds, while he chooses another place to bite you. The delay could save your life."

For a big man, his touch was gentle, his fingers nimble as they brushed against her skin and sent goose bumps all the way to her toes, while her heart bounded like a Russian dancer.

Because the necklace was more than a gift. In her mind, it symbolized the bond between them. And, now that she'd accepted it, there was no going back.

In spite of her chest acrobatics, she played it cool. "I thought all you otherworldly types were allergic to silver."

He leaned into her, his hands cupping her shoulders, his ripped belly flush against her back. His breath, a whispered breeze over her ear, drove another rush of shivers over her flesh.

"Some of the folklore is rooted in fact. But a lot's been distorted over the years. I can handle silver, but if I'm shot with it, I'm hooped. Vamps are the opposite. Silver burns their skin, but if it enters them, they easily expel it and heal."

Stacy touched the cross, tracing its design with her fingertips, as her body recorded each hard line of the man pressed against her back. "I guess this means you do care."

She'd meant to keep it light, to ease the intensity of the moment, but he brushed his hand across her cheek and turned her face toward him, answering her with a kiss.

At first, it was tender, a sweet caress. Then he traced his tongue along her lips, demanding admittance. She opened to him on a moan, as his arms curved round her waist, pulling her closer.

The loud bang at their side tore them apart.

Tala stood at the open door. Though her eyes were hidden behind dark glasses, they still carved a chunk out of Stacy.

Rafe stepped between the two of them. "Tala—you okay in this light?"

The vampire gave a slight wince, fine stress lines appearing on her brow. "I'll manage."

"Good. You got enough cash on you for a hotel room?"

"Should have."

Rafe dove into his pockets and handed her more. "Book one for tonight and tomorrow. Take Stacy there now. Make sure she eats. Caleb and I will join you after the dig. We can sleep on the floor, so go cheap."

"I know the drill."

The next part of their conversation whizzed by, as Stacy struggled to catch up to her new reality. Was this Rafe's solution to save her from the darkness? Pair her up with Tala?

Talk about a rock and a hard place.

Since Stacy's Blue Lagoon moment with Rafe on the beach, Tala took every opportunity to shoot daggers at them. Poison-tipped ones. Stacy couldn't help but wonder if the necklace Rafe had given her was a protection against his vampire colleague.

Tala's grimace sealed the deal. "I should be with you in the tunnel. I'm stronger and faster than either you or Caleb."

Touting greater machismo than your male superior wasn't the smartest move on Tala's part. Rafe lowered his chin, the gaze he leveled at Tala…deadly. "So you keep telling me."

"I'd be far more of an asset to you here than babysitting Stacy."

"Those are my orders."

Tala stood rigid, her shoulders guardrail stiff. "Yes, sir," she said, though with her delivery it might as well have been, "Fuck you."

Stacy braced herself, sure blood was about to flow. The adversaries stared each other down, two pit bulls ready to rumble. Stacy summoned her courage to intervene, but feared her involvement would only escalate the situation. Before she could speak, Tala blinked and looked away.

"Yes, sir," the vampire repeated, the words hushed.

As Tala turned, Rafe caught her arm. They gazed at each other again, hostility drained, their eyes filled with remorse.

Stacy felt like an intruder, a supporting actress who'd jumped her cue and walked in on the stars as they were about to film their make-up love scene. Rafe and Tala shared a commonality that reduced Stacy to a bit player. They were both from the future, of another species, and stubborn as hell. In short, they were made for each other. But neither wanted to be the first to fall.

In an argument. Or in love.

No matter how much Stacy felt for Rafe, no matter what the attraction, she had no place with him. He'd never be hers.

"Send me your coordinates when you're settled," Rafe said at last, his voice low and gravelly.

Tala nodded then jerked her head at Stacy, signaling her to follow. As Stacy trudged behind the vampire, she looked back at Rafe.

She willed him to glance her way, hoping for a last smile, a last anything. But he kept his back to her as he gathered up the rest of the packages and disappeared into the Underground.

As Stacy passed a garbage bin, she pulled the pharmacy purchase out of her pocket and chucked it into the trash.

* * *

TOMAS LIKED THE downtown building, especially in the dead of night. He preferred it to Andrion's movie studio. Too much hurry up and wait, there. And far too many naked females.

The office was ordered and smelled like the one he'd had in Germany—filled with paper, pencils, and regurgitated air. He drank it all in as he strolled the dim, empty corridors—the odors, the sound of his muffled footsteps on the carpet, the canned tunes soaring from invisible speakers.

There'd been no muzak during Hitler's reign. Who the hell wanted to listen to Wagner 24/7, with Amazonians wearing armor-plated bras and screeching like fire trucks?

Nein, danke.

But, in those early days, Tomas would have sucked it up and started a Valkyrie sing-a-long, if that's what it took to get noticed.

With an eye to detail, in a few short years, he'd transformed himself from a pansyfied loser who couldn't afford a loaf of bread, to the rank of *Obergruppenführer*. Even chummed around with Eichmann. Much as anyone could hang with that bore. As long as Tomas made sure the paperwork flowed across his desk and *Sieg Heiled* whenever anyone walked by, life was a dream.

He'd kept his personal business private. As an SS officer, he knew what happened to sodomites. And the idea of going to a concentration camp wearing a pink triangle on a drab prison jacket was enough to shrivel his balls to the size of raisins.

Then he'd met Andrion and Tomas wanted him. At any cost.

But, after checking into a discreet hotel, the tables turned. Andrion pinned him to the bed—bit him, drank him, drained him. Then offered Tomas his wrist and filled him back up with eternal life.

The war meant nothing then. Europe became a happy hunting ground for blood. And Tomas no longer needed the Nazis to get respect. He had the ability to take life and raise the dead. More power than the Führer.

More than God.

Yet, here he was, three-quarters of a century later, still acting as Andrion's errand boy.

He longed to supersede his vampire creator. But overstepping the natural hierarchy came with retributions. Tomas had to bide his time as a flunky. Had to stand back and wait for Andrion to dig his own grave.

Fortunately, WWII taught Tomas patience.

And there were perks to the current job. He enjoyed helping Nikolas with his experiments. So reminiscent of Mengele. And he liked messing with the stock market. Especially with his knowledge of the future. He'd made more than enough money to keep Nikolas in supplies and himself in the high life, complete with designer clothes. Like his present ensemble—a Dolce & Gabbana three-piece suit in coral with a black floral pattern overlay. No more hiding his light under a bushel basket.

He hung a right and cruised into the big man's office. Early, as usual. He needed to get back to his basement lair before the sun rose.

"What's up, T.J?"

Tomas forced his mouth into a happy curve. One day, he'd stand over his creator, and make Andrion pay for his rejection, as well as the nickname. For now, he got down to business.

"Your ruffians turned Miss Cadell's apartment upside down."

"Did they find anything?" Andrion right-angled a stack of movie scripts on his desk, looking far more interested in perfecting the tidy column than hearing about the B&E.

"Not the girl. And, with the mess they left, she's bound to go into hiding. Which will make her that much harder to find."

"But you have a plan." Andrion smiled, showing perfectly straight, white teeth. His canines, even retracted, were long and sharp. Urban myth had it that you could measure a vampire's dick by his fang size.

138

Tomas licked his lips. Why did the guy have to be so gorgeous?

"I've been tracking her credit cards. She used one today."

"Excellent, T.J. Handle it."

Tomas would have liked to handle it back at that hotel room so many years ago. And a million times since. But Andrion never put out. Not for Tomas, anyway. No matter how much he begged, his hunger went unsatisfied.

Andrion came around his desk and clapped a hand on Tomas' back, the physical contact a tease. He let his creator lead him down the deserted hall, picturing himself shoving Andrion up against the wall and stealing a kiss. Then he'd use the knife concealed at his waist to hack off his escort's head.

Love hurts.

As they neared the exit, Tomas felt a touch of vertigo. For a split second, he blamed it on the approaching sun. Or the need to feed. Then he realized, the floor was rumbling below him, as if he were standing near an escalator. "Did you feel that? Must be an earthquake."

Andrion stiffened. He sniffed the air, dropped to the floor like a cat, and placed his ear to the ground.

"My lord?"

Tomas' Maker held up his hand for silence, a slow smile spreading over his lips. "Not an earthquake. Something far more wicked this way comes."

CHAPTER TWENTY-FOUR

AN HOUR BEFORE daybreak, Rafe followed Tala's coordinates to the hotel, the bag of clean clothes he'd purchased at Pike's Market feeling like a fifty-pound sack in his hand.

As soon as he made it past the lobby, he forgot the name of the place. At least, it had been easy to find—a short stroll from the Space Needle— looked recently refurbished and, as long as the walls weren't paper thin, they'd score some downtime.

Caleb searched for the room, while Rafe pulled up the rear, watching their backs. Probably not necessary so close to dawn, but training overrode his fatigue. He was *dog* tired, as Blaez used to joke, but the quip held little humor now.

Rafe coughed, as much to clear the rawness of grief from his throat, as the dust from his lungs. He rolled his shoulders, needed to feel the ache of strained muscles and the itchy tightness of his grime-coated skin. Those pains he could handle, far better than the loss of his teacher. *His friend.*

He was getting too old for this shit—the missions, the anguish, the weight of the vendetta that drove him. Caleb looked beat, too. Not a bad consolation, since Rafe had a good fifteen years on the pup.

Still, he'd give his buddy first dibs on the shower. Rafe wasn't sure he could stand up long enough to wash, anyway. Sleep sounded a whole lot more inviting. If he still felt rough before their clash with the vamps, he'd snag a couple of uppers and a pot of coffee—black. Anything to keep him going.

They stopped at the last door on the first floor, right next to the emergency exit. A smart pick on Tala's part. Caleb slid the keycard into its slot but, before he could grab the knob, Rafe nudged him out of the way.

"Gentlemen knock."

As Rafe lifted his hand to rap, the door flew open. Tala stood there, as if stationed behind it and waiting to pounce. Then again, with her speed, she could have been crawling under the bed harvesting dust bunnies and achieved the same record time.

He should have let her do the dig. She *was* faster than him. He just hated to be reminded of it. She could have shoveled her way clear through to China, while he whiled away the afternoon with Stacy, a bottle of wine, and a box of condoms. A great fantasy, but it wouldn't make him much of a team leader. He hadn't come all this way to get laid.

The smile died on his lips as Tala uttered her welcoming line. "You look like crap."

"Thanks." He'd been in the room five seconds and his back was up already. He strode past Tala, looking for Stacy.

She sat in a big wingchair in the far corner by the window, her expression dismal. He'd bet the last fifteen hours with Tala hadn't been a picnic. All he wanted to do was console Stacy, hold her and hang on tight.

Out of habit, Rafe did a quick scan of the room first, looking for escape routes and items he could use as weapons.

The door and windows provided the former. The drapes at the far end were dark-colored and heavy enough to keep Tala safe. As for a makeshift arsenal, he spied a chair, a lamp cord—*hell*, he could even drive a vamp's head through the TV set. *That* would certainly make the sparks fly, considering the box was on—the word MUTE displayed across the bottom of the screen, an early morning news anchor silently flapping his gums.

The rest of the room was done up in soft beiges and browns, like the lobby and hall. The other furnishings—an armoire, a second chair, and a bedside table—had a fake mahogany veneer, more orange than red. In the middle of it all were two double beds.

If he could convince Stacy and Tala to bunk together, he might even score a mattress, though the chances of that were slim given the frost crackling between the two. And, truthfully, he wanted to sleep with Stacy. Not for sex. He didn't have the energy. But to feel her—warm and soft next to him, to bury his face in her hair and inhale her scent. That would be a little piece of heaven. And a big problem for his teammates. He couldn't expect either one of them to bunk on the floor, if he wasn't game.

He smelled chicken and eyed the remnants of a whole one on the desk, along with a salad, and rolls—the perfect bedtime snack for Caleb.

Rafe jerked his head toward the bathroom on his right, and handed his buddy the bag of clean clothes. "You shower first. Chuck your old stuff."

Caleb looked thankful, either to scrub away the grime, or to escape the tempest brewing in Tala's eyes. He disappeared behind the washroom door, as Rafe stepped farther into the room.

The beds looked inviting as sin, but he would have left an earthy imprint on the white sheets, creating an unholy Shroud of Turin. He found a vacant wall, slid down it, and sat on the floor, his legs splayed out into a lazy V.

On his way to the ground, Stacy jumped off her chair and gestured to it, offering him a seat. He gave her a quick, "I'm good," and sagged against the plaster.

"Is the tunnel finished?"

He opened one eye to find Tala standing between his feet. "Yeah. We'll rest today. Attack tomorrow."

Tala squatted, so they were on the same level. "When is Stacy deploying the computer virus?"

His tongue felt thick in his mouth, too heavy to form words. "Tried it. Didn't work."

The vampire's brows bunched together. "Stacy told me she couldn't get through their firewall, but she could deliver the virus in person."

"Too risky." Rafe closed his eyes again, and then felt a shift in the air. The next time he looked up, both women were crouched before him, eyeing him eagerly.

"Ladies, could you give me a break here?"

"Give *us* a break, Rafe," Stacy countered. "Tell us your plan."

"Storm the building with a hope and a prayer, and to hell with the diversion?" Tala interjected, forming a regular tag team with the human.

Details. He was ready to go comatose and the pair wanted details. "Pretty much."

"Are you really that suicidal?"

He shot Tala the most pissed-off look he could muster. "Right now, I'm more *homicidal.*"

"You need a distraction," his fanged colleague continued, talking over him. "And Stacy's come up with a good one." It had been awhile since he'd seen Tala excited. About anything. And the vamp had good instincts.

"Fine," he said. "Before we confront the renegades, I'll go in and deploy the virus."

Tala's lips curled, heavy on the smirk. "You? What the hell do *you* know about archaic computers?"

Rafe's ego winced. "I watched Stacy at her friend's shop. I'll figure it out."

Stacy lobbed her head from side to side—a big, emphatic *NO*. "Being the leader doesn't mean you have to do everything yourself, Rafe. Delegate. Utilize the person who's best suited for the job."

Exhaustion had slowed him down. Now he realized this conversation was headed into territory he had no desire to enter. "I'm not sending you in there."

"*You* can't go waltzing into a vampire den," Tala replied. Had the two of them rehearsed this attack? "They'll cry wolf in two seconds," she went on. "You and Caleb are far too conspicuous. The vampweres even more so."

"Your alternative?"

Tala and Stacy exchanged a glance. He expected the vampire to continue her argument, but it was Stacy who spoke. "Tala and I will deliver the virus."

He was totally awake now. "No way."

"Rafe, it's the *only* way," Stacy said, her voice measured, controlled. "Tala will mix in easily with the other vampires, and the renegades are used to having humans around. We watched them together, going in and out of the office building unharmed. Remember?"

"We'll find a dark wig for Stacy to wear," Tala added. "Change her clothes—"

"Perry's boyfriend can give me everything I need—"

"It'll be good, Rafe. Even if Andrion sees Stacy, he won't recognize her. You know how all humans look alike to us. We'll be in and out, throw the renegades into chaos, and leave you boys to grab the power source and destroy the time portal."

Their logic was tight. And, if Stacy weren't involved, he might have agreed to the scheme. "Not gonna happen."

Tala's eyes glistened. "Because you don't trust me."

The remark smacked him square in the chest, hard as a sledgehammer. It was true. He didn't trust her. Regarded her as a vampire—first, last and always.

"You might be happy playing Russian roulette with Stacy's life, but I'm not. I've already lost someone I love to the renegades and I'm not willing to... *uh... to...*"

What the fuck was he talking about?

He was too tired and too pissed off to think straight. Now he was rambling, suggesting that he felt more for Stacy than he did. He cared about her, of course. Wouldn't have kissed her otherwise. But he didn't *love* her.

Love took time.

Sure, he'd fallen hard and fast for Daciana. Knew she was the one for him after their third date. That kind of lightning didn't strike twice, and certainly not with a human.

He couldn't backpedal. And he sure couldn't look at Stacy. Not after that slip.

The words were out. Retracting them would sound worse. Draw more attention. He might as well write them across the sky, in the same bright orange as the furniture. Throw in a meteor shower, in case anyone missed it. "We can't put a civilian at risk."

Tala's eyes turned to slits. There was no fooling her. He cracked his neck with a satisfying snap. But it didn't break the tension. The redhead went on the offensive again.

"Stacy's far safer with me than you. I'm better able to defeat a fellow vampire."

Ouch. She may as well have ripped off his balls and poached them for breakfast. "I know that. And if there was only one vampire in question, it wouldn't be an issue. But you'll be surrounded by them."

She reached out and touched his pant leg. A low growl rattled in his throat before he could stop himself. Tala snatched her hand away. "Give me a chance to prove myself to you. I can do this."

"And if you fail, you've got one dead human on your conscience. Can you handle that? 'Cause I sure as hell can't."

Tala stood, stretching to her full height. "It won't go down that way, Rafe. Stacy and I can do this."

She pursed her lips, as if forcing herself to keep her mouth shut. But, in the next moment, the vamp let him have it. "If you go with your plan, and it ends in disaster, I'll be filing an official complaint against you." She lifted her chin, the picture of defiance. "I'm not backing down, Rafe. Not this time."

He let the wall behind him support his head and imagined his name in the Guinness Book of World Records for having the shortest stint as a team leader in the history of time travel. When Caleb appeared next to the females, towel around his hips and gnawing on a chicken leg, Rafe let out a long sigh, relieved to have someone on his side.

The teen swallowed, looked at him, and shrugged. "If I get a vote... I'm with the girls."

Great. Even his adopted brother was against him. So far, this command bullshit was proving to be as much fun as a root canal.

Without anesthesia.

* * *

I'VE ALREADY LOST someone I love and I'm not willing to...

Stacy's breath snagged as she remembered Rafe's words and wondered what he was about to say. That he was unwilling to lose another love? Unwilling to lose her?

Her heart came to a dead stop before shifting back into gear. She shouldn't read her own feelings into what Rafe had said. Not in his present condition. The man was beat, his head lolling around on his neck as if it were about to fall off. And all three of them had leapt on him.

Not that she'd rushed to Tala's side as a show of solidarity. She'd moved to block Rafe's view of the television, her hands flittering at her sides from an attack of the jitters.

On the screen, she'd recognized her high-rise condo, seen her name printed across the bottom of the set with the additional tag, 'Governor Cadell's daughter.' The story of her apartment break-in had hit the news. And the last person she wanted to know about it was Rafe. He'd put his life on the line to save her from Andrion's studio. What risks would he take if he thought the renegades had trashed her home?

She'd had plenty of time to review her options, trapped in a hotel room since the previous afternoon. Deploying the virus was the only real contribution she could make to the team—*her* team. She needed to do this, to fight the monsters who threatened her now, the way she never could in her youth. When the monster was her mother.

Even more important than conquering her demons, she wanted to be there for Rafe, to keep him safe. Because the thought of him dying—his body broken, the life seeping out of him—left her hollow inside.

Protecting him wasn't going to be easy, though. Stacy figured anger was the only thing keeping him upright at the moment. The man looked worn out and utterly pissed—his jaw tight, his focus on Tala.

"I'm not willing to put Stacy in that kind of danger."

Time to end this. The vampire had insisted on presenting the plan, but he needed to know the truth. "It was my idea, Rafe," Stacy told him. "All of it. And I'm volunteering."

As soon as she spoke, Rafe's gaze slid over to her. He winced, like she'd stabbed him in the back.

A second later, his mask snapped back into place, cold and brutal. "And I'm off to shower. End of discussion." Rafe hauled himself off the floor and disappeared around the corner. Moments later, Stacy heard the shower running.

Caleb tossed the stripped chicken leg into the garbage can and shrugged at Tala. "Rafe doesn't do well with ultimatums."

"I got that. Thanks." Tala perched herself on the closest bed and sighed. "It was a good plan, but..."

Stacy nodded. "You bet it's a good plan. You bet. That's why we're using it."

Before she could lose her nerve, Stacy marched to the bathroom door. She banged on it with the heel of her hand and entered, without waiting for an answer.

CHAPTER TWENTY-FIVE

STACY HIT A wall of steam.

She closed the bathroom door and the misty air encircled her. The mirror at her side was covered with a ghostly sheen of condensation, her basic shape clear but her features indiscernible.

Not so with the shower's transparent curtain. The plastic barrier left nothing to the imagination.

Rafe had his back to her, water pelting off him as if the droplets were too timid to linger on his skin. He sagged against the far wall, resting his head on his forearms, which were raised and crossed. He bore his weight on one leg, the opposite hip thrown to one side, showing off his tight ass.

Like Michelangelo's David. Only far more chiseled.

Her mouth went dry, and her hands curled as she imagined grasping that tempting tush.

Then he blurted out a sarcastic, "Am I intruding?" His back muscles bunched, ready for a fight.

Stacy lifted her head and pretended she was wearing a neck brace that prevented her from looking anywhere past his shoulders. Those line-backer specials were wide, smooth, tanned to a deep caramel, and...

The confrontation she'd planned wasn't going to happen with him standing in front of her naked. How could she defend her idea when she couldn't think? She was about to murmur a quick apology and get the hell out of the room, when his body lost some of its tension.

"Stacy?" Rafe spoke her name with a deep, husky rumble. He shot a look over his shoulder and gave her a tired grin.

"Did you think I was Tala?"

"I'm glad you're not."

Her stomach did a somersault, scoring a perfect ten. On her short journey to the bathroom, she'd rehearsed a monologue, one that would convinced Rafe to adopt her plan. Now, she couldn't remember a word of it. So she got to the point.

"I want to deliver the virus."

He kept his back to her, his head bowed. "So I heard."

His tone was flat. Probably from fatigue. Or controlled fury. She'd do best not to antagonize him, in either case.

Stacy softened her voice. "If you can recharge your healing thingamajig with Andrion's power source, you can cure Milan and bring the vampweres hope. I want to be a part of that."

He nodded, gave his head a lazy dunk under the spray then let the water drip from his hair. "Compassion and bravery. You radiate them. It's why I like you."

She felt a ripple of optimism. The argument was shifting in her favor. Then she analyzed his words. *Like*. Not *love*. Color her stupid for being disappointed.

She wished he'd turn, so she could see his eyes. Then she'd be able to read him. But he kept his position, facing the wall, as if he'd rather speak to the tiles than to her.

Stacy grabbed one of the large white towels, closed her eyes, and held it out to him. "It's difficult to talk to you when you're... ah..."

So. Incredibly. Hot.

She settled for an innocuous, *"Like this."* She swallowed, caught her breath. "Could you step out of the shower, please?"

Silence. Stacy wondered if he'd heard her over the water's roar. She took a quick peek at him, as he swiveled toward her.

While the rear view had been appetizing, this side vision was jaw dropping. Pecs so tight they looked ready to burst and a ridged torso that narrowed to the flat plane below his navel. Water cascaded over the whole package and led down to the prize hidden behind his hip and thigh.

"Why don't you step in?"

Confusion rattled around her brain. The previous day, when she'd walked away from him, he hadn't even glanced back. Now his eyes were hooded. Simmering.

"What about Tala?"

"What about her?"

"She's very beautiful."

"A knock-out. So what? You see me getting hard for her?"

Was he? Hard? Now? Stacy remembered that make-believe cervical collar and kept her gaze level. "There's something going on between the two of you."

"Yeah. A shit-load of stuff. All bad."

A hurricane meeting a tornado. But beneath that, Stacy could see how much both he and Tala hated the storm.

"I'm in the way."

He faced her full on. "No. You *are* the way. You walk in here, without a stitch of makeup, jeans, a baggy T-shirt that falls past your knees and, as beat as I am, look who's happy to see you."

Neck brace be damned. She glanced down. A very prominent part of him stood at attention. Ready for her.

Dear Lord.

Stacy gulped and forced her gaze upward. She shouldn't want him. They had no future together. He'd already told her that, with cruel honesty. She had to leave. Now. Before she had no choice.

She reached out and felt for the door's handle. But her feet stayed planted, her heart aching for everything she couldn't have.

Namely, him.

As she hung in suspended animation, his voice reached out to her, caressing her like a lover's touch. "You're the only one I want."

Instead of gripping the doorknob to bolt, she used it to keep upright. He may not love her, but knowing he desired her—and only her—turned her knees to jelly.

"Now take off your clothes. Or they're gonna get wet."

She glanced at the door, visualizing the room beyond. Were they actually going to do the nasty while Tala fumed on the other side of the paper-thin wall?

"I don't know if we should—"

That's all she got out. Rafe swept the shower curtain aside, the metal rings jangling. He stepped out of the bath, leaving the water running, and drew her into his arms, her clothes soaking up the moisture from his body, as if she were being drenched in him.

Rafe bent down and took her mouth—firm and fiery—his lips urging hers apart. As he deepened the kiss, she skimmed her hand down the length of his torso—smooth skin over rock hard muscle—her fingers tingling, itching to touch every inch of him.

She felt his smile against her lips and the rest of the world ceased to exist.

Rafe lifted her T-shirt and Stacy raised her arms in response, her body quaking with need. As he drew the top over her head, there was a moment of darkness, and she thought about her childhood prison. But then the light reappeared, and with it Rafe's kisses. He flicked the shirt over her shoulder, tossing it who-the-hell-cares-where.

Her jeans were the next casualty. He unbuttoned and unzipped her, then slid the denim down her legs till the fabric pooled at her feet and breathing became a lost art. With her brain screaming for oxygen, and wobbly with lust, she leaned against him and stepped out of her pants. As soon as she was clear, Rafe picked her up by the waist and sat her on the vanity, his mouth on hers with every step.

He dipped his head, his lips traveling from her throat to her collarbone, each stroke making her gasp. He moved lower until he found her breasts, licking and sucking her nipples through her lacy bra.

Warm, wet, wonderful.

Stacy arched her back, trying to get as much of her skin against his mouth as she could, the sensations playing slingshot around her nervous system.

He reached behind and undid her bra with one flick, then stood back to look at her. "You are so beautiful. You take my breath away."

Tears welled in her eyes. "No one's ever said that to me before."

"Then the men you've been with are idiots."

She reached for him, but he took a step back, her bra dangling from his fingers. "As much as I like to look at you, I want to try something. If you trust me."

She owed him her life. "I trust you," she told him.

His lips curved. "Good."

He locked the door, hit the light switch and plunged the room into darkness.

* * *

TALA TRIED TO focus on something other than the noises coming from the bathroom. Not that Rafe or Stacy were screamers. Not at the moment. But any fool could tell what they were doing in there. The shower's spray hid so little. At least from a vampire's ears.

A hand fell on her shoulder and she jolted. She hadn't noticed Caleb creeping up behind her, a towel still wrapped around his hips. She'd been too distracted by the radio drama going on in the john to notice much of anything else. And that kind of carelessness would get her killed one day.

He apologized for startling her. "You okay?"

"Fine."

She meant to blow off his question, mimicking the indifference of a politician with a majority vote, but her one-word answer came out harsh.

"You seem tense." He gripped her other shoulder, as well, and started kneading.

She jerked away, twisting out of his grasp. "What do you think you're doing?"

"Giving you a massage." His inflection pitched higher on the last word, as if she'd asked him a trick question and he wasn't sure if he'd answered correctly.

"Thanks. But I don't need one."

Tala trudged to the far side of the room and sat on the foot of the bed closest to the window, as far away from the bathroom as she could get. Exactly where she should have planted herself all along. Why the hell hadn't she lived during the Spanish Inquisition? Apparently, she liked torture.

The mattress tipped as Caleb joined her. "I just want you to know, I'm here for you."

His yellow eyes were full of an understanding that belied his years. But then he'd endured so much—the deaths of both parents, a childhood spent on the streets. She'd have thought he'd be filled with hatred. *No.* Whatever pent-up anger he had, he took it out on the renegades. When it came to his teammates, Caleb only wanted to please. Like a big, happy, golden retriever.

She patted him. "You're a nice kid."

He caught her hand and held on tight. "I'm not a kid. And I'm not that nice." His full, pouty lips zoomed in for their close-up.

Christ. Did he really intend to kiss her? She jumped off the bed, breaking his hold. "We're not going there."

He didn't even have the decency to look chagrined. Just tilted his head and gave her those puppy dog eyes. "Why not?"

She paced, her hands fluttering—an exterior manifestation of what was going on inside her. "Because we're teammates. Because we're on a mission and we don't need any personal distractions. Because you're a *were* and I'm a vampire."

Shit. She was giving him the same reasons Rafe always handed her. And she could imagine her new boss ranting if he came out and found her necking with his young ward.

She knew Rafe wouldn't be jealous. He didn't care enough about her for that. His concern would be for Caleb. That she'd somehow corrupt the adolescent. No matter that it was Caleb's idea. Rafe had never trusted her.

Tala planned to do the right thing, regardless. She had one more argument to hand her new admirer, and it was the best of the lot. "Because... you're a teenager."

She expected him to blush and shuffle off in defeat. Instead, he gave her a triumphant smile. "I'm past the age of consent."

Bloody hell.

"Maybe in some states." Tala crossed her arms over her chest, and gave him the haughty look she was famous for—head angled, nose high in the air, the whole works. "And that's probably not a line you want to use on a girl anyway, Caleb. Not a big turn on."

"In Washington, I'm legal."

"Well, where I'm from—"

"In New York, too. I checked."

She snapped her mouth shut and stared him down. "Been planning this for a while, have you?"

Another grin. "I've always liked you, Tala. You're beautiful, smart... and unbelievably sexy."

Damn. The boy left her speechless. Senseless, too. It was great that someone—anyone—found her desirable. But this was Caleb. She liked him, sure. But as a cousin. Or a nephew.

Except, he didn't look like either. He wasn't as tall as Rafe. Probably never would be after all those years of malnutrition. But he was as tall as her. If they did kiss, their toes would touch.

Breath exploded from her mouth with a whoosh, as if someone had plowed her in the gut. Tala hung her head, shocked by her thoughts. She'd seen Caleb naked, dozens of times, and couldn't have cared less. Now that scrap of terrycloth he wore was a little *too little* for comfort.

"Could you put on some clothes, please?"

He shrugged, stood, and dropped the towel.

She clamped her eyelids tight and heard him fumbling with material. Skin slid into denim. A zipper groaned as it ascended. But she couldn't erase that last visual from her mind. Him standing before her—two hundred pounds of solid male flesh—young, alive, and heartbreakingly gorgeous.

When a last rustle of clothing suggested he'd found a shirt as well, Tala opened her eyes and adopted a schoolmarm tone. "Caleb, you're seventeen—"

"Almost eighteen."

"I was turned at twenty-six. That was back in the 1930s. Any way you look at it, I'm too old for you."

"You're not." He cupped his hands together, the muscles in his arms popping. He managed to look vulnerable and totally invincible at the same time. "What you're thinking is that I'm too young for *you*."

He had a point there. She'd never gone for pretty boys, preferred her men rugged. A well-placed facial scar, a broken nose—she'd fall for either before the next sunup. She liked them emotionally wounded, too. Distant. Maybe that's why she'd never had any success with guys. Just spent a lot of time mooning over ones she couldn't have.

Now, an available male was ready, willing and able... and she was ready to run for the hills. Especially when he eased himself from the bed and took a step toward her. She backed away, smack into the wall behind her.

Though he was twice her width, she wasn't afraid of him. She doubted he'd try to force himself on her. If he did, she'd toss him across the room and onto his derriere. Against a male vampire, her age or older, she would have had a battle on her hands. But Caleb's approach was shy, almost apologetic. "I don't have a lot of experience with females—"

No shit. He hadn't racked up enough years on this side of puberty to be a player. "But you've dated—"

"Not exactly."

"Then what? Exactly."

"Don't make me spell it out."

Dear God. He was a virgin. Which put her on the fast track to Hell.

She sidestepped away, the back of her legs smacking into the wingchair. She lost her balance and ended up ass-planted in it.

Caleb fell to his knees in front of her. "You could teach me. Show me how to please you."

He took her hand and kissed it, making her heart do a little skip. It didn't beat anymore. At least, not regularly. Just enough to keep the blood circulating. Like an alligator's when it dove to the bottom of a swamp.

Nice comparison.

Still, her old ticker gave a kick as Caleb's feather-light kisses whispered across her skin, warm against her chill.

She had to shut him down. Close off this line of conversation. Do it now, and do it hard, so he'd never broach the subject again.

But, damn it, a part of her was considering his proposition. Vampire tradition encouraged mature females to instruct younger males in the art of lovemaking.

Tempting. Till she reminded herself, Caleb wasn't a vampire.

As she eased her hand away from his grasp, he flipped her wrist over and kissed her palm. For a guy without practice, he had some good moves. In a couple of years, he'd have the girls lining up to be with him. She hoped no one would brake his heart, in the meantime. That's what turned nice, sensitive boys like Caleb into the indifferent assholes she craved.

She petted his head, ready to put the whole matter to rest, when his tongue brushed against her skin. The reaction was as intense as if she'd been zapped by a live wire. And that wire somehow connected his touch right to her core, which moistened with interest.

She shook him off and reared back. "No. Caleb, we can't do this." At his hurt expression, she clutched his arm. "You're very sweet. And I am so flattered that you want me to be your first. But—"

"You like Rafe."

Did she? Was she in love with a man who was enjoying himself with another woman in the next room?

No. Not anymore. If she ever was. He was just another unobtainable male. Another guy who didn't want her. Like her first love. The one whose rejection still hurt.

For the amount of money she'd spent on therapy over the years, she understood all the *whys* of it. But never figured out the *what now* part. Whatever was broken inside of her, she had no idea how to fix it.

She'd let Caleb think it was all about Rafe, though. It would be easier to let him down gently that way. "Looks like we've got a triangle on our hands," she told him.

"There's an extra side to this, now that Stacy's here."

Tala nodded, thinking she had more in common with the human than she cared to admit. Stacy might be with Rafe now but, by the end of the week, she'd be a thing of the past, trapped in a different century than her lover.

Tala hated herself for the small pleasure that knowledge brought. She may not have had a future with Rafe, but neither did her rival. And, still, she envied Stacy. Even now, she'd give almost anything to trade places with the human. *Man...* she was a first-class screw-up.

She looked past Caleb to the bathroom, her longing turning to confusion. No light shone from underneath the door. And all she could hear was the shower's spray.

If Rafe and Stacy weren't making love, what the hell were they doing in there?

CHAPTER TWENTY-SIX

DARKNESS ENCASED STACY. Panic clawed at her insides and she trembled like a junkie on withdrawal.

Needing to hang on to something, she clutched the edge of the bathroom vanity where she sat and clamped her eyes tight. At least then, it was her darkness, her choice. Better that than staring at the never-ending black wall looming before her.

Through her fear, she remembered she wasn't alone. Rafe was here. She couldn't see him, but sensed his presence, even before he touched her.

His big hands covered her knees. "You're okay. You're safe. We can stop at anytime."

Now, would be good, she wanted to say—but didn't have enough breath to utter the words. She tried to think her way past the anxiety—the lock was on their side of the door, the light switch just a few short steps away—but it only eased her panic a fraction.

Because her terror wasn't rational. She knew that. A team of child psychiatrists explained it to her years ago.

It hadn't helped then. It didn't help now.

She grasped Rafe's hands and inched her way up his arms, clinging to her support, her anchor.

"That's right, Stacy. Use me to get through it. Hold me, scream at me, punch me—whatever you need."

Escape. That's what she wanted. She'd been looking forward to some kissing, some heavy petting, and a whole lot of buck-naked body-checking. Not a visit with her inner demon. Talk about *coitus interruptus*.

Though she did have an urge to sock Rafe, if he was using her fear to prove a point. Like why she wasn't capable of helping them with their mission.

Because she was such a pathetic freak. A grown woman afraid of the dark. A goddamn scaredy cat.

Anger tinged her blood, its taste hot and coppery as she bit into her bottom lip. She'd prove him wrong, prove she could face this baptism of fire, even if it killed her. She sank her nails into his flesh, and held on for dear life.

If he felt any pain, he kept it to himself. "I want to show you the beauty of darkness," he said, his voice husky. "A night in the wilderness, when all that illuminates you is the stars and the moon—that's wonderful, that's paradise."

Thank you, Lord Byron. At the moment, she found more poetry in squeezing his biceps and digging her fingers in deep.

"Open your eyes, Stacy."

Her lashes felt as if they were slathered with cement-based mascara. She forced her lids open and the room tilted on its side.

Dizzy, that's all. Another symptom of the phobia. To stay upright, she wrapped her arms around Rafe's neck and hung on, her knees straddling his hips, her bare breasts flattened against his chest.

"It's all right. You're doing great, honey. Breathe with me now."

Had she been holding her breath? No wonder she was woozy. She gulped at the air until Rafe side-coached her to take it easy, so she wouldn't hyperventilate. He kept offering words of encouragement until they were breathing as one—united.

In... out. In... out.

"The room isn't completely dark. I can see you. Can you see me? Can you see the light on the other side of the door? It's sneaking in around the edges."

Slowly, she made out a faint light coming from under the door, could see Rafe's yellow eyes gleaming.

"Okay?"

Not trusting herself to speak, she nodded against his chest.

"Okay." He took a half-step away, his hands still on her, his body still close. "All that fear from the past, I want you to pretend you're stuffing it in a suitcase and sending it on a one-way flight to Greenland. Next time you're in the dark, instead of thinking about that baggage, I want you to remember this."

Her body flared as his fingers slipped beneath her thong.

"No!" She slapped her hands on his pecs and shoved. She didn't want the memories of his touch mingled with her panic attack. But moving Rafe was like pushing a loaded dump truck uphill.

His hands retreated to rest on her thighs. "You want to stop, that's fine. But you said you trusted me, Stacy. Trust me, now."

And prove you're not afraid of the dark. That you're worthy of the team.

She stopped fighting but remained on edge, her limbs as stiff as old tree branches ready to snap with the first strong wind.

"All right," Stacy told him. "I will."

He slid a hand up her leg, until his fingers found her.

She was already wet from before, could feel her own slickness as he explored her secret place. His other hand went to her breast, gently molding and tweaking until her nipple tingled. He added his mouth to the mix, scorching his way down her throat—kissing, nibbling.

Stacy skated her hands along his arms to his shoulders, needing to feel him close, but not wanting to restrict his movements and the glorious things he was doing to her. His mouth latched onto her breast—sucking, licking, lapping at her until she was mewling like a kitten. He gave her other breast equal attention before sinking lower to draw lazy circles around her navel with his tongue.

He squatted in front of her. Or knelt. She'd lost track of his body parts, at that point. Except for his mouth.

At first, it was just his breath, hot against her core. He hung there, poised, fueling her anticipation. She wanted him to stop. Wanted him to start.

Then his lips were on her, parting her folds.

He forged a path down her center, ripples of heat curling her toes as she rode the waves. Only when her head touched the mirror behind her did she realize she'd arched against him, pushing herself closer.

Rafe slipped his arms under her legs, so the backs of her knees rested in the crooks of his arms—a man setting up camp, settling in for a *looooong* stay.

He hummed his approval. Knowing he enjoyed pleasuring her, tasting her, made her even hotter. Wetter. The vibrations of his purring lips on her sex almost threw her over the edge.

Then he drew her nub into his mouth, and began to suck.

Forget the darkness. Now she saw explosions of light. She fell apart, coming in surges, her body bucking, sweat trickling between her breasts.

As she tumbled away from the summit, Rafe slipped his tongue inside her, darting it in and out, swirling it around the top of her sex in between stabs.

She gasped as a second orgasm shook her, clamped her lips together so she wouldn't cry out. But she couldn't hold back a deep, throaty groan as her body first tensed then relaxed into a languid bliss.

Before she could catch her breath, he was French kissing her like he had a patent on the art, her own sweet juices still on his lips—the musky scent of their lovemaking perfuming the air, the roar of the still running shower providing an erotic accompaniment that bested any honeymoon suite in Niagara Falls.

"What do you think of the dark now?" he whispered in her ear.

As realization seeped into her sex-fogged brain, her eyes blurred with moisture. "Actually... I'd forgotten about it."

Her chest felt lighter, as if someone had taken a key and unshackled her heart. She looked around the room, batting away tears. It was still dark, and her usual anxiety started to build...but it didn't peak. The volume of her debilitating inner script had softened to a four instead of a *Spinal Tap* eleven.

"But I'm far from cured." She leaned into him, and whirled her tongue around his mouth. When she came up for air, she added, "I'm going to need more therapy, doctor. A lot more."

From the amount of white teeth he flashed in the dimness, you'd think he'd won the lottery. "I agree. Next time you're in the dark, think about this."

He used his fingers to trace a line down her slit, currents zinging over her still sensitive flesh. She let her head fall back, exposing her neck to more of his kisses. "What if I'm in a theater? I can't be..."

She moaned as he found her G-Spot, her A-spot, and her U-Spot. And a few other Spots the men of her time had yet to discover. She panted, murmured naughty words of encouragement, and spread her thighs wider, aching for more.

"I need to be inside you."

"Yes," she agreed, her voice slurred as she dreamed up a name to call the last erogenous zone he'd found. Maybe an R-Spot. For *Rafe*... her werewolf lover.

"Where are the condoms?"

Shit. Her afterglow disintegrated, shattered in a heartbeat. "Gone."

"What?"

"I threw them away."

Rafe growled. "Not funny."

"Wasn't trying to be."

"You threw them..." His words trailed off into a heavy sigh. "Why?"

"I was confused. I thought—"

But he slipped out of her grasp before she could explain, and an arctic front crept into the heated room. "Light coming on," he announced.

She covered her eyes. When a soft glow showed between her fingers, she peeked through them to look at him.

Grooves etched his brow. "I didn't mean to force myself on you. I thought you wanted this. To make love—"

"I did. I do." She struggled to reassure him. "It's just, for a while, I thought you and Tala—" She stopped herself from saying more. They'd already deadheaded that subject. "Look, I was wrong about that. And I really want to make love with you, take you inside me. I don't care about the condoms. Let's just—"

"I care."

Stacy wanted to believe his concern was for her. But she knew differently. And damned if she didn't feel the urge to push for a confession. "Why? Because an unplanned pregnancy would change the future?"

"Yeah. *Mine*."

Rafe reached her in one step, plunking his hands down on the vanity on either side of her thighs. "I know you could raise a child on your own, and any kid would be lucky to have you for a mom. But it would eat me alive knowing I'd deserted you. I'd want to be there. For you *and* the baby." He looked down and let out another sigh, one that smacked of defeat. "And I can't be. So let's just grab our clothes and hit the hay."

As he turned, Stacy tugged on his arm. "But I've left you unsatisfied." She glanced at his still swollen penis, his erection looking downright painful. "I can do what I did on the beach."

He smiled and threaded his fingers through her hair. "Don't worry about it."

"You didn't like it when I took you in my mouth?" If not, he'd be the lone member in that boys' club.

"Are you kidding? I loved it. But I've been hungry to kiss you. That's what I want to be doing when I come."

Stacy grinned. "I'm sure I can accommodate that." She licked her palms, then wrapped them around him and started stroking. "It's why God made hands."

* * *

HAND JOBS DIDN'T thrill Rafe. But these were Stacy's hands. When they glided over him, he could almost imagine being sheathed inside her.

Nice. Very nice.

But not enough to make him come.

Then she clasped his balls. The heavy sack tightened and started a fire deep in his belly.

His hips shot forward, pumping, as he probed her mouth with his tongue, the only penetration afforded him. Her heels curled around his legs as she worked him, putting her in complete control, and Rafe at her mercy.

He was getting close, but needed more.

He tore his mouth away from hers, reached down between them, and gave Stacy's hands a squeeze. She caught on right away and shifted higher, massaging the head of his cock and the meaty ridge just below it. She tightened her grip and moved faster, rubbing his testicles with her free hand until they contracted into his body, building the pressure inside him.

He kept his eyes open to admire the view—Stacy's blond hair spilling over her shoulders, breasts swaying as she gave him the hand-jive, eyes glossy with lust and focused on his...when she wasn't looking down at his dick and licking her lips, like she wanted to taste every inch of him.

That got him harder. He cupped her ass and let his hips piston out of control, while he made love to her mouth.

He put everything he had into the kiss. If this was their last time together, he wanted to make it count. Wanted her to know how much he needed this, *needed her*. And how much he wished he could offer her more.

With a final thrust, he exploded, clinging to her. He kissed her cheek, her neck. Slowly, his lungs remembered how to take in air. He buried his nose in her hair and breathed in her clean, honeyed fragrance.

Then he got his heart under control. Along with the emotions stirring in it.

"Is that better?"

Not the right time to explain his feelings. Especially, when he didn't understand them himself. "Oh, yeah. But I need another shower."

She smiled and licked his essence from her palm. "May I join you?"

Even though he was spent, his balls gave a jerk. "I don't think I've ever had a better offer."

The floor in front of the tub was damp from the shower's runoff. He grabbed a fresh towel and spread it over the wet tiles, then offered a hand to Stacy and helped her into the tub.

Rafe slid the curtain across and reached for the soap. He worked up a lather then dragged it over her skin, across her collarbone, over her arms and up her legs.

He took his time, planting kisses here and there, loving the feel of her silky skin. He lingered on her stomach, following the sensual curve of her belly, and found himself getting hard again. When he brushed the soap over her breasts and her nipples peaked, it was game over. He had to do something to shut himself down. Or he'd be taking her on the bathroom floor, and to hell with condoms.

So he turned her around. But damned if that view didn't make things worse. Her slim waist flared out into a lush bottom. As he soaped her up, he logged a quick fantasy of doing her from behind, but squelched the idea. Even if she were willing, she was too tiny for him to go Greek without hurting her.

Instead, he moved in tight, reached around her, and massaged the soap between her legs. Nice and slow. She sighed as her head fell against his chest, which did great things for his ego. Inflating it along with his cock.

Bad move. Wasn't he supposed to be holding back?

He dumped the soap on the side of the tub, stepped away from her, and adjusted the shower temperature, cooling things off. For a minute, neither of them spoke, and barely touched.

Stacy tilted her head to one side, faint lines appearing on her forehead. Rafe recognized the expression, had seen her wear it many times over the past days. The woman definitely had a question on her mind.

She cleared her throat. "Can we talk about the mission? I need to know that it's okay with you that Tala and I deliver the computer virus."

The topic accomplished what the cold water couldn't. His dick shriveled up like a punctured party balloon.

"No, it's not okay." He pivoted around and grasped her shoulders. "You're the only good thing in my life right now, Stacy, and I want to protect you."

"I feel the same way about you. If there's something I can do to prevent you from being hurt, I want that. I'll be fine with Tala."

His chest swelled, from her words and the way she soaped up his pecs. Too bad she'd added that last sentence.

Damn straight Stacy would be okay with the vampire. Probably better off than if she relied on him.

"I feel safest with you," she told him, as if reading his thoughts. "But you'll be leading the attack. So I'd be with Tala, anyway."

"In a hotel. Not a bloodsuckers' den."

"But during the day. When there're not so many of them around, right?"

"That's the idea. But we're working with Leander's intel. I don't know how accurate it is."

"You trust him though, don't you?"

He did, and was probably a fool to have such faith in a half-breed, but Rafe's instincts told him Leander was sincere.

"He's got a lot to lose if we fail." Namely, his daughter's life. Rafe didn't say that, though. Didn't have to. They both knew what was at stake for the vampwere leader.

"They really appreciated the clothes, by the way." The females had cried openly. Even some of the males got misty. Hearing the news, Stacy blushed.

So pretty.

Rafe leaned in for another kiss, but she held out her hand to stop him. "Don't distract me. I have more questions. And I'm freezing my tushie off. Could you coax a little more hot water out of that shower?"

He chuckled, cranked up the heat, and traded places with her so she could stand directly under the spray.

"Much better." She grabbed the soap and lathered up his lats. "Now, what about your sci-fi doohickeys? Can't they help you determine if Leander's information is correct?"

"Sure. We can detect humans in the building, but vamps are harder to read. And I doubt we'll be able to smell them through a couple of feet of dirt and concrete. It's going to be a guessing game."

"All the more reason for Tala and I to go in first. We can scope out the situation."

Rafe slumped against the tiles. "Damn."

"What?"

"Sometimes I wish you weren't so smart. It makes arguing difficult."

She gave him a sly grin. "Are we arguing?"

"No." He kissed the tip of her wet nose. "But we signed up for this. You didn't. We'll be armed, and so will the renegades."

"So arm me. Show me how to use your weapons."

God, the woman had balls. It made her irresistible. He rested his hands on her hips and took her mouth, their lips mating, his hot and needy. When they came up panting, she wrapped her arms around his waist and clung to him.

He shifted, so he could see her face while cradling her body. "Whatever happens, I want you to know how grateful I am to have met you."

She pulled away, her expression pinched. "That sounds like a good-bye."

"It will be…soon enough. You know I have to return to my time."

She hugged him tighter. "That's why I want to hold on to you while I can." She laughed—a deep, lustful sound. "My dad always said it would take a different kind of man to interest me. But I don't think he ever imagined how different. A werewolf warrior with a velvet touch. A healer. A lover."

"You're a contradiction, too. Sweet and fiery."

"An angel in the kitchen and a whore in the bedroom, huh?"

"You can cook, as well? You're my kinda female." He'd meant the line as a joke, but her blue eyes grew wide, as if she were expecting a real answer.

He stroked her damp hair. "If there was going to be anyone for me... it would be you." He kissed her. Tenderly. Then pulled back. "But I can't stay. As much as I may want to, I can't."

She teared up as she nodded. Her smiled quivered, wavered, then held.

Rafe turned off the faucet and kissed her again before stepping out of the bath. He extended his hand and helped her out, then reached for a towel and dried her.

"You're a pretty chivalrous guy. *Mucho romantic-o.*"

"You should see me on the dance floor."

As Stacy laughed and slipped into her clothes, Rafe tugged on his jeans commando style. He had to talk to Tala before he slept, and he sure wasn't going into battle with the vamp sans pants. "You and Tala take the beds. Caleb and I will sleep on the floor."

She clutched his arm. "I'd rather be with you."

"On the floor?"

"Wherever. Like I said, I just want to be near you. For as long as I can be."

He let his finger trail down her cheek. "That's exactly what I want. To hold you while we sleep."

But he doubted it would happen. Tala was on the other side of that door and he couldn't put off their confrontation any longer.

Rafe shook the excess water from his hair like his canine cousin, wishing he could shake off his sense of dread as easily. He reached for the doorknob, sure the vampire was about to press all his usual buttons.

Hell, she might even discover a few new ones.

* * *

TALA SAT IN the wingchair.

The sound of running water stopped, replaced by the quiet murmur of voices. The only illumination came from the lamp beside her, giving her corner a faint glow. The rest of the room she left in darkness. She had no desire to look at the happy couple once they emerged, to see them flushed with post-coital satisfaction.

To hell with integrity. She should have fucked Caleb while she had the chance.

She stewed, instead—arms crossed, stomach knotted—until the bathroom door opened and Rafe and Stacy emerged.

With that first glimpse of him, Tala's breath hitched. She guessed he was still exhausted, resting one massive shoulder against the wall for support. But a lightness surrounded him—glowed in his eyes, buoyed him up from the grief that had always threatened to drag him under. For the first time in a long while, Tala could see happiness flowing from him. Then his gaze shifted to her, and the light vanished.

Rafe gestured at the nearest bed, inviting Stacy to park it there.

The human's eyes darted between the two of them. "I'll stay in the bathroom, so you can talk in private." Stacy hesitated, as if waiting for Rafe's good-bye kiss, then she disappeared around the corner and the bathroom door closed tight.

Rafe remained in the same spot, hands slipping into the front pockets of his new jeans. He nodded toward Caleb sprawled out across the farthest bed, a tangle of sheets around him, bare butt sunny side up and pointed to the ceiling.

"Seems our pup went out like a light." He took a slow step toward her. Then another. He eased himself down on the one corner of the bed that wasn't taken up by Caleb.

Rafe looked tense, as if he were about to deliver bad news. In that split second, she knew the truth. He was going to shut her out, fire her ass.

As team leader, he certainly could, though the protocol had rarely been used. She wouldn't be able to protest until they got back home. There'd be a hearing, of course, which she'd most likely win. After all, her father ran the program. And she could cite Rafe's obsession with their human captive in her countercharges.

But as much as they butted heads, she couldn't do that to him. Couldn't ruin him in front of his peers. She'd much rather accept a desk job, retire, or don a bikini and face the sun, than destroy him.

She braced herself, sank her fingers into the chair's upholstery, and waited for his verdict.

"I'm sorry, Tala," he began.

Even though she'd prepared herself, and the words were delivered kindly, tears prickled the back of her nose. She couldn't just sit there and take it, wouldn't let him see her cry. She forced herself to her feet, preferring movement to immobility, action to passive acceptance. "I know what you're going to say, Rafe, and—"

"I don't think you do."

She felt a gentle tug on her wrist. All the times she'd longed for him to touch her, and now he did. But like a friend. A brother.

She sat again and met his weary eyes.

"I misinterpreted the situation, Tala. Out of the three of us, you're the one who most valiantly upholds our oath to protect human lives. I should never have doubted you."

Her shoulders relaxed, as her body gave up an inward *whew*. So that's why he'd blown up at her before. He'd thought she was aiming to put Stacy at risk. He wouldn't be quite so forgiving if he knew the truth. That she'd considered it, daydreamed about how easy it would be to ditch Stacy, leave her to flounder in a deadly situation, and thus eliminate the competition. But Tala couldn't do that to Rafe. She knew he cared for the human. It was bloody obvious. Even more so after their bathroom boinkfest. The loss of his wife was still palpable. Losing Stacy on top of it would shatter him.

Tala covered his hand with her free one. "I won't let you down, Rafe. I'll protect Stacy. I swear it."

"I know you will, Tala. I... *trust* you."

Something inside her chest flew apart, as if her dead heart opened up and a ray of sunshine burst in. Rafe's faith in her was like a declaration of love. *Better.*

But he looked three shades of gray, as if the admission took all his strength.

Okay, Rome wasn't built in a day. Bridging a gap took time, and Tala couldn't expect him to do all the work. She had to meet him halfway. "So... when do you want us to deliver the computer virus?"

"Forget the virus. You'll stand by, with Stacy, at a safe distance from the action."

What the fuck? He was benching her? Again? "You're taking Caleb instead of me?"

"He'll be guarding the tunnel's entrance."

Tala flopped back in the chair, confused. Rafe's strategy made no sense. Then it dawned on her, fear turning her cold hands to ice. "In case it's a trap?"

He nodded and she felt the blood drain from her face.

"I'm going in alone, with the vampweres as backup," he continued. "I'll steal the power source and destroy whatever semblance of a time portal is there."

"No." The word flew out of her mouth before she could censor herself. Rafe wouldn't appreciate her emotion. He'd already pulled away, leaning back half a foot, charting some distance between them. She made herself take a deep breath and put her feelings in check before she spoke again. "You don't even know if you can trust Leander."

"That's why I need you to stand by. You have to be ready to take charge and finish the mission with Caleb…in case I don't make it out."

The phrase 'in case' held a shred of optimism, but she doubted either of them felt any faith in the plan. He had to know his strategy held little hope of survival. Dread for him sent her stomach roiling.

"You don't have to do this, Rafe. It's too big a risk. As far as we know, the vampweres don't survive as a species. They're all going to die, anyway. Milan along with them. Our best course of action is to complete our mission, as planned. The *three* of us. We have to focus on the big picture and remember what we're here for, what we need to accomplish. When everything's set to right, we can report back about Andrion and send in a different, nonpartisan team to deal with him."

Rafe dipped his head and scrubbed at his jaw, the stubble on his chin making scratching noises as he stroked it. "According to Leander, Andrion checks in at the office every night at the same time."

Her ultra-slow heart stopped mid-beat. Her fear ratcheted up a dozen notches. "It's pretty clear T.J. is a part of this history tampering, but we have no proof of Andrion's involvement. Killing him won't help our mission. We're not here for a personal vendetta."

He didn't answer. Just kept rubbing. When he finally looked up, his eyes were desolate. "I have to try. For Daciana."

She shook her head, those tears she'd fought earlier blurring her vision. "Don't kid yourself, Rafe. It's not for her. If she loved you, she'd want you to move on with your life. To find some happiness." Like he had with Stacy.

But he wasn't listening, wasn't looking at her. She had to get his attention. Give him a verbal slap and make him change his mind. Tala latched on to his shoulders, and shook. "Daciana wouldn't want you sacrificing yourself. And I sure as hell don't, either. You do her memory a disservice with this recklessness."

His head snapped up, the sadness in his eyes replaced with resolve, hard and unyielding. There was only one other tactic she could think of using to get him to relent.

"Have you told Stacy?"

He stood, as if dragging up a two-hundred-pound weight with him, and slipped out of her grasp. "It's your turn to sleep, Tala. I'll stay up and watch."

Which meant he hadn't mentioned a thing to the human. "Don't you think she deserves to know?"

"She will. When it's too late for her to fight me on it. It'll be better that way. For her." His voice faded to a whisper. "Now, get some rest."

She didn't press him. The male was clearly bagged and their *True Confessions* time was over. "I've been resting since yesterday afternoon. I'm starting to develop bedsores."

When he gave her a tired grin, she dropped the smart aleck routine and smiled back. "You need to recharge your batteries if you're fighting tomorrow. I'm fine. Honest. I'll keep watch."

Rafe let out a long sigh. "Must you challenge me on everything?"

She stood and looked at him, wanting to remember this time with him forever. She needed to freeze the moment, needed to be able to play back this one instant when he'd reached out to her, confided in her, and shown her his trust.

Because this one moment was all she was going to get. Soon, he would be gone.

"Please," she said, her heart breaking. "Go to bed…and take Stacy with you. She's good for you."

She slammed off her tear valve and hid behind another wisecrack. "Just make sure you do all of your kibitzing in the bathroom. If I'm in the mood for adult entertainment, I can rent a dirty movie and watch the pros."

Rafe leaned in and brushed her forehead with a kiss—a brother to his sister, a son to his mother—the most sex-less physical contact she'd ever received.

Damn it.

"I promise," he said, as he pulled back. "No public kibitzing."

Tala watched him walk away from her and go to the bathroom door. When he knocked, Stacy emerged. He took the human by the hand and led her to the remaining bed. They curled up on it together, him spooning her with that beautiful, sun-kissed body of his.

If Tala hadn't figured it out before, that clinched it. Rafe's tenderness around Stacy—the way he looked at her, touched her—it signaled the male was in love. He might not know it, yet. Or admit it. But he'd fallen for the human. Hard.

Tala hung out the Do Not Disturb sign, then returned to the wingchair, where she spent the rest of the night—listening to her comrades' steady breathing, hearing the rustling of material, flesh whispering against sheets as her fellow teammates stirred in the throes of sleep.

When day broke and the light began to seep around the curtains, she moved her chair over by the door, adjusting it without a sound, so as not to wake her napping brood.

Letting them enjoy the calm, before the bloodbath.

CHAPTER TWENTY-SEVEN

STACY WOKE COCOONED in warmth, a solid mass of muscle pressed against her, the clean smell of soap and male flesh tickling her nose.

Her lashes fluttered against Rafe's biceps, her makeshift pillow. In the early morning hush, she took her time exploring him with her eyes—his strong profile, the way his skin glowed in the soft light. From the moment she'd met him, he'd been on the go, slowing only when injured. This was the first time she'd seen him truly relaxed, lying on his back, one arm cradled around her, the hint of a smile on his lips.

Had she put it there?

She snuggled in tight, enjoying Rafe's closeness until she couldn't ignore the call of nature any longer. She eased away from her lover, sat upright, and came face to face with Tala.

The vampire looked intense—hungry. She clutched Stacy's wrist and pulled her out of the bed.

As Stacy opened her mouth to protest, an icy hand clamped over her lips. Once they were at the door, Tala turned to her and whispered. "We have an errand to run."

The vamp held her in place until Stacy nodded, head pumping up and down, keeping pace with her accelerated heart. When Tala loosened her hold, Stacy croaked out a one-word question.

"We?"

"Special assignment," the redhead declared, flashing her fangs as she opened the hotel room door. "Just you and me."

* * *

RAFE CAME TO with a jolt, a heavy pressure between his legs.

He'd had other sexual partners before Stacy. Sometimes, he'd dozed with them after the act. But he'd always split before sunup. Hanging around for the awkward morning after, filled with polite, *I'll call you's* that he didn't mean, held no appeal. *Sleeping* with a female carried an extra commitment that sex never did.

But he'd slept with Stacy.

A grin spread over his lips. Probably a goofy one, given how great he felt. He hadn't had a better night's sleep in months. Holding Stacy, watching her sleep whenever he woke—her luscious body pressed close, her breath caressing his skin—it all felt so right. Something he'd be happy to repeat.

Tomorrow. Next week. Hell, for the rest of his life.

His smile died. Time with Stacy wasn't going to last forever. He probably wouldn't have as much as another day with her. The here and now was all that mattered. So he planned to enjoy it while he could.

He stretched out, sprawling across the mattress, letting his limbs unfurl. The sheets beside him were cold. He scanned the room, looking for Stacy.

The light around the curtains heralded another overcast day. Caleb still slept, someone having covered him with a stray blanket during the night. Tala, no doubt. Her wingchair had moved from the corner and now stood near the door. But it was empty.

He listened. No shower running. No movement in the room. No Tala. No Stacy.

Shot with adrenaline, Rafe threw back the covers and was halfway off the bed when the door opened, a flash of light from the hall invading the room. He grabbed his gun, ready to fire, when the smell of bacon hit his nose, quickly followed by egg, yeasty bread and coffee.

Next to him, he heard a click and knew Caleb had reached for his weapon at the same time, training stronger than hunger.

"It's just us," Tala's voice announced before she and Stacy rounded the corner, brown paper bags in their hands.

Stacy froze when she saw the guns, then smiled and sang out a cheery, "Room service."

That's my girl, Rafe thought, as he holstered his piece. Brave in the shadow of a loaded weapon. Then he frowned. When had he started thinking of Stacy as *his*?

As if signaling a warning, Rafe's stomach grumbled. The last thing he'd eaten was half a Starbucks' sandwich. He didn't usually eat McD's but— even after his fourth McMuffin—the bacon, cheese, and egg combo tasted like ambrosia. Good thing Tala and Stacy thought to buy extras. He settled back, rubbed his full belly, and finished off his coffee.

Tala's sigh broke through Caleb's chomping noises. "You're going to get ketchup on the comforter."

A muffled "*Wha*," came from the young wolf, as he wrapped the word around a mouth filled with his sixth breakfast sandwich.

The vamp went over to him, shaking her head like a disapproving nursemaid and scooped something off Caleb's chin and chest with a napkin.

Rafe chuckled, until Tala scurried back to her chair. He'd never seen her scurry anywhere.

Were vamps allergic to ketchup? Or was she retreating from the window and the sun behind it? Before he could give the matter more thought, Tala was speaking again. This time to him.

"So... the tunnel's finished. What are your plans, Rafe?"

With her matter-of-fact tone, she might have asked who had first dibs on the shower. But he'd spent enough time with her to know the vamp wasn't into small talk.

"Relax for the day. Eat. Snooze. Maybe watch some TV. Any good movies on?"

Stacy set aside her Breakfast Burrito and reached for the hotel guide. "There's a new Bradley Cooper action flick."

Rafe had no idea who this Cooper dude was. And, really, how much action would a guy named Bradley see? Rafe had enough combat in his life, he didn't need to watch make-believe crap. He knew Caleb was itching to see the new Jackass Millennium movie, but Rafe liked the epics. *Ben Hur. Lawrence of Arabia. Doctor Zhivago. Paradise Lost.*

"No, Rafe. I meant, what's your next move?"

This was Tala's second inquiry disguised as chitchat. She was trying to goad him, make him announce his intentions about going into Andrion's alone. And now was not the time.

"Well, Tala... I'm gonna spend most of the day in bed... showing Stacy my gun."

Stacy blushed. Caleb choked on a mouthful. And Tala crossed her arms, giving Rafe a slant-eyed, cheeky look that broached on insubordination.

Rafe drew his weapon from its holster, slipped on the safety, and held it up for inspection. "And... in case there's any confusion... *this* is the gun I mean."

Though he planned to make good use of the other one, too.

* * *

TALA WATCHED FROM the wingchair. She'd given Rafe a couple of openings, baiting him to spill his plans.

He'd ignored her.

Now, he was showing the human how to flick the safety off his gun with her thumb, how to load it and how to aim. By dinnertime, his apt student had received instructions on every one of their weapons. And ordered pizza. Several pies for the boys—packed with meat, meat and more meat—and a small vegetarian one for herself, of which Caleb had half.

Tala ate nothing.

She'd never tasted pizza while alive. Now, she never would. After her transformation, the smell of food turned her stomach. In the nearly 300 years since, she'd found ways to cope, much like homicide detectives who could investigate violent crime scenes without woofing their cookies.

169

Tala became a reluctant spectator—observing her crew joke, reheat leftovers in the complementary microwave, and watch TV—feeling as if she were on the other side of the screen, viewing it all without the ability to interact.

Removed. Apart. Lonelier than if she'd been by herself.

Even more so now as they dozed—Rafe and Stacy nestled together, Caleb propped up by pillows, all lulled to sleep from the drone of the television set.

Tala reached for the remote and lowered the volume, before making her way around the room and collecting the discarded pizza boxes, balancing them neatly on top of the pint-sized garbage can. Disgusted by her self-imposed demotion to maid service, she gave the pile a soft kick and sent the boxes tumbling. Then she extinguished the overhead light, dimming the room.

She sensed a presence at her side and turned to find Caleb clad in jeans, his hair mussed, his chest and feet bare.

"You're hungry," he said, taking in the scattered boxes.

"I'm fine."

"Let me feed you." He walked past her, paused at the bathroom door and looked back expectantly.

His offer tempted her, she couldn't deny it. But she should go out and hunt for her food. That would be less complicated. She could find a human. Bite them, drink them, rob them of the memory, and be done with it. Or she could revisit Discovery Park and prey on a wild animal.

Preying on Caleb... that was a little too wild. Too risky.

But, damn, the guy tasted good.

She was halfway to the door before she realized her feet were moving. Out of view from their comrades, he held out his hand to her. She took it and he led her into the bathroom, locking the door behind them.

Her stomach fluttered in anticipation. She'd pictured herself in this room with Rafe. Now, here she was, but with the wrong male.

At least Caleb was willing. He sat on the edge of the tub and held out his arms. "Come to me."

The flutter spread, making her whole body vibrate. Tala craved what he offered, but not like this.

"Turn around, with your back to me, like we did it before." That's how she preferred it, so her victim couldn't watch her feed.

Caleb didn't move. "Nah-uh. This way."

She stood motionless, listening to the pounding of his heart, the roar of life flowing through his veins.

Her hunger grew. Not only for his blood.

"Forget it then," she said, as she turned away.

He grabbed her hand. She could easily break free, overpower him with little effort. But she didn't want to. She let him pull her back until she faced him once again, a dancer completing a twirl.

Tala watched his chest rise and fall with each labored breath, heat radiating from him. He said her name, another invitation, but she couldn't look him in the eye. She flicked her hair over her shoulder and leaned closer to the pulsing vein in his neck.

"You'll be uncomfortable, bending over like that," he murmured.

"Then stand."

"No. You sit." He patted his thigh with his free hand. "On my lap."

She hesitated. The desire for blood burned through her, but the position he suggested was too intimate. Too sexually charged.

He gave her hand another tug, and the pull was irresistible.

She sat on his lap, as sedately as she could, her hip brushing his ribbed belly, her legs to one side and fused together.

"I was hoping you'd sit astride me," he said. "But we'll start with this."

She felt his hands on her hips and growled a warning. "I do the touching."

Caleb held up his arms as if she were pointing a loaded gun at him. "Okay. No hands." He rested his paws at his sides and smiled. "For now." Then he tilted his head and exposed his neck to her. "Feed."

Her fangs elongated with the command, the pulsing at his neck like a beacon. In her early days, her victims' fears spurred her on as much as the hunger. Once she learned to control her urges, she hunted less—used animals instead of humans, warm blood packs instead of live game.

Now, Caleb's total willingness excited her.

She rested her lips against his vein, felt it throb. He shuddered as her fangs trailed over his skin.

Something hard pressed against her hip. Through the haze of thirst, she realized he had an erection. Her last clear thought was to run, escape into the night and find a stranger. But need overtook her.

She clutched Caleb's shoulders and sank her teeth into him.

The sound he made as she invaded his body—a groan of pain that turned into a heated sigh—was just as intoxicating as his blood. Thick, spicy, like a fine Madeira. As she drank she pressed closer, his rising cock arousing a different kind of hunger.

When his hands slid past her ribs to her rear, it took every ounce of control she had to tear her mouth away from his vein.

"No hands," she said, as loudly as she could, but it was only a whisper.

"Then kiss me. Please."

With his blood still on her tongue, Tala found his lips, taking his mouth with the same frenzy as she'd fed. She clutched his head to lock him in place, and felt his erection grow even more.

So big. So hard. And so very wrong of her to use him like this.

A tear rolled down her face, its salty taste erasing Caleb's sweetness from her mouth. The next thing she knew, she was blubbering—sitting on his knee, crying like a child.

He hugged her to his chest. "I didn't mean to hurt you. Tell me…what did I do wrong?"

Tala shook her head, unable to speak. She slipped off his lap and landed in a heap on the floor in front of him, reaching for the toilet paper to dry her eyes. "You didn't do anything wrong. I did."

She'd used him. When she knew he wanted more from her. Something she couldn't give him. She needed to apologize, needed to explain—but, most of all, she needed to warn him.

"I'm bad, Caleb. Toxic. And you have to stay away from me. Because I can't help myself."

CHAPTER TWENTY-EIGHT

JUST BEFORE DAWN the following day, Stacy couldn't sit still. Scared out of her gourd, she itched for action, looking for some way to burn off her nervous energy.

She'd learned how to handle each of the team's weapons, and felt fairly confident she could carry one of the space-aged pistols without accidentally blowing off her own head. But she hadn't actually fired anything. She didn't want to end up on the front page of the Seattle Times for trashing a hotel room like some drugged-up rock star.

With the patience of a martyred saint, Rafe had explained each item, in detail, until Stacy thought her brain would explode. Already, she couldn't remember what they were all called. Was the machine gun a *blitzzager*? Or was it the pistol that shot wooden bullets? But, as Rafe said, the names didn't matter. She only needed to recognize the weapon, know when to use it and how to operate it. The bayonets were sleek, the throwing knives lethal, the firearms—a cross between things she'd seen on CNN and *Battlestar Galactica*. She could barely wrap her hand around the grips, and her wrist ached from holding the heavy, steel, killing machines.

Meanwhile, Caleb spun two pistols around in his hands like a cowboy from an old B&W movie. He threw them over his shoulders simultaneously and caught them behind his back with the grace of a baton twirler.

"Where did you learn that?"

Caleb looked up at Rafe, hero worship in his eyes. Rafe shrugged and gave his ward a playful nuggie. "He's showing off for you." Then he taught her how to grip the gun with both hands, so her wrist wouldn't fatigue as fast.

Holding the pistol brought home the true nature of Rafe's mission. She'd spent the afternoon half-believing she could be the kick-butt, gun-toting heroine of a *Matrix*-inspired action flick. Her fantasy armory included a pair of inflated breasts spilling out over the top of her imagined skin-tight, latex cat suit.

The pistol reminded her, this was real life, real death.

Stacy wondered again about the identity of the murdered man she'd seen in the alley—the would-be assassin named Smiley. If the vampires had killed him, wasn't that a good thing? Or was the assassin's target a Hitler-wannabe, an evil dictator who had to die in order to prevent another World War. And, if so, what the frig was he doing in Seattle, Washington?

Hugging a tree? Reliving the birth of grunge?

Then a worse thought crept into her mind and filled her stomach with acid. Sometimes, good people got in the way of the future.

Like Abraham Lincoln. His loss was tragic, but it did unite the states after the Civil War, probably faster than if he'd lived. Was Rafe here to prevent an assassination of that magnitude? Or to make sure it happened?

She hadn't heard the current president was planning a trip to Seattle, and prayed to God he wasn't. Stacy had met him a couple of times, even liked the guy. He could visit all he wanted, after the team's mission was over. Until then, she hoped he stayed safe, on the far side of the country, in the other Washington.

Stacy rubbed her shoulders. After her crash course in Warfare 101, they ached as if she'd gone for the world's record in pull-ups. She longed for a hot shower, another that included Rafe. Under the spray that afternoon, he'd kissed and pleasured her until her knees buckled, but denied himself, claiming he needed to keep his edge for the night ahead.

Now, she watched him prepare, his freshly cleaned weapons lined up on the bed. He strapped a leather holster around his hips, settling it between his low-riding jeans and a T-shirt that showed off every hard muscle…and made Stacy wish they'd spent more time in the shower.

"You'll need your jacket," she told him, reaching for it. "You'll be cold."

"Not if I think of you." He sent her a smoldering look, hinting at all the things they'd be doing together later, and her body grew warm.

She glanced over at the black wig Carey lent her that morning when she and Tala had gone out to pick up food at McDonald's. When she'd checked herself out in the mirror at Carey's salon, she hadn't recognized the person staring back at her. Stacy couldn't wait for Rafe to see her in it, and planned to use it to seduce him later. She didn't know if he fancied role-playing but, so far, he'd been game to try anything.

A true adventurer, in every respect.

Stacy suppressed a smile as Tala's voice intruded on her thoughts. The vampire shoved a garment at Rafe—black and ribbed like Batman's muscle suit. "You'll need one of these."

When Rafe shook his head, Tala stiffened. "Stacy... maybe you can get him to wear it." The vampire tossed the thing at her.

The material was stiff, and far heavier than Stacy expected. "What is this?" She looked from Tala to Rafe and back again in the silence that followed, wondering why he hadn't shown it to her earlier.

"It's a bulletproof vest," Tala said finally.

Chills licked up Stacy's spine. She'd come to think of Rafe as indestructible. She'd seen him at death's edge, then watched him rally in an instant. A quick healer, for sure, but he wasn't immortal.

She passed him the vest. "Maybe you *should* wear this."

His upper lip curled as he eyed it. "Takes too long to shed, if I have to wolf-it. I'd be safer going in naked." Rafe reached for the leather jacket she'd offered him a moment before, chucking the bulletproof vest onto the bed. "I'll stick with my old favorite. It'll hide the hardware."

Tala huffed, grabbed the discarded item, and packed it away in one of their equipment bags.

Strange. Even though Tala suggested the vest, Stacy didn't see the vamp wiggling into one. And she assumed there'd be enough of them to go around. Four, in all—a vest for each of the original team members. "Aren't you going to wear one, Tala?"

The redhead looked at Rafe. Again, Stacy shifted her gaze between them, watching another of their non-verbal battles.

Rafe dipped his head. When he finally met her eyes, a sudden darkness brewed in his that turned him into a stranger. "Tala's not wearing a vest... because she's staying here. With you."

Stacy's jaw dropped. She must have heard him wrong. Surely, he hadn't spent most of the day training her so she could spin her wheels in the hotel room watching reruns of *Law and Order.*

"I don't understand," she said, though the icy sickness that penetrated her bones suggested she'd heard him perfectly. She felt Tala's presence at her side and tried to block out the vamp. She wanted *Rafe* to explain, *Rafe* to come clean. Still, it was the vampire who spoke.

"He's going in alone. That's what he's trying to tell you."

Stacy sat on the bed before her knees slid out from under her. She glanced from face to face. Even Caleb stopped his juggling tricks. He looked shocked, as if this was the first he'd heard of it, too. Though, obviously, the vampire knew all.

Stacy focused on Rafe. "Is that true?" In the quiet, she heard the electric lights buzz, the hum of traffic outside their window.

"Caleb will guard the tunnel entrance," Rafe said, at last. "I'll go in with the vampweres, steal Andrion's power source, and destroy the time portal so he can't escape. Then I'll dust him."

She clutched a fistful of bedding, twisted it. "And you couldn't have mentioned this earlier?"

"Would it have made a difference?"

Stacy knew what he was asking. Would she still have been intimate with him, if she'd known? *Maybe.* But, while he'd shared his body with her, he'd shared his thoughts with Tala. "Yes. It would have made a difference."

Stress lines appeared on Rafe's forehead, as if he were in pain but trying hard not to show it. "I'm sorry I didn't tell you sooner then."

The afternoon, their time together—suddenly none of it meant a damn thing. She thought he'd listened. That he'd heard her. That he'd looked at her as a teammate, *a partner*, and taken her advice about the diversion to heart. She'd opened herself up to him. But he'd kept this part of the plan a secret from her. Lying through omission.

"Why did you bother showing me your weapons, if you were going to leave me behind?" She tried to keep the hurt out of her voice and failed.

He didn't want her help. She was useless to him, except for a bit of slap and tickle on the side. And he'd made his opinion crystal clear, in front of the others. Her cheeks burned with indignation.

"I showed you the weapons, because I want you to know how to protect yourself."

"Does that mean *you* don't want the job anymore?" She leapt up, jabbed a finger into his chest. "You've been deciding what's good for me without a thought about what I want from the moment I met you. You arrogant son of a bitch."

She heard a quick intake of breath. In stereo. Both Tala and Caleb shot her wounding stares, as if she'd just used the *were* equivalent of the N-word.

Maybe she had. Probably not a good idea to inadvertently insult someone's mom, especially when she wasn't a member of your species. Rafe looked like she'd slapped him. Stacy wished she had.

He tucked away the last of his arsenal, and then jerked his head toward the door. "We'll continue this in the hall."

How he thought a hotel corridor would be more private than the room was beyond Stacy. At least, it didn't contain his colleagues. He could disgrace her in front of total strangers instead of his teammates.

Rafe told Caleb to join them when he was ready, drew Stacy to his side, and ushered her out of the room. As soon as the door closed behind them, she stood on her tiptoes and wagged her index finger in his face. Before she could speak, he grasped her wrist and held it gently.

"I'm sorry. I thought it would be easier for you, if you didn't know until the last minute. I didn't want anything to spoil our time together."

Pretty words. But Stacy sure didn't feel pretty. She felt used, discarded. "You mean the sex. Because that's all I am to you."

Rafe switched his grip to hold her hand. "How can you think that? I've lived like a monk for the last year. I could have had Tala a dozen times over, and a boatload of my sisters' friends. I didn't want them. Any of them." He pulled her to him. "I only want you."

She rested her palm against his heart, felt it beating, sure and true. This was the Rafe she knew, his eyes no longer shadowed. Still, she doubted him. "I thought you didn't trust me. That you figured I'd let everyone down."

Rafe placed his hand over hers. "I trust you more than anyone. *Anyone.*"

He backed her up against the wall, then bent down to her, so close their foreheads touched. "You're my lifeline, Stacy. It would kill me, if anything happened to you. If you delivered that virus, I'd be so distracted worrying, I wouldn't be able to—" His voice caught. "Please. Let me do this my way. Tala will keep you safe while I'm gone."

The emotion in his plea was more intimate than anything else they'd shared. In the shower, they'd been skin to skin. Now, Stacy felt as if they were soul to soul.

She clutched him tighter, her voice cracking too. "And if you don't come back?"

He didn't answer, which meant he knew the risks. Knew his chance of survival was slim. She buried her head in his chest, so he wouldn't see her lips tremble. She wasn't a pretty crier. When Stacy teared up, her skin mottled and her nose ran. Not a sight that enticed a man. And she needed to entice, beguile, and out-argue him now. Anything to save him.

"You think you're protecting me. Do you know how I'm going to feel every minute you're gone? I'm going to be frantic."

"Andrion killed my wife. I couldn't protect her, didn't see it coming." He blinked, as if waking from a nightmare, then focused on her. "I have a chance to change that. With you. I need to know you're safe, Stacy. Please, don't fight me on this. The only person I'm interested in is you."

"And Andrion."

His expression turned granite-hard, and she knew she'd struck home.

"In a different way."

"Because you hate him."

"Hate doesn't begin to cover it."

"I understand that." As he took a breath to interrupt, she held her fingers to his lips, silencing him. "I'm not pretending I know what it feels like to lose someone I love, but I understand your need for revenge."

He lifted his chin. "*Justice.*"

"Okay. *Justice.*"

"It's all I've thought about for the last year—what I'd do to Andrion once I found him." He kissed her hand, melting her. "Until I met you."

Her heart went wild, swelling with hope. "Then stay with me. Rethink this."

He peeled himself away, ending up at her side, slumped with his back against the wall. "It's all I've been thinking about. How to keep you safe. How to get Andrion without sacrificing the mission."

"You're going rogue to kill him, aren't you?" She stepped in front of Rafe, taking the position he'd held a moment before. Her voice lifted, along with her ire, all fueled by fear—for his life. "If that's not against your rules, it damned well should be."

Rafe reared up to his full height and matched her volume. "This is about honor, Stacy."

"Is it honorable to sacrifice the team and its mission for your own revenge? Blaez is gone. What are Tala and Caleb going to do without you?" What would *she*?

He nodded, as if admitting he'd debated the same question himself. "They'll manage."

"Will they? You're setting them up for failure. You're asking them to function as half a team. Where's the honor in that?"

The door across the hall opened. A red-faced, middle-aged man stepped toward them, took in Rafe's size, blanched, and fled into his room. Stacy took the hint and lowered her voice.

"What about Caleb? He's lost both parents. You're all he has. If you die, what's going to happen to him?"

He gave her a tight smile. "Your talents are wasted in computers, Stacy. You're a sharpshooter, hurling words like ammo."

"I'll take that as a compliment." She returned his grimace, then softened. "If it gets you to change your mind. Because killing Andrion isn't going to bring your wife back. It just might get you killed."

She reached out, needing to touch him again, desperate for him to choose her over vengeance. "That's what I can't handle. The thought of you getting hurt. Or worse."

He stroked her cheek, the anger draining from his face. "Then give me a kiss. For luck."

She wanted to. But it was the only bargaining tool she had left. And kissing him now would only add to her misery later, when he didn't return.

Stacy took a step back and Rafe's hand fell to his side. On cue, Caleb poked his head out of the hotel room. "You two finished talking?"

Rafe held her eye, waiting. Seeing him standing there, tall and strong, like some Norse warrior god, squeezed her chest. Stacy almost caved and gave him a peck on the cheek. Then an old tune her father used to sing played in her mind.

She'd forgotten most of the lyrics, except for the part describing the two lovers—one an irresistible force, the other an immovable object. When they came together, something was bound to give. But that wasn't going to happen here. Rafe wasn't going to change his mind. And she couldn't keep riding the emotional rollercoaster, wanting the impossible. Because he couldn't stay with her. Not when his past and the future stood between them. So she kept her ground, holding his gaze.

When he spoke again, it was to his boots. "I guess we're done. Good-bye, Stacy."

She wanted to take his hand, but one touch would have singed her and she would have taken him on the floor. Stacy watched him turn and walk away, his back to her. She made a fist, ready to punch the wall. Rafe was going off to avenge his wife's murder, and she was...

Never going to see him again.

"Wait."

Both men turned at the sound of her voice. Stacy ran full speed to Rafe, launching herself at him, wrapping her legs around his hips. She braced her arms on his shoulders, combed her fingers through his hair, and tangled her tongue with his, telling him with her mouth what she was too afraid to declare with words.

That she loved him.

When Stacy pulled back to look at him, one last time—to memorize the color of his eyes, the shape of his lips, to feel his body against hers—Caleb gave a low whistle. "Now, that's some kinda kiss."

"Please reconsider," she whispered in Rafe's ear. "Let Tala and me make the diversion first. If I can do something, *anything*, to help get you in and out quick—"

"In and out, huh? That would be good," he said, husky and hushed. "But with you. And real slow."

A tear ripped down her cheek. "Not if you don't come back to me."

He kissed her again, soft and sweet. Though her heart was breaking, she wasn't going to fall apart in front of him. He didn't need to see that. Not now. She'd hold it together and be a brave soldier.

Like him.

She unclasped her hands and let him go, her feet returning to earth. "Take care of yourself, cowboy. You too, Caleb."

"Will do, champ." Rafe grinned at her, and she smiled back, locking her lips in place and holding in the sob battling to work its way free.

As soon as he and Caleb disappeared around the corner, Stacy let go. Her arm shot out as her knees gave way, her palm squealing along the wall as she crumpled to the floor.

CHAPTER TWENTY-NINE

Y OU WANNA GRAB a cab?"
Rafe glanced at Caleb as their boots pounded the sidewalk in sync. "We'll walk."

He needed to blow off tension, shed it. Every step away from that hotel helped. Under the blanket of night, and surrounded by the city lights, Rafe's knotted muscles relaxed and the pressure eased. The fresh air felt good against his skin.

It cooled his head. His heart.

"Stacy really likes you."

He could still taste her on his lips, smell her scent around him. "Seems to."

It had taken every scrap of his willpower to let Stacy go—to end that last kiss and step away from her. He'd always believed that kind of passion came once in a lifetime. He'd found it years ago, only to have it ripped from him. He'd never expected to feel such an intense desire for a female again.

And not for a human.

His heels cracked the concrete for a full block before Caleb's next words. "You like her?"

Not the best topic before a battle. Rafe needed to focus on the operation ahead. He kept his answer short. "Sure."

With her, he felt a heat that went beyond the physical, even when she pushed his buttons. Like when she'd questioned his team loyalty. Thinking about that now put a bad taste in his mouth. Because her opinion mattered, made him question his priorities.

The mission came first. Always. The team second—since they helped you reach your objective. After that, Rafe was duty-bound to protect civilians.

But the action he'd planned for that morning didn't fall into any of those categories. Dusting Andrion wasn't on the list. The only other action that interested Rafe involved Stacy, and a whole lot of heavy breathing.

"Sure, I like her. She's great."

"For a human."

Rafe stopped, in the middle of the intersection, blindsided by the comment. He hauled his ass across the road and spun Caleb around with a smack to the arm. "What the hell's that supposed to mean?"

Caleb grabbed a handful of Rafe's jacket. It might have been to steady himself, but the young lycan's opposite fist popped up at the same time, a kneejerk response to the blow.

Rafe held his ground, staring him down. Caleb caught himself and backed off, his hands up—a gesture of surrender.

"That's what you usually say. 'He's okay, for a vampire. She's okay, for a witch.' So... Stacy's great for a *human*. Right?"

Rafe shook his head, half expecting his brains to rattle. Did he always qualify his appraisals like that?

Maybe he did. He was used to being around his own kind. Preferred it. At work, he didn't have that option. His superiors were vampires. And the beings he encountered? They could be anything—bloodsuckers, shifters, witches. And now he could add goltos and vampweres to the tally.

But Stacy was different. And *vive la différence.*

He'd never imagined being so taken with a human. Rafe knew he had to be careful with her physically. None of the rough and tumble stuff he would have done with a female of his species. Oddly, he didn't feel deprived. If anything, lovemaking with Stacy was more thrilling. Sexier.

He had to be gentle. Take care of her. And that touched him deep down. Made him feel things he'd never experienced before. Not even with Daciana. When he and Caleb stopped at a red light, Rafe almost about-faced back to the hotel. Back to Stacy's arms.

"You waiting for another shade of green?"

Rafe looked up in time to see the light switch from green to orange. How long had he been standing there thinking about her?

Caleb stepped in front of him. "Is that what you meant? That Stacy's great for a human?"

The phrase didn't sound any better the second time around. It came off as a slur, and Rafe wasn't about to have his female insulted. "No. Stacy's great. Period."

Caleb nodded. "And hot."

Oh, yeah. But he didn't want to hear that from his buddy. Rafe's territorial hackles went up, his heartbeat pounding at his temples. "Back off. She's mine."

Rafe frowned. That didn't come out right. A quick look at Caleb confirmed it. The *were* smirked like he'd just heard the declaration of the century.

"No probs. I'm into redheads."

A growl rumbled deep in Rafe's throat as he noticed the fresh bite marks on Caleb. He understood Tala had to feed, but didn't appreciate his friend being served up as the main course. "You okay?"

Caleb blushed and lifted his jacket collar to hide the wounds. "I'm good. Ready to go after Andrion with you." He delivered his famous puppy dog look, his big eyes pleading. "And I *want* to go after Andrion with you."

"No way, Caleb. I can't let you do that."

"Why not?"

Rafe jerked his head toward the fresh green light and they stepped off the curb. "Because it's unofficial."

"So?"

"You could be court-marshaled."

"Then why are *you* doing it?"

Because he didn't have a choice. Rafe had to avenge his wife's murder while he had the chance. If he waited for another mission, Andrion would be long gone—hiding on the opposite side of the world, maybe in a different century. And, if Andrion was also behind Smiley's death, killing him before the big showdown on the yacht would be a good precaution.

Big *ifs*. Rafe had no proof, and his vampire bosses wouldn't appreciate an unauthorized hit on one of their own. No matter what crime the bloodsucker committed.

"You know why," he murmured.

"Because of Daciana."

Rafe didn't answer, didn't trust himself to speak while hatred's slow burn surged through his veins. As soon as he cleared the intersection, Caleb slid in front of him again, this time blocking his path.

"You're not the only one who wants Andrion dead, Rafe. You and Daciana took me in. She treated me like—"

The teen lowered his head. His massive chest heaved as he sucked in a breath. "Like a mother and a big sister rolled into one." When Caleb looked up again, his eyes were glossy. "I loved her, too."

Rafe thumped him on the back—feeling the youngling's pain, suppressing his own. "I know, buddy."

"I don't want to be alone again, Rafe. If something happens to you—" Caleb choked on the rest of his sentence. Seeing the kid broken up about losing him, ripped into Rafe. As Stacy said it would.

Damn. The woman should invest in a crystal ball and put out her shingle.

He wrapped Caleb in a bear hug. "Don't worry. If anything happens to me, Nitsa will take you in."

Mentioning his older sister got a smile out of Caleb. She was mated, perpetually pregnant, and could whip up a mouth-watering feast with whatever wild game you threw at her.

"You're young, Caleb, just starting your career. And you're going to go far. Don't mess it up now."

Rafe released him, but hung close. "Hold the fort for me, while I get Andrion. For both of us."

They walked the rest of the way in silence. When they got to the Underground, Rafe used his *lockepik* to open the door as before. This time, the stairs were lit for their arrival.

Very inviting.

Rafe flicked the safety off his gun, anyway. Just in case. Caleb caught his drift and followed suit. They descended the stairs, hands on their holstered weapons, ready to draw.

As they approached the meeting place, Rafe sensed the vampweres and let out a low howl. Leander's lead warriors appeared from the darkness, bearing a hodgepodge of weaponry—knives, guns, clubs, and homemade stakes.

"Where's Leander?" Rafe asked the biggest male.

The vampwere didn't speak, just tilted his head.

Rafe followed the direction with his gaze and, in a dim corner, saw Leander and his mate holding baby Milan between them. A picture of greeting card perfection, if you liked furry giants with fangs.

A sliver of envy wedged into Rafe's chest. The vampweres were shunned, ailing, and on the brink of extinction, but Rafe would have switched places with Leander in a New York Second to experience that close family bond.

The female swiped at her eyes, but nodded and backed away from her mate, their babe in her arms. Rafe remembered his own parting with Stacy and the fire she'd packed into that one kiss.

Maybe their last.

Even if he survived till morning, he was going to lose Stacy when he returned to his time. Rafe didn't want to go through that kind of pain again—the loss of someone he cared about. He shouldn't have gotten involved in the first place. But he had, and now he wanted her. Needed her. As much as his next breath.

He thought about the things she'd said. The more he replayed them in his mind, the more he wondered what the fuck he was doing here—shirking his duties, chucking his mission, and abandoning his team.

He'd been thinking with his heart, not his head, and that was plain bad soldiering. Especially since he was the one in command. Time to regroup. To get back on track. Make his mission the number one priority.

Leander looked up and approached him. "Are you ready, my friend?"

No. Not anymore.

He nodded and turned to Caleb. "I'll go in and get the power source. That's it."

Then he was getting his sorry ass back to the hotel. To hell with Andrion and the time portal. He'd deal with both later. Alone. After he got his team home safe.

Caleb stopped toeing at the dirt and grinned. "I'll be right here, waiting for you."

Rafe felt Leander's strong grip on his arm. The big male gazed down at him. "Thank you for helping us."

"No probs," Rafe answered, parroting Caleb's earlier reply.

But there *was* a problem. A big one.

Saving Milan wasn't going to help the species. It wouldn't be enough to make a difference. Rafe was fairly certain of that, but not positive. He was still taking a risk. One that could change the future. Perhaps, adversely. He couldn't turn his back on the babe, though. She reminded him of the child he'd lost.

He had to follow through now. His own team needed the power source, too. So stealing it from the vamps was logical, a sound move. He'd help get Leander's warriors in and out, as quickly as possible. Then Rafe would switch his focus back to the main mission, making sure the Governor of Washington fulfilled his destiny.

Leander and his best warriors fell in behind him—two males and one female. All a foot taller than Rafe. The tunnel wasn't high. An average-sized human male would have had to crawl through it. But they had a better option.

Rafe pulled off his jacket and T-shirt and tossed them to Caleb. He unstrapped his weapons belt and set it down on the dirt floor. His jeans were next to go. He slipped out of them, folded them neatly, and placed them under the belt. Then he wolfed-it.

It felt good, freeing. Rafe trotted around the others while they morphed, loosening up his muscles, at home in his animal skin. He picked up his jeans and belt in his mouth, and gave a sharp yelp through his clenched teeth, signaling it was time to move out.

Rafe went into the dark tunnel first, with Leander behind him. The smell of damp earth was all around, making Rafe feel like a rat, trapped in a hole. He kept going.

A car rolled overhead. He was under the road. Halfway there.

He could hear the others behind him, panting as he was, their paws slapping the dirt. This part of the scheme troubled Rafe the most. If they had a cave-in, they were finished. Even once they emerged from the other end of the tunnel, they'd be easy to pick off. Only one warrior could get through at a time.

He saw the dirt wall rise up in front of him. The end of the line.

The tunnel was wider here, taller. Still, there wasn't enough room to stand. Rafe dropped the load he carried and transformed back to human form, crouching low.

From his belt, he grabbed his field *periskope*. They'd drilled a small hole through the floor the night before—the size of an old-fashioned dime. Now, Rafe pushed the long, slim instrument up the opening and looked through the eyepiece.

He swiveled the *periskope* around. No movement in sight for 360 degrees. Just brooms, mops and industrial cleaning supplies.

Knowing the layout, the vampweres had chosen a discreet area for the exit—another part of the plan Rafe didn't like. The janitor's room may have been off the beaten track, but there was no place to run in the event of a retreat. Only straight ahead, over the enemy, or back through the tunnel. Either way, they wouldn't be able to move fast enough to escape the blast of a machine gun. Or the jaws of a hungry vamp.

Leander's troupe had chipped away most of the cement floor during the day, as per their strategy. All that remained was to cut through the floor with Rafe's *zereglazen*. Though the device was relatively quiet, anyone entering the room would see the slicing beam on their side, as he cut a large circle through the layers of concrete and tile. Rafe fully understood he risked death if a passing vamp noticed and blasted him with a *zilva-kieg*. Parts of him would remain splattered on the tunnel walls forever.

When the circle of floor was loose, Rafe held it in place, balancing it on his head. He used his *periskope* again to check for the enemy, swiveling it around to get a full view.

Still no vampires. So far, so good.

He gave Leander a thumbs-up and gripped his weapon. Rafe took a breath and rose, letting the circle of flooring slide to one side.

He pulled himself up, then waited until Leander and one of his warriors were through the opening, weapons ready, before lowering his own gun and stepping into his jeans. Despite what he'd told Stacy, about feeling safer going in naked than wearing one of Tala's bulletproof vests, Rafe had no intention of entering a vamps' den with his gonads flapping in the breeze. He strapped on his utility belt, readied his pistol, and then covered another of Leander's fighters as she emerged through the hole and dressed. A gaggle of vampweres would be hard enough to explain to a human civilian, without having them engage in a streaking party.

When the vampweres were set, Rafe opened the janitor's room door and used his *periskope* to check the hall. Still nothing.

He swung the door wide open. The vampweres took up their positions in the hallway, adhering to the military's 'room entry' techniques that every good warrior learns in training.

Rafe froze, listening while he waited for the rest of Leander's crew to join them. Canned music came from hidden speakers. He smelled stale air... a lingering trace of vampire... and the metallic odor of blood.

A human's.

A sound hit his ears at the same time. A whimper. Barely audible.

Rafe's gut clenched. He wanted to find the victim and help. But he was a soldier first. The objective took priority. They were here for the power source. That was their goal. The victim could well be bait in a trap.

He stepped in front of his troops, paused for a moment, then nodded. Behind him, Leander squeezed his shoulder—their agreed signal to move out.

They made their way down the hall, Leander taking over the lead, guiding them to the lab. Rafe assumed the number two spot, checking on the other vampweres as they passed by each office door, satisfied that they'd remembered and executed the strategic formations he'd taught them.

At the end of the hall, Leander took a right turn and ended up by a heavy, steel door. Rafe slid past him, to the opposite side of the frame.

The smell of blood was stronger, the crying louder. Rafe fought against the wild adrenaline rush flooding his body. He forced himself to breathe evenly, to stay in control. When all the warriors were in place, he used his *lockepik* on the door, then kicked it open and swung to his right, gun high, ready to take out anything in that sector of the room.

Seeing that his area was clear, he glanced back. Leander and his crew were positioned, as planned—weapons poised.

The lab was large and held a hodgepodge of desks, tables, papers, computers, blinking contraptions Rafe could only guess at—and one nearly completed time portal, which dominated the far corner.

It should have been easy to destroy. Except for the human female chained to it. She was gagged, stripped to the waist, and bleeding from several bite marks. Tears rolled down her face, her chest jerking as she sobbed. And, in her position, any sudden movement might prove fatal.

It would likely set off the bomb strapped between her breasts.

CHAPTER THIRTY

RAFE KEPT HIS eyes busy—checking corners and scanning for traps. He spied the curved lens of a security camera overhead. If someone was monitoring the action on a screen at the receiving end, they'd have seen the team storm the lab. But they weren't going to see any more. Rafe took out the camera with a single shot then turned his attention back to the woman.

Suspended spread-eagle over the exposed side of the time portal, she resembled a butterfly mounted on a board. A steel box sat like a diamond in the center of her chest, secured by a crisscrossing of chain. Wires went out from it to the shackles on her bruised wrists and ankles.

Rafe rubbed his chin with his free hand as he gave the setup another inspection. "Damn." The thing looked like an *impalare*—Im-P for short. A device used to protect a valued object by creating a human shield around it. If detonated, the time portal would remain untouched. But the victim would be impaled through the heart with dozens of steel spikes.

Bloodsuckers scored top points in black humor.

The gadget was a mix of twenty-third and twenty-first century technologies. Which meant Rafe was familiar with half of it. Improvised Explosive Devices, he could handle. Im-Ps were Caleb's area of expertise. Rafe wished he'd brought the kid along.

Because, now that the time portal was in front of him, the impulse to destroy it was overwhelming—a bottle of vodka dangling in front of an alcoholic. And Rafe couldn't help but wonder if this little party had been arranged in his honor.

Had Andrion anticipated this moment and set a trap? Or was this how the vampire normally used humans?

As Rafe drew closer to the chained woman, she whimpered louder, her eyes pleading. He lifted his index finger to his lips and made the universal sign for silence. "You're okay. I need you to be quiet."

She immediately hushed and bobbed her head. Rafe peeled the tape from her mouth, but left the gag stuck to her cheek. If she panicked and made noise, he had no qualms about slapping the tape back in place. An easy fix.

Too bad he didn't have an equally simple way to wipe her memory. If he'd brought Tala along, the vamp could have quickly erased the episode

187

from the human's mind—a skill Rafe lacked. Though he had no trouble remembering the woman. She was the same female he'd seen enter the building the other day, looking like an employee. Obviously, she'd received a demotion.

"They're vampires," she told him in a harsh whisper. "They bit me. They—"

He silenced her with a hiss. "I know what they are." Just not what he was going to do about the situation.

Choices.

Rafe could destroy the time portal and the woman along with it. Risk valuable minutes freeing her then deal with the portal. Or screw up, detonate the Im-P, and get her killed anyway. Before he could think of a fourth option, Leander was at his side with the power source.

"Take it back to Caleb," Rafe barked. "He can operate the *heilen.*"

"You come, too."

Rafe examined the Im-P a third time, working his jaw, wishing he could bite through metal. A bolt cutter would be real handy about now. "I can't take out the portal with her in front of it."

"Why not?"

Because she'll die, dumb-ass.

Rafe didn't say it. He could tell from Leander's expression he already knew. His face was hard, cold. This wasn't the father who'd cried over his baby girl's health. This was the mask of a trained killer, and Rafe sure as hell didn't like the view.

Because he could see himself in the vampwere's eyes.

Before Stacy came into his life, Rafe wouldn't have thought twice about sacrificing a human for the sake of the mission. Non-*weres* were expendable, their lives collateral damage, no matter what his vampire boss said. That had always been Rafe's belief. In the past, at any rate. Now, looking at the human, her eyes so like Stacy's, Rafe rethought that mercenary view.

Leander fastened the gag back over the human's mouth. "You think Andrion will spare her after we're gone?"

The woman began to cry again, the tape at her mouth pulsing as she blubbered. Rafe steeled himself, drew on his training as a soldier, and shut her out. He let logic fill his head and ignored that squeeze in his chest—the one he'd felt ever since he kissed Stacy. The one that grew every time he looked at her, every time he thought about her. The one that made him feel as if someone had taken his heart out of the freezer, zipped it back up in his chest, and returned him to the land of the living.

Because Leander spoke the truth. Whether the human was impaled or consumed later by Andrion, death was certain. Before the woman's tears hit the floor, Rafe made his decision.

He clapped Leander on the shoulder. "Go. Milan needs you."

The giant hybrid took a last look at the woman then turned his back on her, as if she were already dead. "I'll leave my two best warriors with you."

The vampwere leader snapped his fingers and gave the orders to his crew. Within seconds, he was gone, leaving the largest male guarding the door and the lone female jogging toward Rafe.

"Armina," she said, by way of introduction. A surprisingly feminine name for the husky-voiced, muscle-bound Amazon now towering over him. Then she smiled, and it transformed her face into something beautiful, while her deep brown eyes gleamed with intelligence.

"Stand ready, Armina."

"To destroy the portal?" The vampwere raised her gun, aiming it at the device…and the human.

"Yes." Rafe caught Armina's hand and gave it a push, until the weapon again pointed at the floor. Then he holstered his own gun. "*After* we free the woman."

He saw Armina raise an eyebrow before he turned back to the device, planning his next move. Releasing the human's shackles first would be foolhardy. Any disturbance would send a message through the wires and detonate the *impalare*. Cutting the lines was out, too. All of them were black and Rafe didn't trust his luck to pick the right ones. Dismantling the Im-P was an even worse choice. It was delicate work that demanded time and patience, and he didn't see a screwdriver in sight.

His best option was to remove the mechanism. His *zereglazen* came with a slicing beam that cut through steel. And flesh. Leaving the woman scarred for life. Which was a damn sight better than killing her. But he couldn't risk her making any jerky movements and setting off the Im-P. He needed something to protect the human from the beam. And the only thing he had on hand was…himself.

Rafe looked for some slack in the chain around the gadget at her chest. Once he found it, he eased in two fingers and started slicing.

He trained the beam on the center of the steel link, working outward. Rafe smelled his flesh burning before he felt it, heard it sizzle. Beads of perspiration popped up on his forehead as the beam cut further into him— the burn sinking deep, like a line of liquid metal from a soldering gun. Only instead of joining his flesh together, the meat on his fingers was melting away.

He'd heal. Faster than the woman. He focused on that, gritted his teeth, and kept his eye on the beam. While letting his mind wander. Back to the hotel room, to Stacy, and how good it felt to be in her arms. To smell her. To taste her. To hear her voice. To lie with her at his side, her head resting on his shoulder, her hair fanned out across his chest. Just holding her—feeling the gentle swell from her waist to her hips, her breath against his skin.

Just being.

With a whispered *chink*, the steel link opened. Rafe unhooked it from its neighbor, the *impalare* flopped to one side, and the spikes shot out. The woman took one look at the contraption and fainted.

Armina ripped the tape from the human's mouth and let her breathe freely. "At least we don't have to worry about her screaming." Then Armina tore off a strip from her top, ran to the lab's sink, doused the material with water, and hurried back to hand it to him as a bandage.

"Thanks." His fingers still throbbed, but the coolness of the fabric on his skin eased the pain and stopped the burn from going deeper. "Search her after she's free. In case she's a plant."

The muscled female nodded. "Got it."

Armina moved in front of the human, holding her under the arms, taking the pressure off the woman's limbs as Rafe used his *schlu-locke* to spring the catches on her ankle shackles, then on the cuffs binding her wrists. The unconscious human slumped over the vampwere's back. Rafe thought to be chivalrous and help the hybrid carry the load, but Armina handled the woman as if she weighed as much as a pillow.

As the vampwere settled the human down on the long table, gun blasts erupted in the hall.

Rafe looked up to see the male vampwere exchanging fire with an unseen assailant. Until, in a blur of motion, the shaggy male's chest exploded and his body slid to the floor.

Andrion appeared over the remains—the vampwere's heart in his hand, blood dripping from his mouth—and grimaced. "I forgot how bad you things taste."

Rafe drew his *blitzzager* just as TJ appeared at his master's side, his gun poised. Without stopping to aim, Rafe cranked off a round of cover fire. If the bullets found flesh, bonus. As soon as the vampires retreated to the hall, he threw the unconscious woman over his shoulder, upended the heavy table, and took cover behind it—the female vampwere at his side, the human on the floor at their backs, as safe as she could be under the circumstances.

The animal in him fought to break free. But with his left hand out of commission, he'd be screwed wolfing-it. Limping around on three paws would put him at a severe disadvantage. He'd have better luck in his current form.

Armina had no such problem. She'd already shifted—her lower body more wolf-like, her upper body shaggy, but with the arms and hands of a human. She used them to continue the firepower against the now advancing vamps, giving Rafe enough of a distraction to peek over the top of the table and aim. He felt a surge of satisfaction as his shot caught Andrion in the head and spun him around. Unfortunately, it wouldn't be enough to keep the bloodsucker down.

Focused on the threat in front of him, Rafe had no warning when the jolt came from behind. At first, he thought it was Armina, giving him a hard thump on the back as a congratulations. Till he saw the horror in her eyes.

He shot a look behind him. The human crouched there—wide awake and breathing hard. In her hand, she held the Im-P, blood glistening off its spikes and streaming down her arms like ribbons.

His blood.

With the visual, the pain kicked in—like he'd been on the receiving end of a horse's hooves. He struggled to take in a breath and knew from the strange crackling sound that his lung had collapsed.

He coughed—the stab of agony slumping him to the floor, the taste of blood filling his mouth. His vision blurred. He could make out Armina's face, see her mouth moving, but no sounds reached his ears—as if he were underwater, caught in a wave that pushed him farther and farther away from shore. He battled against the current—body heavy, limbs aching—and fought to stay afloat.

Fuck. He'd been so close to getting his revenge, only to be carved down by someone he was trying to help. Vengeance seemed so meaningless, now.

He should have listened to Stacy. Stayed with her. Spent the day making love to her. Told her with his body what he hadn't said in words.

What he'd never get to say.

As the cold of shock set in, he imagined the warmth of her kiss, of her wrapping herself around him.

Until the black waters pulled him under for the last time.

* * *

STACY SURFED THROUGH the hotel's TV channels, pressing the buttons on the remote with a vengeance that made her thumb burn.

Carpel Tunnel Syndrome, here we come.

She lay on the bed, legs crossed hard at the ankles, elbows tight to her ribs—a rigid log of anger and worry with no place to vent.

Again, the stations flipped by—a wash of sound and color. She wanted to throw the remote against the wall and watch it shatter into a million pieces. Or crack it against Tala's skull. But, try as she might, Stacy couldn't fault her babysitter. Tala was probably just as pissed with the situation, and only following orders.

Rafe's orders.

He was the one who deserved a smack upside the head.

Stacy jabbed the OFF button on the remote and sighed. As she dumped it onto the bedside table, the digital clock caught her eye. Even though she'd promised herself she wouldn't look at it again.

Was the damned thing stuck? Or did time really move so slowly?

Next to the clock, the phone sat mute. Rafe could have at least called and given them an update. Then again, maybe the guy wasn't into AT&T. For all Stacy knew, phones were obsolete in the twenty-third century.

She glanced over at her jailer. Tala still sat in her corner chair, fiddling with one of her thingamagadgets, which bleated at irregular intervals. The vampire's brows reached for each other—as if she were having trouble concentrating, or fighting a headache. Then, with a sudden cry, Tala arched her spine. She gripped the arms of the wingback chair, pushed herself up, and hovered there, swaying.

Stacy was off the bed before the vamp hit the floor—the dull thwack of bones cracking as Tala's body landed, the room's thin carpet providing no padding for her fall. Stacy's heart shuddered into high gear—afraid to approach the vampire, but equally determined to help. She knelt at Tala's side.

"Are you okay?" Stacy brushed her hand over her patient's forehead, sweeping away the curtain of hair that had fallen across the redhead's face. Tala's skin was warmer than usual, and Stacy wondered if she was experiencing the vampire equivalent of a fever. Her lips quivered, then pursed, as if she were trying to form words.

Stacy leaned in, tilting her head so that her ear hovered over the vamp's mouth. Then thought better of it. The position put her exposed neck within inches of Tala's fangs—a move that ranked right up there with waving a red cape at a bull. Stacy inched away, clamped a protective hand to her throat, and tried again to hear Tala.

"*Rafe.*"

The murmured name poked at the jealousy neurons in Stacy's brain and left her jangling, until she registered the strangled undertone in Tala's voice.

Cold panic coiled in Stacy's belly. "What about Rafe?"

The vamp made a feeble attempt to rise. Stacy looped her arms under Tala's, lifted, and staggered with the added weight. She managed to half-walk, half-drag the vampire to the chair and deposit her in it. Sucking in air, she gripped Tala's shoulders and shook.

"What about Rafe?"

Tala's head fell back against the upholstery, but her eyes were open. "He's hurt," she said, wincing. "Bad. I can feel it."

Stacy prayed the redhead was wrong. Tala couldn't feel Rafe's pain. Not from across town. Could she?

"How?"

"My blood. He drank from me. He—"

As Tala paused for air, Stacy interjected, her chest knotting with the desperate need for assurances. "Can you contact him? Or Caleb? Make sure?"

Tala blinked, as if waking. She unhooked a small box from her waist, punched a button on the device, and waited. "No response from Rafe." She repeated the action, pressing a different selection and frowned. "No response from either of them."

No response? Stacy couldn't imagine a more heart-crushing phrase. Any lingering anger she felt toward Rafe melted, replaced with dread. Her face must have shown it, because now Tala took a turn playing nursemaid, leaning forward to touch Stacy's hand.

"It could be that I'm not getting a signal because they're underground."

A lie. Stacy recognized it immediately. She'd grown up with them, heard one too many bullshit promises from her mother ever to be taken in by false hope again. "You people can time travel, but you haven't mastered radio waves? *Riiiiight.*"

To hell with this.

Rafe needed help. *Now.* And, with Tala out of commission and Caleb MIA, Stacy was the only resource he had.

Calling the police would have been her first choice. Let the professionals go in, guns a-blazing. But tying up the 911 operator with talk of vampires and werewolves from the future would get her slapped with a hefty fine. Or a competency hearing. And it wasn't as if Stacy had a squadron of beefy drinking buddies skilled in barroom brawling to draw on. She couldn't expect Perry and Carey to meet her at Andrion's packing a lethal supply of graphic comics and hairspray.

Even though she was shaking, her knees wobbling as if they'd been replaced with springs—even scared shitless, she had to be the one to go after Rafe. Because, God help her, fangs and futuristic mumbo-jumbo aside, she had feelings for him. *Strong* feelings she couldn't deny.

She ran to the bed, pulled on her denim jacket and reached for the team's kit. Stacy slipped a *blitzzager* into one pocket and a *holz-kieg* into the other. She just wasn't sure which was which. The one on the right shot wooden bullets, the other was a mini machine gun. She knew how to load them and how to pull the trigger, and that's all she needed to know. Like Rafe said, who the hell cared what they were called.

"Where do you think you're going?"

"After them." Stacy jammed extra clips for both weapons into the pockets of her jeans. "After *Rafe.*"

"I forbid it."

Stacy gave the vamp a quick appraisal. The redhead tilted to one side, a shade paler than a goth girl in the dead of winter.

"It doesn't look like you're in a position to stop me." Stacy reached into the bag and gripped one of the team's knives, but decided against taking it. She didn't plan on getting close enough to the enemy to use it.

She buttoned her jacket, grabbed the black wig, and strode to the exit. As Stacy reached for the knob, she was bulldozed from behind, the impact slamming her into the door and knocking the wind out of her.

The floor came up to greet her. Stacy landed hard—arms trapped under her, left cheek grinding into the hotel carpet, Tala's knee crushing her spine. She heard the click of fangs snapping into place and froze. A ragged breath tickled her ear.

"Never. Underestimate. A vampire."

Face crushed, lips pushed into the middle of her face, Stacy could barely form words. "Good advice," she grunted. "But I'm still going."

She made like a bucking bronco to throw her rider. Unfortunately, the saber-toothed cowgirl on her back was going nowhere. She'd have to bide her time until the vampire slept. Stacy just hoped Rafe could hold out that long.

As soon as she stopped struggling, she felt powerful hands lift her from the floor and set her on her feet. She tried not to gush in admiration at Tala's reserve strength—one minute the vamp was lolling in a chair, the next minute she was freaking Dwayne "The Rock" Johnson. But the effort cost the redhead, big time. She fell against the armoire, breathing hard.

"We'll...go together."

No way Stacy could keep her jaw from dropping after that announcement. What a way to negotiate a *yes*. She'd lost the catfight but somehow won the war. Along with an ally. Because if Tala could kick ass like a pro even while she was hurting, it behooved Stacy to bring her along.

Especially if they were about to break into a vampire's den.

"Sounds like a plan, Wonder Woman. Lead on."

CHAPTER THIRTY-ONE

TOMAS ALMOST DOUBLED over.

He fumbled for his cell phone, eager to catch an on-the-fly video of Rafe, and his reaction when the human he'd just saved stabbed him in the back.

Literally.

The werewolf's expression was a mash-up of shock and confusion worthy of the top prize on *America's Funniest Home Videos*, a show Tomas found almost as amusing as the evening news.

But the moment was lost. As soon as Tomas palmed the phone, Rafe slid from view, disappearing behind the table barrier he'd created. Then the crazed, bare-breasted creature who'd skewered him bolted from the room screeching, her cry plummeting in both pitch and volume as she ran down the hall.

Tomas thought to catch her—he could use a tasty snack—but another YouTube moment beckoned: Andrion throttling a female vampwere. She dangled a foot off the floor, her legs peddling for purchase.

Now, this was a video Tomas had to get.

He found the app but, as he set up the shot, someone jostled him from behind and ruined his framing. His responding curse stuck in his throat, as he saw the perpetrator striding into the room.

His Maker's Maker.

Tomas bowed in supplication—something he'd learned to fake back in the thirties. And, with his head still lowered, he snuck a peek at the vampire.

Lean and striking, like a young Franz Liszt, and packing the same raw charisma, Nikolas seemed to glide across the floor. He arrived at the center of the action in a nanosecond, gently freeing the vampwere and bringing Andrion to a position Tomas had only fantasized about.

To his knees.

"Armina is my creation, as are you," Nikolas declared, his voice a smooth baritone even in anger. "You will respect the life I gave her."

The veins at Andrion's neck bulged. "She was shooting at me."

"Which you did nothing to provoke?" Nikolas clicked his tongue. "I will have no sibling rivalry in my lab."

Tomas sensed a fight coming on. A big, juicy one. He hit RECORD. Or thought he had. On second glance, he realized that Nikolas' body check had scooted him over to the wrong app. He'd taken a snapshot of his favorite Gucci moccasins, instead—the off-white ones, with the silver horse bit across the top. He already had a complete photographic account of his shoe collection, so he deleted the picture, all the while keeping an eye on Nikolas, watching as the scientist reached for the female—his long fingers weaving into her hair with the tenderness of a father, the sensuality of a lover.

"Are you all right, my dear?"

The vampwere nodded, her face a mix of wariness and awe. A mirror for Tomas. He felt exactly the same in the Master's presence—the vamp's power forcing the fuzz on his arms to attention.

Nikolas gazed down at the floor, his shoulder-length hair spilling forward, the cravat at his neck—an antiquated style he somehow made fresh and hip—wrinkling as he bent his head. "Whom have we here?"

Tomas sidestepped to his left to see past the upturned table. There, lying in a pool of bright red blood was the werewolf he knew only too well. But it wasn't his place to explain. Tomas kept his mouth shut and played Switzerland, staying neutral.

Ditto Andrion. Though not for long. Nikolas grasped his progeny's hand, as if in greeting. Then twisted Andrion's arm until he achieved a satisfying pop. With an accompanying scream.

Tomas licked his lips, savoring the moment and anticipating its aftermath. In his bedroom, later. There, Andrion would come crawling for sympathy, and Tomas would supply it with murmured reassurances and open arms. They'd lie together on Tomas' big, and usually lonely bed, the length of Andrion's body making his own harden. These were the only times nowadays, when Tomas was allowed such intimacies.

"I asked a question."

Nikolas' words brought Tomas out of his reverie. He focused on Andrion and willed him to answer. The longer the kneeling vamp remained defiant, the less ego-soothing he'd need later.

"It's Garrett." The name came out as a cry—Andrion's vowels elongated, his consonants slamming into the hush of the room.

Nikolas kept twisting. "The one whose wife you murdered?"

No hesitation now. Tomas' soon-to-be bedmate answered with a whimpered, "Yes." Tomas replied with a silent, enthusiastic one—his free hand fisting in triumph. *Yes!*

Suddenly released, Andrion stumbled off-balance, his displaced arm hanging several inches lower than the other. Nikolas moved past him and, with a flick of his wrist, righted the overturned table.

"Armina, place our patient on this, if you would." Nikolas may have phrased his sentence as a request, but Tomas knew it was an order. Taking compliance for granted, the scientist didn't dally to see if the female obeyed. He headed straight for the sink.

As Armina scooped up Rafe, Andrion turned to Nikolas, flinging out his good arm to point back at the injured *were*. "*He's* your patient? What about me? You want me to heal like this?"

Nikolas swiveled to face his creation. "Take a deep breath."

And count to ten. Tomas mouthed his mother's usual line when he'd had tantrums as a boy, and expected Nikolas to give the same advice. However, as soon as Andrion inhaled, Nikolas grabbed the injured arm and popped it back into its socket, producing another yowl.

"Now, to the wolf." Nikolas removed his jacket. He kept his vest on and rolled up the sleeves of his pristine, white shirt. "I've been working on a new operating procedure. This is the perfect time to practice on a live guinea pig." He squirted soap into his palms and lathered up. "Well…*live* for the moment."

"You're going to save him?" Andrion flushed—quite an accomplishment for a vampire. "He tried to kill me."

"Sounds as if they're lining up for the job. Time for you to do something positive for a change." The Master turned off the tap with his elbow, dried his hands and snapped on a pair of latex gloves. "Give him your blood."

"What?" The double-take Andrion executed was something to behold. Another missed video opportunity. Tomas stopped gawking and started filming.

"Your blood is strong," Nikolas explained, as he strode back to the table. "He's only got a few more minutes of life left. Let him drink from you."

Open-mouthed, Andrion blinked. "What do I look like? A water fountain? I want him dead."

Tomas held back a laugh and kept his device steady—capturing the moment—the perfect cheer-up for the next time Andrion bruised his psyche.

Nikolas looped his hand in the air—a king dispensing with a trivial matter. "You can dispose of him later, if you wish. For now, he's my new science project."

"Then *you* play donor."

"*I'm* operating."

"And you can't do both?" Andrion sneered. "I thought you could do anything."

"Enough," Nikolas roared, then sighed and lowered his voice. "Tomas? Are you willing to assist?"

Momentarily stunned by Nikolas' outburst, Tomas recovered, slipped the phone into his pocket, and approached. Time to leave the role of passive observer and, like the damned Americans in forty-one, step into the war.

But on which side?

Nothing spelled success like getting himself into Nikolas' good books. At the same time, Tomas didn't want to completely screw up his relationship with Andrion. Not yet. Not until he came into his own. And not while he could still play both ends toward the middle.

Nikolas was so preoccupied with his patient he didn't even glance up, which gave Tomas the chance to flash Andrion a sympathetic look. Part of his sacrificial lamb routine. Let Andrion think he was doing it all for him. Let Nikolas think the same. Soon, Tomas would be running the show. The only one of the three left standing.

"As you wish, Nikolas." Tomas bared his fangs and lifted his wrist to his mouth, prepared to bite into his flesh, but Nikolas caught his arm.

"The blood may be unnecessary, after all."

Tomas eyed the body on the table—marveling at the hard lines, the firm planes. Those well-defined muscles now rested, inert and powerless. The tanned skin encasing them paled to a shade nearly matching his own.

He met Nikolas' eyes, and saw something like regret in them. "Garrett's gone into cardiac arrest."

* * *

STACY FIDGETED IN the backseat of the cab. She rammed her feet against the floor mat as if it were a giant-sized gas pedal, willing the vehicle to move faster. She died a little at each red light, all of them looking like a puddle of blood against the cloudy morning sky.

Watching Tala didn't help. The vampire was clearly trying to hold it together but, every few seconds, she'd grimace in pain. Or slump in her seat, head drooping.

Stacy laced her fingers with Tala's deathly cold ones, offering what comfort she could. At first, Tala tried to pull away but Stacy wasn't having any of that. The redhead kept her eyes closed, but a barely there smile flickered on her lips and, after a moment, she returned a faint squeeze.

They sat together, a united team, as the taxi made its way to the corner where Stacy and Rafe had eaten their morning Starbucks. With her consuming most of his. The guy's generosity and protectiveness made her chest ache with longing.

What if he were gone from her life? What if she never saw him again? Never shared another kiss. Or felt him close to her—inside her.

She reminded herself, it would be the same when he returned to his time. He'd be lost to her then, too. But at least she'd know he still lived. Something she didn't know now.

The only thing that gave her hope was Tala's condition. Hope and dread. Because every time Tala flinched, it meant Rafe was still alive, but suffering. Just like Tala. Stacy hated that her desperate need for reassurance came at the price of their pain, making her feel as guilty as if she were the one causing it.

"Here," Tala announced, and Stacy told the cab to stop. She handed the driver a fistful of Tala's cash and jumped out, then ran around to the other side of the vehicle to help the vampire from the backseat. She coiled her arm around the redhead's waist, turning herself into a human crutch, and got Tala onto the sidewalk.

Across the intersection, and a half-block up, a crowd gathered and huddled around two police cars and an ambulance. Red and blue lights whirled over shocked faces as paramedics loaded someone into the back of their white van.

Stacy's heart skittered. Did the emergency crew have Rafe? Were they treating him? And, with his biology, would they give him the wrong medications?

Too impatient to wait until the traffic light turned green, Stacy made her way against the tide, dodging cars as she muscled Tala along with her. Horns blared, curses flew and middle fingers pointed to the sky.

Fuck them all. Only one goal screamed in Stacy's mind. She had to get to Rafe, to see if it was him on that stretcher.

She reached the edge of the crowd—tried to see over the people. In the end, she shouldered her way through the horde, never losing her grip on Tala. She emerged at the front of the pack in time to catch a glimpse of the patient, before the doors closed.

Not her man. A woman—thrashing and kicking at the EMS medics as they tried to apply pressure to her various wounds.

Bites.

As the ambulance pulled into traffic, Stacy saw another vehicle, previously hidden from view. A news van.

She recognized the female reporter standing close to it, looking even thinner than she appeared on TV. The newscaster faced the camera, a half pound of makeup on her face and a microphone in her hand.

"...injuries similar to the woman, now in hospital, who worked a short distance from here. She was rushed to Emergency yesterday, when a group of concerned citizens found her on the street in front of her clothing store, bleeding and hysterical. Police aren't releasing either victim's name at this time..."

Stacy didn't hear the rest. She spun around, feeling her way along the cool brick of the buildings as she tore from the scene, her breath catching in her throat. The nearest clothing store she knew of was where she'd made purchases with her credit card the day before.

Had the vamps traced the activity? And terrorized the salesclerk to get information? Stacy felt sick. Without knowing, she'd placed an innocent person in harm's way.

The vampires first came looking for Stacy at her condo, ransacked it, then continued their hunt—tracking her down. Which meant Rafe had been right all along, and going into the vamps' den now would be walking into a trap.

But would it be a *death* trap?

Andrion captured her before and hadn't killed her. He'd used her as bait to get to Rafe, and warned her to keep her identity a secret, as if it held some importance.

Stacy couldn't imagine Andrion's interest stemmed from her career as a website designer. Or her skill at spider solitaire. Since he hadn't held her for ransom, it had nothing to do with her father's position, either. Whatever Andrion's fascination with her, it made Stacy a valuable commodity. A fact she could leverage, if need be, possibly trading herself for Rafe's safety. Or pretending to, until she could get away.

Till then, Stacy planned to stay hidden under her new wig, since she wasn't sure how much help Tala would be as a bodyguard in her current condition. So far, the vampire had proven herself to be an excellent GPS, at least for honing into Rafe. Which made her the best partner around. So Stacy wasn't about to let her walk into a possible ambush without knowing the truth.

"That store the reporter mentioned—Andrion's henchmen followed me there. I think he's after me because I'm a witness."

Tala tugged on Stacy's arm, forcing her to stop. The redhead bent over and rested her hands on her knees, panting. "That wouldn't bother him, generally. Andrion doesn't view humans as threats. Only as food. To him, you're as menacing as tuna salad on rye."

Stacy curled her upper lip. "Then let's hope I'm packing a strain of deadly bacteria."

"There must be another reason for his interest." Tala faced Stacy, her skin taking on a greenish tinge. "Maybe he knows of something you do in the future that assists him. Or obstructs him."

Assist him? Stacy would sooner die. And Rafe surely would, if he didn't get help. She battled the last of her lingering doubts, her fears. Was she truly willing to put herself on the line for the sake of a man—strike that—a *werewolf* she'd just met?

Hell, every time she crossed the street, she took her life in her hands. Nowadays, you couldn't go for a stroll in the park or a movie premiere without wondering if a crazed gunman was lying in wait. At least with her present plan, her death would have meaning. She'd be doing her part for the future, and for the brave soldier who already filled a big place in her heart.

"Andrion's office is two doors down. And we still haven't heard from Caleb." God only knew what happened to him. He could be in the same shape as Rafe. Worse. Guilt prickled Stacy again, for worrying far more about her lover than his buddy. "How do you want to play this?"

"Without my wuss factor running at full throttle." Tala gritted her teeth and straightened. "I don't know how long I can keep it together, so we'll try the direct approach." The vampire marched up to the entrance of Andrion's building. "He won't be expecting us to walk in the main door. *Surrrrprise*."

Tala pulled back on the handle and the door swung open. Inside, the air was cool, a super air conditioner on max. Stacy felt like a slab of meat in a walk-in fridge. She took a quick scan of the place, checking for exits as she'd seen Rafe do. So far, it looked like the only escape was back the way they'd come. But the long hall to their left contained several doors, any one of which could have led to another way out.

In front of them stood a receptionist's desk, amidst a waiting area with couches, all done in gray, burgundy, and black. Sleek, sophisticated…male. But the person at the desk was definitely a woman. A twitchy one.

She sat twirling her multi-layered black hair—dyed that color, Stacy surmised, after noticing her skunk strip of blond at the roots. She wore the remnants of dark polish and had several piercings—nose, dimples—but the jewelry was gone. Stacy guessed the vamps didn't want anyone with hardware on their frontlines. How conservative of them.

Tala pitched herself Stacy's way and whispered. "Follow my lead." She stepped up to the receptionist and flashed a friendly smile. "Hi, I'm Theda Bara, the new temp worker from the agency." The statement was delivered with an upward inflection and packed with a nonthreatening likeability.

The woman behind the desk blinked several times. "A vampire temp worker?" Obviously, the receptionist had seen enough of the toothy creatures to be able to recognize one on sight. Frowning, she rifled through the papers on her desk and muttered, "No one tells me a darn thing."

The chameleon Tala giggled. "I hear you, girlfriend." Who knew the leggy redhead was another Nicole Kidman?

The receptionist slapped her hands against her work surface. "Nope. I don't see your file anywhere, Theda. How typical." She opened a drawer at her side. "Let me at least give you a timecard to punch." She handed Tala a rectangular sheet, eying Stacy as if noticing her for the first time. "What about the human? Does she need a card?"

"Oh, no." Tala's grin showed off her fangs. "She's my lunch."

Stacy gulped, remembering the vampire's crack about tuna on rye.

"Guard her like a hawk, Theda. The guys around here like to nibble." The woman pulled her collar tighter, her fingers trembling.

Tala looped a possessive arm around Stacy. "Will do. Now, if you could just point me in the direction of the lab…"

The receptionist's brow crinkled. "The lab?" Her right hand disappeared under the desk, as if she were fumbling for a security button.

Stacy reached for her gun, but Tala caught her arm. The redhead leaned forward and gazed into the receptionist's eyes. "Point me to the lab. Then have a little nap and forget you ever saw us."

"Last door at the end of the hall…" The woman's voice was soft, dreamy. Stacy and Tala stayed only long enough to see the receptionist fold up on the desk, her head resting on her crossed arms, a soft snore escaping her lips.

That's what Tala tried on me, Stacy thought. *A freaking eon ago.* "Life's easier when you're not a *memansaan*."

"You got that right. Let's go."

"To the lab? You're sure Rafe's there?"

"That's where he was headed."

Weapons out and ready, Tala led the way, Stacy guarding their rear. But soon, Stacy was performing double duty. The energy Tala used to hide the pain during her role-playing stint as Theda Bara had cost her. She moved in slow motion, stumbling down the hall, unable to hold her gun level. When they were ten feet from the final door, Tala flung out her arm, reaching for the wall to support herself.

Stacy caught her before she fell. "More pain?"

Tala blinked. "No. Nothing."

Relief flooded through Stacy. If Tala was no longer suffering that meant Rafe was out of danger, but the look on Tala's face was dire.

"I don't get it. What's the problem?"

"I feel nothing," Tala repeated with urgency. "A total release. As if Rafe has…"

Died?

Stacy shook her head. "No. That can't be."

Surely, she'd know—feel his loss deep within her. Still, she almost dropped Tala, almost took a nosedive and planted them both on the floor. She batted away tears and clutched at her chest, gasping as her heart shattered.

"No," she said again. "It's not true."

It wasn't too late. She could still help him. Stacy knew CPR, Tala had healed him with her blood before—certainly there was something they could do.

"I won't *let* it be true."

Tala didn't argue, just ran the last few feet to the lab with Stacy. Putting their combined force into one solid kick, they trashed the already dented door and entered—Tala covering the left side of the room, while Stacy swerved to the right, her gun high.

What she saw made her drop her guard—Rafe's lifeless body on a table, blood everywhere.

Stacy bit back tears and aimed at the vampire who hovered over her dead lover—the front of his lab coat more crimson than white. "Get away from him. Now!"

The vamp stayed in place, looking imperturbed and not the least concerned for his own safety. Then Stacy heard a series of clicks and understood why.

A half dozen vampweres, Leander among them, emerged from their hiding places, machineguns raised.

Not at the mad scientist, but at her and Tala.

CHAPTER THIRTY-TWO

TALA FORCED HER vision to go tunnel. She blocked it all out—the blood, Rafe's body on the table, and the holy mess of wires and tubes invading him. She trusted Stacy to stick a mental dartboard on Nikolas' chest and aim well.

That left Tala free.

Squinting one eye, she pointed her *blitzzager* at Leander's fat, ugly head. If she was about to die, Tala planned to take the traitorous bastard down with her. And hoped to score more vampwere kills before she hit the floor, picking them off like ducks in an arcade.

Big, hairy ones.

"Stand down." Caleb's voice came from behind her, and damned if it didn't do crazy things to her hormones. She'd been dreading the worst when he hadn't responded to her calls, but the feeling that flowed through her was more than relief at knowing her youngest teammate was alive and had her back. Even while she held another creature at gunpoint, even while hatred for that shaggy fuck poured out of her like sweat, Caleb's presence sent heat to parts of her body she had no business thinking about in a combat situation.

"Stand down," Caleb repeated, and added a confusing addendum. "Everyone."

Then he was in front of her, blocking her shot, putting himself in the path of any bullets she might trade with the vampweres. She looked into his eyes—sober, rational—though what he was doing and saying made no sense.

"It's okay, Tala. Stand down and I'll explain."

She glanced past him. The vampweres already stood at ease, their weapons limp at their sides. Stacy had dropped hers altogether, abandoning it on the table where Rafe lay as she clung to him.

Tala swallowed and raised her gun to the ceiling, elbow bent. From there, it would be easy to switch back into a firing position if need be, gravity's pull on the weapon working with her rather than against her. After all, it was a female's prerogative to change her mind. "Start talking."

"Leander returned to the Underground. Without Rafe." The smooth skin between Caleb's brows puckered, as if merely imagining Rafe alone and in a dangerous situation caused him physical pain. The older *were* was best friend, brother and father, all rolled into one.

"I had to come back for him. Convinced the others to follow me." He touched her arm, stroked her flesh with the rough pad of his thumb. "Sorry I didn't respond to you earlier. It wasn't safe."

No doubt he'd been slinking through halls, unable to send back a signal. Understandable. But she wasn't about to be distracted by his touch. No matter how good it felt. She shook him off.

"And what's with Josef Mengele in the lab coat?"

The lines between Caleb's eyes traveled up to his forehead, worry shifting to confusion. "That's Nikolas."

No shit. The vampire was legend, as a philanthropist, a lover and a cold-blooded killer. Tala made a mental note to ease up on the World War II quips around Caleb. Obviously, Junior had skipped out on his history lessons.

"I know who he is. What the hell does he think he's doing?"

"Saving Rafe's life."

Tala took in the doe-eyed expressions around the room and gripped her gun tighter, anxiety transforming the back of her neck into a pincushion. Had Nikolas hypnotized them all to receive such awe? Was she the only sane person left in the room?

Rafe was beyond saving, his chest motionless, as Stacy kissed his cheek and tangled her fingers through his hair. Any second now, he'd be transported back to their time. The same as Blaez.

"Please, Tala." Caleb's voice cracked with emotion. She had a sudden impulse to take him in her arms and comfort him.

She squashed it. Bad enough he was going soft without him dragging her along.

He cleared his throat and leveled his gaze. "Let Nikolas finish what he started."

Which was what, exactly? Nikolas had crossed *weres* and vampires to create Leander and his kind—a Heinz 57 smorgasbord. Going by that experiment, and the amount of mad scientist paraphernalia plugged into Rafe, her team leader could end up with wings. Or a pair of flippers. And be just as miserable as the vampweres he'd tried to help.

Caleb's full lips pulled tight. "What other choice do we have? Rafe's wound is too serious for the *heilen* to fix. The only thing that's kept his body from shutting down completely is T.J.'s blood."

Tala swung around, a sweeping three-sixty—her knees bent, her trigger finger hungry. "Where is he?"

"Gone to lick Andrion's wounds."

It was the first time Nikolas spoke, and he did so without looking up from his patient. She'd heard his voice before, in documentaries and recorded interviews, but those few sound bites didn't do him justice. With his dark tones and faint European accent, the smart-ass comment rolled off his tongue as if he were purring a love sonnet. Now she understood why females grew moist just listening to him.

He met her eyes, his smoldering. "But I have no doubt they'll return. Soon."

That spelled trouble. Andrion was lethal. But T.J? At first sight, he'd struck her as a simple yes-man, insipid and weak. But at Andrion's trial, she'd seen something else behind his public mask. Something dangerous.

"That's why we were hiding," Caleb explained. "And why the vampweres drew on you. We thought you were them."

It also explained why she'd had trouble sensing Rafe toward the end of her search. Judging from the bag of vampire plasma pumping into her team leader's arm, T.J. had made a significant donation, muddying Tala's bloodtracking markers, and delaying the automatic transport of Rafe's body back to their time.

Useless efforts both.

Tala laid her palm on Rafe's chest and felt nothing. No heartbeat. Not even a flutter. He was past help now.

She locked her teeth together. No way would she sob out loud. She'd spent the better part of a year wanting him, pining for him. She'd only begun to realize there was no future for them. Especially with Stacy in the picture.

In the last few days, she'd grown to admire the human. Even like her. Because, in the harsh light of reality, Stacy was no competition. A couple hundred years separated her and Rafe, an unbreachable chasm. Easier for the woman to fly across the Grand Canyon using a feather in each hand for propulsion than to have a lasting relationship with the werewolf. And, God help her, there was a part of Tala that found comfort in that knowledge.

Until now.

Yes, she'd hoped for an end to their romance. But not like this. Not at the expense of Rafe's life.

"Do the right thing."

It could have been her conscience talking. But it was Leander, who'd sidled up to her without warning.

Instinct took over. Tala snapped her arm around and hooked the barrel of her gun under his chin. Again, the sound of metal clacking against metal reverberated through the room as the vampweres cocked their weapons.

"Hold," their leader ordered. His hands drifted up and he assumed a position of surrender, even as Tala's gun dug into his flesh.

"Kill me, if you wish," he whispered. "But please, let Nikolas help your friend."

Leander gained a point in Tala's scorebook. Bravery wasn't easy with a loaded weapon at your throat in place of a necktie.

She backed off. A smidgeon. "You show a lot of confidence in someone who abandoned you."

"Actually…" The giant vampwere took a breath and let it out on a sigh. "We ran away." Then he knelt, a repentant sinner. Only he wasn't asking for Tala's forgiveness. He was looking at Nikolas.

"I wish you'd come to me when your illness began," the Master vampire said, making his way around the table. He placed his hand on Leander's head. "We could have worked through it. Together."

Tala choked on the heavy dollop of sentimentality. "Great. So you've kissed and made up. Now, you trust him?"

Leander blinked and gazed at her in confusion. "Nikolas is my Maker," he said simply, as if it explained everything.

The quick retort Tala planned stopped short of her lips. Like a wary diver on the ten-meter platform, it clung there, refusing to leap off her tongue.

She couldn't fault Leander for his eagerness to lap up every breadcrumb Nikolas offered. It didn't matter who you were—male, female, vampire, *were*—*hell*, even Frankenstein's monster. Every sentient creature sought acceptance from their creator, craved approval from their father, longed to kiss the hand of God.

You didn't have to be a monster to understand that need. Tala knew it well, from experience.

Still, she wasn't about to leave Rafe in Nikolas' hands. "Well, he's not *my* Maker. Or Rafe's. And he wouldn't want this."

She reached for the tubes in Rafe's arm, ready to set him free, but a firm hand caught her wrist.

"How do you know that?" Caleb asked, pulling her to him. "Things have changed since he met Stacy. If there's a chance to save him, we should take it."

His close proximity brought back the intimacies they'd shared in the hotel room. Kissing him had been a mistake. It muddled her thinking. Damn Rafe, but he'd been right all along. Sex with colleagues made for a toxic cocktail.

Tala tore out of Caleb's grasp and pointed to the body on the table. "Look at him. It's over. He's finished. Let him go."

"I can't." Caleb shook his head, his eyes clamped tight, as if he could block out the reality of losing Rafe if he only tried hard enough.

"You have to. I know you care about Rafe, but you must put feelings aside. Focus on what's best for him." Again, she wanted to comfort Caleb, to enfold him in her arms and rock him. She cradled her gun instead.

"Please, Caleb. Don't let Nikolas use him as a lab rat. Or turn him into something he'll loathe. Rafe won't thank you for saving his life, if that life's not worth living."

"It won't be that way. It won't." The words held conviction, but the shaky tone revealed Caleb's doubt. He coughed, pulled himself together and met her eye. "I vote, yes."

As gently as possible, Tala trained her voice to deliver the final blow. "And I say, no. Stalemate."

"Not quite." Caleb reached across Rafe's body and touched Stacy's forearm. The human lifted her head, her eyes red-rimmed, her expression dazed. "It's your call, Stacy."

An hour ago, Tala would have been pissed if one of her teammates asked for the human's opinion. Now it seemed right. Stacy was one of them. More than that, Tala knew Stacy would be on her side. On *Rafe's* side.

Stacy had seen, firsthand, how proud Rafe was of his pureblood heritage. How reluctant he'd been to accept vampire blood—vampire anything. She wouldn't want him poked and prodded after death any more than Tala did. Wouldn't want him coming back as anything other than himself.

"Caleb's right. It's your call."

The human pushed herself up from the table, as if it took all her strength. She looked almost as pale as Rafe—cheeks sunken, mouth turned down—like a wax candle, melting with grief.

She winced, as if engaged in some internal battle. Then her face went blank, save for the one tear that trickled down her cheek.

"Do it."

* * *

RAFE WALKED DOWN a long corridor. When and how he'd arrived here were questions he couldn't answer. His last memory was of pain, struggle. Now there was none, a strange cessation of feeling, as though he were caught between sleep and waking.

Weightless.

Warm air surged across his flesh. His bare feet padded against a marble floor, but made no sound. On either side of him, the walls shimmered like a desert mirage.

Was he dead? Hallucinating?

He slowed and fought to remember how he'd ended up in this strange place.

Nikolas' lab… stabbed…darkness…

Then there was light.

At the end of the hall, it shone. Its warmth, its beauty, reached out—urging him closer.

Rafe took another step then hesitated. He heard a whisper, a soft breeze caressing silk.

"Stay with me, Rafe."

He glanced back. Though he'd only taken a few steps, the corridor stretched on for miles behind him. Blackness closing in.

The light ahead grew warmer. He focused on it again, shielding his eyes. Silhouetted in the glow, was the figure of a female. He couldn't see her face. Didn't need to. Everything in his heart told him she was Daciana. Come to take him to the other side.

How many times had he wished for this moment? At the bottom of a bottle, at the end of a dream. Now that it was here, he wanted something else.

Life.

And Stacy.

Rafe wheeled around and headed back the way he'd come, his steps labored. He forced his feet to move, stumbling through the black void.

He fell, pulled himself up and trudged on.

Every mile brought more sensations. His body became heavier, a deathly cold surrounding him. Even so, he persevered. Desperate to reach his goal. *His love.*

He fell again—farther, harder. Back first, he slammed against ice hard steel. He gasped, opened his eyes and saw her—at his side, holding his hand and pleading with him.

"Rafe...don't leave me."

Dear God. Red-faced, tear-stained and her dark wig askew, she was still a beautiful, brave woman. *His* woman.

Through cracked lips, he managed to croak one word. "Never."

He cupped the back of her head with his miraculously healed hand, ditched the fake hair, and drew her to him, giving her a kiss to prove his vow. A brief one, packed with as much promise as he could muster. The tension in the air told him he didn't have time for more.

He kept his hold on her and looked around. Tala and Caleb were there and armed. The vampweres, too. And a stately bloodsucker in a lab coat whom Rafe recognized from photos.

Nikolas?

"What the fuck?" Grudgingly, he realized the expletive might be his last word. For, at that moment, in through the broken door, streamed a horde of goltos.

Ready for a late night bite.

CHAPTER THIRTY-THREE

STACY WINCED AS Rafe ripped the wires and tubes from his body. He seemed fine. A damned sight better than fine. Energized with a power beyond his own. And that kiss of his came packed with enough passion to curl her toes and inflame every inch of her.

It felt so right to have him back. His touch and the way he held her— *perfect*. Still, she wanted to freeze frame, take a moment, check him out and make sure he was *her* Rafe, not some warped Nikolas version.

With the goltos pouring into the room, there was no time. A tremor of fear and disgust laced through her as the things streamed in the open door, their pale arms hanging rubbery at their sides.

An inhuman wail followed the crunch of bone and the first victim fell. The male vampwere's blood sprayed onto the ceiling, droplets raining down onto Stacy's cheeks. Her heart and stomach lurched when three goltos raised the warrior's dismembered arm and proceeded to chomp on the limb.

Stacy clung to Rafe and hid her face against his chest to block out the image, but it replayed on her closed lids in gory detail. She inhaled Rafe's scent, used it to calm her, and turned back to the carnage in time to see Nikolas chuck his stained lab coat and step into the fray.

"Please. No snacking on the prisoners. They'll spoil your dinner."

So they were prisoners again, as well as the Catch of the Day. Stacy wiped the cold sweat from her upper lip as she wondered what Nikolas switched most, sides or his boxers.

He stretched his arms over his flock and cooed to them like a mother hen, which tempered their feeding frenzy somewhat but not enough for Stacy's comfort. In the absence of moveable lights to attract the goltos' attention, the team flung tables, lab equipment, whatever they could grab, into the path of the creatures.

Stacy hurled a couple of chairs at them and a clear trail to the lab's computer station opened up on her right. Her survival instincts screamed at her to stay with Rafe, but a deeper force drew her to what looked like the central processor.

"Time for our diversion," she told him and broke away.

Rafe shouted her name. Stacy didn't dare waste the time to look back at him. She yelled over the din as she ran to her goal.

"Cover me for ten seconds."

Behind her, the fight kicked up a notch. The screech of bullets mingled with cries of pain. Quickly, Stacy pulled the thumb drive from her pocket, steadied her hand and shoved the device into a free port. When the launch question appeared, she chose YES.

"Champ," Rafe called to her, his voice raw, urgent.

"Done." She whirled around to catch a clear, plastic bag with several metallic squares inside—all the size of Chiclets, but more weighty. The power supplies they'd come for, she presumed, and no doubt given to her by Rafe as a shield. Nikolas wouldn't risk anything happening to her while she carried his precious cargo. Holding it blanketed her with protection and left her heart belting out a top forty love song for the man who'd placed it in her care. In that moment, she knew Rafe had come back to her—unchanged, whole.

Hopefully, her plan would keep them all that way, because their side was losing ground fast. The goltos outnumbered them and, despite Nikolas' charisma, she doubted his ability to corral the herd. The once-human eating machines were relentless, ambling along with their zombie-like gait. Blood-tinged drool dripped from chins, mouths hung agape, teeth gnashed, ready to gnaw on flesh.

Thoughts of a painful, gruesome death would have crushed the breath from her, if not for Rafe. His strength and that determined jut of his chin injected her with another shot of bravery. She ran to him and, with a sweep of his arm, he tucked her behind him and whispered into her hair.

"Stick close this time, babe."

Taking the brunt of the threat himself, he cut a semicircular course to his left, his plan apparent to her. He was drawing the goltos in, maneuvering them away from the door, clearing a route for the team to escape.

Her muscles tensed as one of the creatures made eye contact and licked its lips. If Rafe couldn't coax the brainwashed horde to swing around just so, the goltos would end up forming a solid wall between them and the door, trapping everyone.

Fortunately, Nikolas was cooperating. Whether he realized what Rafe was trying to do and assisting them, or playing the Pied Piper to round up his ragtag crew for their own protection, the creatures followed him, lured by his presence like moths to his flame.

With the army now well into the room, Stacy's computer virus kicked in. The overhead fluorescents blinked on and off, and the words, 'Grab some jelly, this computer is toast,' streamed across the giant screen. She smiled, in spite of the threat around them. She'd forgotten Perry had added that bit.

Transfixed by the light show, the goltos stopped to *ooh* and *ah*. Rafe used the few seconds of reprieve to push a weapon into Stacy's free hand. He tilted his head toward the target and, together, they turned and fired on the contraption in the corner.

It exploded in a burst of color, a thousand sparklers set off at once. Glowing embers from the debris fell onto Stacy's clothes, leaving black dots the size of pinpricks. The odor of sulfur, strong and sharp, burned her eyes and stung the back of her nose, while Nikolas' shrieks of indignation jabbed at her ears.

With the room in chaos, they burst through the exit, the surviving vampweres bringing up the rear, all running full speed down the hall. Until Caleb's strained cry brought them all to a dead stop.

"We lost Tala."

* * *

TALA STOOD ON the opposite side of an upended desk, blocked from the doorway and her team. The goltos faced away from her, but she could tell by their bent heads and restless feet, their interest in the light show had waned. She knew it was stupid to speak, to do anything that would draw the attention of the mindless guards, but she had to confront the vampire scientist. Justice demanded it.

"Nikolas…come back with us."

He approached her, circling his salivating army, as if they were nothing more than a litter of playful puppies. "You need to go. Now."

She trained her gun on him. "Not without you."

"How touching." His smirk oozed matinee idol sex appeal. "Do you really expect me to return? To face charges of history tampering and genetic experimentation? To spend the rest of my days in a prison cell?" Nikolas' gaze flicked over her in a soft caress. "That doesn't sound very *pleasurable*, does it?"

Ignoring the seduction in his eyes, she focused on his list of crimes. Damn, she hated this part of the job. Arresting her own kind made her feel like the bad guy. Guilt whittled away at her conscience, the jagged splinters of it digging into her chest. It didn't help that she admired the vamp's accomplishments. That, and his age, put her in a tight spot. If Nikolas didn't come voluntarily there was no way to force him. He was, most likely, faster than her bullets. Tala had nothing but words and chutzpa with which to convince him to accompany her and face the music. She lowered her weapon and tried a different tactic.

"We can explain that Andrion coerced you—"

"A protégé coercing his Maker?" He snorted and somehow made it sound elegant. "I'm here of my own accord. To study the vampire virus and how it's adapted over time. A new strain developed in this year, replacing the one before it. Only through this type of hands-on research, will we find a cure. I've devoted myself to it."

"And you really believe the ends justify the means?" Since sweet talk hadn't worked with him, Tala summoned up a jab. "I always thought you were better than that."

"Better? No. When you've survived as long as I have, you'll understand that trite ideologies offer little comfort. Passion is all that remains, and nothing will keep me from mine."

His eyes were intense, probing, as if able to see into her soul. Whatever he found in that dark, empty spot must have suited him. He drew closer. "I want to walk in the sunshine again. I want to father children…the human way."

God help her, but the low tones of his voice made her womb quiver. A growl from his offspring quickly put that shit in check.

"I want to age and truly die," he went on. "As old as I am, those are sensations I haven't experienced. I want them." He pointed at the ruined tripping portal, at the sabotaged computer, and heaved a sigh. "And this is how you repay me for saving your friend's life? You destroy my equipment and steal my energy supply—which I'd have willingly shared. You've set me back months."

"That's the idea." Tala kicked the toppled desk into the path of the nearest golto. The bottom edge landed with a crack against the thing's shins. It staggered, fell and then managed to right itself—making more progress in its goal than Tala had, so far.

"If you don't come voluntarily, we'll be forced to return for you. Without the portal, you'll be stuck here. The world's a big place, but not large enough to hide from us indefinitely."

"I'm not hiding." His smile reminded Tala of a patient teacher doling out information to the class dunce. "I'm going farther back, step by step, century by century. In each new time, I'll build another portal, journeying closer and closer to the beginning, noting all the mutations of vampirism, until I find him."

"Him?"

Nikolas' face glowed in rapture. "The cure. The Savior."

"Jesus Christ," she swore, and then took in the upward rise of Nikolas' brows, his excited step toward her. Belatedly, she realized *Jesus Christ* was the answer to her question.

"You understand," he crooned, mistaking her for a kindred spirit. "Christ's blood is the cure. I know it."

The statement unnerved Tala, made her scalp crawl. She'd expected their conversation to be difficult, not downright eerie. Genius and insanity—Nikolas tread the fine line between them. She'd heard rumblings of secret sects of vampires who performed strange acts, believed in oddball fantasies. Did he honestly think a biblical character held the secret to his quest? Most deemed the idea an old wives' tale, ranked right up there with warnings about saucy looks freezing on faces.

If mental illness proved to be a factor in his case, the courts could grant leniency. Pity tinged her next plea. "Come back with me, Nikolas. Please."

The light in his eyes faded. Their camaraderie ended with his scowl. "You're not a believer. No matter. I will never submit. How could I leave my creations so abruptly? I am their father."

"I can't say much for your parenting skills." Especially now as the goltos zeroed in on her, chewing on air as they warmed up for the next chow-fest. She withdrew a step and collided with a solid wall, the hard, cold finality of it seeping into her back.

"Your own Maker isn't a saint, Tala."

A warning tingled at the top of her spine. Tala had always suspected the vamp who'd transformed her had an unseemly past. There'd been whispers. Sly looks exchanged between associates. She longed to ask Nikolas what he knew, but feared hearing his mad recollections.

What if she believed him?

"Go," he told her. "I can't hold them back much longer."

Looking at the mob, she knew he was right. She lifted her gun to defend herself. In an instant, Nikolas was at her side, his hand on hers, aiming the weapon at the floor.

Tala was powerless to protest. He was too strong for her—both physically and mentally. She stood there, paralyzed and at his mercy, her heart equally scared and excited by his control. Until he leaned in and kissed her cheek, his lips gentle. Loving.

"Go now, Tala. Save yourself."

At his touch, something inside her cracked open. Her rusty heart beat faster. Every nerve awakened, as if an unseen hand was stroking her skin with feathered softness. She blinked and snapped out of it, to discover Nikolas had already slipped away and now formed a barrier between her and his creations—his arms outstretched, like the Savior on the cross.

"This way, my children."

In a daze, Tala opened the door. She turned back to look for him and caught one, last glimpse—an angelic smile on his face—before he was engulfed by the throng.

* * *

RAFE SPRINTED TO the lab, the last place on earth he wanted to revisit, all the while praying Tala was okay. He'd already lost Blaez on this mission; he wasn't about to see another team member fall. No matter how much she pissed him off.

She'd disobeyed a direct order. Tala was supposed to have stayed in the hotel and kept Stacy safe. She'd done neither, jeopardizing both their lives.

While saving his.

He wanted to thank her. After he tore a strip off her. *If* she were still alive.

Damned if Caleb didn't have it bad for the headstrong female. Rafe saw that now. The fear in the kid's eyes when he'd reported Tala missing, and the way Caleb had fought to join Rafe's one-man rescue mission, it was heart-breakingly obvious. He'd been so emotional, Rafe ordered him to stay behind. Uncontrolled passion made soldiers do dumb things. Rafe could testify to that, firsthand.

He slowed a fraction—his ears pricking at the grunts of feeding goltos, his nostrils stinging with the scent of fresh blood. He scanned the area ahead for Tala and, as though his thoughts conjured her, she stepped into the hall, visibly shaken but all right. A dozen curses were ready on his tongue, any one of which would have turned her into vampire flambé. Instead, he closed the distance and clasped her to his chest in a fierce hug.

"Don't ever scare me like that again." Worried she'd misinterpret, he backed away and added, "Lieutenant."

The vibrancy of her eyes softened, all the sexual interest he'd ever felt from her replaced with a general amity. "Understood…*sir.*"

One problem solved. "Where's Nikolas?"

"He's…" Her voice cracked. "Gone."

Rafe sensed a story there. He'd get a full report from her later. For now, he needed to take advantage of Nikolas' departure and get out of this hellhole.

Rafe led the way, his mind racing. They couldn't exit the building the way they'd entered. That would force Stacy to endure a trek through the Underground again and he wouldn't—couldn't—do that to her.

He decided on the path of least resistance: to leave via the front doors.

Sure, there'd be people on the street that would witness their mass exodus, and the vampweres were as conspicuous as a troop of gorillas, but Rafe hoped twenty-first century folk would assume the lot of them were mascots for a new sports team, or costumed fans on their way to a local sci-fi convention.

He reached his compatriots, Stacy's smile and the touch of her hand filling his soul. And, when Caleb first eyed Tala, Rafe thought the pup would break into a cheerleader's pike jump.

At a half-jog, they made their way through the remaining corridors, weapons drawn and ready. He rounded the last corner, the main doors in view, just as a SWAT team stormed the building.

Rafe threw out his arms, driving his teammates and the vampweres behind a protective wall, but they'd already been spotted.

"Police! Drop your weapons!"

The sound of heeled boots squeaked across the tiled floor. Before his speedy dive for cover, Rafe had caught a glimpse of eight men, all heavily armed. The thud of footfalls told him more followed behind that first wave.

Great. They couldn't risk using the rear exit and meeting up with the goltos. Now, moving forward wasn't an option, either. Plus, he didn't know when and where Andrion and his flunky might pop out at them.

Time to think three-dimensionally. "Does this building have a stairwell?" he asked Leander. If they could make it to the roof, they might be able to jump over to another building, hopefully one with a fire escape.

"The goltos are blocking it."

"Fuck me." Their choices just got reduced. To *one*, if he were any judge. And it happened to be the worst alternative he could throw at the woman by his side.

* * *

STACY FELT ANOTHER tug on her arm, as Rafe switched directions again. He started back the way they'd come and then turned down a different corridor. One with a dead end.

He waved the others on ahead. As the army of bodies streamed past them, he cupped her shoulders and whirled her around.

"There's only one way out. Through the Underground."

Her body seized up, fear freezing her to the spot. She barely registered his next words.

"I need someone small and agile to lead the way. Someone who can get us to the other side fast."

He looked at her expectantly. Did he seriously want her to crawl through a tunnel? An enclosed space? In the dark? Her throat felt as if she'd inhaled sand. She pried her tongue from the roof of her mouth and took a gulp of air. "I'll go back to the entrance. Talk to the police."

"And maybe get shot in the process." His grip tightened.

She shook her head from side to side, her hair creating a curtain, shielding her from his scrutiny. The police wouldn't hurt her. She could walk out with her hands up, explain she was a victim—attacked and kidnapped by Andrion. "I can tell them you're helping me. To escape—"

"The vampires could be anywhere. More goltos, as well. It's not safe." He smoothed the strands away from her face and lifted her chin until she met his eyes. "I need you to lead, Stacy. The rest of us will be firing on our enemies, should they follow."

Lead the way? Through the blackness? With the others depending on her? Panic fisted in her chest. She curled her arms over the pain and squeezed in a breath. "I can't."

He took her hands, held them in his. "You can. You will. For the team."

Without waiting for a response, he led her down the hall to the others. The passageway distorted, the walls seeming to close in on her. Instinct told her that death waited at the end of the corridor.

Stacy locked her knees and dug her heels into the floor. Her palms were so slick with sweat she easily slipped out of Rafe's grasp. She backed away, using the wall for support. "No. We'll be better off with the cops. You and Caleb look human. Tala could pass—"

"And the vampweres?"

She hadn't thought about them, only wanted to find a way to avoid the terrors of her past. No matter the cost.

A chicken.

"We can't be captured, Stacy. There's no record of our existence. And if a doctor should examine us…"

They'd be poked and prodded within an inch of their lives, more interesting lab specimens than a troop of Sasquatch. Without ID, they'd be unable to explain their presence in the twenty-first century. Unable to complete their mission if they were locked up.

She balled her fists and stomped her feet—her regular routine when dealing with her phobia. It didn't help in the least. Until Rafe drew her to him. The sheer breadth of him and the warmth of that rock solid chest made her feel safe in the middle of all the madness.

"I won't let anything bad happen to you, Stacy. I swear it."

She grabbed onto that promise, remembered how he'd pleasured her in the darkened bathroom to replace her trauma with something beautiful. If she could hold onto that, lock all those old fears into the metaphorical closet where she'd once been held captive, and walk away from the past, she could get through this.

Maybe.

The sound of approaching gunfire decided it. Stacy jumped as each staccato shot cracked her eardrums. The police were closing in fast. Perhaps the vampires, too. She nodded and Rafe smiled. He grasped her elbow and led her down the hall, overtaking the team, all of them moving as silently as a mass of muscle-bound, weapon-packing, otherworldly creatures could.

He stopped at some sort of closet, its floor marred by a gaping hole, reminding Stacy of an open grave. A shiver rattled through her, until Rafe put his arms around her.

"You go in first. I'll follow."

Yes. If he were right there with her, she'd be okay. She hoped. She'd imagine him holding her, sheltering her, just like this, and she'd make it to the other side.

"Armina, you and your two male buddies will be next. Then you, Tala," Rafe continued, issuing orders. "And, because we don't want to lose you again, Lieutenant, Caleb will be right on your ass."

In spite of her fear, Stacy caught the gleam in the young man's eye. "Best view in town," he declared.

Tala's schoolmarm glare didn't dampen Caleb's mood one iota. He grinned like a kid holding a sack of candy on Halloween.

Speaking of scary days…

Stacy turned and peered into the hole, her heart pounding as loudly as the sporadic gunfire down the hall, her legs numb from fright.

"You can do this, champ," Rafe whispered, his breath fluttering over her skin. "I know you can."

Thoughts of a cave-in, of being eaten alive by rats—both images thrashed around her brain, along with the hundred other nightmares she'd imagined in her childhood prison. But Rafe believed in her. She concentrated on that and tried to believe too, as he lowered her into the gloom.

Below the earth, the temperature dropped. Noises from the world became muted. She heard only the sounds of her body—her quick, shallow breathing, her hair scraping against her neck.

She peered into the pulsing blackness, feeling as if her eyes were cranked opened to twice their normal size. Still, she saw nothing. Now she knew how Jonah felt when he began his slide to the whale's gullet. Or a mouse, swallowed whole and sucked down into the belly of a snake.

Panting, her breaths echoed off the dirt walls. At first, she tried crawling, her progress slow. Small enough to duck walk through the passage, she found that worked better. Faster. And, Lord help her, all she could think about was reaching the other side as quickly as possible.

She could sense Rafe in wolf form behind her, and hear the rustling progress of the others as they moved through the tunnel. When he used his nose to nudge her, she realized she'd stopped without knowing it.

A car rumbled overhead. She must be under the street by now, halfway there. Too far in to go back, too scared to move forward.

She forced one foot in front of the other, her shoes scraping against rubble, her shoulder bumping into the sides of the tunnel, her knees screaming.

The walls started to widen. She was almost there. A few more yards and she'd be home free. Pride replaced her lingering fear. Euphoria followed, whispering in her ear that she could accomplish anything. That she didn't have to hide from the public behind computers and websites anymore, worried that someone would discover her secret and expose her phobia.

She'd conquered it. Nailed it to the wall and used it for dart practice. All thanks to Rafe.

Then a howl reverberated through the passageway, followed by gun blasts that left her ears ringing. Something was after them—vampires, goltos or the cops.

She had to hurry. Now able to walk in a crouched position, she increased her pace, her legs straighter, her back bent.

At the end of the tunnel, she could see light, and a group of female vampweres waiting for them. Stacy bolted forward, clear to the other side— the aches of her body forgotten, the horror of that darkened place, a memory.

Rafe emerged from the tunnel and transformed to human. Naked, he reached for a gun, kept it trained on the opening.

One by one, the team emerged—Tala, Caleb, a vampwere, another— and then a second God-awful shriek ripped through the tunnel and burrowed deep into Stacy's bones. Without pause, Rafe and Stacy raced to either side of the opening, lending a hand to pull their comrades to safety.

Finally, Leander appeared. "The vamps took down the two males behind me. I'm last."

Rafe and Stacy grabbed Leander by the arms and tugged. The vampwere's head snapped back, his mouth open with an agonized cry. No sooner had they freed him from the tunnel than T. J. emerged from the darkness, blood dripping from his fangs.

Stacy reared back, desperate for something to use as a weapon, a short-lived hunt that ended with Rafe's one word command.

"Detonate."

Armina hit a switch and an explosion brought the cave entrance tumbling down. T.J. shot a look overhead, hissed, and was buried in a pile of rubble.

Cheers erupted. Stacy threw her arms around Rafe's neck, while Caleb gave a vampwere male a high five, and hollered, "At least we got one."

"I wouldn't make that assumption," Rafe said.

Stacy agreed. She'd seen Andrion come back after a police car squashed him. She doubted a bunch of rocks would hold T.J. for long. "We need to get out of here."

"And fast," Rafe said as he slipped into his jeans. He led the group down a passage and away from T.J. "Is there somewhere we can go, Leander? Somewhere your people aren't going to be noticed?"

The leader looked up from the two puncture wounds on his meaty calf. "There *is* a place. Nikolas knows about it, but I doubt he'll follow. Not now."

Tala joined them, her expression grave. "Not ever. If my guess is correct, the goltos are picking him out of their teeth."

Stacy grimaced. If she'd had any appetite, that picture squashed it.

Rafe wrapped an arm around the vampwere, becoming a crutch to help the injured hybrid walk. "Then this place sounds perfect. Because we have to get out of here. ASAP."

Stacy followed Rafe's gaze and saw a stirring in the rubble. Her skin rippled in response, a thousand goose bumps crawling over her flesh. If T.J. was digging his way out, they needed to be long gone before he succeeded.

She helped the vampweres grab their few possessions and, as a group, they headed off at a run into the crisp, night air—refugees in search of asylum.

CHAPTER THIRTY-FOUR

LEANDER'S 'PLACE' TURNED out to be the vampweres' old training barracks, far from the city, in the middle of a wooded area that they reached on foot. The spot was deserted, and had been for some time given the dust tickling Stacy's nose. Still, the quarters came equipped with a rustic dining hall, dorm rooms with beds and a good supply of hot water for the showers. There was also a fully stocked freezer filled with steaks and frozen vegetables. Not exactly Home Sweet Home, but it sure beat the bejeebers out of the Underground, and contained everything they needed to relax and regroup.

As long as the vampires didn't show up looking for a fight.

To be on the safe side, three of Leander's followers patrolled the periphery. While Rafe pulled out the meat to thaw, Stacy played with Baby Milan, now completely cured of her skin lesions, thanks to Rafe's *heilen* and Nikolas' power supply. The child held court from her blanket on top of one of the mess hall tables, surrounded by cooing vampweres—both female and male. Heck, after some initial hesitation, even Tala made goo-goo noises, showing a softer side that surprised Stacy all to hell.

Stacy had always wanted children of her own. Now, she couldn't imagine having them with anyone other than Rafe. He'd avoided unprotected sex with her, worried she'd become pregnant, so apparently he could father a baby with a human. But would their child be like her? Or a werewolf? And, if otherworldly creatures weren't accepted in the twenty-first century, how would a kid of mixed species fare?

Thoughts of what might lie ahead for her imagined child hurt her brain, though fantasies of practicing baby-making spread warmth to her cheeks and fire to her parts down under. When the man of those dreams approached and leaned close to her ear, his breath on her neck made her shiver with anticipation.

"Why don't we grab a shower and claim a room?" he asked, his voice deep and husky—intoxicating as a fine brandy. In her stomach, butterflies flapped around like mad things.

Stacy craved another bathroom session with him, wet and wild. She figured she'd earned it after coming through the tunnel like a trooper. But the shower wasn't private. Two large, communal washrooms stood on opposite sides of the long hall—one for females the other for males—and, with a gaggle of vampweres lathering up under the spray, it wasn't quite the intimate setting she envisioned for a romantic tryst.

When she emerged from the shower room, Rafe was loitering in the hall, waiting for her. He'd found some clean clothes, as had she, from a supply intended for the vampweres during their training. With Rafe's large size, the combat-style cotton pants and shirt fit him perfectly, and made him look doubly lethal, especially with his leather jacket slung over top. Meanwhile, Stacy had to roll up her sleeves and her pant legs to keep from tripping over herself.

Rafe clutched her hand and led her to the end of the corridor, and the dorm rooms. He opened one door. Inside were two single beds, already made up with linens and blankets. A bedside table separated them.

"We're going to need more room for what I've planned." Rafe made short work of redecorating, pushing the two mattresses together. "Shall we give it a try?"

He grasped her around the waist and then she was airborne. In a backward swan dive, she hit the mattress, giggling. Rafe followed her down, his lips on hers, his hands reaching under her clothes. When the rough pads of his fingers found her breasts, she had to bite down on her lower lip to keep from screaming out a hallelujah. She pulled her mouth away from his and filled her lungs with air, ready for more touching, more kissing. A rumbling noise stopped her. Not an earthquake, not a bear. The sound came from Rafe's stomach.

"Hungry?"

"For you? Famished."

She drew herself up, supporting her weight on her elbows. "Slow down, cowboy. I don't want you running out of gas halfway through because we haven't filled your tank."

He reached for her again—God, she loved his enthusiasm—but she thrust her palm against his chest. "We'll have plenty of time after dinner." She scooted out from under him and adjusted her shirt. "Right now, I'll get started on those steaks. Bet you like yours rare."

"Blue. And I'll cook. Steaks are my specialty. Just a little more appetizer first." He nibbled on her earlobe, producing a rumbling sound out of her. A moan of desire, not for food, but for him.

"Do you think this place comes stocked with condoms?"

"I'll get some," he whispered. "If I have to manufacture them myself."

She smiled against his cheek. It was almost perfect. She had her man—alive and sound. Even though their time together was coming to an end, and he couldn't promise to stay with her, she still wanted to make love with him. Nothing in her life had ever felt so right. But it didn't stop her from wanting more.

He hooked a finger under her chin, bringing her lips to his in a sweet kiss that defied the heat of the last few minutes. "I'd give anything to stay with you, Stacy. Believe it," he said, as if reading her mind. "But it's not in my power to change time. All I can do is love you now."

She blinked back tears. "Love?"

"Stacy, you must know…I'm in love with you."

His simple declaration took her breath away. A good thing. It made room in her chest for her heart to swell. She clung to him, her head on his shoulder, his next words releasing those tears.

"I fought it at first. I can't anymore. I know the timing is wrong. We met in the middle of a war you should never have been a part of. And, in a few more days, a couple of centuries will separate us. Please know, if there's a way for me to come back to you, I will." He bent his head. "I don't expect your love in return—"

Dear Lord, he already had it. Couldn't he see that? "I won't regret tonight with you, Rafe. If that's what you're wondering."

A sad smile spread across his lips. He flopped back onto the bed, bringing her with him, his arm around her.

Damn it. That's not what she meant to say. He'd just given her his heart, and she'd agreed to sleep with him, as if it were a business transaction.

She'd risked her life for him. *Of course,* she loved him. But how could she share the truth of her feelings while still being dishonest about herself? He didn't even know who she was. Not really.

"How long do we have?"

"Till Saturday. My mission comes to an end then."

End. Did he realize how apt the word was? If he didn't accomplish whatever it was he had to do, and survive all the danger it entailed, the mission could lead to his end, too.

She had to tell him. Now. Disclose her identity. She'd known men who wanted to sleep with her because of her last name. An equal number ran the other way when they learned it. But Rafe was different. He loved her. He'd said so. And, coming from the future, he wouldn't give a damn about her father's occupation. Whatever vague warning Andrion had given her about keeping her roots a secret had been rendered moot. The vampire had shown he was the bad guy in all of this. And his words of caution? A simple tactic to make her doubt Rafe.

It hadn't worked. She trusted the brave werewolf with her life. He'd proven he deserved that faith. She ran her fingers through his hair and took a breath…

* * *

223

RAFE TUCKED STACY against his side. Holding her, feeling her ribs expand and contract with each intake of air, feeling her heart beat next to his—this was what he wanted in life.

He'd remember her scent, her taste... forever. She'd healed the ache in him with her spirit. Her *human* spirit.

And if she didn't love him?

He'd survive the blow to his ego. It was better that she didn't return his feelings. She deserved so much more than he could give her.

She shifted her weight, leaning over him, cuddling close. "Saturday's going to be a busy day. For both of us."

Was this her way of asking if she'd be part of his mission? She'd become an integral member of the team, still he didn't want to endanger her life any longer. He'd have to rely solely on Caleb and Tala from now on, leaving the freshly healed Leander and the vampweres to protect Stacy. Though, truly, he wanted to be the one to shield her, to keep her safe.

"Gee, you really tensed up there," she told him, patting his biceps. "It's not like I'm going shopping for engagement rings, or anything."

Rings? That sounded good to him. *Weres* didn't normally do the gold band thing—just another item to take off and lose while shifting—but if that's what it took to mark Stacy as his, he was all for it. He fingered the silver necklace he'd given her. At the moment, it was a far better piece of jewelry than a ring. It would give her some defense against the vamps.

"Maybe we should get matching tattoos," he joked. "More permanent."

She laughed and shook her head. "Might not work with the dress I've picked out for Saturday. I'm going to a swanky yacht party."

Rafe swallowed, felt the tension creeping back into his body. A yacht party? What were the odds of two unrelated gatherings scheduled for the same day?

He'd always had a niggling feeling that the ripples in time had brought them together for a reason. That Stacy was somehow involved in the damage he was here to repair. Was she killed in the original skirmish? Struck by a stray bullet? If he had to lose her that way, he needed to know.

Tonight, he'd comb through the detailed information Blaez had on the mission, and familiarize himself with every last scrap of material, intel Rafe hadn't needed to concern himself with when he was second in command. As team leader, he wanted all the facts he could get his hands on. As Stacy's lover, his heart burned for it. In combat, in the heat of battle, he'd have seconds to make life and death decisions. He had to be prepared. Know the information as well as Blaez did—as well as Blaez *had*—and somehow find a way to safeguard the woman he loved.

"Who's party?"

"It's for my father." She gave him a shy look. "He's going to announce his presidential candidacy."

Rafe felt sick—his chest heavy, blood pounding in his ears. "Your father? Is he…"

"The Governor of Washington? Yes." She giggled again. "That's another reason I like you. Most guys want into my pants because I'm the Big Fella's daughter. You want me for me."

"You're Stacy…*Cadell*?" He hadn't asked her last name before, hadn't come across a Stacy in any connection to the governor.

"Anastasia Cadell, actually. Stacy's a short form. Hey, you really know your history? Does that mean my dad makes it to the oval office?" She covered her ears and laughed. "I know, you can't tell me." She kissed him, her lips lingering on his, innocent of the repercussions of her news. "I'll get those steaks started." Rafe watched her leave then turned over on his side.

Governor Cadell—the focal point of his mission. Before the vampires changed history, the dead man in the alleyway had assassinated Jonathan Cadell.

Rafe wondered—when Blaez had told him to look after Stacy, had his mentor understood who she was?

No. Blaez would have mentioned it. No matter how pressed for time they'd been. Blaez hadn't realized the truth, either.

Tragically, Rafe knew it now. To complete his mission, he had to hurt the woman he loved. By eliminating the man she adored.

Rafe scrubbed one hand down his face, the thought of eating now making his stomach turn. To restore history, the governor, Stacy's beloved father, had to die.

CHAPTER THIRTY-FIVE

STACY SIPPED HER champagne and tapped her toe to the DJ's Motown tunes, her stylish shoes pinching her feet. She teetered on them precariously under her full-length, backless gown, while Mr. Fitzhenry, her father's campaign manager and the yacht's procurer, droned on about strategies to the accompaniment of Mary Wells' *My Guy*.

Stacy hadn't heard from *her* guy in two days.

They hadn't made love, either.

Although she'd longed for Rafe's body, the memories he'd left her with that last night were more enduring.

"As much as I want to be inside you," he'd said, "I need you to know my desire for you goes deeper." After giving her a bouquet of wildflowers, he'd held and kissed her all night, revealing a romantic side she'd hardly expected from a big, bad werewolf.

Then he was gone. Did he regret his words of love? Words she hadn't returned?

She shook her head, dying a little. What the hell was wrong with her? Every time she'd thought to tell him, those old insecurities left her mute. Instead of blurting out her feelings, she'd waited for an opening line, for him to say those three words to her again.

He hadn't.

Now, forty-eight hours later, there was still no Rafe. No Caleb, either. And she'd hardly seen Tala.

Rafe had explained they needed to do damage control after the debacle at Andrion's. Wipe the events clean from the minds of the humans involved. More importantly, they had to prepare for the crucial last leg of their mission—to right the wrongs created by the murder of that man in the alley.

Stacy understood. She'd willingly endure anything to help them succeed and survive. So she'd stayed at the vampweres' camp and worried, under Leander's watchful eye.

She could only pray the team was okay. That Rafe still lived. It killed her not knowing. Though, once he returned to his century, she'd be in exactly the same boat. She'd drive herself crazy stressing over him, wondering where he was, *how* he was. She had to force herself to focus on what they'd had, cherish the time they'd spent together, and hold that last night in her heart forever.

Late this morning, a tight-lipped Tala had appeared at the vampweres' barracks to escort Stacy to her condo. The redhead waited in silence while Stacy dressed, and while Carey weaved her hair into an elegant updo. Tala then brought her to the yacht and promptly disappeared, leaving Stacy nervous and edgy.

She fidgeted with her lacquered hair to make sure it was still in place, catching a view of the clouds streaking across the sky, like white ink dispersed in blue water. Vulturous seagulls careened overhead, searching for any stray hors d'oeuvres that landed on the yacht's deck. Stacy sidestepped as one bird flew directly above her, sure it planned to dive bomb her with a big splat of guano.

Oh, well. Wasn't that supposed to be good luck? She'd happily take a direct hit, if it somehow helped Rafe.

The campaign manager touched her arm, jerking Stacy out of her daydream. "Hope to see you on the dance floor," he said, and wandered off to speak to the press.

Her dad rested a hand on her waist and sent her a smirk. "I thought he'd never shut up." Always the consummate politician in public, her dad said the darnedest things when it was just the two of them, solely to crack her up.

She clinked her glass against his. "To the next President of the United States."

He sobered, his eyes moist. "To *you*, Stacy."

The last time she saw him looking this sentimental was when he'd pulled out the old home movies and made her suffer through endless hours of...herself. *Stacy* cutting her first tooth, *Stacy* riding her first two-wheeler, and *Stacy* trick-or-treating dressed as an iPod—her all time favorite costume, an outfit they'd created together.

"I want you to know how very proud I am of you, Stacy. I only regret I wasn't there for you when you needed me most—"

She lifted herself up higher on her aching toes and kissed him on the cheek. "You didn't know, Dad. Once you did, you were there for me one hundred percent. A hundred and *fifty* percent." Damn. She was tearing up, too.

"I'm not always going to be here for you, honey. But you'll manage just fine without me. You've got the brains and determination to do whatever you set your mind to. You're the bravest person I know. You make me fearless."

That did it. She gushed like a fountain. Why hadn't she worn her waterproof mascara? "I'd better fix my makeup in the ladies' room."

"One last hug, before you go."

She slipped into his familiar embrace, filling her lungs with that aftershave he'd worn for as long as she could remember—some cheap stuff she'd bought him for Christmas when she was a kid, which he still insisted on wearing. A scent he managed to pull off with aplomb. When she made a move to go, he held on for a few more seconds.

"Okay, now I'm getting your tie wet," she said with a watery laugh, digging in her beaded purse for a tissue to dab her eyes. "Give me ten minutes. Promise you won't make your announcement until I get back."

"Promise." He let her go with a smile and a wink.

She mopped herself up as she steered through the clusters of people, her heart kicking into gear when she spotted him on the far side of the dance floor.

Rafe.

Like the other male guests at the black and white event, he wore a tux. But he filled it out like no other man on the planet. His wide chest tapered down into slim hips. His muscles rippled, barely concealed beneath the fabric of his clothes.

God help her, everything about him screamed *wild*—untamed despite the suit, and hot enough to use as a griddle.

She couldn't stop the grin that stretched across her face, so wide it almost hurt. He'd come back. Come to surprise her. To let her know his job was finished and to wish her a final good-bye. Her thighs practically hummed as she looped her way around the gyrating dancers to reach him.

"Tell me I'm not dreaming."

His eyes shone. When he licked his lips she almost leapt into his arms, eager for some tongue action herself. Then his expression changed. He dipped his head and looked from side to side, checking out the crowd before meeting her gaze again.

"Miss Cadell, I presume."

So that's the way he wanted to play it—casually, as if meeting for the first time. To protect her, as always, she imagined. Reporters were in attendance. After her father's announcement, the paparazzi would be watching her every move, eager for gossip.

The driving beat of *My World Is Empty Without You* replaced the last song, another classic by Diana Ross and the Supremes.

"Do you dance?"

He gave her a quizzical look, his brow furrowed, as if her query was the most ludicrous one he'd ever heard. The next moment, the breath whooshed from her lungs as he crushed her to his chest and began whirling her around the dance floor, like Gene Kelly on steroids.

"I'm beginning to think there's nothing you can't do."

"I don't knit."

She laughed. "Good. Sweaters are overrated."

He led her past the refreshment table and Mr. Fitzhenry, who stared at them open-mouthed, an hors d'oeuvre slipping from his fingers and falling onto the deck. Another treat for the gulls.

Rafe danced her right into the interior of the ship. Was he hoping to find a cabin? To get her alone somewhere private?

"Couldn't stay away from me, huh?"

His lips curved into a smile. A sad one. "Something like that."

Was he upset about leaving her to return to his own time? Or was there more to it? "Is your mission complete?"

He avoided her eyes, his gaze slipping down to the chain he'd given her. He ran a fingertip along it and her skin, making her tremble. "You're still wearing the necklace."

"I've never taken it off," she murmured. "I never will."

"Good. The vamps...we're expecting them."

The news doused her ardor like a bucket of ice water. Now, she trembled with fear. "Here? Why?"

She could only assume the team had succeeded in their assignment and Andrion was after them, bent on revenge. Only that didn't make sense. Rafe would have led his nemesis to a secluded place for their final confrontation. Not to a boat filled with innocent humans. He wouldn't put their lives at risk. Or hers.

Before she could question him further, a couple of guests wandered through the passageway. Rafe clutched her arm and eased her to one side, speaking in a hoarse whisper. "If they come at you, do whatever you can to escape. Don't put yourself in danger."

"Rafe... you're scaring me."

"I mean to. You know what they're capable of."

Stacy felt a presence slip in behind her. A hand seized her wrist. She turned to find Tala, her grip like iron.

"We're ready, Rafe."

He nodded to the redhead. "Stay with her, Tala. Keep her safe."

Rafe took a step closer, as if he might give Stacy a final kiss. Then he fisted his hands, swiveled on his heel, and strode away.

"Wait!" Stacy bucked against her captor, but the vampire's grasp was firm. Tala easily hustled her into the nearest cabin, the guest bedroom Stacy's father had used to rehearse his speech. She released Stacy, secured the door, then planted herself between it and her captive, an impenetrable wall.

"What's going on?" Overhead, Stacy heard shouts and the thud of heavy boots.

Tala looked at the ceiling, her mouth a tight slash. "It's started."

Stacy's stomach lurched up under her diaphragm. Whatever *it* was, she had to get to her father. Warn him about the attack.

After she got through Tala.

Strength-wise, the vampire outmatched her. Playing the sympathy card wouldn't work, either. Stacy knew she had to find a way to outsmart her prison guard. Just no idea how.

As if in answer to her prayers, the cabin door burst open, knocking Tala clear across the room. In her keeper's place stood a vision that was anything but heaven sent. Andrion, dressed to kill in a white, ruffled shirt, leered down at Stacy, strangling her next breath.

In a blind panic, she ran her hand over the desk, searching for anything to use as a weapon. A pen, paper, her dad's computer tablet—hell, didn't anyone buy letter openers anymore?

The lamp would have to do. Lungs bursting, she pulled it off the writing table and raised it above her head, trying to look fearsome even while her hand shook.

Andrion only chuckled. "What a pretty picture you make."

His laughter stopped when she smashed the bulb on the corner of the desk, shattering the glass. If she couldn't electrocute the fucker, she could damn well rub the broken ends into his flesh.

Working up her courage, she let out a rebel yell and began her charge. That's when Tala intervened, launching herself full speed at Andrion. With a simple, effortless swing, he bashed her across the face. The redhead crashed into the wall, leaving it dented, and slid to the floor. Motionless.

A scream locked in Stacy's throat. She retreated as Andrion approached—his fangs extended, his eyes eating her up.

CHAPTER THIRTY-SIX

STACY DOVE FOR the opposite side of the desk, her weapon held high.

"Resistance," Andrion purred, "usually makes me harder."

The vamp didn't lie. She could see the outline of a huge erection through his pants. Her horror ratcheted up another notch as she imagined all the ways he could violate her.

Before using his fangs.

She remembered the tunnel and embraced the fear, willed the primal rush to bubble up into rage. Losing wasn't an option. She would survive, help Rafe, and escape with her father. No matter what. She gritted her teeth as Andrion undulated toward her, a lounge lizard trolling for fresh meat.

"You've seen what I can do with a woman, Stacy. I did that to entice you into my world. To show you how it would be with me. Don't pretend you weren't watching when I made love to the twins."

Stacy swallowed to suppress her gag reflex. "What I saw didn't involve love."

"They enjoyed it."

"Not for long. The goltos attacked them."

"An occupational hazard." He shrugged and took another step closer, while undoing the top buttons of his pretty shirt. "That wouldn't happen to you. Not if you were my mate, if I made you immortal."

Without missing a beat, Andrion sneaked a hand under her raised arm to trace the curve of her breast. Stacy yowled with indignation and brought her weapon down hard, barely grazing him, his vampire speed giving him an extra advantage. As if he didn't already have weight, height and might on his side.

A lucky break—that's all she needed. Heart pounding so fast she thought it would short-circuit, she clutched the end of the lamp tighter and took a batter's stance, ready to hammer the crap out of him.

His red eyes darkened and she cringed, prepared for his assault. Andrion didn't advance; instead his expression turned contrite. He sat on the bed and crossed his wrists over his lap, hiding the bulge, his body language subdued.

Though he'd given her space, she didn't relax her guard. Stacy had no doubt her adversary could snap her neck in the time it took to blink.

"I've had several lifetimes to perfect my lovemaking skills. Rafe's only had this one. Five minutes with me and you'll forget all about him."

Five minutes? Is that all you've got?

She almost blurted out the taunt, but stopped herself. Mocking him wasn't going to save her. Andrion could easily take what he wanted by force—her blood, her sex, her life. Still, he hesitated? Was he toying with her? Or was it possible he wanted her consent?

"Tell me more." She surprised herself with the coolness of her delivery. Andrion looked intrigued, too. He patted the mattress beside him, offering her a seat, reminding Stacy of the spider and the fly story.

She remained standing and locked her gaze on him, while checking her peripheral vision for Tala. From Stacy's vantage point, she could no longer see the redhead's crumpled body on the opposite side of the room. The bed blocked her view.

Was Tala unconscious? Truly dead? Either way, Stacy couldn't get to her. She couldn't rely on her fallen comrade for help, either.

"I can offer you more, Stacy. Starting with protection for the ones you love. Your mutt has a bad track record with that."

A bitter taste flooded Stacy's mouth. No one belittled her man. "None of that was his fault. It's because of you Daciana and Blaez are gone."

Andrion hung his head low, while his eyes danced with mischief. "What can I say? I'm a prick. Reform me."

In spite of her revulsion, his half-assed attempt at repentance made her laugh. "I should look at you as a make work project? No thanks."

"I thought women liked bad boys."

"Bad, maybe. Evil, not so much."

"Evil?" He winced. "Oh, Stacy. Do you think this is about good and evil? That the world and its people are so neatly divided into two groups? Hitler was an artist at heart, who loved his dog and lavished friends with expensive gifts. I once saw him rock a crying baby to sleep in his arms."

Not something she wanted to hear about the most hated man in history. Of course, sociopaths made a charming bunch. She didn't doubt Andrion could soothe a fussy child, himself. If he stood to profit by the action.

"I'm the hero here, Stacy," he said, the grandiose line voiced with a lover's hush. "Rafe's the bad guy. He *will* hurt you in the end."

Another warning about Rafe. This one prickled. The werewolf had been missing in action for two days and had behaved strangely when he finally showed up on deck. Was Andrion jealous? Or was there more to his words of caution?

"Why are you trying so hard to convince me?"

"I want your loyalty, Stacy. Need it. Because what happens here today decides the future for all of us."

He glided to the window, his back to her. Now was the time to run for it. She'd never get a better chance. Curiosity, though, secured her feet to the floor, stickier than flypaper. Andrion controlled her as much with it as he'd done before with her fear.

"You have two paths, Stacy. Go along as you are, safe behind your computer monitor. Or fulfill your political destiny."

She snorted at the notion. *Political destiny?* She'd always avoided public life—afraid someone would discover the severity of her panic attacks and use her terror of enclosed, dark places to ridicule her. A fear that was now in the past, thanks to Rafe.

At the sound of her derision, Andrion swiveled and faced her. "I knew you'd feel that way. That's why I sought to protect you from it. By protecting your father." He leveled his gaze and approached. "I ordered the murder of his assassin...Paul Smiley."

Stacy went numb. "The dead man in the alley?"

The killing seemed a lifetime ago, but that was the start of it all, the moment when she first became enmeshed in this dangerous, new world.

When she first met Rafe.

He'd told her the team was there to protect the assassin. Now, Andrion was saying that his intervention, his hit on Smiley, had saved her father's life. If Rafe had intervened...

Andrion gave her a solemn nod. "I arranged the meeting that brought you to the alley. I wish I could have spared you from the violence, but I knew you needed to witness Smiley's demise, and understand my part in it, to fully appreciate how our interests are linked. You love your father. You don't want to see him hurt. *I* don't want the *weres* to come out of hiding. Both things hinge on you."

On *her*? Was that possible? And why hadn't Rafe told her? He'd never mentioned her father. Then again, until that final night with him, she hadn't revealed her last name.

Even though she didn't trust Andrion, on a gut level, she feared what he said was true. She'd been a pawn from the start, each side kidnapping her, fighting over her. She grasped the desk behind her, desperate for something real to hang on to.

"If you're with me," Andrion continued, "you can, if you wish, still take over your father's role as Governor. As you originally did before history changed. However, instead of doing it for boring altruistic reasons, you can work for our personal interests."

"Which are?" The question came out in a whisper. She couldn't manage the strength for more.

"Gaining power. Building wealth. Having fun." He leaned in, his lips inches from hers. "What do you say, Stacy? Be with me forever."

She wrenched away, spitting out all her hatred in words. "I'll take Rafe's right now over your forever."

The vampire pouted. "I'm sorry to hear that, Stacy. You can never be with him. You know that, don't you? He'll be leaving on the next express back to his time. But *I'll* be here."

He reached for his fly, unzipped it. "And, if you treat me *very nicely*, I can still save your father from Rafe."

Stacy struggled for air, but a heavy weight pressed against her chest, as if all the oxygen had seeped out of the room. Andrion's mouth moved, but she couldn't hear him, her own thoughts tumbling over each other, drowning out everything else.

Rafe was here to kill her father? *That* was his mission? The murder of a good and kind man would fix history and make everything right? How could that be?

Tears blinded her as her hearing returned—the light rustling of clothes taking on the harsh finality of a death knell as Andrion lowered his pants, eager to barter sex for her dad's life.

"If Rafe is successful, I will have to kill you, Stacy. I can't risk you destroying everything I've worked for. Unless you're willing to join us."

Could she make the trade? Let him fuck her? Turn her? In order to save her father?

Stacy dropped her weapon. She let the tears roll down her cheeks. Mopping them up would take too much energy, and she had none to spare.

Andrion stepped out of his pants, slithered closer, and grasped her limp shoulders. She let out a sigh—hoping he'd mistake it for passion instead of revulsion——and tilted her head, offering her neck to him.

"Lovely," he crooned. "I knew you'd see things my way."

His fangs elongated as he inched forward. He lifted a curled tendril of Carey's creation then jerked away with a cry. Smoke spiraled up from his fingers, followed by the odor of burnt flesh. The impression of her silver necklace branded his hand.

Summoning a roar from deep within her belly, she swung back her knee and, with every ounce of strength she had, rammed it into his crotch.

The maneuver worked as well on this male vampire as it did on human ones. Andrion toppled over, his torso bowing to meet his thighs, his eyes rolling back.

In the next instant, a loud blast deafened Stacy. Cool droplets hit her face and dress, as Andrion's blood fell down around her like a spring shower.

The vampire kept his hands busy—one trapped between his legs, shielding his injured gonads. The other, Andrion used to apply pressure to his new injury—the bloody mess left of his shoulder. All while he howled in pain.

Stacy looked past him to see Tala leaning against the door, a smoking gun in her hand.

The redhead clicked her tongue. "Andrion…haven't you ever heard that *no* means *no?*"

* * *

TALA'S AIM WAS off. The broken arm she nursed sure didn't help. She fired again, but Andrion dodged right and the bullet screamed into a wall.

Damn it. Her weapon that shot wooden bullets had ended up skidding halfway across the cabin in their earlier skirmish. She couldn't do much damage to him with her full silver jackets, but she had no other option, so continued to pump the remaining bullets into his chest. He stalled each time she hit her mark, but didn't stop. When the *zilva-kieg* was out of ammo, she knew she was done for.

But she didn't plan to go down without a fight. Not when Rafe was counting on her to protect Stacy. So she belted Andrion across the chops, the empty gun now a club.

That got a reaction. From him and her throbbing arm. The pain ripped into her like a jagged edge through flesh. A sob shot out of her mouth before she could stop it. She felt ready to collapse, but held tight to her momentary lead. While Andrion was doing his best imitation of a yogi in a back bend, she used her *zilva-kieg* as if it were a set of brass knuckles and plowed it into his gut.

The shots may not have killed him, but they'd weakened him. That much was clear. Or she wouldn't have lasted this long. While he was bent over, she took the opportunity to knee him in the face.

The last move in her.

Andrion came up swinging. While she blocked, expecting a blow to her upper body, he kicked low, smashing bone and knocking her leg out from under her. She fell hard, used her good leg to trip him, but missed.

He grabbed her by the hair and bashed her head against the wall. White flashes exploded across her closed lids with each whack, until she saw nothing—felt nothing. Her last thought involved Stacy and a hope that the human had escaped. Then darkness embraced her.

CHAPTER THIRTY-SEVEN

RAFE TOOK IN the beauty around him—the elegance of the yacht, the grace of the dancers, the warmth of the sun on his face—and felt every kind of rotten he could name.

He'd disobeyed his own first rule as an assassin: Don't get close to the subject. Not *emotionally*. Although he'd never met Jonathan Cadell, Rafe knew from Stacy he was a devoted father, an honest politician, a good man.

And, to restore history, Rafe had to take this good man down.

The act would rip into Stacy. That truth alone made it hard for Rafe to breathe, made his heart feel like a traitor for continuing to beat. He'd sooner die than hurt her.

He remembered that iconic picture of Anastasia Cadell from his research. The blurred B&W newspaper photo showed her cradling the dying governor, her lips pulled back in a silent scream, her features twisted with anguish. No wonder Rafe hadn't recognized the woman as Stacy, or understood her connection to his mission.

Until she'd told him her full name.

Damn it to hell. Right where he was going to land in her books, if she figured out what he'd really been sent to do.

He'd spent the last few days trying to come up with some way to complete his mission without executing the governor. It wouldn't be the first time the team had staged an assassination. But, at a public event, out in the open, Rafe doubted the Great Houdini could pull off such legerdemain.

Above the salty tang of the ocean breeze, Rafe smelled vampires and every fine hair on his body rose. The urge to wolf-it, overwhelming—the need to tear the bloodsuckers apart, insatiable.

He battened down the animal within and focused. He had only a short window of opportunity. News reports of the time suggested Jonathan Cadell would be alone at the bow of the ship for a mere three minutes. Still, it would have been long enough for Smiley to make his move.

It would have to do for Rafe, too. Between Tala guarding Stacy, and Caleb on vamp watch, the team was stretched as far as it could go without snapping.

He spied his target against the ship's railing—a tall man with a kind face, silhouetted against the open sky. Rafe clutched the handle of his twenty-first century gun, the weapon Smiley would have used if he'd lived long enough to steal it, its weight light compared to Rafe's conscience. Once he set this in motion, there was no going back. He'd be gone—dead or returned to his time—and Stacy would have to deal with the misery of his actions.

He raised the gun to hip level, shielding it from view with his body as best he could, and prayed his plan worked.

"Rafe!"

The one-word cry bored into him. Shooting a glance over his shoulder, he saw Stacy racing to him on a full-speed collision course.

As much as he'd longed to see her again, his heart plummeted as though it were attached to one of the ship's anchors. The thought of her witnessing what he was about to do flayed him. Worse, if she'd escaped from Tala, it could mean only one thing. The vampires had attacked Stacy, and his female team member had died defending the human. *Really* died. Another fatality on his watch.

Stacy flew at him, her eyes wild. "Please, don't do this."

The plea left him speechless, horrorstruck. She knew the truth. Or, at least, part of it. And he had no time to explain the rest. Thirty seconds had ticked by and the governor was already in motion. Soon, he'd be out of range, lost in the crowd. Rafe's window of opportunity was closing fast.

Stacy looked down at his gun and then back up at his face. Her grip tightened, her fingers clawing at him. "You're going to kill someone I love. You, more than anyone, know how that feels."

He did, and wished with everything in him that he could hold Stacy in his arms one last time and give her the reassurances she needed. Instead, he pushed her out of his way and took a step toward his mark.

She latched onto him again. "How can you do this to me? Why didn't you tell me? Prepare me?"

He drew her aside, slipping behind a bulkhead, placing it between them and the unwanted gaze of any curious partygoers. "I didn't know you were his daughter until our last night together."

He couldn't tell her more. A million things could go wrong in the next few minutes, so he couldn't make any promises. They might *all* end up dead. And now that she'd appeared on the scene, he needed her genuine reaction for those jerks behind the cameras to immortalize her pain. To snap the photo that would help catapult her to fame and change her destiny.

"It has to be this way, Stacy. If I could have found a way to spare you, I would have." Rafe reached out and dried her damp cheek with his hand. "Trust me."

"Trust you?" Stacy recoiled from his touch, her eyes turning from fire to ice. "I *hate* you."

She may as well have eviscerated him on the spot, cut him open for all the world to see. He gritted his teeth and swallowed his own tears before they could form. "And I don't blame you for it."

* * *

STACY HAD KNOWN exactly where she'd find her father. Before a speech, he always needed some private time to collect his thoughts. That she'd discover him on the secluded bow overlooking the harbor was a given. That she'd found Rafe there too, stirred a feeling of dread deep within her. At that moment, she knew everything Andrion had told her was true.

Rafe was here to kill her dad.

She'd thought she could get through to the werewolf, use his professed love for her to change his mind. She'd fallen for his heart-on-sleeve pillow talk, but all of it was a lie. She could see that now. His eyes were cold, his face stone. Words and tears were useless against a trained killer.

So she ran to her father, intent on shielding him with her own body. If she were truly needed to secure the future, Rafe wouldn't dare risk killing her.

As she raced to her parent, he turned, saw her and smiled—a smile filled with so much love and pride her heart splintered. His gaze shifted higher and she realized he was looking at Rafe. Her father's smile faded and he nodded, just once, as if he recognized the werewolf and was giving him the green light. But how could that be?

Her question floundered on her tongue as four vamps appeared behind Rafe. The sound of breaking glass split the air and her former lover crumpled.

T.J.—dressed in a candy pink tux and looking no worse for wear after the cave-in—stood over Rafe's lifeless body clutching the neck of a broken bottle. Champagne mingled with the blood oozing from Rafe's head, making the deck sticky.

She made a move to help Rafe, her turncoat of a heart remembering only the love between them. Before her brain clicked in to stop her, Andrion stepped forward, blocking her way.

"What a waste," he said. "Dom Pérignon '96 was an excellent year."

Stacy had no stomach to discuss vintage wines with the vampires—either the two she knew and feared or the duo of muscled flunkies guarding their flanks. She darted around the bulkhead and waved her arms over her head, hoping to draw someone's attention. The D.J. still blasted out his tunes. The dancers swayed and mouths were flapping in conversation, no one yet registering the danger nearby. Only her father saw her need and rushed to help her. The very person she wanted to protect.

She motioned for him to stay put, just as a sharp tug on her gown pulled her back, face to face with Andrion. He clutched Rafe's gun in his hand and pointed it directly at her.

"Sorry, Stacy. I offered you a way out, but I can't have you ruining my empire. No one kicks me in the balls twice."

She screamed a pathetic squeak that didn't carry over the roar of the music, but left her throat raw and her lungs desperate for oxygen. With nowhere to run, and sensing her sacrifice would save her father's life, Stacy held to the spot, even as her legs quaked and her knees threatened to buckle. When Andrion pulled the trigger, she saw the gun's flash, heard the loud crack. She anticipated the pain and waited for death's embrace.

It didn't come. Her ears rang and she'd almost wet herself, but she was still alive.

Andrion stared at the gun with incredulity. "Blanks?"

As T.J. drew his own weapon and aimed it at her, Rafe stirred, grasped the vampire's ankles and pulled his pink clad legs out from under him.

T.J.'s gun discharged as he crashed to the deck. Seconds later, the possum-playing Rafe leapt at Andrion, transforming mid-jump and shedding his clothes as he sailed through the air. Teeth bared, he clamped his powerful wolf jaws around his enemy's throat.

Andrion's cry was almost as loud as T.J.'s next gunshot. The bullet streaked past Stacy's shoulder, taking a strip of her with it. She clasped the stinging gash with her free hand, just as Rafe gave a final twist and ripped Andrion's head from his body.

Stacy cowered against the wall to shelter herself from the blood's spray, but the vampire turned to dust before he hit the ground. Blown away on the wind.

Seeing the carnage, T.J.'s cocky expression crumbled. His face scrunched up, as if he were about to cry, his pain so tangible, Stacy almost felt sorry for him. Until a sly grin twisted his mouth. He signaled to the other two vamps and they ran. The trio jumped onto the dock, lost from view in the time it took Stacy to draw her next breath.

As she fell to her knees to embrace her wolf savior, to sink her face into his warm, thick fur, she was startled by the silence. No music played. All she heard were a few isolated gasps from the crowd and the sound of waves as they slapped against the hull.

She pivoted to find her father, the front of his white shirt turning red. She barely acknowledged the blood before he stumbled and fell.

He'd taken the bullet meant for her.

"No!" She ran to him, sliding the last few feet that separated them, and cradled him in her arms.

"Someone, get a doctor," she hollered at the inert crowd. "Right fucking now!" A few people sprang into action. Most stood staring.

"Don't blame yourself," her father murmured, choking on his words. "Or Rafe. He came to me. Explained. Planned another way out. One with special effects that would have made George Lucas jealous." He tried to laugh and coughed instead, blood bubbling past his lips. "We knew it might not work. That it still might come to this. But I'd do anything to keep you safe."

"Shhhh. Save your strength." Stacy wanted to show him a brave face but her hands trembled as she undid his tie, loosened his collar. She needed something to apply pressure to his chest injury and reached for his pocket handkerchief. Wrapped up in it, she found the remains of a fake blood pack, punctured by a real bullet. Stacy palmed the evidence of Rafe's failed solution, and held the white pocket square against the real wound, from which real blood flowed.

She clasped her father tighter, hoping sheer willpower would somehow keep him alive. "Daddy, please. Stay with me."

He shook his head, a tear splashing onto his cheek. "Love you, Stacy. Always."

Her dad smiled and then the light in his eyes dimmed. With a last sigh, her father's body went slack, and the ocean air grew heavy with sorrow.

Screams erupted from the crowd, matching the screeches of the gulls overhead. People turned away, bunched together and rushed toward the exit. Some stood in shock, pushed and jostled by those trying to escape.

Through her tears, Stacy saw a bruised and bloody Caleb carrying Tala's broken body. They stood at the far edge of the yacht with Rafe, who was now back to human form and clutching the remnants of his tattered clothes to his waist for decency's sake. As if there was anything decent about what had just occurred.

Stacy's heart swelled, knowing Rafe had planned a way to save the future without killing her father. Then that same heart broke, knowing her last words to her lover were said in hatred. And that her father was still gone. Lost to her.

She'd caused this. By interfering. She should have trusted Rafe and let him do his job. By stepping in, by trying to change the events, she'd actually caused them to unfold.

As reporters crowded around her, a team of security guards let loose with a hail of bullets, jolting her from her self-recriminations. Rafe and his team fell backward off the deck, amidst a barrage of gunfire and a twinkling of lights. They disappeared before they hit the water.

Stacy rocked her father and wailed, mouth open, regret and sorrow tearing her apart. She barely registered the flash of bulbs as reporters captured the moment. Forever.

CHAPTER THIRTY-EIGHT

Ten years later...

GOVERNOR ANASTASIA CADELL woke with a start. The drone from the private jet's engine that had first lulled her to sleep, now changed pitch and roused her. Just when things were heating up.

She'd been dreaming about Rafe. Again.

His mouth on hers—as well as on other, more intimate parts of her anatomy. Kissing, licking, teasing, and all of it ending right before they made love.

Talk about a familiar refrain.

Slick with sweat and groaning in disappointment, Stacy sat up to get her bearings. The small sleeping compartment at the back of the plane was dimly lit. She'd neglected to close the window shade before retiring but, as it was night, no illumination came from that source. Likewise, no towns or cities twinkled from the darkness below. Since the forecast called for clear skies, she guessed they were somewhere over the Pacific, heading back to Seattle, as planned.

The only light in the room, in fact, came from the TV. A muted Judy Garland, wearing a snug blue dress with white collar and cuffs, was giving it her all. Stacy recognized the movie, the moment. Judy was singing about the man that got away, and Stacy knew how that felt.

She leaned over and clicked on the bedside lamp. The room came into view with its dark wood accents and leather upholstery, buttery in both color and feel.

Stacy swung out her legs from the hot, tangle of sheets and tiptoed to the bathroom in her bare feet. She grabbed the facecloth and ran it under the tap. She wrung out most of the water and then swiped the cloth over the back of her neck, cooling her heated skin. She doused it again, this time patting her chest. Lukewarm water trickled down her breasts, reminding Stacy of her dream, and the path of Rafe's tongue.

"Get over it, girl." She needed to face the harsh reality of the waking world.

The mirror above the sink revealed the passage of time. A few fine lines scored the skin around her eyes but she'd kept in shape, despite an exhausting work schedule. Since her father's death she had, as predicted, taken up politics and been elected governor. It proved to be a better fit than she'd expected.

During her term, she'd fought to bring in several new bills, the most controversial of which ensured the rights of the first *weres* to reveal themselves to humans. Of that, she was most proud. And now, like her father, she was thinking of running for president. If she won, she'd be the second woman in history to hold the office. A busy time, indeed.

All the same, she'd been lonely.

She missed her father. Knew she always would. The pain of losing him wasn't quite as raw. Still, whenever she spotted a young girl with her dad, sentimental tears gathered in her eyes. Even a Hallmark card could set her off. Fortunately, constituents loved Stacy's mushy side as much as her kickass legislator persona.

She'd been so keen on work, and trying to forget the tragedy on the yacht and her lost love, that she'd long ago scrapped any kind of social life that didn't involve her job or extremely close friends. Sure, there'd been a few dates. But no one compared to Rafe.

After all these years, that was the one undeniable truth she couldn't escape. In only a few days, she'd fallen in love with a wild man from the future. And Stacy hadn't stopped loving him in the time since.

She'd even seen him. Or thought she had. Whenever trouble brewed around her, she sensed his presence. Sometimes, she'd spot his face in the crowd, or catch him in her peripheral vision. But when she looked again, he'd be gone.

Had she only imagined him near her? Probably. It didn't deter Stacy from watching for him, though.

Rafe might well be dead, for all she knew. On that last, fateful day, authorities had searched the waters for the bodies of the three suspected assassins but found no trace of them. Did the team make it back to their time in one piece? Or had they appeared in the twenty-third century riddled with bullets?

And why did she keep dreaming about Rafe, anyway? Even wide awake, he appeared in her thoughts. More now than ever.

"Maybe a cold shower will give me a jolt of common sense."

She reached for the bottom of the oversized T-shirt she wore to bed and yanked it over her head. While blinded by fabric, she heard a sound in the bedroom. Hadn't she locked the door? Was her assistant coming in? She was on good terms with the young man, but flashing him wasn't part of her public relations platform. She jerked her shirt back into place.

"Hello? Is that you, Andrew?"

No answer. She called out again. "Andrew?"

Still nothing. Was she mistaken about the noise? The plane's engine did seem awfully loud. Different, somehow. Now she wished she'd closed the window shade. All she needed was to find a gremlin on the wing like in *The Twilight Zone.*

Unnerved, she peered around the bathroom door and her heart staggered. Air swooshed out of her lungs and, for a few seconds, she forgot how to take in more. All she could do was stare—her jaw slack, her mouth watering.

The man of her dreams stood there, looking very real and very solid, his eyes glowing from a fire lit within.

"Rafe?"

"Hello, Stacy."

God Almighty. The sight of him, and the low timbre of his voice, made her knees quake.

Stacy reached for the doorjamb to steady herself. How could this be? He looked exactly the same as when she'd last seen him, as if no time had passed between them. Was she still dreaming? If so, she planned to enjoy every minute of it.

She took the few steps that separated them at a dash, jumping into his arms and wrapping her legs around his waist. Strong hands cupped her bottom and she wriggled against them with a sigh. She melded her breasts to his chest—felt the heat of him and the rapid thump of his heart.

They clung together, murmuring each other's names, stroking each other's hair, hanging on for dear life.

"You feel so real."

"I am real."

His kiss proved it. A new lover might have been tentative and gentle. Rafe's lips were possessive, demanding. And Stacy gave as good as she got. She darted her tongue around his mouth, receiving a hoarse growl in response that fired up a deep, raw need in her lower belly.

She slid down his torso, enjoying every bit of the ride, and then threaded her fingers through his hair, framing his face with her palms. "You haven't aged at all. It's been ten years."

"Only six months for me."

Of course. Time wasn't linear for Rafe. He could travel back and visit her at any moment—when she was five, or fifty. For him, it would be all in a day's work.

"The others...Caleb and Tala...did they make it? Are they okay?" Stacy was sure Tala had died that day but it felt wrong to ask about one and not the other.

"Tala recovered from her injuries. I doubt Caleb ever will." Rafe glanced down at the floor and then back up at her, a grin tugging his lips. "He's got it bad for that vampire."

Knowing Rafe's former prejudice against Tala, the lightness of his tone surprised Stacy, as well as his apparent acceptance of Caleb's new relationship. She couldn't imagine how a union between two such opposite species as vampire and werewolf could occur, and it reminded Stacy of her own impossible situation with Rafe.

He kissed her mouth, and then the tip of her nose. "What if there was a way for us to be together? Would you take it?"

Cue the zillion-dollar question. Did they have anything in common now? What would they talk about over breakfast? And what about their Golden Years, when they were old and wrinkly? Would she still be his girl? Would he still be her guy?

"Oh, Rafe. Of course, I would. I'm proud of what I've accomplished, and I know I'd be able to give so much more if you were by my side."

Too bad this was a game of Let's Pretend. Unfortunately, her soul didn't realize it. She could feel it soaring around inside her, hoping there was a chance for them, in spite of their time barrier.

He looked away, his gaze dipping down to the silver necklace at her throat. The one he'd given her. The one she always wore. "Our parting words were angry ones."

Stacy's cheeks heated. She'd said she hated him. "I'm sorry." She whispered his name and waited until their eyes met before she continued. "I should have trusted you."

"I need you to trust me now. We've reached a political crisis in my century. The world is on the verge of another great war. And, this time, with the weaponry at our disposal, we might just wipe out the planet. We need your help—your negotiating skills, your political savvy."

She backed away from him. "I don't understand. Are you here to consult with me?

"No. I'm here to take you with me. To my century."

Her knees gave way and she sank to the bed. "Is that even possible? You can take me to the future? Is that what you'd intended for my father? He told me you came to him with a way out."

Rafe hung his head. "I'd planned to fire off a fake shot, grab him and take him overboard with me. I hoped his presumed death would be enough to complete our mission. He could either go into hiding, or be carried away with me to my time. But that had never been done before. Our scientists have since told me we would most likely have fused together and died." He searched her eyes with his sad ones. "I'm sorry I failed you."

He'd been prepared to die to save her dad? She wouldn't have believed she could love Rafe more but, after that confession, Stacy did. "Failed me? You're the best thing that ever happened to me."

With one step, he joined her on the bed. After another lengthy kiss, curiosity got the better of her. "So how would *I* get to the future?"

"We've been working on the technology. We've tried with animals and have been successful. Now we need a human to volunteer. I convinced my superiors you'd be the perfect subject, because of your bravery and adaptability. And, frankly, we need you."

"But won't that change history? You said yourself I was a risk with what I already knew about your time. If I visited you in the future, when I returned—"

"You would never return. You'd live out your days in my century."

He held her hands. Until that moment, she hadn't realized they were shaking. Could she leave everything she knew and go to a completely different time? She'd be like a woman from the 1800s transported into a world of computers and cell phones.

Utterly useless. For a while, at least.

She could think of it as moving to a foreign land—learning a new language, new customs. She remembered the early settlers, abandoning Europe and sailing across the ocean to reach America. There were great hardships but they made it.

"Will you come, Stacy? For our country's survival? For me?" Rafe kissed her hands and then held them over his heart. "I'm not going to pretend the transition will be easy. It will be challenging, overwhelming, aggravating... but exciting and rewarding, too."

"What about my life here?"

He looked deep into her eyes. "Your life in this century will end very soon. Within the hour."

Her stomach dropped. Stacy might have blamed a patch of rocky turbulence, though she would have been lying. Is that why Rafe had come to her? To deliver a death sentence?

"This plane never reaches its destination," he continued. "There's a mechanical problem. Bits of wreckage are found floating in the Pacific for weeks. Your body is never recovered."

She thought about her father's friend, Mr. Fitzhenry. He'd loaned Stacy the jet so she'd be fresh for a television interview in Seattle the following morning, instead of drained after a day of cross-country airport stopovers. He'd be devastated when he learned his act of kindness had led to her end.

"Then everyone else on the plane..."

"Miraculously, your assistant and the flight attendant are found clinging to some of the debris. For the others... it's their time."

Her throat tightened. Did she have any right to live while the others perished? "Did you know about this crash ten years ago? You never said my days were numbered."

"I didn't know then. And I'm glad. No one should have to live in the shadow of a ticking clock. The terminally ill come close, but even they don't know the exact moment of their mortality. Nor should they." Rafe cupped her face and ran his thumb over her cheek. "If you'd known, you would have worked yourself harder, tried to accomplish even more and made yourself ill. Knowing wouldn't have freed you. It would have enslaved you."

His argument made sense. But how would her friends handle her disappearance? "I should call Perry. Say good-bye. Tell him I—" She stopped herself mid-sentence as she realized her request was impossible. If she let something slip, said the wrong thing…

She'd left everyone on great terms. Since the incident on the yacht, she'd understood how precious every moment was. She praised colleagues regularly and made a point to tell good friends like Perry and Carey that she loved them. Often and with meaning.

She hoped the others on the plane had lived their life the same way. Stacy had an urge to warn them, but knew it would only prolong their fears. Still, she felt guilty, knowing she would live, while they would die.

"Why didn't you tell me about the plane straight away. Choosing between life and death is pretty simple."

"There's nothing simple about this. The risks of taking you to the future are huge. For one, it might not work. You could still die. Or, you could survive the trip only to succumb to a common virus in my time that your twenty-first century immune system can't handle."

Forget survivor's guilt. This news flash made her feel less like a rescued damsel and more like a science experiment. Perishing in a plane crash lost some of its horror.

"Don't make your choice between life and death," Rafe went on. "But between this life and a new one. "

A life filled with purpose, adventure… and Rafe. She looped her arms around his neck. "What are we waiting for?"

"The moment of impact. Sorry I have to put you through it, but I'll be right here with you."

He clasped her to him and nuzzled her. If she made it to the future, no doubt she'd end up with an old-fashioned hickey. For now, though, all that mouth action on her skin was making her moist down below. If this was what life with Rafe entailed, she might end up dying after all. From unfulfilled lust.

"If this hour is going to be my last, I have only one wish… for us to be together."

"I want that, too."

Rafe kissed her again, his fingers slipping beneath her panties to caress her. She tried to hold back, to savor the sensations, but he knew exactly how to touch her—how hard and how fast. Within seconds, he made her forget about everything but his touch. She moaned into his mouth as he took her over the edge.

He grabbed the TV remote and turned up the volume on Judy. "To mask any sounds. From what I just heard, you're still pretty vocal."

"Don't talk, wolfman. I plan to make you howl."

He stood and peeled off his shirt and her vocalizing began with a weighty sigh of approval. *Man, oh man*, he was a sight to behold, a landscape painting of muscled hills and rock hard valleys. On looks alone, he could win any woman he wanted, but Stacy knew he was so much more. Brave, smart, funny, loyal—a guy who always tried to do the right thing, even when it hurt. Rafe was the whole package and she loved all of it. All of him.

And couldn't wait to show him how much. Especially if this time with him was all she was going to get.

She crouched on the floor in front of Rafe and freed him from his pants, letting the black jeans fall to the floor. The groan that rumbled in his chest was all the encouragement she needed to begin stroking him, the rigid flesh of his erection both hard and supple—steel sheathed in silk.

He dragged her top over her head and tumbled back onto the bed with her, bracing himself on one elbow to support his weight. Rafe's other hand located her knee and hugged it against his side. He nibbled kisses along her mouth, her neck, her breasts, tasting her as if he couldn't get enough and making her body throb.

Once more, the delicious pressure started to build. He shifted slightly, changing the angle and found a sensitive spot deep within her. Every time he nudged her there, she called out his name, and God's, punctuating both with loud cries of, "Oh."

Rafe was hers. The only man she wanted. And now, they were finally united. The feeling of oneness with him, mixed with the recollection that time was still their enemy, filled her with such joy and sadness, her eyes misted.

Stacy recovered the remote and pressed the red OFF button, because she wanted Rafe to hear this next part without any accompaniment from Ms Garland. "There's been no one else for me. I love you. I always have and I always will."

A smile curved his lips. "So you want to be with me? Truly? *Weres* mate for life, you know. You can't back out once you've committed."

For life? That had a very nice ring to it. "I won't back out," she assured him. They kissed and cuddled, their touches no longer frenzied but slow and thorough, as if memorizing each other.

"Since we're going to be together, will you turn me into a *were* like you?"

He shook his head. "The way it's portrayed in your movies isn't far from the truth. It's a very painful process for the convert. So no, I wouldn't turn you. Besides, I love you the way you are."

Finally, he'd said the L-word. Just when she heard the engine wail. The altitude dipped suddenly and the FASTEN YOUR SEATBELT sign flashed.

"It's started, Stacy. Take your seat."

He retrieved her clothes and they dressed, while the pilot's calm voice relayed what Stacy already knew—that the plane was experiencing mechanical problems and for everyone to remain calm. Rafe sat beside her, only a small end table separating them, and secured his belt, too. He held her hand while the plane shuddered.

"It'll be okay. Trust me."

He'd asked her to trust him a decade earlier and she hadn't. No matter what happened, she vowed to do so now.

She squeezed his hand as the plane bobbed, leaping and diving like a dolphin. The papers she'd been working on before her nap flew around her head. The bathroom door banged out an SOS against its metal frame.

Without warning, the plane's nose tipped at a sharp angle and Stacy was thrust forward, suspended by her seat belt. The strap slammed across her like a steel pipe, stealing her breath. Amidst the chaos, the cool-headed captain spoke over the intercom. "Brace for impact."

Shrill screams pierced the engine roar. The smell of jet fuel hit Stacy's nose and burned its way down her throat and into her lungs. Her heart boomed in her ears, her composure plummeting faster than the plane. Until she looked at Rafe, who radiated confidence, his hand still wrapped around hers. She held on tight to him—her love, her rock—knowing that, with him by her side, she could get through anything. Death included.

The blow on impact wrenched Stacy's seat from the floor and she flew, her connection with Rafe lost. She heard the screech of tearing metal, felt a split-second of blinding pain, and then nothing.

CHAPTER THIRTY-NINE

Were Force One Outpost, Spring 2284…

TALA WALKED AT a clip, leaving her compartment in the blue-walled module of the station's private apartments section, and headed to the red corridor of Command Central.

When she'd first taken up residence in the rotating wheel space station, the trip around the color-coded and never-ending circular hallway confused the hell out of her. She always screwed up and took the long way around to wherever she went. Trust a female to have a wonky sense of direction. Especially in space, where *up* and *down* were relative terms.

She appreciated the artificial gravity the design created, though. Fewer blood drops on the ceiling.

Nowadays, she didn't give a thought to her route. Not with Caleb at her heels. The wolf could sniff out the way blindfolded. Still, she felt uncomfortable about arriving at their destination together. Would colleagues guess that they'd started their trek from the bedroom of her cabin? If not, the doe-eyed looks Caleb sent her way, even now as they walked, would have told the rest of the story. That he'd singlehandedly nursed her back from the edge of death with a steady diet of TLC and the tastiest blood she'd sampled in decades.

Sure, she'd taken from his vein, but she'd saved his virginity. *So far.* Once he blew out those candles on his twenty-first birthday cake, she planned to chuck her restraint in a drawer.

Tala reached Rafe's office and scanned the room through the half-opened door. Instead of going on missions, her former crush was now in charge of them—a newly appointed Colonel. He sat at his desk, absorbed in reports, his expression dark and troubled.

He'd been like this for months.

She paused, hesitant to intrude. She rested her knuckles against the door and then gave a faint rap.

"Come," he said, without looking up.

They took positions in front of his desk, standing at attention. Once Rafe made eye contact, he waved away the formality and motioned for them to sit in the faux leather club chairs.

He manufactured a smile. "How's it going?"

"Good," Caleb answered, for both of them. "Antsy waiting for our next mission, and sorry you won't be joining us, but good."

Rafe remained silent while he studied them, and Tala's gut sneaked up under her ribs, looking for a place to hide. Past due for a dressing down, she expected the 'Don't mess with my little buddy' speech. She'd given herself the same tongue-lashing for using Caleb.

That's not what Rafe gave her, though. "From recent, subtle changes in timewave dispersement, we have reason to suspect Nikolas is still at large," he said.

Tala's mouth flopped open. "But that can't be. I saw him—"

"Surrounded by goltos. You didn't see them attack. Maybe they were protecting him. From you."

She supposed that could be true. Still, she couldn't imagine anyone surviving the dog pile of bodies she'd witnessed. "Where do you think he is?"

"1930s New York."

The city of her birth, and the decade she became a vampire. She'd always wanted to revisit it and take care of some loose ends. The kind that resulted from a love affair gone horribly wrong. But it would be risky. If she should run into her past self...

"I'll brief you on the mission later today. First, I want to introduce you to your two new teammates. We'll meet up with them in the mess hall. Both excelled during training and did well in light field missions. This will be a big leap for them so I want to pair them with the best."

Cripes. Was Caleb blushing? Tala couldn't blame him. She also basked in Rafe's praise.

"Who are they?" she asked.

"Gage Jackson and Catalyn Elliott."

Tala knew the male as a mighty fine looking werewolf—as big as Rafe and a serious heart-breaker, with a penchant for hard work, hard play, and for leaving a squadron of satisfied females in his wake. Elliott, she'd seen once or twice. The female was definitely a *were* or shifter of some sort— intelligent, steady under pressure and reserved to the point of being icy. Tala figured that armored exterior hid its share of inner secrets.

Caleb scratched his chin. "Will it be a five-person crew? You haven't mentioned a team leader."

Rafe perched on the edge of his desk, his arms crossed over his chest. "You're sitting next to her," he replied. "That's why I wanted a moment alone with the two of you. I'm promoting you, Tala. You're a huge asset to this operation. I'm just sorry I didn't see it sooner."

If the buttons on her shirt were any tighter, she'd have busted them. Advancement in the *Were* Force was cause for celebration and a swollen head, as much from pride as over-imbibing. Knowing Rafe recognized and valued her efforts, gave Tala's dawdling heart reason to dance. She made a couple of attempts to speak, and ended up stammering something unintelligible, before squeaking out a respectable, "Thank you, sir."

"After you get back, we'll go after Tomas." Rafe rose and steered for the door. "As far as meeting the rest of your crew, I thought we'd start with lunch. It'll give the four of you a chance to get acquainted." As he led them down the corridor toward the mess hall, Caleb grasped her hand and gave it a congratulatory squeeze.

Such a nice male. She didn't deserve him. He'd realize it one day and be gone. Her eyes misted at the thought of losing him, knowing she'd be the one to drive him away. Such was her nature. He smiled at her, probably mistaking the tears for joyful ones. How could she be joyful crushing his innocence?

Up ahead, a blue-eyed blonde stepped into the corridor like a burst of spring. In contrast to the combat fatigues everyone else on the station sported, the blonde wore a simple floral dress, the material flowing over her baby bump.

Rafe came to an abrupt stop and then broke into a run. He scooped the woman off her feet and twirled around, his serious expression lost to a toothy grin.

Stacy laughed. "Put me down, Rafe. I must weigh a ton."

"Light as a feather and made for kissing." The one he planted on his wife's lips left Tala fanning herself.

"You're a little heavier than you were two centuries ago, but I can handle it." Rafe's quip earned him a playful swat.

Tala blinked to avoid tearing up again. When the hell did she get so sentimental? Before life as a vampire, having a husband and child had been her biggest dream. She put her feelings of loss aside and gave her human friend a hug. "How much longer?"

Stacy patted her belly, the diamond wedding set on her ring finger twinkling almost as much as her eyes. "Another two months. I can hardly wait. My feet are killing me. I never realized how difficult campaigning would be in this condition."

Tala knew, from observation, that aching feet were the least of it. She'd seen how hard Stacy had worked to bring herself up to speed with their time—the decades of information she'd absorbed, the technologies she'd had to learn. Not to mention the hoops she'd jumped through to quell the unrest between current world leaders, and to win a place in the hearts of her new in-laws.

"Boy or girl?" Tala asked. "Do you know? Are you telling?"

"We do know." She looked up at a beaming Rafe, who winked and wrapped an arm around his bride's waist. "We're having a boy, and we're calling him Jonathan Blaez Garrett."

Tala smiled. "A perfect name."

With all the couple had overcome to be together, Tala could only feel happy for them. And hopeful. They'd found a timeless love.

Maybe there was a chance for her, after all.

* * *

If you enjoyed *WOLFEN TIME*,

please help other readers find it by recommending it to friends

or writing a review on whatever platform you purchased it from and on Goodreads.

ABOUT ROXY BOROUGHS

Before turning her attention to fiction, Roxy appeared in numerous TV commercials and movies.

In addition to *WOLFEN TIME*, she's also published sexy romantic suspense titles, and is one of three authors involved in the Frost Family Christmas series, combining sweet romances with cozy mysteries.

Visit her at http://www.roxyboroughs.com where you can sign up for her newsletter to get the latest information on everything Roxy.